CRESCENT MOON : TRINITY CURSE

STEPHANIE HONEYCUTT

CONTENTS

		V
Prologue		1
1.	Silent Retreat	4
2.	Parent Talk	10
3.	Power of Two	17
4.	Long Lost Brother	23
5.	Old Acquaintances	33
6.	Making Plans	37
7.	Change of Plans	44
8.	You Can't Change Fate	55
9.	Aftermath	65
10.	Morning Surprises	75
11.	Surprise Visitor	79
12.	Processing	91
13.	Family Dinner	97
14.	Transparency	103

15. Dead Ends   111

16. Hard Goodbyes   116

17. Alpha Problems   123

18. Challenged   130

19. Connections   140

20. Plans Revealed   147

21. Brother Broken   154

22. Taking a Piece Off the Board   166

23. Operation G.A.B.   173

24. History   182

25. The Other Woman   194

26. Intrusion   203

27. Best Laid Plans   214

28. Life for a Life   220

29. History of the Moon Goddess   229

30. Bloodlines   240

31. Race Against the Clock   250

32. Binders Protection   264

33. Through the Tunnel   280

34. Bonding   292

35. Call to Battle   299

36. Moonstone   315

37. Celebration of Life   331

Epilogue   336

Thank you! Thank you! Thank you!   340

Thank you to my husband and children whose continual support and encouragement have pushed me through times when I questioned what I was doing. Thank you to my parents and brother who always believed in me, even when I didn't, and who would entertain all of my crazy ideas. And to all the other friends and family who have been with me on this journey. Your support means more to me than words can express.

And thanks to all the readers who saw the first book and gave it a shot!

PROLOGUE

ASHER CALLED A MEETING with Liam and several other neighboring pack alphas. The mission was clear- find Kayden and bring him to our pack house alive.

We had less than two weeks before I was in whatever coma like state Chloe was in and even that was an estimate since we didn't know how my previous situation effected the timeline. I could feel it in me, growing stronger, whatever *it* was. Every night I went to sleep I feared I wouldn't wake up.

After breakfast one morning, there was a soft knock on the door.

I went to answer it, hopeful it was a pack alpha with news of Kayden but standing there was a woman who looked as old as the Earth, but still held a youthful glow. Her skin was a deep tan and worn like old leather and her hair was a bright silver color that flowed all the way down to her knees. I felt like I should bow in her presence even though I had no idea who she was because she carried herself with elegance and royalty.

"Hello. May I help you?"

She smiled warmly at me, her bright white teeth sparkling, carrying up to the twinkle in her eye. "My dear Camilla." She rested her hand on my cheek and I felt a warmth flow across my skin. "How big you have grown. You are strong just like your mother and loyal, just like your father." Her words lightly drummed into my head, with a steady beat.

I smiled back at her, not really sure what to say.

"I'm here to see Alpha Asher. I have news for him- for both of you, really."

My brow furrowed. For both of us? "Asher." I called to him softly.

He was by my side a second later, with his hand on my back. He saw who was at the door and bowed immediately. "Elder Heldalore."

I looked between the two of them and bowed, embarrassed I hadn't already done so.

When Asher stood back up, so did I. "What can I do for you Elder?"

She smiled. "I have news for you, for both of you." She stepped out of the door, inviting us to step outside with her - a modicum of privacy.

Asher closed the door and I could feel worry pulsing through him, twisting knots into his stomach. This last month has been one hit after another and I don't think we could take another right now. I reached my hand out and slipped it in his, giving a gentle squeeze and a silent show of support and strength.

"Asher Evans." She smiled, letting his name play on her lips, a hint of excitement woven throughout. "After we spoke about the letter you found, we were able to decode it."

"And?" Asher asked breathlessly, tension laced in his words.

"Not yet." She placed her hand on his shoulder. "I want you to know that what I have to tell you will come as a shock, but will also clear up some other questions that have been weighing on you."

My head snapped to Asher. What had been weighing on him he couldn't or hasn't talked to me about?

He looked at me and smiled even though it didn't reach his eyes.

"We had to do a lot of research, which is part of the reason it has taken so long. Your mother and father took great care in concealing this particular piece of information that was in the letter you found."

I squeezed Asher's hand again and he squeezed mine in return.

"Asher." Elder Heldalore started.

My heart was nearly pounding out of my chest, as a nervous anticipation was flowing through our bond.

"Your mother was a Crescent wolf. You are part Crescent. Cami is your bonded mate."

I looked from Elder Heldalore to Asher and tears started streaming down my face as Asher stood there in shock.

Elder Heldalore smiled. "Your mother, wanting to protect you, came to the Elders and requested they suppress the Crescent gene in you. It was not impossible because your father wasn't a Crescent, so you technically are only half Crescent." She grabbed his free hand. "The letter was the contract of the agreement."

"I'm part Crescent?"

"If you want, we can reverse the suppression. That's not to say your Crescent will activate, but it would at least have the chance to."

I looked at Asher, my eyes wide with excitement.

He looked at me and softly rubbed my cheek and then turned back to the Elder.

"Reverse it."

SILENT RETREAT

WAS THIS WHAT DEATH *felt like? A silent abyss of nothingness...*

I felt my body floating through the air, the world deathly quiet as I watched everyone below me move in slow motion. Shifters, werewolves and part of the Ellsmire Coven were united against the Red Crows... even Luna was fighting alongside Drake and Ruthy.

I should care about what was happening to all my friends and family instead of retreating into silence... but it was hard. I felt the darkness tugging me away and felt myself drifting towards it.

There was no more pain.

I felt tired.

I felt free.

The display of animals fighting with vengeance and passion felt like I was watching a show on Discovery- something filmed in the wild... but this was not the wild. This was my home and it was being destroyed and people were dying. I saw bodies scattered, unmoving, across the scorched ground.

I should care.

I wanted to care.

I looked around slowly, my eyes felt like they were attached to fifty-pound weights and every millimeter moved took great effort. I continued to search, knowing what I was looking for, and landed on a black speck on the ground.

The cause for all this.

Laying inconspicuously in the middle of all the chaos was a small black rock. But not just any rock- it was the moonstone. The first moonstone created in over fourteen hundred years.

It was laying there all by itself, looking innocent, as chaos unfolded around it.

But it was not innocent.

It was evil.

I felt my head slowly swivel as I looked around and found Kayden and Chloe floating in the air with me. Were they feeling the same thing as me?

Kayden's eyes were focused on the stone and as I turned to Chloe, her eyes were focused on me. They were saggy, like she was fighting exhaustion, while at the same time more intense than anything I'd ever seen. It was like she was trying to talk to me, communicate something to me, but all that was here was silence.

I don't know how long we stayed like this, staring at one another, but something caught my attention. I felt a pain, so brief and so light that I don't know if one could call it a pain, maybe a prickle on the skin.

I looked down and saw Asher's wolf trying to shake off another wolf- Lucian's wolf. His jaws were clamped like a vice around Asher's back leg and Asher's wolf cried out in pain, neck arched to the sky- I couldn't hear it, only see it. Is that what the sound of pain looked like? Asher's wolf turned and snapped at Lucian's leg but missed, so he tried again and was able to contact just enough to break the grip on Lucian's bite and pull his leg free.

Asher squared off against Lucian, hunched close to the ground like a coiled spring ready to release. Lucian, full of rage, took no time and launched forward, missing Asher as he jumped out of the way before turning back and clamping down on Lucian's back leg. Lucian quickly pulled out of it and lunged after Asher's throat, catching a tuft of hair. Asher barreled into the side of Lucian, knocking him down and then moved to bite on his neck. He centered his body over Lucian's and bared down even harder, twisting his head with a ferociousness I've never seen before.

There was no mercy.

There was no hesitation.

Asher twisted and Lucian's body shifted into a human seconds later.

He looked up at me, his eyes filled with something- a feeling. Satisfaction? I looked just beyond him and saw a Red Crow charging towards him and panic filled me. I could feel something, perhaps a stirring inside. I tried to reach out to him!

Asher! I yelled out.

His eyes were focused on me, but he needed to look to his right! Could he hear me?

Asher! To your right! I yelled again, but his head didn't turn away from me. Why was he staring at me? He needed to mind his surroundings.

I saw Xander a distance behind him and could tell he saw the Crow bearing down on Asher. He started running towards him with what looked to be lightning speed, even though everything was moving in slow motion.

I looked between Asher, the Red Crow, and Xander and could tell by the pained expression on Xander's face that he knew he wouldn't be fast enough. Asher must have caught him out of the corner of his eye and turned just as the Red Crow approached him and lunged forward and swiped hard against Asher's throat and face. Asher fell to the ground in shock and lay there, moving slowly- too slowly. The Red Crow took the opportunity and bit down on his neck and twisted.

Asher's body shifted into a human- his beautiful human body- at the same time Xander launched at the Red Crow, killing him.

On the ground lay Asher and the Red Crow, both in their human form and Xander looking up at me with an unreadable expression.

I felt a brief pain that tore through me like a knife through butter, and then it vanished.

Asher was gone.

Asher was dead.

Everything started to fade to black.

"Asher!" My eyes shot open as I sat up in bed. Panic and fear coursed through my veins, making me nauseous as my eyes quickly darted around the room, searching for him, but he wasn't here.

I was alone.

"Asher!" I yelled out again, tears streaming down my face.

I clamored out of bed and raced towards the door just as it swung open.

Asher!

I jumped onto him, wrapping my arms and legs around his waist, squeezing.

He chuckled, "Good Morning to you."

I continued to hold on, scared if I let him go, he would disappear.

"Cami?" He patted my back, his tone dropping. "What's wrong? You have me worried."

I slowly sat back so I could see his face, but still refusing to release my hold on him.

His brows raised, when I just silently stared at him for a minute, feeling his face to make sure it was real. Of course it was real- he was real. The nightmare, it just... it just felt real, too.

"Now you're freaking me out."

"I'm sorry." I wiped the tears from my cheek.

"What's going on?" He gently stroked the back of my head.

I hesitated telling him, scared if I spoke the words out loud, that would make them come true.

"Cami." He tilted his chin down and looked at me between his lashes.

I hopped down and grabbed his hand, pulling him into the room and shutting the door. "Sit." I pointed to the bed.

He cocked his head to the side and studied me.

"Sit." I commanded in a softer voice.

He sat on the edge of the bed and put his hands under his legs. "Ok. Can you please tell me what's going on? I don't like whatever has you like this."

I took in a deep breath. "I think I had a dream or a future dream... a vision." I was flustered and shaky.

"That's great!" He studied my face and adjusted, "That's not great?" He said, shaking his head.

"Asher." I started, then stopped as the words got stuck in my throat. "You..." I started crying again.

"What? What? What is it?" He was rubbing the back of my head, trying to soothe me, but little did he know, nothing could soothe away the fear and pain I felt.

"Asher." I swallowed hard. "I had a vision of a battle. It looked to be just after the ceremony for the moonstone was performed and... you..."

"Me what?" His tone was somewhere between concerned and frustrated he was having to pull it out of me, but he didn't understand.

"You were killed. They killed you!" I blurted out.

He looked at me, his hand frozen on my back as the weight of my words hung in the air like a lead balloon.

"They killed you, Asher," I whispered, nuzzling into his chest. "I watched it happen and I couldn't do anything to stop it. I just... watched it." I pulled away from him quickly and defended, "I couldn't do anything to stop it. I was still in the air above you, while you were all fighting. It was like everything was in slow motion."

He continued slowly rubbing my back. "It's ok." His words wandered away.

"Asher, it's not ok!"

He pushed me away and cupped my face in his hands. "That's not what I'm saying. What I mean is that we know what's going to happen so we can change it."

I stared at him for a moment as realization set in. "We can change it." I repeated quietly.

"Yes." He pulled me back in for a hug and buried his face in my hair, squeezing me tightly. "It's going to be ok."

I leaned forward and planted my lips on his and felt a surge move through me, filled with so much emotion it was hard to contain. Even though he was telling me it was going to be ok, parts of me still had a hard time believing it, but I didn't want to ruin our morning by continuing to focus on it.

It had been just over a week since Chloe had fallen into her unconscious state- a result of the unfinished Trinity curse weakening her. I wasn't there yet because after Mira tried to kill my brother, Kayden, at the Red Crows compound, I had jumped in the way, taking the brunt of the curse. Luna was able to act quick enough and bring me back, but it took several weeks as I floated in and out of consciousness. We think that had somehow slowed down whatever it was- the thing inside of us we could feel. It needed to finish the curse and until we did, it made us weaker and weaker, forcing us to find one another.

Soon after Chloe fell into her state, we learned Asher was part Crescent. His parents had taken great caution in protecting him from the Crescent world, which meant his mother, the Crescent, walking away from her family. His parents had gone to the elders and requested they suppress Asher's Crescent gene, just in case, and when we found this out from Elder Heldalore, Asher decided to reverse it. We didn't know if it would work or how long it would take, but the idea he could shift with me, potentially fly with me... I tried not to let myself dream, so I wouldn't be disappointed, but I couldn't get the image out of my head I had of him when I was held captive at the Crows compound. He was a beautiful dark brown owl.

"So..." I asked, forcing a smile. "What do you want to do today?"

He smiled knowingly. "We can go talk to your parents if you want."

I had wanted to talk to my parents, to tell them about Asher, because along with everything else, I was scared of how they would react. Would they see us as a threat to their pack? Would they expect us to give up our pack and move in with them?

So much stress and what-ifs that I wanted to ignore. "In a little while." I smiled playfully, pushing him backwards.

PARENT TALK

WE WERE WALKING UP the front stairs of my parents' house and I felt like I was going to be sick. This was the first time I had been here and I didn't know what to expect. The house was slightly smaller than our pack house, but was all white with black trim around the windows and door. The front yard had several large patches of flowers that were probably tended to daily by my mother. I could easily envision her with a wide-brimmed hat on her knees tilling and pruning each flower by hand while she sang to them.

They had invited me over on several occasions, but it didn't seem like the right time, but now, with everything going on, I was starting to see I had to make it a point, because tomorrow wasn't guaranteed.

I raised my hand to knock on the door, but before I even touched it, the door swung open and Xander was standing there. "Welcome to the dark side." He laughed.

"Hi Xander." I smiled.

Asher nodded. "What's up, man?"

"Just preparing for your arrival, of course." He clasped his hands together and spoke in a higher pitched voice. "The house is so excited! Abuzz with excitement, some would say."

I shook my head, laughing at him.

"Please come in." Xander took a step back, waving his arm out, like a butler in those classic movies.

"It smells delicious." I took in all the aromas, landing mostly on basil, oregano and other Italian spices. The front room was a large open space with chairs and couches spread throughout, with a piano and several other instruments tucked in the corner. I couldn't help but wonder if my parents played, and if they did, which instrument they played. There was still so much I didn't know, I thought regrettably.

"Nothing but the best for you." Xander retorted, bringing me back to the present.

"Do you have a comment for everything?"

He looked at me, but pressed his lips together.

"Hilarious."

"I try!"

"I thought I heard you." Liam boomed, walking into the room, smiling. "Your mother has me in there cutting up onions and I swear, no matter how hard I try, they get me every time."

He held his arms out, so I moved to give him a hug. "You could be like Ruthy, who insists on wearing a gas mask when she cuts them."

"She's always so dramatic." Xander poked.

I cut my eyes at him. "Careful." I teased. "She could also take you down."

He shrugged. "I'm not scared of her... well, maybe a little, but if you tell her I'll deny it!"

"Noted."

Asher crossed his arms in front of his face and bowed. "Alpha."

"None of that nonsense. You're family." He added. "But I thank you." He waved us back to the kitchen. "Let's go meet the rest of the pack."

For some reason, when they invited us over for dinner, I had assumed it would just be the four, maybe five, of us, if you included Xander.

As if answering my thought, Liam announced. "Don't worry. Xander is taking them out tonight for dinner. I just thought it would be nice to introduce you, since they've heard so much about you."

I smiled, feeling slightly uncomfortable, and tried to make a joke. "You trust Xander with your pack?"

Liam's lips pinched in a hard line. "I'm not sure." He laughed, then patted Xander on the back. "Only kidding, of course. I trust him with my life and yours." He looked down at me very fatherly, causing my skin to prickle.

"Thank you, sir." Xander said in all seriousness. It was hard seeing him that way, because he was always so playful.

We walked into the kitchen, and huddled around the island and adjoining living room were about twenty people ranging in age from teenager to early fifties. They all stood up and crossed their arms in front of their faces and bowed. "Alphas."

Asher and I returned the gesture.

Anastasia floated around the kitchen island with her customary flowing dress and held her arms out. "Thank you so much for accepting our invitation. I wasn't sure with everything going on..."

I smiled. "It's because of everything going on."

Xander interrupted. "Pack. That's our cue." He waved his finger in a circle in the air.

"They don't have to leave on my part." I glanced over my shoulder at him.

"We aren't. I'm starving." Xander grabbed his stomach. "And as you can attest, it's always about me."

I cocked my head to the side and stared at him. "Very true."

"Do you think Levi or Ruthy would want to join?"

I studied him for a moment. "You can ask. I'm not sure what their plans are."

He nodded, then clapped his hands together. "Ok. Well, I'll see you both later!"

"Have fun." I chuckled.

"Don't get in trouble this time, please." Liam warned playfully, but also with a note of seriousness. He looked at me. "Last time they got booted out of a go-kart track because they decided to form teams and play chicken on the track."

"How's Chloe?" Anastasia called over her shoulder, clearly wanting to change the topic. She stirred the pot of boiling water before turning to face me.

"She's the same. I don't know if that's a good thing or a bad thing." I rubbed my hands together.

"What's wrong Cami?" She sat the spoon down and looked at me. "There's something weighing on your mind."

"I'd rather enjoy our dinner and talk about it after, if that's ok?"

She stared at me for a moment. "Yes, of course. We'll be ready to eat in about fifteen minutes. Liam, do you want to show them around while I finish up?"

"Of course, darling." He said, planting a quick kiss on her forehead.

Asher grabbed my hand as we followed him out of the kitchen.

"You've already seen the kitchen, front room and living room."

I nodded. Their living room was large and held more couches, and several large televisions spread out across the wall. They had the bedrooms upstairs on the second and third floors with a fourth-floor loft that had pool tables and more televisions. In the basement was a large pool that carried through under a retractable wall to an even larger outdoor pool.

"How long is that pool?" I asked, picking up my jaw off the ground.

"About a hundred feet."

"Wow." Asher commented.

"We need it long since we swim so fast." He chuckled.

"We need one of those!" I squeezed Asher's hand excitedly.

Liam raised the wall as we walked outside. There were several oversized hot tubs lining the edge of the pool, with a large outdoor kitchen to the right.

"Wow! I really love your outdoor setup."

"Thanks. Your mother did a lot of the work herself."

"Really?"

"Yes." He chuckled. "She is quite handy. Plus, when she gets stressed, working on projects helps set her mind at ease."

"Makes sense."

Dinner time.

"There she is now!"

Dinner went by quickly, or maybe that was just my perception because I was dreading the upcoming conversation. How would they react when they learned Asher was part Crescent?

Would they feel intimidated, like we were going to challenge them to alpha over the Crescents? I hope not, because we would never. We are happy with our pack.

Oh, goddess.

What would *our* pack think when we told them?

They say they're fine having me as their alpha because they have Asher, a werewolf, but what will they think when they find out he is half Crescent?

Would they really want two Crescents being their alpha?

What's wrong, babe? I can feel your nervous tension flowing through me in waves.

What's going to happen when we tell my parents? Tell our pack? Will my parents feel intimidated by us? Will our pack want two alphas who are Crescents? They're fine with me, because they have you, but both of us?

We don't know anything yet. We don't even know if my crescent will activate.

He was right. We didn't know, but deep down, I wanted it to. Ever since the dream I had of him flying in to protect me when the Red Crows had me, I have wanted nothing more than to share this part of me with him.

He grabbed my hand and planted a kiss on my head.

"Do you all want to go outside on the patio and talk?" Liam suggested.

"Sure."

"Do you want a lemonade or anything to drink while we're out there?"

"Yes. Lemonade sounds nice." I wasn't super thirsty, but I wanted something in my hands to stop them from shaking. Why was I so nervous about this?

I can remember not too long ago I didn't care if they were in my life and now I was terrified of losing them.

We took our seats outside and before I could say anything, Liam started. "If you feel pressured to have a relationship with us, or if it's too difficult, we can give you more space. We just felt like things were getting better between us and with Chloe... well, before she..."

I stopped him. I hadn't thought they could misinterpret my nerves, but wanted to set everything straight. It was time. "It's not that. I'm glad we could finally come over. Mom's spaghetti was delicious and I'll definitely be taking some home so I can snack on it later."

She smiled, placing her hands on her lap.

"Ok then. What seems to be bothering you? Is it Kayden? Have you found him?"

"No, not yet. We have scouts all around the country looking for him." I swallowed hard and looked between Asher and my parents. "But we found out something."

"About Chloe? Kayden?"

I shook my head, trying to gather the words. "About... Asher."
Their brow furrowed.

Asher jumped in, thankfully. "When the Red Crows had Cami... I
may have lost my temper." He bobbled his head from side to side.
"The floor may have been ripped up in the alpha's room and hidden
under a panel was a piece of paper. It was in another language with
an Elder's signature on it." He paused, squeezing my hand. "I took
it to an Elder and they recently just told me what the document
was."

Liam grabbed Anastasia's hand. Did he already know?

"She said that it was a contract. Apparently... my mother was a
Crescent and when I was born, she was scared for my safety... so
she worked with the Elders and had them deactivate the crescent
trait, since my father was a wolf. When the Elder told us, she said
she could activate it again... so we said... yes."

"Wow." Liam looked at Anastasia, a heavy silence filling the air.

I quickly added. "We don't want you to view us as a threat or
anything like that... because..."

Liam laughed and looked at me. "Cami. We know and trust you
both. We don't think either of you would do anything untoward."

I let out a sigh of relief.

"Is that why you were so nervous?"

I nodded.

"Cami." Anastasia chuckled. "We have been through so much. We
won't let this come between us."

I took in a deep breath.

Liam stood up. "If anything, I like him better than I already did,"
he put his hand by his mouth like he was whispering, "which was
already quite a bit."

Asher shook his hand. "Thank you, sir."

Liam batted the air.

Anastasia walked over to give me a hug and rubbed the back of
my head. "You mean so much to me- to us. We are so thankful
you're back in our life."

"Me too." I stared at her and something happened. My legs felt
weak and everything started spinning. "Mom?"

"Cami? What's wrong?" She panicked, sensing something was
off.

"Mom?" I said again and my legs buckled.

Anastasia caught me in her arms and guided me to the ground.

"What's happening?" I looked around, panicked. My heart was racing and my entire body felt weak. Even if I wanted to stand, I could tell my legs weren't strong enough to hold my weight right now.

Asher dropped to his knees, grabbing my hand. "Cami."

"Asher." My heart was pounding out of my chest. "What's happ-"

Alphas. Ruthy chimed in.

What is it? Asher demanded. I knew he didn't mean to come across as impatient as he sounded, it was just the wrong time.

It's Chloe. Something's wrong.

Shit. Cami too. She just collapsed. Asher softened his tone. Fortunately, Ruthy always looked at intentions versus actions.

Asher looked at my parents. "Something's wrong with Chloe."

Without hesitation, Liam scooped me in his arms and took off out the front door.

POWER OF TWO

I WAS GOING IN and out of consciousness the entire way back to the house.

Asher... what's happening? I looked over at him and saw him keeping pace with us as the world flashed by behind him. I don't think I ever realized how fast we could move in human form.

I don't know.

Did Ruthy say something's wrong with Chloe? I was sure that's what I heard, but panic over what was happening to me interfered with the conversation.

Yes.

You don't think... I couldn't say the words for fear that would make them true. I would feel it if she was dead... right? And I don't, therefore she's not.

A moment later, I felt myself being catapulted up and recognized the familiar landing- we were at the back of the pack house. Asher burst through the doors, nearly knocking them off their hinges, causing the entire pack house to go into alarm. When they realized it was Asher and me, they relaxed, but only for a minute until they saw me in my father's arms.

"Alpha?" I heard a young voice ask, followed by hushed whispers.

I'm... fine. Just a... little... tired. I mindlinked the pack.

Another second later, we were in the foyer and making the giant leap to the fourth level. Liam landed with ease.

We walked down the hall to the right, into a room we had converted for Chloe.

"Oh my God." I heard Anastasia gasp. The pain and worry in her voice caused me to use all the strength I had to lift my head and see what was going on, while dread filled every fiber of my being. It felt like someone had tied sandbags to my head, weighing it down, but I fought.

I strained.

When I had my head more vertical, I had to fight to keep it up. Ruthy was straddled over Chloe, pressing down on her chest over and over again. She glanced over her shoulder and I could see the beads of sweat rolling down her face. Her eyes darted from Asher to me, and her face fell as she turned back to Chloe.

Anastasia moved so fast to Chloe's side she looked like nothing more than a blur.

"Move... closer." I commanded. I had to be near her.

I wanted it.

I needed it.

Liam moved closer.

"Clo... ser."

I felt like I was fading fast, or was it Chloe? It was hard to tell sometimes where one of us started and the other ended. It had been days, maybe even weeks, since I'd heard her laugh or seen her smile.

"Ruthy..." Asher hesitated.

She looked up but didn't stop pressing on her chest. Anastasia moved by her side and started feeling around Chloe's neck for a pulse.

"Take a rest, Ruthy." Anastasia commanded softly. Ruthy climbed off and Anastasia climbed on.

"I... I..." I saw a tear forming on the rim of Ruthy's eye. She closed them, took a deep breath, and when she opened them again, Ruthy was back. Our Ruthy was back. She stood erect and began spitting out the details. "We were eating downstairs when the alarms started going off. I called for Levi."

Levi and Xander burst through the door at nearly the same time. I watched Xander rush to Liam's side, I'm sure getting directions.

Ruthy continued. "Drake has called for Mira, or anyone at this point who can help."

"Liam." Anastasia cried out.

He rushed to her side and his head fell.

I felt myself getting weaker and weaker.

"Ash... er..." Blackness was creeping in. This was it... this was my time.

I heard another commotion by the door, but I didn't have the energy to look. I felt my eyes closing and then my body being jostled around.

And then nothing.

I felt like I was floating in a cloud as my body and mind were drifting away into nothingness and then as if being pulled from raging waters, I felt my body take in a deep breath, like I was being jolted back to life with a pair of jumper cables.

I felt my body lurch itself upright. My back was fully arched when my eyes opened and then I crashed back onto the bed.

"She has a pulse." Anastasia exclaimed.

I looked down and saw my hand holding onto Chloe's. "What happened?"

"We almost lost you... both of you." Mira said, pressing her hand to my forehead and then grabbing my wrist to check my pulse. "Chloe's still in a coma, but she has a pulse and is breathing again."

I moved to roll out of bed, but Mira stopped me. "No. You need to stay here beside your sister. You can feed off each other's energy, which will help." She shook her head and looked down briefly. "This is why you all need to complete the ceremony, and soon."

I panicked and looked at Asher. "We can't. I can't."

She shook her head in disbelief. "You have to. You will both die if you don't. Your brother too."

"I can't." I said again, shaking my head quickly.

Asher looked between the two of us, his expression clearly torn.

"I don't understand. I came to you weeks ago and told you about this... right when Chloe fell ill. It's because you all have started the Trinity curse and left it unfinished."

"I know." I yelled in exasperation. "I know." I repeated, this time more defeated. "I feel it... whatever it is, inside of me... I can feel it sucking my energy, making me weaker every second of every day."

"Cami." Asher whispered, grabbing my hand.

"I didn't tell you because... I know what has to be done... but we can't. I can't. I can't lose you."

Mira snorted. "You won't lose him."

I looked between her and Asher. "If I complete the ceremony... if we complete the ceremony... Asher will be killed."

Mira shook her head. "No."

Ruthy gasped.

I nodded. "I had a dream... a vision." I squeezed Asher's hand. "We were at the end of completing the ceremony out in the field, and there was a fight. Our pack and your pack," I looked at Liam and Anastasia, "we were fighting the Red Crows. I saw the stone. It was laying in the middle of the field, completely unattended." I felt a tear trickle down my face. "I couldn't do anything. We were still above you all. It was like everything was in slow motion. I couldn't move. I couldn't speak. I couldn't mindlink."

"It's ok Cams." Asher pulled my head into his chest.

"Asher was killed."

"No. That's not... no." Ruthy exclaimed.

Xander grabbed her hand and she looked at him, then accepted it.

Ruthy continued, "Just because you had a vision, doesn't mean it's going to come true. I mean that's happened before, hasn't it? Right? Right?" I could feel her raw emotion at the thought of not only losing her alpha, but her brother. Her best friend. "He didn't turn into an owl. He's not a crescent, so your vision got that way off." She laughed a nervous laugh.

I looked at her and then at Asher.

"Right?" she pressed.

I nodded. I wasn't sure if Asher was ready for other people to know about his mother, and it wasn't my secret to tell.

"Right." She said more confidently. "So this is also wrong."

Xander chimed in, trying to help Ruthy. "Plus, we can't perform it because we don't know where your vicious, traitorous brother is."

"Hey now." Liam reprimanded.

He shrugged and stretched his lips, nodding to Ruthy.

"It's true." I defended.

Xander gave me an appreciative head nod.

I looked at Mira, who had taken a seat by Chloe, holding her hand. "Are you closer to finding us a way out of this that doesn't involve completing the ceremony?"

"No. I'm afraid there isn't much to go on. We're looking through all the documents and books Maye had gotten out of our library to try to piece some things together, but all things curse related have been mostly witches and since none of them made it..."

I heard a knock at the door downstairs. We all turned but continued talking. "There has to be something. There was the one group of shifters... I know you all think it didn't happen, but what if it did?"

She nodded. "We're working with your Elders to see if they're aware of anything or can corroborate the story in the book."

I nodded and then every hair on my body stood on end, like someone had just zapped me with electricity. I looked at Ruthy and Asher and could tell they felt it, too. The pack was on edge. Angry.

"Something's wrong." Asher said.

"You stay here. I'll go." Ruthy said, without waiting for an answer.

"I'll come too." Xander followed her.

"What's wrong?" Anastasia asked.

"The whole pack house just went into high alarm." And then I smelled it.

I smelled him.

Asher looked at me as an understanding washed over his face. "Kayden."

The one word felt like a black hole had opened up in my stomach.

"Kayden?" Anastasia whispered.

I couldn't help but notice the look of dread and hopefulness on her face.

"I have to go see him." I said, looking at Mira.

She took in a deep breath.

"I feel fine." I corrected. "Fine enough. I have to see what he wants and then I'll come back."

"I can't stop you, if you want to be reckless, but it's not just you I'm worried about." She said, rubbing Chloe's hand.

"I love you Mira." I said before sitting up. "I promise I'll come right back."

"I'll carry you." Asher scooped me up without asking. I ignored the defeated tone in his voice that told me he agreed with Mira.

As we approached the platform, I curled my hand behind his neck. "I love you too."

He rolled his eyes and kissed me on the forehead.

"You're stubborn."

We landed and saw Ruthy and Xander standing at the door with the rest of the pack right behind them. Liam and Anastasia landed just after us.

I walked to the door and saw a very weak Kayden who was being propped up by Maye.

He glanced up. "Hello sister."

"Kayden." I seethed.

"I see mom and dad are here too. Family reunion, is it?" He coughed, then slumped further to the ground, dragging Maye down. He looked up at me and smiled. "Help me?"

Long Lost Brother

I STOOD THERE IN complete shock as my head reeled.

Kayden looked up at me from his knees, slumped over with one hand on the ground. "Sister?" He heaved dramatically.

"You've got to be kidding me." I heard Ruthy exclaim, but I ignored her.

Mira was down a moment later and gasped.

"Maye?" she whispered.

Maye looked at Mira, her expression cool, but not cold.

"Sister?" Kayden asked again. "I'm literally dying here."

"Damn it." I mumbled. "Bring him in."

Ruthy, followed by Xander, stepped outside and roughly grabbed Kayden under his arms. I could tell by the look on Ruthy's face, she didn't agree with me, which she would let me know in private later. For now, she would play the part of the dutiful beta.

Maye started following them in, but I held my hand up. "I didn't say you." I snapped.

"But..." She leaned forward, holding out her hand, watching Kayden.

"He's my family, unfortunately. You killed yours."

I closed the door in her face, not feeling the least bit guilty about shutting her out. She was a friend, well, I thought she was a friend and she betrayed me. For what?

"Where do you want him?" Ruthy asked, shifting him around in her arms.

I didn't know. I hadn't thought through any of this.

I looked around and saw the house was still in shock and on edge. Ruthy was pissed and Xander was along for the ride and my parents were... I don't know what they were. Happy? Relieved? Scared?

Let's put him in one of the rooms on the second floor.

Ruthy nodded and leapt up, while my parents followed her, and Mira walked outside.

I looked at Asher. "I'm sorry. I didn't know what to do."

He brushed my hair back with his hand, then pulled me into his chest, cradling me. "It's ok."

I felt my legs get weak for a second.

"Let's get you back up to Chloe."

I nodded, and he scooped me up and leapt to the fourth floor. We walked into the room and found Chloe sitting up with her hands clasped in her lap. Her eyes looked tired, but she was alert and looking around.

"What the? Chloe?"

She smiled, weakly.

I jumped out of Asher's arms and ran over, sitting on the bed beside her. I grabbed her hand and felt a spark and realized she felt it, too.

"How are you feeling?"

She looked from her hand up to me. "He's here, isn't he?"

I glanced at Asher in surprise. "Yes. How did you know?"

"I can feel him. It... can feel him. I think it's why I woke up."

"Mira was here–"

"I know. I heard her." She glanced between Asher and me. "Do you really think Asher's going to die?"

I nodded.

Her lips pinched into a flat line. "What are we going to do?"

"I don't know." I held up my fingers as I listed all the possible outcomes. One finger. "If we don't perform the ceremony we're all going to die." Two fingers. "If we do, we *could* all die, and if we don't then a stone will be created." I held up a third finger, then put it down, then put it back up again, shrugging. "If we complete said ceremony and create the moonstone then the Red Crows could get ahold of it and then... we could all die." I said waving my hand around in a big circle to indicate the entire species would die. "And then not to mention during all of that, during the completed ceremony before the Crows get the stone, Asher dies!"

"Well..." She smiled at me. "We could all not die and the Red Crows don't get it and we all live happily ever after?"

I chuckled and wrapped my arms around her neck. "Goddess, how I've missed you."

"I've been right here... and apparently so have you. I mean seriously... I was starting to get stalker vibes." She grabbed my hand and squeezed. "I missed you too."

"We probably need to let the others know... about you." Asher cautiously entered the conversation.

"How about we go surprise them?" Chloe suggested.

"You realize you almost died like an hour ago?"

She shrugged and winked. "I heal quickly."

"Not that quickly."

Her eyes focused on me, "Hey." Her tone became more serious. "Do you feel it? Inside of you?" She reached up to grab at her chest.

"Yes... it's buzzing... almost like before at the Crows compound."

She nodded. "We have to do the ceremony... soon."

I shook my head. "We can't."

Asher interjected. "Cami. You have to. If you don't, you will die. You all will."

"And if we do it, YOU will die! No! I'm not doing it! I'm not losing you!"

"You're willing to risk your life and your sisters," he bobbled his head back and forth. "And I guess your brothers, for mine?"

I took a deep breath. I knew I wasn't being rational, but I didn't care. Mira would find another way. She had to.

"Look." Chloe stood up and then fell back to the bed. "Ok that was less dramatic than I wanted. What I was going to say was look... you had a vision... you know what's going to happen."

Her eyebrows raised in excitement, but I missed what she was getting at.

"She is trying to say the same thing I told you." Asher helped. "We know what's going to happen so we can be prepared for it. We can stop it or at the very least, prevent it from happening."

"But-"

"No, buts." She reached for Asher, clearly ending the conversation. "Help me up. Let's go shock some faces." She pumped her eyebrows.

"I don't think this is a good idea." I mumbled.

"Apparently neither of us is listening to logic right now."

Asher rolled his eyes. "One of you is hard enough, I can't deal with two of you."

Chloe patted him on the chest. "Up, up and away good chariot."

"At least you didn't lose your sense of humor while you've been in a coma for weeks." Asher lifted her up.

"Weeks?" She looked over his shoulder at me, the shock clear on her face.

"Yea." I said cautiously, not knowing how she would take to missing out on so much time.

Without missing a beat, she replied, "No wonder my legs are so weak. I need to start building the muscle back."

I stood up and reached for her hand, holding it the entire way down the hall and let go when Asher made the leap to the second platform. A sudden dread filled me as I looked at how far down it was. Even though I had felt more strong in the last ten minutes than I had felt all day, all week even, I was still nervous.

Asher looked back up and before I could do or say anything, he sat Chloe on the ground and leapt back up to get me.

"Someone call for a Wuber?"

"Wuber?"

"Yea." He scrunched his nose playfully. "It's the newest in were-wolf and shifter transportation." He picked me up in his arms and leapt down to an impatiently waiting Chloe who was pressing onto the railing trying to stand up when we landed.

"Busted." She said, holding her arms up.

"I'm getting my work out in today, between the two of you."

"Such a good brother in law." She smiled.

We walked down the hall and I entered Kayden's room first. It was a smaller bedroom than the ones on the fourth level. There was a window on the right side of the room with a dresser on the left and the bed in the middle, against the back wall. The dark blue duvet had been folded down and rested at the foot of the bed, while Kayden was propped up in the middle.

Anastasia and Liam were standing by his bedside, while Ruthy and Xander were in the corner with hawk eyes on him.

Ruthy turned to look at me. "Cami! You shouldn't be out."

"She's not the only one." Kayden said, shifting in the bed.

Liam and Anastasia looked at the door just as Asher was walking in with Chloe. Anastasia cried out and ran over as Asher was sitting her in a chair in the corner of the room. She fell to her knees and grabbed Chloe's hands as tears started trickling down her cheek.

"What's going on?" Ruthy asked, confused.

"It was me." Kayden answered.

"I'm not talking to you." Ruthy snapped, then looked at me.

"Well, technically you just were..." Kayden retorted.

I saw red flash across Ruthy's face so I grabbed her hand to calm her down. "Ignore him." I turned to Kayden. "Shut up."

He drew an invisible line across my lips.

I turned to face Ruthy. "So, you obviously know when we started the ceremony at the Crows compound, we were sort of bonded together. There was this energy flowing through us, connecting us and then you all showed up and we were able to terminate the connection. The thing is, that it's still there. Chloe and I, and I'm sure Kayden as well, can feel it inside of us, growing and buzzing. It's why when Chloe and I were- are- around one another the synergy created, brought us back to life. When Kayden showed up, the thing inside of us... whatever it is, started vibrating even more and it's probably what helped Chloe out of her coma. The thing inside of us... it wants us around one another... it wants to complete the ceremony."

Ruthy held up her hand. "Please, please, please, can you stop saying it- that it wants this and it wants that? You're giving me the image of a worm or something inside of you, living off you." She shuddered.

"Ew Ruthy. That's just nasty. Now I have that in my head." Xander said nudging her shoulder.

She gave him the side eye and he retreated.

"We aren't there yet." She said holding up her hand.

"But you're saying there's a chance!" He laughed. "Plus, I really thought we bonded over our mutual hate for that guy." He nodded towards Kayden.

"I can hear you."

"I don't care." Xander snapped back.

Mira entered the room a second later and grabbed her chest in shock. "My word."

"Surprise." Chloe flashed her hands in the air not missing a beat.

Mira glided across the room and checked Chloe in several places, her forehead, her wrist, her neck. It was like she was having a hard time believing what was in front of her face.

"Where's Maye?" I asked, halfway caring.

"She's still on the front porch, waiting."

"She's not coming in. I don't trust her."

"And you-" Ruthy started but stopped. *Sorry alpha. I just... I don't get why we let him in. He's a conniving, vindictive, selfish, little shit stain.*

I looked at her and smiled. *I know. I don't trust him either, but he's my brother and I don't say that in a familial sense, rather, he's part of the Trinity and without him here we could- no, we will die.*

What are you going to do?

We have to perform the ceremony. I know we do. Everyone has told me as much, but I just need to buy as much time as possible. I have to put safeguards in place to ensure Asher makes it through. If he dies... well...

Stop. We aren't going to think about that. You know what's going to happen and we're going to prevent it. End of story. She looked at Kayden. "Where are your friends?"

"You left her outside." He smacked his lips. "Rude, I may add."

"Shut up." I barked. "You don't get to come here and tell us we're being rude. You should be thankful you aren't outside with her after what you did."

Ruthy continued. "No. I'm talking about the Crows. We heard you were the alpha of the pack. Loyal packs don't go far without their alpha."

He scrunched his nose. "Yea... they aren't really my pack anymore. After the whole incident at the compound they felt I was a liability."

"So you have what... been on your own?" I corrected before he could remind me, "Aside from Maye."

"Yes."

"And you just decided to show up on our door today?" I asked.

"I felt..." He looked out the window like he was trying to gather his thoughts, "I got this feeling tonight like something was wrong and then I got really weak. I thought I was going to die. Maye used some of her magic and was able to bring me back and then we portaled here." He fumbled with his hands. "Even just being here, I can feel it... the energy between us all."

I heard Xander mumble something about the term it, but ignored him.

"We're not going to perform the ceremony. Thought you should know." I said matter-of-factly.

"If we don't we'll die. Maye said as much."

"Well, Maye doesn't know everything. She's a young witch with no loyalty who betrayed her coven."

"Maye is smarter than anyone in this room."

"I'd be careful what you spout off. You're an enemy in the eyes of most of the people in this room."

"You're right. I'm sorry. Your... bluntness just hit me the wrong way, I suppose."

Anastasia spoke for the first time. "Would you like something to eat? Chloe? Kayden? I made some spaghetti and there was plenty left over. I can have someone bring it by."

"Mother's cooking. I would say I missed it, but I don't remember it." Kayden remarked.

"Kayden." Asher bellowed, using his alpha voice. It commanded the entire room and caused the hairs on the back of my neck to stand up. "You are a guest in our house and as such you will remember your manners. I'll not tolerate you speaking ill of anyone, especially my family. I have no problems kicking you out on your ass since you're the reason we're all in this situation. So don't forget that."

I grabbed his hand and squeezed. I'd never heard him use his alpha voice and I felt uncomfortable and it wasn't even directed at me, while at the same time, feeling excited with the power it commanded.

"Yes, alpha. My apologies." Kayden retreated. "I would love some of your spaghetti, mother."

She smiled, a flurry of emotions were flitting across her face. "It will be here soon."

"Well, I think this has been enough excitement for one night." Chloe said. "Would you have my food brought to my room?"

"Of course, darling." Anastasia said, rubbing her head affectionately.

Asher moved to the door, but Chloe stopped him. "Xander. Can you help me?"

He looked around the room to see if there were any objections. "I would be honored. Plus, there is so much gossip to catch up on." He winked.

Ruthy was fighting the smile on her lips as she was shaking her head.

I know she was still trying to pretend she didn't like him, but I knew she did. It was almost impossible not to like him. He had that way that made you hate-like him. It also helped Levi seemed to tolerate him more, even though there was still something there. Tension? Uneasiness?

"I think I'm going to go too." I yawned. "Mira. Would you walk with me?"

"Of course. Let me just check on Kayden. I want to make sure you're all safe tonight."

I watched Mira walk over and feel his forehead and pick up his wrist. I presume to check his pulse. "How are you feeling?"

He looked up, surprised. "I'm feeling better than an hour ago."

When we were outside of the room, I looked up at the platform, nerves getting the better of me again.

"Let me help you." She waved her arms in a circle and we began floating into the air, landing softly on the fourth platform.

"That is such a nicer way to travel. Easier on the knees." I laughed.

"Making jokes?"

"I do it sometimes when I'm nervous." I shrugged.

Her lips flattened into a hard line and her face fell in sympathy. "I know you're concerned."

I waited until we were in the privacy of the alpha suite before I talked about my intentions of our little meeting. "Do you think Maye is a threat? She has her brother's power after the Gemini transfer." I still couldn't wrap my head around the fact she was so eager for power that she sacrificed her brother's life for it.

"I don't know yet. I was trying to gather that earlier. She was just very concerned about Kayden, so it was hard to get a good read on intentions. She's always been so good at masking them, and now... with so much at stake, I'm just not sure."

"Can you put extra protections around the house? I don't want her sneaking in and causing problems. We'll have wolves on guard throughout the entire night, but still."

"I've already done that. She won't be able to enter the house unless she gets expressed permission from only you or Asher, and I've added some blocks on Kayden as well. I don't know if he's telling the truth about the Red Crows, but he won't be able to communicate with them."

"I remember when Maye did that to me. It was so frustrating."

Mira laughed. "The magic will fade in a few days, like it did with yours. As long as we keep Maye and him apart, then she won't be able to reverse it."

"Ok. So we've taken all precautions we can to keep everyone in this house safe from Kayden and Maye?"

"Yes. If it would make you feel more comfortable, I can have a few of my most trusted stay here."

"Let me talk to Asher about it first."

"Talk to me about what?" Asher asked, walking in.

"Do you want some extra Ellsmire coven witches to stay here to help monitor things concerning Maye and Kayden?"

"Sure, that would be great." He nodded, looking at me. "Is that what you want?"

"It would make me feel safer." I was thankful Asher was not like most other alphas who tried to handle things on their own. Asher understood the meaning of teamwork and was happy to take help when needed.

"Perfect." Mira clapped her hands. "I'll have them arrive tomorrow." She pulled her lips.

"What?"

"One of them may be Luna..."

"No." I said immediately. "She..." I couldn't even get the words out.

Mira nodded. "I understand. The last time you really had any interaction with her was when you thought she was working with Dixon."

"I'm not convinced she wasn't. Ten years is a long time to be with someone and not end up following their same ideologies. She was vile. I'm sorry. I know she's your daughter, but she was horrible to me."

"She was angry at the coven, and rightfully so. Look." She patted the air. "She is one of the best. She was always one of the brightest before everything happened, even though she had a bit of a reckless streak... and I've been working with her for the last several months. And she has saved your life twice now."

"Don't remind me," I huffed, crossing my arms.

"I won't force it, but I think she'd be a great addition to the team and if you decide it's not working out, then I'll pull her back to Ellsmire."

"She's there," I stated, drawing confusion from Asher and Mira.

"She's where?" They asked in unison.

"Fighting with us in the vision I had." I looked at Asher and sighed. "I guess if you trust her, then I should, too. People can change, right?" It was more of a rhetorical question. I still didn't trust Luna... I couldn't. Too much had happened between us, even though she saved my life.

"Thank you." Mira clasped her hands together and started to leave.

"Mira. Wait."

"What is it?"

"I know we have to complete the Trinity, and I know it's going to be soon. Days away even. But you need to tell Luna and the rest of the coven... they need to protect Asher."

"Babe." Asher noted, slipping his arm around my waist.

"I'm serious Asher. I can't lose you. I've already seen it once... I can't see it again. I can't feel it." I started crying. All the emotions I'd been bottling up for the last few hours just came pouring out of me.

He pulled me into his arms and pressed his lips to my forehead. "I love you Camibear."

I looked up at him and smiled.

"I will leave you two to it. Luna and the others will be here tomorrow."

"I want Drake here too, if that's ok." I added, "When he's done helping my brother."

"Of course. I don't think I could stop him even if I wanted to." She raised her eyebrow at me. "He and Ruthy seem to be getting pretty serious. I only hope she doesn't hurt him when her mate comes along."

I scrunched my nose. "Me too. They're a nice compliment to one another and both mean so much to me."

"Take care, darling. I will see you later."

"Oh, Mira." She paused at the door. "In my vision... there were a lot of Red Crows. A lot. We had your coven, our pack and my parent's pack and it was barely enough. I'm not sure of the outcome because I woke up... but there was a lot of death on both sides."

She nodded solemnly. "I will let everyone know."

OLD ACQUAINTANCES

"AGAIN!" ASHER YELLED.

The pack held in their sighs of annoyance and continued to race and fight one another. Asher had been pushing everyone to train for the last two days. Each time getting them up before dawn, taking a break for breakfast and then resuming until lunch.

I walked across the field to stand beside him, gently placing my hand on his back. *I think we can give them a break now. You've been running them ragged the last couple of days.*

Dixon was worse than this.

Doesn't make it right.

They need to be strong. You said it was going to happen soon.

It will. I can feel the buzzing growing stronger every day, and I can tell Chloe is getting weaker, even with me beside her. And I'm getting weaker. I can feel it.

So they need to practice.

We can't have them too tired and sore when the time comes. They need to rest and recover.

He cut his eyes at me and smirked. "Pack. Good work today."

They all stopped and looked at us both.

"Does this mean we're done for the day?" Ruthy asked, bent over with her hands on her knees.

"You're done until you're needed to fight. That could be a day or a week. But just be prepared."

I grabbed onto Asher's shoulder for support.

He glanced at me, worried, but I nodded. "Pack. It doesn't go unnoticed. Your hard work and dedication. The time is coming...

soon. There will be a lot of them. More than I have ever seen, but we won't be alone. We will have the Crescent pack with us and the Ellsmire coven. When the day comes, we will be victorious."

The entire pack thrust their arms into the air and shouted in exhilaration.

My legs buckled just a bit, but I tried to play it off. "Go enjoy the rest of the day! Who knows what tomorrow will bring."

I heard a slow clap echo in the distance and turned to find Luna walking up with a few other witches from Ellsmire. "That was a beautiful speech. Amazing."

The pack house tensed up immediately. I could feel their energy flowing through me, through everyone. Ruthy was standing just to my side a second later, but I put my hand on her shoulder to hold her back.

"Luna."

"The one and only." She said, spinning in a circle.

I was already regretting allowing her here, but Mira ensured she could be trusted.

"I see you haven't changed much since we last saw each other."

She shrugged and stopped just in front of me.

I took in a deep and calming breath. "I would like to thank you for saving my life."

"Again." She added.

"Again," I nodded, trying to hide my irritation. "I also want to welcome you as a guest to our house."

You can't be serious. Ruthy mindlinked.

I'll explain later.

"Thank you for the invitation. I would say I was eager to be here, but you know..." she snarled.

I was finding it really hard to see how she changed, but I had to go back to what Mira said and I trusted her with my life.

"Do you have our rooms ready?"

"Yes. We have done some remodeling and have converted some of the unused space in the basement to bedrooms."

"We're in the basement?" She sneered.

"I wouldn't think about it like that. You are just on the lower level. I feel you will find the rooms to your liking."

She rolled her eyes.

My legs buckled again, but this time I wasn't able to hide it and I swear I saw Luna break for a second. A flash of concern, perhaps, but she rebounded quickly.

"I'm going to get you up to your sister." Asher grabbed me. "Luna, thanks for coming."

"You know I always had a soft spot for you, Ash."

"You know they've marked one another." Ruthy snapped.

"A girl can dream, can't she?"

"No. No, she can not." Ruthy answered matter-of-factly.

Asher started walking away and I looked over his shoulder at Ruthy and winked at her. I thought it would make her smile, but she was still fuming that Luna was back.

I should have warned her, but I knew it wouldn't have helped either way and maybe part of me was hoping Luna wouldn't show up and I would have stressed Ruthy out for nothing.

When we got inside, Asher looked down at me. "You know, we probably should have told her... but her face." He chuckled.

I cocked my head to the side, feeling guilty for agreeing with him.

We were in my sister's room a few minutes later.

"What did I miss?" She asked, sitting up in bed. Her eyes looked weak and her skin was pale.

"Luna and some of the coven just showed up."

"Eesh. I remember what you told me about her, so I know that couldn't have gone over well."

Asher laid me on the bed beside her and I grabbed her hand.

She looked at me with sad eyes.

"What's wrong?"

"This isn't really working anymore." She lifted our hands.

I knew it. I could feel it. "Don't say that."

"You know it's true. You can't want this into existence. We have to perform the ceremony... soon."

"I know." I frowned.

I hadn't checked on Kayden, but I imagine he's the same as us. Perhaps even worse, since we weren't visiting him as much.

I snarled my upper lip.

"I will have a meeting with our parents, Xander and Ruthy tonight... and I guess Luna and the others. We will plan on performing the ceremony tomorrow."

"Evening?"

"Sure." I furrowed my brow. "Why tomorrow night?"

"Your vision had it during the daylight, right?"

I nodded. "Yes."

"Look at that. Changing your vision! Now Asher won't be hurt."

"I like where your head's at, but I don't know if it works that way. I can only hope, I suppose." I smiled at her as she laid her head back down.

She was getting weak and fast. It scared me to leave her and have the meeting with the others, but I knew I had to.

We had to prepare, because if what I saw in my vision came true... it would be a day we would never forget.

MAKING PLANS

I COULD HEAR THE room buzzing with conversation before I walked in. I paused at the door with my hand on the handle, gathering my thoughts and getting my emotions under control.

This was it. The moment we'd been preparing for and dreading.

Asher put his hand on my lower back, reassuring me. "You got this."

I glanced over my shoulder at him and reached to grab his hand before pushing the door open.

The room stopped talking at once and everyone looked at me.

"Thank you all for coming." I moved to the head of the table to stand beside Ruthy.

"Alphas." She nodded and the rest of the room followed suit, except the coven. It wasn't out of lack of respect, it was just a shifter and werewolf thing.

"As I'm sure you all know, we called you here to inform you..." I took a deep breath. "We're going forward with the ceremony tomorrow night."

"Night?" Anastasia asked.

I smiled. "Because of my vision, Chloe thought we should do it at night." I shrugged, "so the vision can't be right."

There was a small chuckle amid the growing tension in the room.

"I know this is scary for everyone. But Chloe and I," I looked at my parents, "And Kayden, are getting weaker. Chloe can barely keep her eyes open and I feel it inside of me. It's killing us. So we can't wait any longer."

Asher walked over to the cubbies on the back of the wall and pulled out a map and spread it on the middle of the table while I started laying out the plan. "This is a map of our house and grounds. Mira said she cast a spell on Kayden to prevent him from communicating with the Red Crows, even though he says he hasn't been. No one believes him, so we took precautions."

"I can confirm the presence of magic in the room." Luna interjected, without any sign of sarcasm or added snide remarks.

I looked at her.

She shrugged. "My mother, Mira, told me what she had done. I wanted to make sure all safety measures were still in place when I arrived."

"Thank you Luna."

She rolled her eyes. She was back.

I continued, "We plan on doing it in the field here." I pointed to the place just past the fire pit and decking, but further away. "With the winds and such, I don't want to risk damaging our property."

"The pack thanks you." Asher said, smiling.

"Anastasia, Liam. We will need your pack around the border here," I said, pointing to the row of trees on the back of the property. "Our pack will cover this tree line to the west, and Luna if you and the Coven could take this space to the south." I pointed to the spot between the field and the house. "If we can create a circle around us, that will help protect us in case the Red Crows show up."

"How will they find out?" A boy from the coven asked.

Luna shot him a nasty side eye and he retreated back into the shadows.

"It's ok. It's a good question. I don't know how they would find out, but I want to plan for the worst outcome and hope we don't have to deal with those consequences."

"Some of the pack has reported the feeling of other shifters in the area, but some of them are newer and I think, are just anxious." Ruthy said.

"We should still check it out."

"We did and came up with nothing."

I smiled at her. Of course she'd take every feeling as a potential threat.

"We'll eat dinner, or at least try to, and then get Chloe and I set up, then bring Kayden down at the last second. The more we can keep him in the dark, the better."

"How long will it last?" Luna asked.

"I don't know. Last time, I felt like it happened both, within the blink of an eye, but also lasted an eternity. Things move differently when we're in the middle of the ceremony. Everything feels like it's slow motion, but I don't know if that is reality or not. It feels disconnected."

"The books have said it happens fairly quickly... in real time." Liam added.

"But we don't know how accurate those are since no one has ever successfully performed it." Luna retorted.

"She's right. We have no idea, really. There are so many unknowns- how long it will take, if we will survive, if the Red Crows will show up. I will just say that if the Red Crows show up, the number one priority will be preventing them from getting the stone. In my vision, we had created the stone, and it was lying on the ground, but we were still in the air. The fight was already happening below, but I don't know how long they had been there." I shook my head and took a deep breath. "All I can say is that I hope what I saw in my vision doesn't come true. Because if it does... many people will die."

Asher gripped my hand.

"I won't force anyone to fight tomorrow. If they do, it needs to be their own choice. I can't have those deaths on my conscious."

"Was Maye in your vision?" Luna asked, a hint of worry in her voice.

"I don't remember. I don't think she was, but I also can't imagine her not being there."

"I will handle her." Luna snapped.

"Your priority needs to be Cami." Asher jumped in.

Her head lurched back in surprise.

"No. It's ok. With Maye's increase in power since the Gemini bond, she may be a bigger problem. I will let Luna make that decision. I trust her judgment."

"You do?" Luna asked.

"You do?" Ruthy chimed in a second later.

"I do. I trust Mira with my life, and she trusts you. So, by default, I trust you."

Luna and Ruthy both looked at me without speaking. I hope I wasn't making a mistake.

We discussed a few more plans regarding placement around the perimeter and other safeguards we could take just in case the Crows showed up, and then sent everyone away so they could rest and prepare for the conversations with their packs and covens.

As everyone was leaving, I stopped Xander.

"What's up, buttercup?" He asked, making a dramatic entrance back into the room.

I smiled, thankful for the constant cheer he always brought. "Tomorrow. I need you to protect Asher."

He laughed. "You two."

"What?"

"He already pulled me aside and told me my priority tomorrow is you."

I rolled my eyes. "It needs to be him. I saw him getting attacked and killed. Lucian will be there with the Red Crows and Asher won't be able to stop himself. He will go after him and not think about anything else. That is when he is killed. He kills Lucian and is looking at me, in satisfaction and doesn't see the other wolf bearing down on him. By the time he realizes, it's too late and you look up and you see it. You race towards him, but you can't get to him fast enough."

"Eesh."

"Just... don't get too far away from him and if you see him fighting with Lucian... then... just be prepared."

"I love your confidence in me."

"Hate to burst your bubble, but you aren't the only one I'm talking to."

"Ouch." He grabbed his chest. "Right through the heart."

"Well, I feel like we can be honest."

"Remind me of that when you ask me about your cooking or some other thing."

"You wouldn't."

He raised his brows. "I wouldn't. I'm obviously a better friend and a nicer person than you."

I rolled my eyes. "Oh my Goddess. You can leave now."

He started walking out of the door.

"Xander?"

He looked over his shoulder at me.

"Thank you."

He winked, and a second later was skipping down the hall, calling Levi's name.

I looked around the empty room while the weight of tomorrow lingered in the air. I knew we had to complete the ceremony, and I was no longer scared about surviving that, but scared of everyone else making it through the day. Dark images were on a loop in my mind, replaying my worst nightmare. No matter how hard I tried, I couldn't get the image of Asher's limp body laying on the ground out of my head.

I stared at the map and wished it could speak to me and tell me where the Red Crows were or show me the future, but I knew that wasn't possible.

A wave of exhaustion passed over me, so I decided to head down the hall to see Chloe. She always managed to put a smile on my face, even in our darkest moments.

"Hey there." She said, opening her eyes when I walked in the door. I could see how weak she looked, and it broke my heart.

"Hey." I pinched my lips together in a hard line.

"That good?" She patted the bed slowly.

I walked over and laid beside her, grabbing her hand. "Just got done with the meeting discussing tomorrow."

"Are we ready?"

"As ready as we're going to be." I squeezed her hand. "How are you feeling?"

"I feel fan-ratty-tatty-tastic."

"That good, huh?" I looked at her and saw her eyes were closed again.

She sighed and mumbled something, so I thought it best to let her sleep.

I crawled under the covers and laid my head on her shoulder. "Goodnight Chloe."

She crooned.

There was a frantic knock on the door.

I leapt off the platform and landed in the foyer.

"Sister."

"Kayden?"

He was covered head to toe in scrapes and cuts.

"Help me."

"Help you? Get the hell off my property."

"Please sister. They're coming for all of us."

"Who?"

"The Crows."

"Why would they be doing that?" I held up my hand. "That's right, because you betrayed us. Do you know how many people died that day because of you?" I let out a frustrated sigh. "You better be thankful I haven't killed you yet!"

"Alpha?" I turned to find Ruthy walking over to me. "Do you need help?" Her face was seething with restrained anger.

"No. I can manage." I turned back to Kayden. "You may leave." I closed the door, but Kayden's hand smacked against it, pushing it back open.

"I can't do that. With Asher gone, your pack is weak and vulnerable."

I stormed out of the door and grabbed him by the collar of his shirt, slamming him against the side of the house and lifting him off the ground. "What do you know about our pack? Nothing!"

He was gasping for air.

"You're the reason he's gone!" I felt my blood boiling.

"Cami? Cami!" Ruthy said, walking outside grabbing my shoulder.

I shrugged her hand off. "You're the reason for all of this! How could you be so stupid? So naïve?"

I felt Ruthy's hand on my shoulder again. "Alpha!" She said sternly.

I dropped Kayden back to the ground, who immediately bent over, grabbing his knees, sucking in air.

"Thanks."

"Shut up." Ruthy snapped. "I didn't do it for you. You mean nothing to me. I did it for her. After everything she's had to go through, the last thing she needed was your death on her conscious."

I walked back inside and waited for Ruthy to walk in before I slammed the door shut.

Kayden banged on the door. "Damn it! They're going to kill everyone... all the Crescents. She's going to come for you." He yelled in exasperation.

I looked at Ruthy and shook my head, fighting with myself. I couldn't let him in, not after everything he's done. Everything he's responsible for.

"I'm sorry." He whined softly.

He couldn't be trusted.

He only looked out for himself.

Where was Asher when I needed him most? I felt a deep ache.

I was the alpha of the house so I had to act like it. Pull myself together.

I stood up straight and opened the door.

Kayden must have slid down and was sitting with his back against it, because when I opened it, he fell backwards into the foyer. He scrambled to his feet.

"Ruthy. Take him to the cellar."

Her eyebrows raised, and she nodded without speaking.

"The cellar? Sounds ominous."

"It was created for assholes like you." Ruthy said, yanking his arm into the house.

By now, several other pack members had gathered in the foyer and were watching. Levi and Xander helped to part the crowd so Ruthy could walk through and then followed her.

I closed the door and took in a deep breath.

Asher... I wish you were here... I need you so badly. I sank to the floor, sitting against the door and put my head in my hands.

I realized it wasn't the alpha wolf thing to do, but I didn't care right now.

What were we going to do?

CHANGE OF PLANS

I BOLTED UPRIGHT IN bed.

"What's wrong?" Asher asked.

I looked around, trying to get my bearings and realized I was in Chloe's room laying beside her. "Asher?" I found his electric blue eyes shimmering in the chair beside me and let out a sigh of relief.

He stood up and walked over to the edge of the bed and sat down. "What's wrong? Was it another vision?" He asked, wiping the hair out of my face before letting his hand rest on my cheek.

The small gesture was what I needed to calm me down. I tilted my head to fully rest it on his hand. "Yes."

"About tomorrow?"

"No. After... several weeks after."

"And?"

I took in a deep breath. "You weren't there. You were gone." I could feel my chest getting heavier and heavier as I spoke the words.

"Maybe I just wasn't in the room or in your vision."

I raised my head and cupped his face in my hands. "You weren't there. Kayden came back to the pack house, bloodied and bruised and said the Red Crows betrayed him and they were coming after us, after all the Crescents. Apparently, a lot of people are going to die tomorrow and then he even said with you gone, our... my... pack was weak. I then yelled at him and said that he was the reason you were gone." I couldn't hold the emotions back anymore. I broke down and started sobbing.

He pulled me into his chest, holding me tightly. "It's ok." He was rubbing my hair. "It's going to be ok."

I pulled away from his hold and looked at him. "It's not. You're going to die tomorrow and so are a lot of others. I know Ruthy, Xander and Levi make it, but I didn't see Drake, or Anastasia, Liam... or Chloe. Oh Goddess. What if they also die?"

I felt myself hyperventilating.

"I can't. I can't."

"You don't know they're dead and just because you saw it doesn't mean that something else can't change."

I didn't have it in me to argue with him anymore. He was trying to console me and I needed to believe he was going to live and survive.

"Lay with me?" I asked, laying down beside Chloe.

Asher climbed in bed and wrapped his arms around me. "I'm surprised we didn't wake her up." He whispered in my ear, before he gave it a gentle kiss.

I couldn't speak as worry weighed heavy on me.

A second later, I felt a wave of comfort spread over me and squeezed Asher's hand.

I felt the bed shaking and woke up to find the sun filtering in through the windows. I rolled over and saw Asher standing up, stretching his arms towards the sky.

"What time is it?

"Just before eight."

"I can't believe I slept that long."

"You were exhausted." He bent over and gently brushed a kiss across my forehead. "I'll have Ruthy or Xander bring you both some breakfast."

"Xander?"

"Yea. He stayed the night last night. I think Ruthy, Levi and him were making plans." He cut his eyes at me. "Something about a secret mission. Xander said he wouldn't tell me the mission, but that they were calling it operation SALT."

"SALT?"

"Save Asher's Life Tomorrow." He rolled his eyes.

I laughed, shaking my head. "Well, I need to protect you, especially now that I've had another vision."

He gave me one more kiss on the nose before he left.

"Where are you going?"

"I have to go talk to some people about my own mission. Mission SCLT."

When Asher walked out of the room, I glanced at Chloe, who was still sleeping. She looked so peaceful. I was almost envious.

I laid back down and stared at the ceiling, mentally preparing myself for the day, but was interrupted by a soft knock on the door.

"Come in."

Ruthy.

"Good morning." She said, looking down her nose at me.

"Good morning."

"Is she still sleeping?" She asked, shocked.

"Yea."

"I wish I could sleep that hard. The smallest noise wakes me up." She laughed, walking the tray of food over. "Should I let her sleep?"

"Yea. She needs it."

"She looks so peaceful."

"I know." I said, stuffing a bite of toast in my mouth.

"What do you think she's dreaming of?"

"I don't know, but I hope it's good thoughts." I put the piece of toast down. "Did Asher tell you?"

"Tell me what?"

I stared at her for a second, trying to figure out if she already knew the answer, but she wouldn't betray his trust if she did. She was a lockbox of secrets.

"I had another vision last night."

"You did?"

"Several weeks after today."

Her nose scrunched. "And?"

I replayed the entire vision from start to finish.

"That little shit."

"Yea."

"So we think he's still working with the Red Crows?"

"Yea. We have to assume it."

"But I thought Mira put a spell on the room."

"That's what she said."

"And Luna confirmed."

I nodded.

She reached across the space and grabbed a piece of toast off my plate and took a bite. "So what are our thoughts on Maye?" She waved the toast in the air as she spoke.

I shrugged. "She wasn't there with him this time and he said the Red Crows were going to kill all the Crescents and that she would be coming after me."

Ruthy nodded, taking another bite of toast.

"Have we been monitoring her?"

"Yea. We've had someone watching her the whole time. Well, just after we moved Kayden in."

"And she hasn't tried anything?"

"Nope. Just sitting there at the door."

"I don't get it."

"You think it's love?"

"It would have to be at this point... I mean, what else could it be?"

"A means to an end? They're both using each other."

"What does he get out of it? She gets the stone and gets rid of the Crescents. Her brother is gone. It's been too long since he died, so there's no hope of bringing him back. What does he get? Revenge on his family?"

"Maybe she's using him. Can we use that against them? Try to drive a wedge."

"Good luck. Chloe and I tried that at the compound and they were prepared for it."

Ruthy grumbled.

"I know."

I glanced at Chloe. "Let's get out of here so we don't wake her up."

"You think it's ok to leave?"

"I've been with her all night. I will go do a few things, then come back and lay with her."

"Does one of those things involve checking on your brother?"

I rolled my eyes. "I feel like I should."

"Your parents have been in there with him a lot."

"I know. I'm sure part of them feels guilty about the way he's turned out."

"You don't?" She asked, shocked.

"I feel like the old me would have, but he's pissed me off so much. Even the coven said they felt a darkness in one of us all those years ago. Well, technically Maye said that, so I don't know if it was true."

Ruthy shrugged.

I took a quick shower, then headed to Kayden's room. Liam was standing by the window looking out at the front grounds, while Anastasia was parked next to the bed. Kayden was on his side, turned away from her, but she didn't seem to care. She just wanted to be near him. I watched him for a minute and saw he looked to be as weak as Chloe.

"Ah, the prodigal sister returns. Tell me. How do you have so much energy?"

"Maybe it's the fact I almost died and was in a coma for a while after I saved your life. You wouldn't know anything about that because you bolted the chance you got."

"Not the entire truth."

I raised my brows at him.

"Sure. We portaled out of there, but to the ridge where my guys got you the first time. I watched as everyone skittered around you, worried. When Mira portaled you out of there, I left."

"So thoughtful."

He raised his voice. "What was I supposed to do? They just tried to kill me and you risked your life for me. Did you really want me to stay around so they could try again?"

I shook my head.

"I know you can't admit it because I'm the bad guy, but you would have done the exact same thing and you know it."

"Don't compare us. We aren't the same. Tell me... Are you still working with the Red Crows?"

His head snapped in my direction with a look of shock on his face, and then his eyes narrowed on me. "Why do you ask that, sister? Have another one of your future visions?"

"Why are you avoiding the question?"

"Why are you avoiding mine?"

"Because I asked you first!" I yelled. "Are you still working with them? Tell me! What's the plan?"

He causally rolled and looked out of the window.

"Damn it Kayden! People are going to die."

He didn't react, but continued staring out of the window.

"I think that's enough for now." Anastasia whispered.

I looked at her and then at Liam before storming out of the room.

"Ta-ta sister." I heard echoed behind me.

I didn't even bother turning around. He wasn't worth my time.

I leapt downstairs and felt my legs give a little when I landed. It was hard to remember I wasn't as strong as usual when I was this angry.

There was a knock on the door at the same time I landed. Part of me hoped it was Maye so I could lay into her for all that she's had a part in, but when I opened the door, Drake was standing there.

"Drake!" I wrapped my arms around his neck then popped my head outside, looking behind him for Maye, but she was gone. I pushed the door open. "Come in. Where have you been?"

He laughed. "I was helping your impossible brother out."

"How is he?" I felt bad I hadn't talked to him much since I had been back from the compound. I had let them know I was ok and promised to stop by for dinner one night, but I just hadn't made it over yet.

He cocked his head to the side. "Good. You need to call him though. He's worried sick about you. It took everything I had to get him to stay at Leo's. I almost bound them both to the house."

I puckered my lips. "I know. I'll call them now." It was hard to remember Leo and Will couldn't mindlink. They had been- are- such an important part of my life, but things have changed so much after I learned I was a Crescent Moon shifter. They had been so great after they learned the truth at the end of last year, but it definitely put a strain on the relationship. Not so much because of anything they have done, but because so much had been going on with me. I wanted to keep them safe, so that meant keeping them in the dark, or lessening our talks, which hurt almost as much. But I would explain everything when this was over. The priority right now is keeping them safe and alive.

"What are you doing down here?" Xander asked me, then saw Drake. "Hey man." He grabbed his hand to shake. "So glad you're back. Ruthy has been a bear," he paused, "since you've been gone." He sang the phrase from the Kelly Clarkson song.

"No she hasn't." I defended.

"Glad to see some things haven't changed." He rolled his eyes, laughing.

"Ruthy's in the kitchen." Xander thumbed over his shoulder.

"Thanks man." Drake patted his shoulder and walked past him.

"What's up?" I asked Xander.

"You tell me."

I furrowed my brow.

"Don't pretend you weren't coming down here to find me to have a talk."

"You're irritating, you know that?"

"Because I'm right?" He wrapped his arm around my neck. "You love me."

I rolled my eyes and we walked into one of the sitting rooms off the main foyer.

"What's up, buttercup? Let me have it."

"Did Asher tell you?"

"No. But he looked slightly more stressed than usual, so I figured it was something."

"I had another vision last night."

"I see."

"Xander. It basically confirmed the first one. Asher is going to die, lots of people are going to die and the Red Crows are going to get the moonstone."

He looked at me without speaking.

"I don't know what to do." I laid my head on his shoulder. "What do you do when you see the tsunami coming, but you and all your loved ones are cemented to the ground?"

"That was a nasty visual."

I popped my head up and glared at him.

"I'm sorry. I joke in awkward and tense conversations."

I sighed and laid my head back down.

"We'll figure it out. You and Asher are the alphas of the house. You'll be protected."

"I hear what you're saying, but I can't unsee what I saw."

We sat in silence for a little while.

"Luna was looking for you." Xander chimed.

"She was? Why didn't you tell me before?"

"Because you needed to talk and rest and I needed you to think I was omniscient."

"You're an ass, you know that."

"A cute one… I'm sure you accidentally left that part out."

"Yea." I rolled my eyes. "Completely by accident." I stood up. "Do you know where she is?"

"I think she's downstairs in the cellar."

"The what?" I snapped my head at him. "We don't have a cellar."

He laughed. "Calm down. I was only kidding. She's downstairs."

I studied him for a moment, letting my mind calm back down. Was it only coincidence that he called a room downstairs a cellar after I just had a dream- a vision- about that?

"Thanks."

"You ok? You look like you've seen a ghost."

"I'm fine."

I walked across the kitchen to the door that led downstairs to our workout room and new bedrooms for those without levitating or jumping powers.

It was an open area with padded floors and exercise equipment scattered around, with televisions hanging on the walls and arcade like games on the back wall. Down the hall on the back side, we had added doors to the rooms to close them off. I didn't know which room Luna was in and didn't want to knock on every one.

"Luna?"

Silence.

"Luna?" I yelled a little louder.

"Coming!" she barked from one of the back rooms.

A door, three doors down, opened, and she walked out, putting her hair up.

"Good morning. I heard you needed to talk to me?"

"I just wanted to finalize the plans for today. After the meeting last night, I had some ideas.

I nodded.

She started rambling off her entire list and places she could have her people stationed and admittedly, they were good ideas.

"So you think Maye is going to be a problem?"

"I do. I don't trust her. She's always been jealous of my rank and power within the coven." She bobbled her head from side to side. "It's probably why she went after me in the first place."

I snarled. "She made a mention of Drake when I was at Ellsmire before."

She nodded. "He may want to watch his back, too. He moved up through the ranks fast, especially when he was the one chosen to look after you at such a young age. He's been a favorite of Ellsmire and his parents are damn near royalty."

"Really? He doesn't talk about them much."

She nodded. "They're very good at what they do and get tasked to several high-profile cases, probably another reason he was chosen for you... he used to travel with his parents, so he's familiar with protocol. Now he's managing you on his own."

"Managing me?" Sounded like a job, rather than him being a friend.

"Yes. He's your general protector and conduit to the coven. Granted, his role has increased exponentially since you found out the truth about everything. Prior to that, he had it kind of easy." She shrugged. "You and your family are a top priority for the coven. Implications of this Trinity curse are still not fully known. I just know it won't be good if Maye gets her hands on the moonstone."

"You think she would try something?"

"I think she's an opportunist and while most of us are distract-ed trying to prevent the moonstone from being taken, she'll be working on something else." She added. "She didn't come from a powerful family and her whole life she has been obsessed with that- it's power. She strategizes and manipulates to get what she wants." She took a deep breath. "I wouldn't put it past her to use your brother too, especially after what she did to hers." She shook her head in disgust.

I raised my eyebrows in agreement. "I still can't believe she had him killed for more power."

"That's dark, even for me." She smirked.

Were we bonding? This felt weird. "Look. I want to thank you again for your help today."

She shrugged.

"Also... can you help keep an eye on Asher?"

She furrowed her brows.

"Long story short, I've had several visions or dreams or whatever you want to call them and he dies today... in all of them."

"Shit."

"Yea. I can't let that happen."

She took in a deep breath. "He'll probably be near you because he can't seem to stay away." She rolled her eyes and then caught herself. "So I guess that means I'll be near you as well."

"Thank you."

We stared at each other quietly for a minute, both wanting to say something, but not having the guts. I needed to find it. "Luna. I'm sorry for what happened to you years ago. I'm sorry your coven turned its back on you, and I just wanted to thank you. After all of that, you saved my life not once, but twice, which I will admit is a little hard for me to accept." I smiled slyly. "But I have. So, thank you."

She scrunched her nose. "You're welcome. But don't think I did it for you."

I could tell she was still trying to keep her wall up, even though she didn't want me to see.

"Mira and the Council are on standby. If we need them, they'll portal here."

"Why can't they just be here? I've seen them in the vision. Why don't we want to show our force against the Crows to stop them?"

"It's a political landmine for us."

"I don't understand."

"You wouldn't. Respectfully, you haven't grown up in this life to know any better." She sighed. "Ellsmire is a witch's coven, obviously." I nodded, and she continued, "They look after you and your family, but mostly you, because my mother has a connection with you. However, the coven needs to remain as neutral as possible in most situations, intervening only when completely necessary."

"So they don't care if the Crows get the moonstone?"

She cocked her head to the side. "They obviously don't want that, but... if by some chance the Crows don't show up and they are there, then it will look bad."

"And if they don't show up and the Crows are, then..." I was having a really hard time understanding.

"I agree with you. I also believe you, but the Council is not Mira and while she holds a lot of sway with them, she also burned some bridges when..."

"When what?"

"When she brought me back into the fold. She had to do a lot of negotiating and explaining."

"Oh."

"The Council doesn't... they don't believe you have visions." She shrugged, "Well, really, just one is the biggest hold up and they need full support."

"Let me guess Madame Lydia?"

"Yes."

"I don't understand what her problem is with me."

"She doesn't like many people."

By the look on her face, I could tell Luna also had some run-ins with her.

"It's not typical for shifter or Crescents to have... extra powers and, well, you seem to."

"They think I'm lying?"

"No, they are just... confused and probably a little nervous."

"I still don't understand. They'd rather wait for me to be in a dire situation and prove that I'm right, instead of trust me and end it before it starts?"

She shrugged.

There was no way I was going to convince them with the time I had left before the ceremony that they needed to be here. The best I could hope for was to tarnish my credibility in hope the Crows didn't show up and kill everyone I love. I shook my head and tried not to sound too defeated. "We have some time. Do you want to come up and grab some lunch?"

She narrowed her eyes.

"I'm not asking for us to be best friends."

"Good." She tilted her head down and I thought I saw a hint of a smile. "We'll be up in a little while. I want to go over the changes with the team first."

"Sounds goo-"

The house started going into alarm.

"What's that?" Luna asked, her body getting tense.

"I don't know."

Alphas. It's Chloe! She's not breathing.

"It's Chloe. She's not breathing." I called behind me as I was taking the stairs ten at a time.

You Can't Change Fate

By the time I made it to her room, our parents were in there with Kayden.

"What's he doing here?" I barked.

"She's not breathing. I thought he could help." Anastasia answered from Chloe's bedside.

Ruthy was on top of Chloe, pressing on her chest. She looked over her shoulder at me and her eyes told me all I needed to know.

I ran across the room and grabbed her hand. There was a slight flicker, but it didn't help.

I looked at Asher and he shook his head slightly. I felt the rock forming in my stomach.

It was happening.

It was time.

We couldn't wait any longer.

I looked outside and saw the sun shining brightly, just like my vision. We tried to change it, but you can't change fate... you can't change the future.

"Well, I guess we're performing the ceremony now." Kayden said apathetically.

No. We can't. It was too early. I wasn't ready to say goodbye to Asher because part of me knew that no matter how many people I talked to, something bad was going to happen today.

I couldn't change the future...

"Ruthy?"

She continued to press on Chloe's chest.

Luna entered the room a second later and walked over to Chloe. She grabbed her wrist then swiped her hands across her body, not touching her, but swirling them around her chest. She looked at me and shook her head.

"Damn it."

"Sister. Just think. The sooner we complete the ceremony, the sooner I'll be out of your hair."

"Shut up Kayden!"

Luna held her hand up and clasped her fingers together quickly.

Kayden went to say something, but Luna magically sealed his lips together. He threw his hands in the air in frustration.

I took a deep breath and looked around the room. "Drake, find Maye. Xander, get your pack here. Levi, prepare our pack. Mom, can you get Chloe? Dad, you need to keep an eye on Kayden. Let's move to the field and get ready."

Kayden reached up and pried his lips apart. "Ouch."

Everyone started moving out of the room. "Asher. Wait." I called after him when he got to the door.

He stopped and walked over to me, and I wrapped my arms around his neck, burying my face in his chest. He held me tightly and we just stood there. The weight of the world felt like it was crushing me. We had talked about this, made plans, and yet they had still changed. I wondered if part of me knew they were going to change, but I was just unable to admit it to myself.

I could feel anxiety and fear pumping through our bond, coupled with love and anger. So many emotions...

I felt like my heart was going to break, terrified of what was to come. "Asher."

He pushed me away and looked into my eyes before pressing his lips to my forehead.

"I can't say goodbye to you." I started crying.

"Then don't." He smiled, trying to hide his own worry.

"Asher. You know what I saw. We tried to change it, but it didn't work."

"You don't know if something else doesn't change the future."

"What if it doesn't?" I could feel my wolf whimpering, which caused my chest to get tight.

He pulled me back into him.

"I love you so much, Asher Evans."

"I love you too, Cami Evans."

I looked up and pressed my lips to his, holding him against me. I didn't want to stop because I knew this could be the very last time that I kissed him- that I felt his lips on mine, his body pressed against me. We didn't have enough time. I had this whole life planned for us- a future and now... it was all coming to an end.

Alphas. Ruthy said solemnly.

She knew too.

"We have to go." Asher gently pushed me away.

I shook my head. "I can't."

"You said I'm killed after I kill Lucian. I just won't fight him or I will know and be prepared. Ruthy knows, Drake, Luna, Xander. Everyone knows."

I kissed Asher one more time. "Don't leave me."

"Never." He ran his finger from my forehead down the bridge of my nose before tapping the tip gently.

We ran down the hall, leapt down the foyer, and ran outside.

I looked around and saw everyone in their places and felt the anxiety and tension oozing around the entire field. There was no sign of Drake, Maye or the Red Crows.

Liam was standing behind Kayden and Anastasia was holding a limp Chloe up.

"Let's go." I said, grabbing Kayden's hand.

He grabbed Chloe's hand and I looked at Asher and mouthed, I love you before I grabbed Chloe's hand. Instantly, her body stiffened and her eyes opened as she sucked in a large breath of air. Anastasia and Liam backed away, and Lily and Theo joined them. I saw them say something, but I couldn't hear it.

The buzzing was pulsing through us, almost singing like it was happy we were all connected again. I felt the wind pick up around us and saw the clouds overhead get dark. It was happening so much faster than last time and there were still no Red Crows. Maybe my vision was wrong. This would happen too fast for them to show up.

I felt my body floating up. I looked from Kayden to Chloe and was thankful to see she was fully alert.

I felt this pulse moving through us like it was passing in one hand and out the other, getting faster and faster. My back stiffen and I had to fight my neck from straightening so I could watch Asher. I had to know he was going to be safe.

I looked behind him and saw Xander, Levi, and Ruthy with Luna off to the side, and that's when I saw it. The ring of light forming in the field behind them.

Asher! Behind you!

Silence.

My heart was sinking.

The blue portal opened all the way up and wolf after wolf leapt through.

And so it started.

I tried to break my hands free, but they wouldn't budge. I had to go fight. I had to protect him.

The whole pack shifted in unison and charged the Red Crows, followed by Liam and Anastasia's pack, who came out of the woods surrounding the field in a variety of creatures- mostly wolf and bears. A Crow wolf ran after one of the bears and leapt through the air, clamping down on its arm. The bear shook violently, throwing the wolf across the air landing on its side. The wolf took a moment to get up, but ran off in an opposite direction.

I watched Asher and Ruthy race through the crowd- sleek, determined. He would turn, she would turn. He would stop, she would stop. Xander and Levi were right behind them, following their every move, causing my heart to swell. They would protect him. Everything was going to be ok.

Above the buzzing, I heard a clack of lightning, then felt a surge of electricity shoot through us, filling us with a charge... with power. The others on the ground seemed unfazed, their attention solely focused on the Crows.

It felt like there was another surge building up and then, as if shooting from the middle of each of us, then up to the sky, another clack of lightning snapped through the clouds. I realized the energy was coming from us into the lightning, not the other way around.

I fought with all my strength to turn my head back to the ground to watch the scene unfolding. There were flashes of lights from Luna and her team as they huddled on the southern side of the field, closer to the house, shooting off spells. Behind her, another portal was opening, and I panicked. More Red Crows lunged from the blue circle, attacking them. It was pure chaos on the ground with Crows coming in from all angles. When one portal would close, another would open. I had never seen so many Crows before... how was this possible?

I stared at the ground, trying to comprehend everything, and that's when I saw it. I was the only one that could see it too, well me and my siblings.

The Crows were disappearing into thin air. They weren't real. Not all of them, anyway. They were sent to distract and to overwhelm.

I panicked, my heart nearly pumping out of my chest.

Asher! Ruthy! They aren't real! Watch your backs! They're decoys! Silence.

I knew they wouldn't be able to hear me, but I had to try.

I felt my neck wanting to be turned up to the sky, but I fought with all my strength to keep it angled towards the ground to watch everything. I saw a few of the wolves attack holograms before they realized they were decoys because they paused and then the rest of the pack stopped and waited.

The field started dwindling in size as Maye's spell seemed to wear off.

I felt a surge of wind around us and I looked down the field to see Mira and the Council gliding across with their staffs in their hands. Maye must have realized because I saw her launch something at them and a second later, the ground in front of them was exploding up, knocking a few of them down, while the rest of the holographs vanished.

I felt another pulse building between us as lightning spouted off rapidly, and then silence.

Everything stopped moving.

Time was frozen.

One last surge moved through us, circling with such speed that I felt like I was on the fastest merry-go-round, even though I wasn't even moving. It felt like my body was being cut through with the smallest razor blade and all I could think of was death by one thousand paper cuts.

This was it.

I knew it. I could feel it with every fiber of by being and so could Kayden.

The loudest clack of lightning, the actual zap as it moved through the air, surrounded us and then shot straight from the sky to the ground.

I felt breathless, like all of my air, all of my energy had just been sucked out of me.

A second later, the clouds disappeared and the blue skies returned, but we were still floating in the air and there was silence.

The kind of silence that was suffocating- almost deafening. The kind that makes you question whether you're alive or dead.

This was it, I slowly realized... this was the moment from my vision. I was floating through the air, and it was deathly quiet. Everyone was still fighting below, moving in slow motion, completely unaware we had completed the ceremony. I watched as everyone attacked one another, fur and blood flying, bodies scattered across the grassy field laying on the ground in the fetal position- dead. Streaks of black grass lined the fields where spells had been cast.

There, in the middle of the chaos, was the lone black stone. The moonstone. The power that one little stone held...

My eyes swept across the field and landed on Maye, who was still standing by the portal, out of the chaos. I could see it on her face. She knew we were done. The portal closed, and she started walking towards us. Not too fast though, she didn't want to bring attention to it, just slowly walking, throwing out a spell here or there as others came near her.

No!

This could not be happening.

I looked at Kayden and then to Chloe. Kayden was focused on the stone. Did he look worried? Panicked? He saw Maye making her way over to us. Why was I getting the feeling that's not what he wanted? I looked back at Chloe and she was staring at me with such intensity that I felt like I should be able to hear something- a thought, a whisper, something. But there was nothing.

Just silence.

I felt a twinge in my leg.

No!

I knew what was coming next. I had replayed this moment over and over in my head, dissecting every detail. I looked down and saw Asher's wolf kicking off Lucian's. Levi, Xander and Ruthy were nowhere around him because they were all fighting with other wolves, and Luna and Drake had their backs to one another, circling.

They had been separated!

Asher turned around as his wolf hunkered down on all fours, ready to attack and then realization set in. He knew what was coming. He knew he was going to be killed after Lucian's death. Yes! Yes! It was changing! He was changing the future. This was different!

Asher's wolf looked up at me- he was telling me he understood! His bright blue eyes pierced through the haze that surrounded me. I watched as Lucian lunged after Asher, but he sidestepped him. Asher squared off again, keeping his head on a swivel, and then Lucian lunged again. Asher snapped at his neck, missing. This was all different. A modicum of relief crept in as I dared to hope for a second that my vision would be changed.

I looked down at my hands - our hands. We had to break apart. I had to get down there and help him.

Lucian lunged forward again and Asher's wolf reared up on his hind legs and caught Lucian's wolf around the arms, locking him there in a standing stance, while his mouth latched around Lucian's neck. Asher twisted and Lucian's wolf let out a scream, but he was able to get out of the hold.

I could feel my heartbeat pounding a hole in my chest.

Xander! Ruthy! Levi! Liam! Anastasia! Anyone!

Silence.

Lucian was limping around shaking his head from side to side, like a boxer whose bell had just been rung.

Asher took the opportunity and lunged forward and knocked into the side of Lucian, causing him to fall on his side and skid. Asher glanced at me and then stood over Lucian's lifeless body and bit down on his neck and twisted.

No mercy. No hesitation.

Lucian's body shifted into a human seconds later.

Asher looked up at me and my heart sank.

This was it. It was like fate had known we ventured off track and it course corrected.

Asher knew this was it. He had to know! Why was he looking at me? He knew this was the moment. Why? We had talked about this on repeat. He knew. Goddess! He knew!

I was screaming... rather, I was trying to. I could feel this energy moving within me, but it was different than before. This was not a unified energy between us. No. This energy was within me, boiling up.

I felt this heat surrounding me and saw a light dancing around my hands, around my arms. Chloe was looking at me, her eyes were wide with surprise. Could she feel it too?

I looked back down at Asher and saw the wolf charging him and looked in the distance and saw Xander running towards him. Just like my vision, he was going to be too late.

I couldn't let this happen. I couldn't lose him.

I saw the wolf leaping after Asher.

I screamed out and used all the strength I could to break our hands apart. I felt the burst of energy shoot out of me, blowing Kayden, Chloe and me apart, throwing us on the ground. As if someone had removed the cone of silence from above our head, the noises of the field rushed around us. Sounds of growling, ripping, and screaming. It was horrifying. I stood up as quickly as I could and saw Asher lying on the ground.

"Asher!"

Xander got there the same time I did and leapt on the back of the Red Crow that was hovering over Asher.

I fell to my knees by his head. I picked it up and cradled it on my lap. "Asher!" I yelled. "Don't you do this to me! I told you! I told you this was going to happen!"

A howl echoed in the distance and the remaining Red Crows backed away.

The moonstone!

I looked to where I'd just come from and the stone was gone.

They'd gotten the moonstone.

I looked up briefly to see Kayden holding it in the air between his thumb and his forefinger just before he winked at me and ducked into the portal.

I looked back at Asher, rocking back and forth as tears streamed down my face.

"Asher. Please, please, please, open your eyes."

I looked over his body and realized he didn't have any visible marks on him. Did the Crow not bite him? I replayed those last seconds in my mind, but couldn't remember him being bitten or swiped.

"Asher Evans! You come back to me!" I smacked him in the chest repeatedly, rage and sadness driving me. "Asher! Asher! Open your eyes." Tears continued to stream down my face as I shook him. I couldn't lose him. Not now! We didn't have enough time together.

"Asher." I sobbed as I continued to hit him until a hand gripped my wrist. I tried to jerk out of it, but my arms were exhausted and I was weak.

I looked up and saw Luna standing above me, her eyes broken as she looked between Asher and me. "You need to stop."

Mira was beside her. "Cami, are you ok?"

I shook my head, confused by her question. "Yes, yes. I'm fine. It's Asher! Help him! Fix him!"

"What happened?" She asked, dropping to her knees.

"I don't know." I shook my head, trying to remember exactly, but reality was blurring with my vision.

I rolled Asher's head over, looking for the gaping wound on his neck, but it wasn't there.

"Did you see?" I asked Xander.

He shook his head. "It happened so quickly. I saw the Crow running after him and then there was this flash of light from you and it knocked me back."

"Me too." Levi, Drake, and Luna said at the same time.

Ruthy came up and skidded to a stop when she saw me on the ground holding Asher. She started shaking her head and a second later, her legs gave out. Drake caught her just before she hit the ground.

Mira looked at me, her expression torn.

"What is it? What's wrong?"

She shook her head. "I don't know."

"You don't know?" I shouted in shock.

"He's alive... but..."

"But what?"

"I don't know.

"He's alive?" I whispered. "He's alive." I said, a little louder. I looked at Ruthy. "He's alive."

She nodded her head, but didn't speak.

"He's alive." I repeated to anyone who would listen.

"Let's get him back to the house." Mira suggested.

Xander scooped him up without waiting.

I looked at Liam and Anastasia. "Kayden took the moonstone. I saw him holding it between his fingers before he walked through the portal."

Anastasia's face fell like she had failed. Liam wrapped his arm around her for support. I think on some level, she had hoped these last days she could undo years of pain and damage. She had hoped he would have changed, that he would have chosen us, but she didn't know him, albeit I didn't know him either, but I had a fairly good sense of who he was after he kidnapped me.

He wouldn't change.

Ruthy stood up and wiped her face. "I'll handle the pack. You figure out what's wrong with Asher and bring him back to us." Her words were curt and without emotion.

I nodded in a partial daze.

He was alive. The words were on repeat in my head. He was alive.

As I was walking back to the house, I heard Ruthy giving orders to compile all the bodies into two separate areas.

Asher was alive.

That was all I needed to focus on right now.

AFTERMATH

Xander had brought Asher upstairs to our room and laid him on the bed.

This damn bed! I wanted to throw it through the window!

I felt like every time I thought about this bed, it only held memories of bad things. Me in a coma, me weak, Asher now... I don't even know what he was.

When all of this is over, we're going to get a new bed! An enormous bed! A fluffy bed with a white comforter that feels like silk!

I scolded myself for thinking about the bed right now when everything else was happening, but I felt weak and broken. Useless. I had to focus on something that was definite.

"Cami?" Xander was looking at me like he had called my name several times.

"What?"

"Are you ok?"

"What? Huh? Yes. I'm fine." Just having an inner dialogue about a stupid bed because I'm spinning out-of-control right now.

"Mira and Drake are coming up." Chloe said, walking into the room.

I hurried across the room and wrapped my arms around her, squeezing her tightly. "Are you ok? How do you feel?" I pushed her away and looked at her, lifting her hair, squeezing her arms.

She laughed and looked over her shoulder at Mira and Drake walking in with a few other Council members. "I'm fine. It's getting a little crowded in here. You focus on Asher and we'll talk later. I'm going to make myself useful to Ruthy and Levi."

"Me too." Xander said, pointing in the air.

"Thank you." I mouthed.

He winked at me. "Call if you need me."

My lips flattened as I nodded. "Mira."

She held her hand up, acknowledging me, but didn't turn around to look at me.

I glanced at Drake, who was standing across from her.

I didn't know what to do- didn't know if I should stay here or leave. Leaving wasn't an option, though. Part of me was terrified if I left, if I took my eyes off him for one second, he'd be gone, like this was all some kind of dream.

Terror filled me.

What if this was a dream? What if I was still on the field and everyone was still fighting beneath me?

I felt my heart race and got light-headed, stumbling backwards and bumping into a table.

"Luna!" I heard Mira shout.

Fighting through the haze, I felt a hand on my arm guiding me to the chair by the door.

"Dreaammm." I mumbled.

"Cami!"

I shook my head, feeling like I was in a daze.

"Cami!" I was being shaken.

I felt my head wobbling around like it wasn't properly affixed to my neck.

"I think she's in shock!" Luna yelled. "Cami!" I felt the sting across my face before I heard the slap.

It shocked me back to present and squatting in front of me was Luna.

"Thank Goddess!" Relief swept across her face.

"Did you slap me?" I asked, grabbing my cheek. I could feel the heat radiating under my touch.

"You wouldn't listen."

"You didn't have to slap me."

"You could have listened. Are you feeling ok?"

This was not a dream. In my dream, Luna wouldn't give two shits about how I was feeling, if she was even in it to begin with. "I'm fine. How's Asher?"

"Mira is still looking him over." She placed her hands on my head. "Let me look at you."

I batted her hand away. "I'm fine."

"I will look over you. You can choose how painful it will be."

I glared at her and let my arms fall to my lap.

"Stafford." She called out and a tall lanky man walked over.

"Yes, Luna."

"Get my mother's bag by the door."

"I don't-"

"Now!" she demanded.

He was back a second later with the bag. She sat it on the ground and immediately began rummaging through it. She grabbed something out and then thrust the bag in the air. "Take this to her."

He nodded and walked away.

Luna began checking my vitals, among other things, before she held up a needle.

"Nope." I said, pulling my arm from her hand.

"Cami. We have to. We need to check your blood for anything... odd."

"Odd?"

"You three are the first that have survived the Trinity ceremony."

"We aren't lab rats."

"No, but wouldn't you want to know if there's something different about you... see if it changed you? You... your body... went through a lot."

"What aren't you telling me Luna?"

"Nothing."

"Luna. I can tell you're hiding something."

She raised her brows at me with the needle causally dangling between her fingers.

"Fine, but try not to get too much joy out of stabbing me with a needle."

"I'm hurt you would even think that." A small smile played on her lips just before she stuck the needle in my arm. "I'm going to need three vials."

"Three?"

"You don't want me coming back for more later, do you?"

I narrowed my eyes at her and she purposefully ignored me.

Mira stood up and looked at me. I wanted to run over to her, but I was stuck in the chair with a needle in my arm.

"Hurry." I said, bouncing my feet up and down.

"I'm sure it isn't anything too serious." Luna said, pulling the needle out of my arm.

I jumped out of the seat.

"Your bandaid."

I grabbed it out of her hand and put it on my arm as I raced over to Mira.

"Is he ok?"

She shook her head.

"No." I cried.

"No, child. Calm down and let me speak." She reprimanded. "He's alive, vitals are strong, but I don't know why he isn't waking up."

"Is he injured?"

"No. I think that blast you emitted knocked him out."

"So I did this?" My hand clasped over my mouth.

"I can't say for certain. Do you know what you did?"

I shook my head. "It just happened. I didn't mean to. I thought he was going to die. I was so scared and now..." I buried my face in my hands. "I did this to him... me."

"No, I know you didn't do it on purpose. It's a rare gift, hardly even seen."

"What is it?"

"I don't know what your Elders would call it, but we call it a Shiban Sori."

"A what?"

"It's a burst of light- a power source. I don't know much more about it, but I'm having others find more information."

"It happened another time at the Red Crows compound. I remember it scaring Maye, but she didn't say why. She just ran away."

Mira studied me for a minute, then continued, "We will continue to monitor Asher. How are you doing?" She swiped her hand across my forehead and gently brushed my hair behind my ear, cupping the back of my neck.

"I'm fine. Worried about Asher, but fine."

Alpha. Will and Leo are here.

I looked at Mira. "Are you going to stay with him?"

"I have to get yours and Chloe's blood back to Ellsmire. We need to better understand what the Trinity curse does, if it changes you at all." She sighed. "But don't worry. Luna and Drake will stay behind to monitor things."

I looked at Luna, who had her arms crossed in front of her chest, and then to Drake, who was standing beside Asher. "I'll be right back. Leo and Will are here."

Drake pulled his face.

"What?"

"Nothing. They're just worried about you. They knew you were going to finish the ceremony today."

I nodded and then walked down the hall. I heard Ruthy talking to Leo and leading them into the kitchen, warning them of the scene they were about to walk into.

When I landed in the foyer, Will turned to look at me, then tapped Leo on the arm.

"Hey sis." He said concerned, having seen the several pack members sprawled across the kitchen and living room floors, with bloody wraps laying beside them.

I exhaled and ran over to him, wrapping my arms around his neck. All the worry and stress of the ceremony melted away when I saw him. He had always been my rock growing up, the one who stayed with me when I had my night terrors, the one who made me feel safe. I needed his stupid face right now, squeezing harder.

"Everything ok?" He laughed, pushing me away after a second.

I tried to regain my composure, so I didn't worry Leo. Will had seen me broken many times, but not Leo. I tried to keep it hidden from him. I never understood why, my only guess was when I was younger, I was scared if he saw the real me- the broken me- he wouldn't want me. I know now I was being crazy because Leo was the best thing that could've ever happened to me and he seemed to love me unconditionally, almost from the moment he and Will found me clinging to life on the edge of the creek bank. "Yes. Well, no, but yes."

"Sounds ominous." Leo said, looking over his nose.

"Want something to drink?" Ruthy offered while the rest of the pack gathered their bloody clothes and cleared out of the kitchen.

"No thanks. Drake told us about the ceremony tonight, and we wanted to be here to support you." He said, watching them leave with a grimace on his face. "But it looks like we're late."

"They'll be fine." I nodded at the pack. "We heal fast." I took in a deep breath. "We had to do it earlier because Chloe was fading fast."

"I see." Leo waited for me to finish, knowing I had more I wasn't saying.

I blinked hard. "I don't know how bad the damage is yet. I've been upstairs... Asher was injured." I scrunched my nose. "Well, more knocked out or something. Drake's with him now."

"Is he ok? Drake said you were nervous about today."

"I was... I still am."

"Do you want to talk about it? It's no front porch swing, but I know you have rockers outside." Leo said, grabbing my shoulder.

I nodded.

"I'm going to see Drake." Will looked at Ruthy. "Give me a lift?"

She scooped him up and laughed when he flailed out like a child throwing a tantrum. "Imagine if you and I had ever been a thing." He purred playfully. "You could carry me around like this all the time!"

Ruthy muffled a laugh. "You couldn't handle me, princess."

"I..." He chuckled, "No, you're probably right. You definitely ended up with the better one of us. Who knew he was a witch... or warlock... that's what they liked to be called, right?"

"What's going on butter bean?" Leo asked, pulling my attention back to him.

"Butterbean? It's been a while since you've called me that."

He smiled, patting my shoulder as we walked outside. "I use it on special occasions."

"I had a vision Asher and a lot of others were going to die today. Some did. I just don't know who or how many."

"But Asher?"

"He's alive. He's just knocked out. I don't know if it's a coma or something else. I was up in the air like my vision and I got scared. I saw a Red Crow coming after him and I panicked and all the sudden this light, or energy," I shook my head, not sure what to call it. "Exploded out of me. It knocked everyone back and broke us from our bond, tossing us to the ground." I shifted in the chair. "Mira thinks that's what knocked him out."

He sat there, rubbing his chin for a moment. "What can I do kiddo?"

I looked at him lovingly. "You're already doing it." I grabbed his hand and smiled. We sat like this for a while, just looking out across the field. The grass was still green, but showed streaks of black throughout where spells had been cast. Aside from that, it looked like nothing else had happened.

Like today hadn't happened, but it did.

There were a few people on the perimeter of the field in the distance... a gentle reminder that danger still existed. One that Leo couldn't see, and it had to stay like that.

He had been so accepting of me when I finally got the courage to tell him the truth and while he never wavered in his love and affection, there were still things I had to protect him from. He could know what was happening, but not in every detail. I wanted him to live in a world where he wasn't as scared as I was. Scared that a group of people- wolves- hated me because of something that happened years and years ago and now that same group had the moonstone- the thing they planned on using to wipe us out of existence.

What would it be like if they succeed? To have no powers again...

How would Leo feel if he knew? Would he be excited? Worried?

Cami. Alpha. Ruthy interjected into the silence.

Yes?

When would you like to know about the fallout from today?

I looked at Leo and then back out at the field. I wasn't ready to let him go yet, to let this go.

Now is fine. How many did we lose?

I gripped the handle of the chairs, anxious.

We lost three, your parents lost two.

The Red Crows?

Six.

I felt sick, but it wasn't as bad as I thought it was going to be.

Who were the three?

Samson, Willem, and George.

They were new... so young.

Yes.

We need to have their ceremony tonight.

Of course. We're already setting it up for after dinner.

Good. What do you need from me?

Nothing, alpha. With your permission, I can handle all of it.

Yes. Ruthy. Of course. I paused for a moment. *Ruthy... how are you doing?*

Silence.

We don't have to talk about it if you don't want to.

No, it's not that. It's just that... I'm worried and I'm sad. Worried about Asher and that this whole thing with the Crows isn't over. And I'm just sad... sad we had to lose five people because of their greed and hatred. Do you really think they're going to get rid of the Crescent curse?

I don't know.

I heard dishes smashing inside and knew it was Ruthy throwing pots and pans around.

Do you need to go for a run?

I can't leave you.

I'm fine for right now. You go on a run and I will handle things here. I have the pack with me if I need anything.

She hesitated. *Are you sure?*

Absolutely. You need to focus on yourself right now.

I love you, sis.

I love you, too.

If anything happens, you mindlink me immediately.

You got it.

A minute later, Ruthy was tearing across the grass.

"Was that Ruthy?" Leo asked, watching her wolf dart across the field and into the woods.

"Yea." I chuckled. "It amazes me how you can distinguish our wolves."

"It isn't that hard." He laughed. "Well, you, Asher, and Ruthy aren't that hard. You all are very different and I guessed with the smashing dishes she needed to run."

"You're an amazing person, Leo. I'm so lucky to have found you... or rather, so lucky that you found me."

"Oh, kiddo... I'm the lucky one."

"You mean you aren't disappointed the little girl you found turned out to be a Crescent Moon shifter, who has a whole family that was kept from her and a group of wolves that want to kill her because of what her ancestors did years ago?"

"Not for a second." He squeezed my hand. "I love you, kiddo."

"I love you too, Leo."

Ruthy got back just after dinner, but before the burning ceremony. The sun was slowly setting in the sky, casting an ominous orange and purple haze over everything. We were standing around the edge of the water with lit torches in our hand while our fallen had been laid on three separate wooden rafts that were several feet high and almost seven feet in length. Branches and twigs were intertwined with a small bunch of dried sticks in the middle. The rafts were slowly drifting into the water.

I stepped forward and said a few words, followed by Ruthy. As I was listening to her speak, I was filled with an immense amount of guilt. I had been their alpha and barely knew them. I had talked to them a few times, but I had been so consumed with my own problems, I hadn't made time for them.

I looked around at the pack and realized that was the case with several others. I knew of them and had several small conversations with them, but I didn't *know* them. That had to change.

When Ruthy finished speaking, she made an announcement, and everyone stood on guard. She spoke another phrase, in a language I'd never heard, and everyone tossed their torches at the rafts, so I followed.

A second later, the rafts were engulfed in flames and black smoke billowed towards the clouds above. I felt numb. I was numb. We all stood there and watched the flames grow as the heat tickled the hairs on our skin. After the rafts burnt out, people started walking back towards the house. I stayed though, along with Ruthy.

She wrapped her arm around my neck, but didn't speak.

"You sure you're ok?" I asked.

"Yea. I'm just pissed."

"Me too."

"Any news on Asher?"

"Not yet. I checked on him before we came down here, but he was still the same."

"He's going to be ok."

"He will be." I yawned.

"Let's get you back. Asher would have my head if anything happened to you."

I smiled. "I'm getting tired, anyway."

"It's been a long day. Hell, a long few months for you."

"It's not over yet."

She looked at me. "Let's not think about that right now. Tomorrow, maybe the day after, sure. But not tonight."

When we got back to the house, I spoke to a few people, then went upstairs and crawled into bed, curling into Asher.

What I would give to feel his arms wrap around me and have him rub my head until I fell asleep.

"Night Asher."

I waited, but there was nothing but silence.

"I love you." I gently pressed my lips to his.

Morning Surprises

WHEN I WOKE UP the next morning, I was lying on my side with my arms entangled around Asher's. I loved being the little spoon to his big spoon.

I squeezed his arms and slipped my hand in his and felt a gentle squeeze. "Good Morning." I mumbled absentmindedly.

I froze.

He was lying on his side, holding me.

He squeezed my hand.

I felt a small chuckle from behind. "Good Morning babe." He whispered.

I rolled over instantly and looked at him and saw his beautiful face smiling at me. I grabbed it in my hands and pulled him to me, planting my lips on his in an unapologetically hard kiss. I pushed him away and stared at him in disbelief. "When? Why? How?"

He laughed again, his blue eyes sparkling.

I smacked him on the arm. "Why didn't you wake me up?"

"Ow." He smiled, rubbing his arm.

I raised my eyebrows at him impatiently.

"Pup." He said in that low sultry voice that made me melt.

"Don't. Don't do that. I'm mad at you and you know that makes me definitely not mad at you."

"Pup." He lowered his head and looked at me between his lashes.

"Asher." I raised my eyebrows.

He laughed again. "Goddess, I love you." He put his hand on my cheek and stared at me for a minute... the kind of stare that leaves you breathless and wanting and swooning and everything else in between... but not mad. "I'm sorry I didn't wake you up... you just looked so peaceful and I know how nervous you were going into yesterday. You needed the sleep."

"What happened? I was so worried."

"I know. I could hear you... I could feel your worry and that killed me."

"So what happened?"

"I was in this dark space, like a cave... kind of like what you described."

"The mind temple?" I said with apprehensive excitement.

He nodded. "I think."

"What else did you see, or hear, or feel?"

"It was dark... pitch black, but I heard animals and a whooshing sound kind of like big gusts of wind."

I nodded. "Asher, that is so exciting! It must have worked! Elder Heldalore said she didn't know... but!" I shook his arms excitedly.

He smiled.

I pushed him on his back and threw the covers off and straddled him. His hands rested on my legs and we just stared at each other for a moment, letting all the worry of the past few weeks, hell, the last few months wash away.

"Asher. I was terrified I was going to lose you."

"Welcome to my life for the last... well, pretty much ever since we met." He chuckled.

"Oh, you mean when you ghosted me?"

He cocked his head. "You know I did that for your own protection."

"Doesn't mean I liked it."

He squeezed my leg. "So Lucian..."

I nodded and realization hit me at the fact I'd never acknowledged he was gone. Like, I knew he was gone. I saw Asher kill him, but I was so focused on Asher not being killed, I never really took the time to relish that Lucian was out of our lives. "He's gone." I whispered.

"How do you feel about that?"

"Honestly, as sad as it is to say, I hadn't thought about it until this very second. I had been so consumed with you I didn't even process."

He didn't speak, but just watched as I processed my feelings.

I continued, "It's weird." I shook my head. "It's like this enormous weight has been lifted off my shoulders. I feel a little guilty because I should wish no one dead, but him and Dixon... they were pure evil. Lucian wouldn't stop coming for me, so it was something that had to be done."

He nodded.

I felt my face contort. "I shouldn't be happy about it, should I?" I leaned over and laid on him, nuzzling my head in his neck as he rubbed my back.

"You can feel whatever you need to feel about it."

"I do... I feel happy that he isn't here anymore."

"That's ok. I feel the same way... I felt the same about Dixon, too. He had tortured me for years, and Lucian was no different. Sure, he wasn't the leader of the pack, but he followed those others blindly. He would have killed you without hesitation because you intimidated him."

"I know."

He stroked the back of my head as our thoughts drifted off on their own.

I sat up. "I'm not sad he's dead."

"Ok." He let his hands fall back to my legs.

"For the first time in a long time I feel... free?" I shook my head. "I don't know if that's the right word... but I don't know."

"I get it."

Did he though? I'm sure he understood some of it, but ever since I found out the truth about who I am... I was immediately thrown into this battle that had been waging on for years. I had an enemy that hated me with such vitriol, when I didn't even know the players in the game. So much was thrown at me so quickly that I didn't even feel like I had time to process, and then, on top of that, I had to play this chess game with Dixon and Lucian. I had been on edge from the moment I found out and now... now I felt like I could relax some.

"Are you ok?" He gently pressed.

After a moment, I nodded. "Yea."

"Did Kayden get the moonstone?"

"He did."

"So..."

"So... I don't know. My vision said the Red Crows are going to betray him and he will be here in the coming weeks."

"So we have some time off?" He chuckled.

I smiled. "Yes, but you aren't here."

"Well, we know that's not true."

I shrugged.

He grabbed my legs. "I didn't die during the ceremony."

"Yes, I know. We were able to change that part... but I don't know. It seems like I have a vision and part of it happens, with you, with Chloe. They are never exact, because maybe me knowing what's going to happen changes it a little." I gazed out of the window. "The Red Crows plan to wipe out our existence. I don't know if they can do that, but Maye seems convinced they could. At least that's what she's spouting."

"How would Maye know, but not Ellsmire?"

I shrugged. "She seems to know quite a bit more. I don't know if she found other documentation or proof." I laid on his chest. "She allowed herself to be more open to possibilities of the impossible, where the other's dismissed it. Who knows what other papers exist we don't know about because someone, somewhere, at some time, thought it wasn't important?"

He nodded. "So we need to find Kayden, Maye and the Red Crows and stop them from going through with this spell, or whatever you want to call it."

"Yes." I sat up and looked at him. "But not today. Today, I want to just enjoy your company."

He pumped his eyebrows. "You do?"

I leaned down and kissed him. "I love you."

"I love you." He grabbed me and in one quick move flipped us over so I was laying underneath him.

SURPRISE VISITOR

ASHER AND I WALKED into the kitchen close to an hour later.

"Shut the front door!" Ruthy dropped a bowl in the sink and rushed over to wrap her arms around Asher. She pulled back, grabbing him by the shoulders, and then looked at me. "Why didn't you tell me he was awake?"

"I figured you'd want to see him. I just found out a little bit ago." I smiled.

"Are you ok?" She turned back to Asher.

He nodded, chuckling. "I'm fine."

"Good." She punched him in the arm. "Don't scare me like that again."

He grabbed his arm. "Sorry."

We took a seat at the bar and Ruthy put a plate in front of us. "We're having pancakes this morning."

"Sounds delicious. Do you need any help?" I asked.

"No. You can just sit there and relax for two seconds." Ruthy demanded lovingly.

Drake walked in and wrapped his arms around Ruthy, and then looked over at us. "Well, well, well."

"Hey man." Asher said, nodding.

"How are you feeling?"

"Feeling good."

Drake looked at me and then back to Asher. "I'll let Mira know. Does Luna know?"

I shook my head. "We just came downstairs a few minutes ago."

He nodded.

"I didn't even know she was still here." I said, looking around, half expecting to see her sitting at a table.

"Her and the others are going back to Ellsmire today." Drake offered.

"Oh."

Ruthy looked over my shoulder. "Speak of the devil."

"And she shall appear."

I turned around and saw Luna walking through the door with her arms in the air.

Her eyes fell on Asher. "Well, hello there, stranger. Glad to see you're up and about." She sat her shoulder bag on the table and walked over to Asher, grabbing his wrist, and then looked over at me. "Need to check his vitals."

I shrugged, rolling my eyes.

"Leaving so soon?" Ruthy interjected.

I glanced at her and gave her a 'cool-it-down' stare, causing her to raise her eyebrows in innocence. Everyone, including Luna, knew Ruthy wasn't happy about her being here, but Ruthy also knew it was a necessary evil. Ever since Asher and I became alpha of the house, Ruthy didn't hold her tongue when it came to Dixon's old squad, even though it seems like Luna was only on it to get information.

Luna dropped Asher's wrist. "You know, I may stay around a little longer. You've all been so welcoming."

"Luna." Asher reprimanded quietly, trying to keep the peace.

I interjected. "Luna. I really appreciate all the help you've provided since you've been here. How does Asher look?"

"Handsome as ever."

"Luna." He warned a little louder.

She rolled her eyes. "Fine. He looks fine... his vitals. He doesn't seem to have any residual damage from your blast."

I felt the pointed comment.

"Luna." Asher whispered again, pleading with her.

She let out a loud, dramatic sigh. "No fun." She looked around the room at the few pack members that were in the kitchen helping get breakfast prepared. "Well, we need to get going."

"No... don't go..." Ruthy exaggerated.

"You know. It's amazing how much mouthier you are with Asher as alpha."

"Asher and Cami. They're mated." Ruthy corrected.

"Whatever. I liked you better when you didn't speak as much."

"I like you better when you're not around."

Luna's eyes thinned into slits as she glared at Ruthy.

I jumped in again. "Luna. Would you and the others like some breakfast before you head out?"

"I'll pass. May find a wolf's hair in it or something."

I shot Ruthy a look and she turned around to join Bryson at the stove.

"Was it something I said?" Luna mumbled.

I ignored her little jabs, even though it was getting more difficult. "Thank you again for your help."

"Whatever. I'm sure I'll be seeing you again soon. You seem to have a knack for getting yourself into trouble."

"That's what I've said too!" Chloe announced, walking into the room, completely missing all the little torpedos that had been launched.

"Ugh. Two of you." Luna said.

Chloe looked confused.

"Chloe, can you help me over here?" Ruthy asked.

"Sure thing!" Chloe chirped.

Luna watched her for a minute. "How is she always so cheery?"

"It's a talent." I laughed.

Luna laughed and then caught herself. "Drake. You need to come with. Council wants to meet with you."

Ruthy and I both looked at one another before settling on Drake.

"What's this about?" Ruthy asked, walking back over to stand beside Drake, grabbing his arm.

Luna snarled. "This doesn't involve you."

"Drake?" Ruthy looked up at him, her eyes full of worry.

He shrugged. "I'm sure everything's fine. I'll be back before you can miss me." He kissed her forehead.

Luna made a gagging sound, but we all ignored it.

"Ready?" Drake asked to Luna.

She looked around. "Yep."

Asher, Ruthy, and I followed them through the main door and watched them open a portal back to Ellsmire. With a gust of wind, the portal closed and we were standing outside, looking at an empty field.

"What do you think that's about?" Ruthy asked.

"You seem really worried. What do *you* think it's about?"

"I don't know, but I don't have a good feeling."

"I'm sure it will be fine."

"I don't know."

The bell in the kitchen chimed.

"Time to eat." Asher said.

We walked back into the house and Ruthy followed, but she was quiet. I don't think Drake had done anything wrong, so there shouldn't be a reason he'd be in trouble.

We ate breakfast and the rest of the pack house came over one at a time to check on Asher and offer their help if he needed it after we finished.

"Ruthy." Asher called.

"What's up?" She asked, walking over to us, then paused when she saw the look on this face. "Are you ok?"

"We need to talk. Are you available right now?"

She turned her head to the side. "I don't like the sound of this."

Asher chuckled. "Everything's fine. I just need to talk with you."

"Why are you so nervous about everything all the sudden?" I inquired.

"I don't know. I feel like something bad is going to happen. I just haven't been able to figure it out."

"So you're going to worry about every little thing now?"

"No," she huffed, crossing her arms. "If it deals with both of you, though... I probably will. You both seem to attract danger and problems."

I laughed.

"It's true."

"We're working on that."

Alphas. Bryson called out.

What is it? Asher asked.

Alpha Benji says he's here to see you.

"Benji?" Ruthy and I asked at the same time. "Why is he here?"

"I don't know." *Let him in.* Asher responded.

A moment later, Bryson and Benji were walking into the kitchen. Benji was a big man, towering over six and a half foot tall and muscular with wide shoulders, causing most to dwarf in his presence. Bryson wasn't small by any means, measuring at over six feet tall with a wide upper body from playing football, but next to Benji he looked tiny.

"Benji!" I said, running over to him.

"Hey there!" He gave me a quick hug, then backed away and crossed his arms in front of his face, bowing.

Asher walked up behind me and we both returned the gesture.

"Sorry. I still forget sometimes." I blushed, picking at my fingers.

Bryson watched us for a second, then walked away.

"It's ok. Me too." Benji winked.

I knew he was lying to make me feel better, but I appreciated it none the less.

"What brings you to our pack, old man?" Ruthy chimed in. "Sorry alpha old man." She bowed her head, showing respect.

"Ruthy." He held out his arm, inviting her in. "Still with that witchman?"

She wrapped her little arms around his torso. "Yes. I'm still with that witchman."

"Well, when you decide you're ready for a change, there are a lot of eligible wolves in my pack that would love to meet you."

It wasn't customary for other packs to openly recruit, or for the beta to talk to an alpha the way she does, but Benji and Ruthy had a special relationship and it was all said in jest.

"Benji. If you need me to alpha your pack because you can't, just let me know. I would happily make you my beta." She lightly punched him in the side.

"Glad to see some things never change." He chuckled, then looked at Asher and me.

"How are you both?"

"We're doing good."

"I heard about the ceremony and the Red Crows attack. I was on my way to offer my pack's services when I found out I was too late, but I still wanted to come out and make sure you all were ok."

We nodded. "Yes. We're doing good."

"Who is this man God?" Chloe asked, walking into the conversation.

Benji looked between us.

I smiled. "Benji, this is my sister, Chloe. She doesn't really have a filter."

"I was never allowed around people, so blame my parents." She smiled, holding her hand out.

"Chloe, this is Asher's god-father, and alpha of the California pack." I emphasized the alpha for good measure.

He reached out and shook her hand. "Nice to meet you Chloe. I've heard a lot about you, and I'm glad to see you're feeling better."

She frowned.

"What's wrong?"

"No spark. He's not my mate."

We all chuckled. "He's not a crescent." I realized too late what I had said, rather, implied. They were no doubt looking at Asher and me, thinking the same thing.

"Well-" she started, then stopped when she looked at me, then continued, "Well, a girl can dream."

Silence filled the small space as we all looked at one another.

"Ok. I can see you all need to discuss alpha stuff, so I'm going to find Levi and Xander and see if I can't bother them for a bit."

"They were out in the fields this morning. They've been out there a lot lately." Ruthy noted.

"Perfect!" Chloe bowed as she exited the group. "Nice to meet you."

Benji chuckled as he watched Chloe leap over the balcony. "She's fun."

I smiled. "She's great."

"I'm so glad you were able to find her."

I nodded. "Me too."

Another heavy silence filled the air.

"Benji." Asher started. "I want to talk to you about something."

Benji nodded.

Ruthy looked at me, confused, and I shrugged my shoulders.

Asher and Benji headed towards the foyer and Ruthy walked over to me. "What's that about?"

"Not sure."

"Cami." Asher called out.

I looked up and saw he and Benji were waiting for me.

"Oh." I said, looking startled. I didn't know what was going on. I thought Benji showing up was unplanned, so it surprised me that Asher seemed to have something so pressing to discuss.

Ruthy raised her eyebrows at me.

Ruthy, we'll talk in just a bit. Asher said.

I followed Asher and Benji into the library on the fourth floor and shut the door. I was getting a strange vibe off Asher and could tell he was anxious about something.

Benji sat down and must have also felt the same thing because he joked, "I feel like I should sit for this." He chuckled. "Is everything ok?"

Asher stood at the end of the table and gripped the back of the chair. "I need the truth from you."

Benji shifted uneasily in his chair, confused. "Ok?"

"I recently just found out something about me."

Benji nodded like he knew what was coming, but he still didn't speak.

"I have to know." Asher looked at me, then back to Benji. "Did you know my mom was a Crescent?"

Benji's lips flattened into a hard line and he waited a beat before he spoke. "I wasn't certain."

"But you knew there was a possibility?" Asher pressed.

Benji took a deep breath. "Your parents never really talked much about your mom's past. I don't think they ever told anyone. I mean, I was your dad's closest friend and he never told me. How did you find out?"

Asher seemed a little more relaxed. "When Cami was being held at the Red Crows compound, I lost it. I destroyed Dixon's room and in the process, I found a document rolled up under a floorboard. I took it to an Elder, and she didn't recognize the writing at first. She did some research and discovered it was a binding document. My parents had deactivated the Crescent curse, trying to protect me, and the document was proof of it."

"I see. I didn't think they could do that."

"I guess because I'm a hybrid, there was a better chance of it."

"Does anyone know?"

"Not really. We told Cami's parents, since they're the alphas of the Crescent pack. We didn't want them to feel like we were keeping things from them that could create tension between the packs."

"I see. How did they take it?"

"Fine, although, right after we told them, everything happened with Cami and Chloe and then Kayden showing up and the Trinity curse being completed, so we really haven't had a chance to talk with them in depth to fully gauge their feelings." Asher took a seat at the table. "Why didn't you say anything?"

Benji shook his head. "Again, I wasn't certain. I had an idea when I learned you and Cami were mated, because I've never heard of a cross species fated mates."

"My parents weren't?"

Benji shrugged. "I'm not sure. I know they loved each other very much and they talked about their mated bond, but again, I can't say for certain. I know they definitely wanted people to believe they were mated, obviously to protect your mother and you. A few times, your mother would speak about her sister or her family, but when I asked questions, they would always change the subject."

"What about at their marking ceremony?"

"They had a private event, just the two of them."

"It didn't even cross my mind when I saw the transition cage in the basement of their old house. I had assumed it was there from the previous owner."

Benji shrugged. "I imagine it's part of the reason your dad didn't want to alpha a pack and wanted to keep his space. He was probably nervous the more people they were around then the higher the chance they would find out about your mom."

"Oh my Goddess." I blurted.

"What?" they both asked, looking at me.

"Do you think that's why Dixon killed your mom? He found out?"

Asher studied me as the realization hit him. "I don't know. It would make sense, but he was also a sadistic bastard who wanted power and my parents stood in the way."

I nodded. There was no way he could've found out.

Silence filled the air again as I'm sure thought after thought filtered through Asher's mind.

Benji hesitantly asked, "So, you said they suppressed your curse..."

Asher looked at him, like he'd been pulled back to reality from his thoughts. "Yes. Elder Heldalore visited and let me know what the document was and gave me the option to reverse it." Asher looked at me. "So I did."

"And?"

"After Cami and her siblings created the moonstone, there was fighting still going on. In the process, I was knocked unconscious."

"By me... by accident, of course." I interjected.

"Yes, but apparently I went into the mind temple."

"Mind temple?"

Asher looked at me to explain it.

I took a step closer to the table. "So basically, it's the space that houses our other animals. At first, it's like a large black void, like a cave maybe, but the more you visit it and build the relationships and bonds with your animals, the more the darkness fades. It takes some time, but..." I shrugged, not really sure what else to say.

"So you had this? Benji asked.

"I did."

"How do you feel about it?"

"I'm excited." Asher laughed, "And nervous."

"How did Ruthy take it?"

"We haven't told her yet."

Benji's eyes grew large.

"We were planning on it, then you showed up."

"Don't blame me." Benji said, holding his hands up. "I don't want any part of her wrath."

We all chuckled.

Benji spoke quietly. "I wish your parents were still here to help you navigate through this."

"Me too."

"Did you say Asher's mom mentioned a sister? Maybe we can find her or something?" I looked at Asher, smiling.

Benji nodded. "Yes. But it was only a few times in passing. I have no other information, not even a name."

"I wonder if the Elders know? They should, right?" Asher asked, looking for encouragement.

"I would think so." Benji said.

"Wait." I said, a little too excited.

"What?" Asher asked, confused by my sudden outburst.

"Theo."

"I don't think she ever mentioned a brother." Benji said.

"No." I laughed. "Remember when you came to visit me at Theo and Lily's house after I found Chloe? Remember when Theo said Evans sounded like a familiar name?"

"Yea, but there are lots of Evans."

"I know. But what if it was your parents?"

Asher shrugged. "Evans was my dad's name, not my moms."

I shrugged. "I know... it was just a thought."

Asher moved around the table and wrapped his arms around me. "That's one of the reasons I love you."

I cut my eyes at him. "Why?"

"Because you're just so cute... and hopeful... and always trying to find the light in any situation."

"You two lovebirds." Benji teased.

I snaked my arm around Asher. "So what does this mean? What are we going to do?"

He gave me a quick kiss on my forehead. "Well, if what Benji says is true..."

"Which it is." Benji interjected.

"Then that means I have family out there." Asher said in a hopeful tone.

"You have family." I repeated, smiling from ear to ear.

It had been hard for me when I found out my parents were alive and I had siblings. I felt Asher and I had bonded over that commonality in some ways, but that all changed once we learned the truth. I felt guilty. I know it made little sense and I shouldn't feel that way, but I did. I was mad at my parents for abandoning us and splitting us up, even though I now know, and can agree with, why they did it. And now Asher has a chance of reconnecting with his family.

"I have a family." He smiled apprehensively.

"Do you think they know about you?" I asked.

He shook his head. "I have no idea."

"This is why you leave."

Benji looked at me, confused, but Asher understood and nodded.

I looked at Benji. "I have these visions."

He nodded. "Asher's told me."

"Well, I had several leading up to the ceremony. The first was that Asher died, which is part of the reason I had that blast thing which put him in a coma... I was terrified I was going to watch it in real life and couldn't bear the thought of losing him." I shook my head, not wanting to relive it again, "Anyway, the second vision was several weeks after the trinity ceremony," I clarified, "In my vision time, not actual time." Benji looked confused, so I kept talking. "The second vision was Kayden coming here looking badly beaten. He said the Red Crows had turned against him and were planning on using the moonstone to destroy the Crescent curse, making us all human. Ruthy, in the vision, was angry with him and said that Asher was gone because of him and said I had dealt with a lot over the last several weeks. So that is the time we are talking about...

we think Kayden will come back, but Asher won't be here. So all that to say, I think this is why Asher isn't here, because he goes to find his family."

Benji sat there nodding, trying to process it all. "I'm glad I'm sitting down." He scratched his head. "So you think the Red Crows are going to use the moonstone to get rid of the Crescents?"

"I do. Maye mentioned it before when I was at the Red Crow's compound."

"So she thinks she can play goddess? Does she even have the power? I thought the Ellsmire coven was the most powerful..."

"They are and she came from the Ellsmire coven, but while we were at the Red Crows compound, she performed the Gemini bond with her twin brother and killed him to absorb his power. She was going to bring him back to life with the moonstone after we completed the ceremony, but we didn't and too much time has now passed, so her brother is gone."

He pulled his face. "How does she feel about that?"

"I don't know."

"So you feel you have some time before anything crazy happens?"

I shrugged. "I don't know, but I'm hoping. We need the time to figure out how to stop them."

"Can you just get the moonstone back?"

I cocked my head at Benji.

He laughed. "Ok. I realize now I oversimplified an arduous task."

"Yes. I would love to get the moonstone back. I just can't understand why the moon goddess would give us the ability to create something that would kill us."

"Are you sure that's what it does?"

"No. There are a lot of things we don't know. For starters, all the other trinities died on their nineteenth birthday when they completed the ceremony. We didn't, because we completed it before we were nineteen. Granted..." I just did the math. "Our birthday is a little over a month away."

Asher looked at me and shook his head. "No."

"No... right?"

"What am I missing?" Benji chimed in.

"In the book, or what little documentation that exists, the other trinities were called together on their nineteenth birthdays. The way it was written was basically they had no control, that fate drew them together. What if, in my vision, fate calls us back together, and that's why Kayden shows up?"

Asher shook his head.

I felt this weight on my chest. I had been so hopeful that most of this was behind us, but I felt like we were right back where we were last week.

"I don't think that's the case." Asher said unconvincingly.

"But we don't know." I said, sitting in the chair.

Benji stood up. "We don't know anything... much... so let's try not to dwell on what we don't know."

After a minute, Asher agreed. "Let's focus on what we do know."

I looked at them both, feeling like my head was in a haze, and nodded. The possibility of the Trinity curse not being complete never crossed my mind. Did Mira know? Luna? Is that why she said she would see me soon? Is that why she took my blood? All these thoughts started rapid firing in my brain.

"Cami." I looked at Asher. "It's ok. We'll figure it out."

Processing

ASHER, BENJI, AND I walked into the kitchen. Ruthy was sitting at the island flipping through a magazine when we walked in. She looked from Benji to Asher to me.

"Is everything ok?" she asked, mildly concerned.

"Yea." I said, walking to the refrigerator to grab a drink.

"Asher. Benji. What did you do to my girl?"

I laughed, trying to sound more confident. "They didn't do anything. You want to go for a run?"

She narrowed her gaze on me. "Yes. I would love to."

I glanced at Asher. "We'll be back soon."

He nodded, then winked at me. "Relax and have fun."

Ruthy and I were outside five minutes later, running across the field.

We passed Xander, Levi and Chloe laying in the grass looking at the sky.

What in the world is going on over there? Ruthy asked.

I laughed. *I have no idea.*

We ran and ran, ducking under branches and swerving around trees, running alongside the river. We finally came to a stop at the top of a cliff, Ruthy's cliff. This is where she had brought me one time before, when she was freaking out about Drake admitting his true feelings towards her.

So we're here. Ruthy said, sitting on the edge, looking out.

Yea. It's beautiful up here.

We sat in silence for a while, looking out. I could tell Ruthy was dying to know what was going on, but she was giving me space to process and open up to her. That was one of the many things I loved about her.

So. I started, then paused.

So?

I was talking with Asher and Benji when I realized something.

What was that?

So in all the books, it says the trinity comes together on their nineteenth birthdays.

Ruthy looked at me but didn't speak.

And I had a vision of Kayden coming here in several weeks, all battered and bruised.

Your birthday is in a month...

Yea.

So you think you three are going to be drawn together again to complete the ceremony?

I don't know. I just assumed that we did it and it would be over, but I don't know. Luna was so cryptic when she left, saying she will see me soon. She took my blood... why? And then Drake... I don't know. I just feel like Mira may know something or at least suspect something and isn't telling me.

Do you want me to find out from Drake?

Do you think he would tell you?

I don't know why he wouldn't.

I just have a really weird feeling about this.

Could you complete the ceremony again and get another moon-stone?

I have no idea. I still don't know why it was created to begin with.

Do you think the Elders would know? Maybe you should talk to them. I saw Elder Heldalore here a few weeks ago.

I couldn't tell if she was making a general statement or was fishing for information. Ruthy typically wasn't one to beat around the bush.

Yeah, she had some business with Asher.

Would your parents know anything?

I don't-

I stopped talking when I heard branches breaking in the distance. Ruthy turned around and hunched lower to the ground, ready to pounce if needed.

I come in peace. Asher said at the same time his wolf was coming through the trees. *I thought I would find you two here.*

You know this is my spot. Ruthy pounced.

I do. Asher's wolf sat beside me and my wolf hummed excitedly. *I wanted to talk with you, Ruthy.*

If it's an arranged marriage with Benji, the answer is no. I like him and I love you, but no. I draw the line at arranged marriages.

What are you talking about?

I couldn't help but laugh.

You aren't trying to marry me off?

Why in the world would you think that?

I'm going to kill him. Ruthy seethed.

Kill who? Asher asked, still chuckling.

Xander. He said he overheard you all talking about an arranged marriage for me.

Oh my. No. Not even close.

Why is he such a little shit?

Why did you believe him? I asked.

I have no idea. Levi was there too and... they are both dead.

No arranged marriages, but there is something I wanted to talk with you about. I wanted you to be one of the first, for many obvious reasons. Asher said, refocusing her attention.

Ok. This seems kind of important.

It is. So do you remember when I sort of lost it after Cami was taken?

How could I forget?

Well, I found the rolled-up piece of paper. I took it to the Elders, and they came back and told me what it meant.

And? The anticipation is killing me!

My mother was a Crescent wolf. I'm a Crescent wolf hybrid.

Oh shit.

Yea and Cami and I are true bonded mates.

That's fantastic. Wow. Ok. Wow. Ok. Ok. Wow. That's a lot to process.

I know.

Ok. Wow. Geez. I'm going to stop saying that. I will. So that means you're part Crescent. But...

The document was proof they had my crescent traits deactivated, and Elder Heldalore gave me the option to reverse it.

And you did, of course.

Yes.

Apparently, part of the coma, or whatever state he was in, was because he was transitioning. I added in.

Transitioning? So you're a Crescent?

I don't know. I mean, I was in the mind temple, but I don't have any other animals, if that's what you're asking.

What does this mean for the pack?

What do you mean?

Are you going to leave to join a Crescent pack? Liam and Anastasia's? What are they going to say?

We told them already, when we had dinner with them. We didn't want them to think we were hiding information or come across as a threat.

Ok. Ruthy walked around in a circle, clearly still trying to process. What does Benji have to do with this?

His showing up was purely coincidental, however, when I told him he didn't seem too surprised.

He knew?

He didn't know, but he suspected after he found out Cami was my mate and the fact my parents lived a fairly solitary life until they ended up being alphas to this pack. He said my parents never really talked about my mom's family. A few times she mentioned a sister, but when he pressed, they would shut down.

Wait! She stopped walking. You have family out there.

I do.

Oh my Goddess! You have to go find them.

I know. He laughed. But I don't know where to start.

Talk to Liam and Anastasia!

And Theo and Lily. I added.

And them too and then if you don't find out anything there, then go to the Elders. They would have to know. They know everything. She paused for a second. This is so exciting! Her wolf jumped on Asher's back. You have family out there!

I watched her jump and pounce and circle Asher for a while. He just stood there, letting her get all of her excited energy out. Part of my heart hurt though, because I couldn't help but wonder if her excitement for Asher, and even me, when we found out about my family, was partly because it gave her hope that she would one day find hers. We've only talked about it a handful of times, but I know she wonders where her parents are and if they're alive and wants to know why they left her.

Man! You two with your bombshells today.

That's all we have thank goodness. I chuckled.

When do you leave?

I don't know. I just found out I have an aunt not even an hour ago.

Well, I'm just saying. I got it covered here.

Geesh. Trying to get rid of us. I laughed.

Never. Although, when you were both gone last time, I rocked at being alpha. Just saying.

We started walking back to the house, and the conversation was quiet. I'm sure everyone was thinking about different things, but not me. I was trying my hardest to not think about a single thing. I wish I had a magic switch that could cut off my thoughts and emotions, so I could just be... for like five seconds. No worries, no planning, just quiet.

When we got to the field, I saw Ruthy take off running and I couldn't understand at first until I saw a hawk soaring into the sky.

Xander.

He was circling around, while Levi and Chloe were rolling on the ground in fits of laughter.

You can't stay up there all night!

Ruthy, love! What's going on?

I'm not your love. She snapped.

Well, I'm not your enemy.

An arranged marriage. You're an ass!

It wasn't my idea.

It wasn't?

No. Ask your BFF, Levi.

Dude. No. Not cool. Levi retorted.

Ruthy adjusted her stance and looked at Levi, who started frantically scooting backwards on the ground.

Levi?

No. No. He said, holding his hands out in front of him. *I didn't.*

Liar, liar, pants on fire. Xander chimed in.

Shut up, Xander!

Chloe stood up and held her arm out, giving Xander a place to rest.

Levi?

Levi shifted into a wolf and started running across the field. *I'm sorry, Ruthy. It was only...*

Ruthy's wolf tore off after him while we all watched.

Xander jumped off his perch and landed on the ground, shifting back. "Well, that was unexpected." He covered himself. "Does anyone have something for my naughty bits?"

Chloe laughed, grabbing the blanket off the ground and throwing it at him.

"That wasn't a very funny joke you two played on her." Chloe reprimanded.

Asher and I strolled back to the house, and I walked to one of the shifting rooms and grabbed a loose dress to put on while I headed to our bedroom.

"What do you think she'll do to him?" I laughed.

"I have no clue. I just feel sorry for him. I pranked Ruthy once, and let's just leave it at that." He walked over to his dresser to pull out some clothes. "I will also add, I don't think I would ever prank her again, even if my life depended on it."

I glanced at my phone and saw a missed call from Leo.

"What's that about?" Asher asked.

I shrugged, listening to the voicemail.

"He invited us over for dinner tonight."

Asher's brow furrowed. "Seems odd."

"Yea. I mean, there's been a lot going on, so maybe he just wants to see how we're doing." I slipped on a pair of shorts and a shirt. "Do you have a problem going over tonight?"

He walked over and wrapped his arms around me. "Not a one!"

I called Leo back and let him know we would be over in a couple of hours. When I hung up the phone, I texted Will to see if he had any inside information, but he didn't respond.

"I hope everything's ok." I turned around and mumbled into his chest.

FAMILY DINNER

WE PULLED ONTO THE rocky driveway a few hours later. Even though it had only been a couple of months since I officially moved out, the house felt different. On the outside, it looked the same- the tire swing on the tree, the swing on the front porch.

I looked around taking everything in for a moment as flashbacks hit me one after another- the wolf behind the tree, the owl perched on the branch, the first time Asher came to pick me up in his Audi and the time I showed Will and Leo the real me.

Maybe it was me who had changed...

I heard the creak of the screen door and looked up to see Leo walking out.

"I thought I heard you pull up." Leo said from the front porch.

We walked up the stairs to meet him. I gave him a hug, then pulled away, a little too abruptly. "What's going on?"

"Can a dad just want to have dinner with his son and daughter and her... mate?" He looked at Asher questioningly. "I'm sorry. Mate feels too informal, but husband doesn't feel right either." He chuckled softly.

"Mate is fine." Asher smiled.

"And of course you can, dad, but that doesn't mean something isn't up your sleeve." We followed him inside and saw Will and Ems sitting at the dining room table.

"Hey Cami. Hey Asher." Ems said, smiling.

"Hey Ems." I was a little surprised to see her here, because they were still working things out and I didn't think they were back together officially. I would love if they were because she was a calming influence on his rather outgoing and boisterous personality.

"Hey sis." Will said before nodding to Asher. "What's up, man?"

Asher nodded back.

Leo walked into the kitchen to pull something out of the oven.

"What's going on?" I leaned over and whispered to Ems.

She shrugged.

"Also, are you and Will?" I pumped my eyebrows.

She rolled her eyes and smiled. "I don't know."

"I wanted to thank you all for coming tonight."

"I live here, dad."

"Shut it, Will, you're ruining the moment." I snapped.

"What moment?" He shrugged.

"Shut up." I raised my brows to show I was serious.

Leo smiled softly, then continued. "Well, thank you to the rest of you for coming." He sat the casserole dish down on the table. "So, there has been so much going on over the last several months... and it has really put things into perspective for me."

There was a soft knock on the door.

"Ah. Perfect timing." Leo smiled anxiously.

"Who's that?" Will asked, leaning around, but still couldn't see.

Asher and I both instinctively held our noses in the air and could tell it was a female. Asher looked at me, I'm sure to gauge my reaction, but it wasn't me he should be worried about.

"What is it, you guys? I know you know something now."

I nervously glanced at Ems, who was confused by his comment, but before I could answer, Leo was walking back in, holding hands with a woman who looked to be a few years younger than him. She had short brown hair, brown eyes and was wearing black capris pants and a white and pink flowery blouse.

"All. I would like for you to meet Evelyn."

Will looked from me to Evelyn and didn't speak.

"Hi Evelyn," I stood to give her a welcoming hug. "Nice to meet you."

"Nice to meet you, too."

"This is my..." I looked at Asher, not sure what to call him in front of people that didn't know us.

"Boyfriend." He said, standing to shake her hand. "Nice to meet you."

Ems followed then gave Will a look, who begrudgingly stood up and shook her hand.

I saw Leo shoot him a glance and Will plastered a smile on his face.

Leo pulled out a seat at the end of the table. "Evelyn, you can sit here. I will sit on the other end by Will."

"I can move." Asher offered.

"Yea me too."

"Nonsense. You two are fine where you are." Evelyn said, smiling. "I don't want to be a hassle."

Leo served everyone some food, then sat down.

"So Will, I hear you got a scholarship to play at Bellamy." Evelyn said, taking a bite of food.

Will nodded, looking at Leo. "I did. It just came through about a week ago."

"That's great."

"I'm excited, because he'll be there with me!" Ems bounced in her seat.

"You'll have to monitor him." Leo chuckled, looking at Ems.

"I'd love to come see a game sometime." Evelyn said.

"Sure." Will said, taking another bite of food. "But I don't think I'll be playing much the first year."

"Non-sense. I've seen your arm. You're brilliant on the field and my brother happens to be the head coach of the football program." She winked.

"No way. You're coach Goodall's sister."

"I am."

Will's attitude completely changed.

"That's actually how we met." Leo added. "When I was at one of your interviews, Evelyn saw me in the bleachers watching you, and we started talking."

"And next thing you know, he was asking me out on a date." She said, smiling.

"That's so nice." Ems clasped her hands together.

We finished dinner and moved outside to eat ice cream on the back porch. I was happy to see Will seemed more welcoming to Evelyn. He had to be ok with Leo finding someone; it was selfish of him to think Leo should spend the rest of his life alone. Leo had dated no one while we were in school, because he always put us first. Now that we're moving on with our lives, I'm ecstatic to see him doing the same.

"Tell me Asher... are you going to school with Will, Bryson, and Connor? You four boys were quite the thing to watch."

"You saw us?"

"I watched a few videos... those catches you made." Evelyn slapped her knee. "Very impressive. You could probably make it to the NFL if you kept putting up plays like that."

"Thank you, but football isn't really my thing."

"Your thing?" She asked, shocked.

"No." Asher laughed. "My... Dixon," he corrected, "Had me play."

"Well, that man was a smart man."

The entire conversation fell silent as the awkwardness filled the air.

Will interjected. "Let's stop talking about how great Asher is and move back to me." I rolled my eyes and Leo laughed, while Ems patted his leg. "It's ok to share the spotlight every once in a while, babe." She smiled.

I looked at Will, raising my eyebrows and mouthed babe.

He mouthed back, 'Shut it', which caused me to chuckle.

"Beautiful night out." Evelyn said, looking at the moon. "Full moon. Wonder if the wolves will come out."

"Wolves?" I asked before I could catch myself.

She nodded. "If you listen, you'll hear them howling."

We all nodded, but didn't speak.

We all sat on the back porch and talked a little while longer, but it was getting late and Will kept looking at his phone, which meant he had late night plans with someone. I patted Asher's leg. "Well, it's time for us to be going."

"So soon?" Evelyn asked, grabbing Leo's hand.

"Yes." I yawned.

Will glanced over at me and winked. "We better get going, too."

"Where are you two headed?" Leo inquired.

"We're meeting up with some of Em's friends."

"You young kids and late hours." Evelyn teased.

Leo and Evelyn followed Will, Ems, Asher, and I, through the house and out of the front door.

"You all be safe." Leo said, looking directly at Will.

Will flicked his fingers over his head before jumping into his Jeep.

"You kiddies have fun tonight." I said teasing.

"You too!" Ems said.

"Later, sis. Ash."

"Later."

Asher held the car door open for me and I climbed in. We weren't on the road two seconds before I could feel a tension in the air.

"What's wrong?"

"Nothing." He said too quickly.

"Asher." I warned. "I don't think I need to remind you of our mate bond."

He was rubbing the pad of this thumb back and forth on his steering wheel.

"I know something is bothering you, even though I can't read your mind."

He let out a deep sigh. "After seeing your family tonight... having dinner with them... I miss that." He quickly added. "Don't misunderstand, I have a lot of that with the pack... but..."

"It's not the same." I said, finishing his sentence.

"It's not the same." He repeated, softly.

"You want to go find you family... your aunt?"

He looked at me, but didn't speak.

"I figured this was coming... vision and all. It makes sense and I think you should."

"You do?"

"Yes, I do."

"For so long, you've been without your family. You have the chance now to find them and get some of that back."

"But you're my family."

"Duh." I laughed, squeezing his leg. "But I'm not your only family and that's ok. I want you to have them... I want you to find them."

"I was just thinking... your brother and the Red Crows have the moonstone... and they are planning on reversing the curse. Who knows what's going to happen... I don't know. I'm just scared I'm going to lose them again, before I even find them."

"Asher." He looked at me. "I get it. You don't need to explain anything to me. When I needed to go find my sister, you were there to support me... mostly." I teased, trying to lighten the weight of the conversation. "According to my vision, we have several weeks before anything happens. You need to do this."

"I know, but the timing..."

"The timing is why you have to do it. If the Crows and Maye are successful in reversing the crescent curse, who knows what that will do to us- if we will live or what our lives will look like. Like I said, we have some time."

"I love you." He squeezed my leg.

"I love you too... so big." I laughed.

I looked outside and realized we were on the interstate, heading away from the pack house. "Where are we going?"

He cut his eyes, smiling at me. "Our house."

"Our house?"

He winked. "I figured our last night together for a while should just be the two of us."

I reached for his hand, intertwining my fingers in his before bringing it to my lips.

TRANSPARENCY

WE GOT BACK TO the pack house the next day and called Ruthy into the library. We wanted to let her know Asher's decision before we told the rest of the pack.

"Did you two have fun last night? How was Evelyn?"

"How did you know about Evelyn?"

"Leo was nervous about telling you and Will... mostly Will."

"You had a conversation with Leo about his girlfriend... before he told us?"

"Yes." She shook her head, confused why I thought that was so odd.

"Xander was there too."

"You've got to be kidding me."

"I don't kid... well... not about things like this." She sat in one of the chairs in the library. "What's up? I feel you have to tell me something serious."

Asher started. "We just wanted you to be the first to know I'm going to be taking off for a few days... or weeks, not sure really... to find my aunt."

"Oh." She sighed in relief.

"What did you think I was calling you up here for?"

"Nothing." She snapped quickly.

"Ruthy?"

"What?" she huffed.

"What are you not telling me?"

She rolled her eyes. "I may have played a little prank on Levi... for payback."

"What did you do?"

She hesitated for a moment, then took in a deep breath. "I may have chained him up in one of the rooms downstairs."

"I don't feel like that's all."

"I may have also, previously, had Drake cast a spell on the door, so that he couldn't escape."

"Ruthy." He sighed. "How long has he been down there?"

"All night."

"Ruthy. You need to go let him out."

She sighed. "I know. I was on my way to do it when you two love birds got home and called me away."

"Where's Xander?"

"I don't know. It wasn't my turn to keep up with him."

I snorted, then caught myself.

"I'll let Levi out and be up for your announcement." She paused at the door. "Are you going to tell them the truth about you?"

Asher looked at me, like he was asking for permission and I shrugged. It wasn't my place to say whether he should share that news. In my opinion he should, but again, it wasn't my secret.

"I don't know."

She nodded, patting the doorframe twice before heading down the hall.

"Are you going to tell them?" I asked, walking over to stand beside him.

"Yes. I feel it's the right thing to do."

"You don't think they'll have a problem with it?"

"I don't think so. They've been so accepting of you."

"Yes. But that's when they still had you. I don't know how they'll feel having two Crescent alphas leading their pack."

"Well, technically, I'm a hybrid."

"Technically, they aren't going to care." I said, cupping his face in my hands and pulling him in to give him a kiss.

"Well, if they have a problem with it, then we will address it. If they don't want me as alpha, then..." he looked around. "I will step down."

"You would just step down?"

He nodded. "Well, it depends on who it is. I don't want it going back into the hands that went to the same school as Dixon."

"You think those still exist in our pack?"

"I don't know. There are a few I wonder about."

"What... do you think they're just waiting around?"

"No... I don't know. Point is, if it's the right person, I would step down. I never really wanted to be alpha."

"Just like your dad."

He nodded. "I just want to live in our house, raising our children away from all of this."

"They would be more protected in a pack."

"I'm sure we'd have your parents' pack."

I shook my head. "We're playing a lot of what if scenarios. Let's just take this one step at a time."

"Yes, ma'am." He said, grabbing me by the waist and lifting me up. "I do love when you get bossy." He kissed the tip of my nose.

"Asher." I laughed.

We were downstairs five minutes later, with most of the pack in the living room. When Asher sent out the request, a few had responded and said they were hunting and were on their way back.

Everyone continued to talk in their little groups, while a few cast wary glances at us.

Levi walked upstairs ahead of Ruthy and was not happy.

"Everything ok?" Asher asked.

"Did you know?" Levi snapped, then quickly stepped back in apology.

"We just found out."

"She locked me away in a stone room all night. It was like a dungeon or an old cellar... for what? For playing a little prank."

"I said I was sorry."

"I don't care." Levi retorted, then walked away to go talk to Bryson and Connor.

Ruthy frowned. "Maybe I took it a little too far."

"You think?" I raised my one eyebrow at her.

"Ok. Fine I did." She looked over her shoulder at him.

"He's pretty mad."

"Yea." Asher nodded.

"Ugh. I'll figure out a way to make it up to him."

"Please do. I don't need extra drama going around the house." I said.

The two other pack members walked in and stood on the edge of the room, nodding in apology for their tardiness.

Asher cleared his throat and the entire room went silent. "Pack. I know we've thrown a lot at you in the recent weeks and, first and foremost, I want to thank you for your continued support and trust in Cami and myself."

The room sounded in a uniform grunt.

"Cami and I have prided ourself in being an open and forthright alpha to this pack. And in the spirit of being open, there are some things we need to share with you. As most of you know, the Red Crows acquired the moonstone that was created at the trinity ceremony a few days ago. What some of you may not know is they plan to use the moonstone to reverse the Crescent curse... making them all human."

Those that didn't know looked around the room, stunned.

"We are obviously working with Ellsmire to prevent it from happening, because we don't know what that will do to those who are part of the Crescent pack. My fear, along with others, is that it could kill them all."

There were indistinct murmurs spreading around the room. Asher held up his hand to silence the room again.

"Now this next bit of news will come as a shock, as it did me." He sighed and looked around the room. I could tell he was still waging an internal war on whether he should share this next bit of information. "When Cami was taken earlier this year, I may have lost it a little."

"With good reason, alpha!" One boy shouted from the back.

"With good reason," Asher repeated. "In... my outburst, I uncovered something... a document. It was written in an old language I couldn't read, so I took it to the Elders and had them decipher what it meant." He looked around the room, breathing slowly.

"What was it? What did it say?" A handful of people asked.

"It was a binding document."

"What was a binding document doing hidden in your room?"

"My mother..." he looked at me so I grabbed his hand. "My mother and father had me bound. My mother was a Crescent, my dad a wolf."

The room erupted in chatter. I tried to listen to it all to get a general consensus on thoughts and opinions, but it was too much at one time. I glanced at Ruthy who was probably trying to do the same thing. My eyes shifted to Bryson, Connor, and Levi and they looked shocked- but neither happy nor upset.

Asher continued. "I know this comes as a shock. It did to me as well."

"Just because you're a hybrid doesn't mean your curse is active."

"You're right, but after the blast when I was knocked into the coma... I believe I started the transition."

I caught a few people looking around the room nervously.

"This changes nothing here. I'm still your alpha, like I've always been, the same as Cami." He looked around the room, pausing for a second. "I also found out another bit of information."

"If you're a triplet, too." Bryson shouted out, trying to make light of the situation.

Asher laughed, "No. But I found out that I may have an aunt out there in the world. My mother never really talked about her, so I don't have much to go off of, but she exists and I want to find her. I will find her." He squeezed my hand again. "With the Red Crows plans and the uncertainty around the fate of the crescents, I want to find her sooner rather than later. So with that said, I'll be leaving tomorrow to find my family." He quickly added. "Cami will stay here and continue to run the house, so you will all be in excellent hands." Asher continued, "I just want to thank you all for your support on this next adventure. That's all."

No one moved for a moment and then one by one they started trickling up, congratulating Asher on the news of finding out about his family and offering support. I could feel Asher's tension ease away as more people pledged their loyalty to us and the pack. I know he said he didn't want the alpha and would step down, but he's a natural. He's good at it. He has the respect from his pack and is building relationships with others across the country. He is spearheading change and without him in this position, half of what he's been able to accomplish wouldn't have happened.

"Let's have a party tonight!" Asher shouted, and the room erupted.

Once everyone came up and dispersed Benji walked up. "Brave man."

"How so?"

"Telling your pack... I just hope it doesn't come back to bite you."

"I don't understand." Ruthy interjected, walking up, playfully smacking Benji on the back.

"Hey future wifey." He said, laughing.

She rolled her eyes.

"All I was meaning is that typically alphas don't show any weakness."

"Well, Asher isn't your typical alpha." Ruthy defended.

"That's for sure." Benji looked at me. "Listen, if I can do anything to help while he's away, let me know."

"Thank you."

"She has me. She'll be fine." Ruthy said.

She was being kind, but also setting boundaries to protect me.

"Oh, Ruthy. Always a pleasure." He chuckled.

"Are you taking off?" Asher asked.

"Yea. I need to get back."

Drake walked into the kitchen. "Do you want me to portal you back?"

Ruthy spun around. "When did you get back?"

"Just now." He laughed.

"Everything ok?"

He nodded, but didn't speak.

Benji looked between the two of them.

"It's not a problem." Drake added.

"Ok then. Yea. Sure. These old bones get tired a lot quicker now than they used to," he said, patting his thighs. Benji said his goodbyes to everyone, then followed Drake through the front door.

"Thanks again for coming out." Asher said.

"Anytime. You're my family. I hope you know that." He said, placing his hand on Asher's shoulder.

Asher nodded.

Drake started opening the portal, and Benji looked at Drake. "How can I get one of you in my pack? This is definitely the way to travel!" Before Drake could answer, Benji had disappeared into the blue ring of light.

The ring snapped shut and we were stuck looking at Drake, who could sense us all watching him.

He cocked his head to the side. "What's up?"

"Do you want to tell us why you had to go to Ellsmire?"

His lips flattened into a hard line. "Everything is ok, but I really can't talk about it... it's coven stuff."

Ruthy ran her finger down his chest. "You can't talk to... anyone."

He closed his eyes for a second. "I would tell you if I could, babe."

She snarled her lips playfully. "Fine."

He raised his eyebrows in shock. "I didn't think you would give up so easily."

"I haven't... I'm just patient."

He laughed, pulling her to him. "I love you." He tilted her backwards and planted a kiss on her lips, then stood her back up.

"Hubba hubba." She said, regaining her balance.

"Drake." Asher said, bringing the crew back to reality.

"What's up, man?"

"I wanted you to know I found out I'm part Crescent... my mother's side."

Drake nodded, but didn't seem shocked.

"You already knew?"

He held his hands up. "Just found out today."

"How did they..." I started, then stopped.

Asher continued. "My parents had my curse deactivated, and we just found out about it... the coma I was in... well, I assume it was a coma... regardless, I found myself in the mind temple."

"Is that why Benji was here?"

"No. He heard about everything going on and came to check on us."

Drake nodded. "So he didn't know?"

"He says no. He said my parents didn't tell him anything, but he suspected, especially after he learned about Cami." I grabbed his hand. "He also said that a couple of times, they let it slip my mom had a sister."

Drake's eyes grew wide. "That's outstanding."

Asher nodded. "So... I'm going to try to find them."

"You are?"

"Yea. I have family out there... and with the Red Crows threatening to eliminate the Crescents... who knows what's going to happen."

Drake nodded again, and I was getting the feeling he knew something about the curse or the Red Crows that he wasn't sharing with us. I quickly glanced at Ruthy and got the impression she felt the same.

"I think it's really awesome you're going after your family."

"Thanks, man."

"When do you leave?"

"Tomorrow."

"Wow. So soon."

"Yea. Again... Red Crows. Who knows what's going to happen if they're able to pull off this curse."

Drake nodded. "I wish I could help you out."

"That would be nice." Asher laughed.

"Well, let's just enjoy tonight!" I clapped, looking around at everyone.

Ruthy narrowed her eyes and then smiled. "Let's!"

DEAD ENDS

I ROLLED OVER IN bed and saw Asher lying on his back, looking at the ceiling. "You ok?"

"What? Huh? Oh, yea." He turned to look at me, clearly lost in his own thoughts.

"You need to leave soon." I said, propping my chin on his chest.

He looked down at me, but didn't speak.

I started mindlessly tracing the tattoos on his chest, watching it move up and down, and paused when I got to the wolf's bust with his parent's names on either side of it. "You need to leave soon." I said again, less blunt this time.

"What?" He asked confused.

"The last couple of days... you've been here physically, but mentally you're somewhere else." Asher's plans to leave the next day after he made the announcement were disrupted when he realized he had no starting place, so for the sake of time, he scheduled a meeting with Liam and Theo today, hoping they'd be able to point him in the right direction.

He placed his hand on mine. "I'm sorry."

"Let's talk with Liam and Theo... maybe they know something or know someone who does? Theo had said before he thought the name sounded familiar..."

He narrowed his eyes at me. "I love you."

"I love you too." I crawled on top of him. "Now let's go find your family!"

We got to my parent's pack house a few hours later and knocked on the front door.

Liam opened the door with a beach towel thrown over his shoulder. "Well, hello there." He smiled, backing out of the door, inviting us in. "I thought you were coming by later."

"Did we miss the invite for the pool party?" I teased.

"Just a little fun today for the pack house."

Asher nodded. "We need to get a pool."

"Oh my goddess! Totally! We have the space for it." I beamed, excitedly.

Asher laughed, then reached for my hand. "Would you and Theo be able to talk for a bit now? I was hoping you may have some information about my aunt."

"Your aunt?"

I smiled. "Asher found out recently his mother had a sister. She didn't talk about her much, since she was a Crescent and they wanted to keep that hidden from everyone... even his dad's best friend."

"What's her name?"

"I don't know."

Liam scrunched his nose and chuckled. "That's going to make it a lot more difficult to find her."

"I know." Asher frowned.

"I was hoping Theo may have some information. When I was at his house earlier this year, he thought he recognized the name Evans... so I hoped perhaps he could think on it some more... I don't know. I know it's a long shot..."

"Sure." He looked off for a second, then back to us. "He'll be here in just a minute."

"So, do you have any information about your aunt?"

Asher shook his head. "Nothing at all."

Theo walked up in a pair of blue board shorts and flip-flops.

"Sorry to interrupt..." I said, feeling a little guilty now.

"Non-sense. Liam said you needed my help with something?"

"Hopefully."

Asher shifted. "I was hoping you may remember where you recognized the name Evans from. If maybe you had heard someone mention it before, in a certain pack."

Theo studied us for a second.

I added. "We just found out Asher has an aunt. His mom was a Crescent and did everything she could to protect him from that life. Benji, alpha of the California pack and god father to Asher, came to visit and said Asher's mom mentioned her sister on several occasions by accident. When Benji would press the issue, she realized she'd said too much and clam up. So we don't have a name or anything."

Theo thought about it, but after a minute frowned. "I'm sorry. I can't remember. I mean, it would have been years and years ago, at least twenty."

"Ok." I mumbled. "It was worth a shot."

"I'm sorry again. I wish I could help you out."

"It's ok." Asher said. "We will let you get back to your pool party. We didn't mean to interrupt."

"Non-sense. You're always welcome over here. Chloe, Xander and Levi are out back."

"Levi is here? That little traitor." I teased.

"Yea, those three are becoming quite the trio."

I nodded, noticing the same thing. "Well, I'm happy for them. If they can stand to be around Xander for that long, then kudos to them." I laughed. "Only teasing, of course."

"Of course." Liam said.

"We would love to stay, but we need to take care of a few more things before I try to track my aunt down."

"Understood. We will put out some feelers. What were your parents' names?"

"Hunter and Gwendolyn... Gwen Evans."

Liam and Theo both nodded. "We'll let you know if we find anything." Liam said.

We waved and walked outside, pausing on their front lawn. "Want to go for a run?" I asked, pumping my eyebrows up and down playfully.

"Do you think you can keep up?"

"Oh I know I can." I ran ahead of him and shifted, only turning back for a second to watch pieces of my clothes float down in front of Asher.

I liked that dress on you.

I did too. It was one of my favorites, but I got a little carried away. *See you back at the house.*

Oh no.

I heard the huffs of Asher's wolf catching up to me, so I pressed harder.

You've gotten faster.

I've been working out more.

You still aren't fast enough. Asher chuckled.

A second later, I felt his wolf brush up against the side of me and I let out a frustrated sigh. I pushed to the right, knocking into Asher's wolf, whose head snapped in my direction.

That wasn't nice.

I bumped again, causing Asher to laugh.

We were in the field by the house a few minutes later and I could feel my lungs aching for air, but I was determined to beat him back, so I lowered my head and pushed forward. My wolf immediately let me know she was not happy about it, but she didn't slow down.

Oh. We're really doing this. Asher said, surprised, but I didn't answer.

I could feel him catching up to me. So... close.

The high grass was racing past me, flicking across my face and rubbing down my body. My feet were pounding the ground, hit after hit after hit.

Almost there.

I didn't want to chance a look behind me because it would slow me down. I just had to trust he wasn't going to pass me.

Come on Cami. You... got... this. Just... a few... more...

I cleared the field and slowed to a stop, nearly toppling over.

I beat you! I shouted from the ground.

My wolf was laying down on the grass, unwilling to move. Her chest was heaving up and down.

You did good. Asher said, coming to a stop by me.

Thank you.

His wolf laid down beside mine after giving my head a quick lick. "That was some finish." Ruthy said, jumping over the back of the couch to sit beside me.

"I'm so sore."

"I don't think I've ever seen your wolf run that fast."

"She did good, although I don't think she's thrilled with me at the moment."

Asher walked into the living room and sat where my feet were propped, lifting them up, then resting them on his lap.

"You ok?" He smirked.

"I'm so sore."

"You ran fast." He said, gently rubbing my feet. "Faster than I've ever seen."

"I just really wanted to beat you."

"I could tell." He laughed, switching to the other foot.

"You can rub mine when you're done with hers." Ruthy called out.

Asher shook his head. "Not going to happen."

"Well, if you wanted to think about it for a minute... I'll wait."

"Nope."

"I need to find my mate so they can rub my feet." She snarled.

"You'll find it."

"I hope so. Even though Drake would happily rub my feet if I asked. He does have magic hands." Ruthy burst out in laughter. "That was completely unintentional! Magic hands. He literally has magic hands." She stood up from the couch. "I crack myself up."

"I'm glad you do." Asher called after her.

Where do you think Drake is right now?

Asher shrugged his shoulders.

Do you think he knows more than he's letting on about the Crows and the Trinity?

I do, but he can't tell us. I know he would if he could.

I puckered my lips.

HARD GOODBYES

I STOOD ON THE patio off the main floor by the kitchen and watched the rain pour down and listened to the low rumbling of thunder roll across the sky. I hoped this wasn't an indicator of how today and the coming weeks were going to be. Asher left in a couple of hours and I was filled with an immeasurable amount of dread. I couldn't place the reason behind it, and assumed it was a combination of me not wanting to be without him and the fact we had no idea how long he was going to be gone. I also worried he wouldn't be able to find them or worse, he did, but they wanted nothing to do with him. I shook my head. That would not happen. I was letting my own fears about my family resurface and that worked out fine... well, mostly fine.

I snarled at the thought of Kayden and then remembered my vision of him visiting.

"You ok?" Asher asked, walking behind me and slipping his arms around my waist.

I leaned back into him and rested the back of my head on his shoulder. "Yea." I breathed.

"Wow. That didn't sound convincing at all." He chuckled.

"I'm fine. I'm just not ready for you to leave, but at the same time, excited for you to find your family."

"I know." He flexed his arms. "I'm a little nervous, too. What if they don't like me?"

"How could they not? You are Asher freaking Evans!"

"Damn straight I am." He laughed and then silence filled the air. "But seriously, what if... I don't know. Why haven't they tried to find me? Or my parents? Oh, gosh."

"What?" I turned in his arms so I was facing him.

"What if they don't know about my parents? What if I find them and have to deliver that news?"

"I'm sure they know..." I wasn't sure. How would they know? If Asher's parents had wanted to protect their relationship and Asher, they would have gone to any length to do it.

"Then why didn't they come looking for me?" Asher looked off across the field and I could feel his sadness creep in.

I wrapped my hands around his neck. "These are all questions you can ask them when you find them... there will be a great explanation that will make complete sense and you'll understand everything."

He laughed. "I hope."

"I know."

"Where was all this supreme optimism when you were in this spot a few months ago?"

"I doubted myself... and my family... but I had you here supporting me and offering me encouragement and look how it all turned out. My parents... Chloe... it's been great and yours will too."

"Hopefully she doesn't want to kill an entire race of shifters... we already have one of those in the family."

"Har, har har. Hilarious."

He shrugged. "I try."

"So, is Drake going to portal you somewhere?"

"No. I'm going to meet with the Elders again. I feel like they're my only shot right now."

"Yea... makes sense."

"I was even wondering... what if Evans isn't my last name?" He stopped himself. "I mean, I know it is, but what if my parents changed their name to help them hide?"

"You think they would do that?"

"I don't know. I feel like in some ways I don't know them at all... I feel like everything was a lie."

"It could be possible... I mean... it would make sense why your aunt never found you... because she didn't know your name."

"Yea... that's what I'm wondering." He chortled. "It's interesting to think about now... but they could always explain things away and it made perfect sense, but now knowing what I know... it's just different."

"What do you mean?"

"I'm not sure... but the living off the grid... in their house on their own... why they never wanted to be part of a pack. Just things like that."

I nodded in agreement.

"What if the camping trips we went on were for a different reason?" His eyes grew wide with realization.

"What? What is it?"

He shook his head. "Nothing. I thought I figured something out for a second, but it was nothing."

"What?"

"I thought maybe it had something to do with the Crescent mark, but I don't think that's it."

"Maybe your camping trip was just that?"

"Yea... probably. But now I'm going to wonder and second guess everything I remember."

"Don't do that. I know it's easy to do, but you could wander down endless rabbit holes and what-ifs with no answers."

"Yea, you're right."

"Sorry. I had a hard time hearing you. One more time."

"Not a chance." He kissed my forehead and pulled me into his arms while the rain continued to pour.

We stood here for what felt like hours before he released me. "Are you going to be ok here?"

"I have Ruthy. I'm going to be fine. The pack house is going to be fine. All is going to be good. Will you be ok?"

"Me?" He asked confused.

"I know you didn't want alpha, but you're good at it and the pack adores you. Will you be able to leave the pack for so long?"

"I'll be ok because I know it's in excellent hands."

Ruthy interjected. "Oh, thanks for saying that. I'm going to do my best while you're gone."

I laughed. "Hey Ruthy."

"Enjoying the balmy summer weather?"

"You know it's my favorite." I joked.

"What time are you thinking about leaving?" Ruthy asked.

"Already trying to get rid of me?"

"Not at all."

I didn't miss the fact she didn't elaborate, and I wondered if she was planning something for Asher with the rest of the pack house.

"In about an hour. Just wanted to spend as much time with Cami before I left."

"You two are seriously too cute."

"Stop." I playfully punched her arm. "No less cute than you and Drake."

She cocked her head and scowled. "Low... even for you. I expected better Cami."

"What can I say?" I shrugged.

"Oh! Chloe said she had something to give you. Something you left at your parents' when you were there for dinner or something."

My brow pinched into a v. "I did?"

"Yea."

I got the impression she wanted me gone, so I gave this to her and didn't push her on it. "I'll be back in a little." I called over my shoulder.

I walked inside to find a cake on the island and balloons and streamers hung around the living room, and my heart nearly melted. The entire pack house was perched on chairs and stools, quietly waiting.

You ok? Asher mindlinked.

Yea. Why?

You just got... weird...

Oh... I looked around at everyone. *Chloe just had to give me my necklace.*

You weren't wearing a necklace that night.

Yes, I was. His keen observation skills were both a blessing and a curse.

I don't think you were.

Then come in here and look for yourself hot shot.

I will in just a second. Ruthy and I are wrapping up something.

I looked at the rest of the pack and shrugged. Minutes passed, and I looked at my watch. What could be taking them so long? I thought she was just distracting him so I could come in.

What's taking so long? I asked her.

Ugh. We're almost done. This boy. I swear he loves you big.

I smiled and held my finger up, showing one more minute.

Fortunately, it wasn't even that long. Ruthy walked in first, followed by Asher.

"Surprise!" Everyone shouted in unison.

Asher scanned the room and his eyes landed on me and he smiled. I shook my head and pointed back at Ruthy and the rest of the pack.

"Wow. This is such a surprise and so not needed."

Ruthy patted him on the back. "We're going to miss you... but we also love cake and any reason to celebrate."

Everyone laughed while Ruthy sliced and served the cake.

I walked over to stand by Asher and grabbed his hand.

"Did you know?"

"I did not."

He glanced at my neck. "No necklace."

"Seriously, how did you even remember that?"

"I remember everything about you."

"Gross, you two." Ruthy said, walking over holding two pieces of cake. "The pack house wanted to do a little something for you to wish you luck on your journey. Finding out you have family out there is a pretty big deal and we couldn't be more excited for you!"

"Thank you." He looked at the rest of the crowd. "Thank you all. This really means a lot to me."

"Alpha Asher!" someone in the back shouted, causing the entire room to erupt in unison before taking a knee with their arms crossed in front of them.

He crossed them back and nodded.

I ate my cake slower and slower, knowing that when I got to the last bite, he was going to leave and I selfishly didn't want that.

"You could just say you don't want me to go."

I cocked my head to the side. "I would never do that and I hope you wouldn't stay if I asked. This is important. You need to find them." I planted a quick kiss on his lips.

"I know." He sighed.

"You will find them and they will love you."

"I hope so."

"I know so."

Drake walked up to us with a brown satchel. "You two. I swear." He said, handing it to Asher.

"You should patent these. It's great work."

Drake laughed. "Yes, hello United States patent office. Yes, I have designed a satchel using magic that will auto-adjust around a werewolf's arm as they shift from their human form. I've been watching too many movies? No. I'm not playing a prank on you... hello? Hello?"

"Ok. I get it. But it still is an amazing idea."

"Because he's pretty amazing!" Ruthy said, rubbing his chest.

I looked around at everyone and then at my watch. "Well... it's that time." I prompted, knowing if I didn't, he would likely stay.

He scrunched up his face.

"You got this!"

"Pack." He announced and everyone stopped talking and looked at him. "I want to thank you for this little surprise. It means the world to me. I don't know how long I'll be gone, but you're in excellent hands with Alpha Cami and Beta Ruthy."

The whole pack house erupted into howls.

"You all take care and I will see you in..." he shook his head. "I don't know when, but I will see you again."

He walked outside and Ruthy, Drake, and I followed him out.

"I will see you again?" Ruthy smacked his arm. "You could have lied and said soon, or in a few days or maybe a couple of weeks, but see you again... that could be freaking forever."

"You aren't crying, are you?"

"No. Your face is crying." She retorted.

I wrapped my arms around Asher's neck. "Go find your family and hurry home."

"Yes ma'am!" He cupped my cheeks in his hands and leaned in to give me a long, hard kiss.

Ruthy walked over and gave him a quick hug, then pushed away and then Drake walked over, holding out his hand for the weird hand shake chest bump thing.

"Take care of our girls." Asher said.

"You got it, bro. Take care of yourself."

"I will."

"You're sure you don't want a portal jump?"

"No thanks. I'm going to see the Elders, so I can't portal there."

"Right."

Asher adjusted the strap on his arm and then gave me one more deep kiss and then shifted.

"Go get 'em babe." I said, and he was off.

I watched as he ran further and further away and I had to fight the urge to call him back or run after him, because, Goddess, I wanted to. I already missed him and it hadn't even been a minute.

I took a step towards him.

"Please don't." Ruthy said.

I looked at her, studying her face.

"Would you stop me?"

"I would." She said simply and then shrugged. "He made me promise."

"When you were outside before the party?"

She nodded.

"What else did you talk about?"

"I'd rather not say." She shifted uncomfortably.

I stared at her, debating on whether I should make her tell me, but decided against it. If she needed to tell me, I had to trust she would.

I looked out in the distance and saw just a speck of black, just before it vanished from sight.

He was gone.

Asher was gone.

ALPHA PROBLEMS

THE LAST SEVERAL DAYS had passed without incident, thankfully. Everyone seemed to be on their best behavior for me, and I was thankful. I had the southern pack reach out to discuss a treaty issue with their western border neighbor, but we were able to get it resolved pretty quickly. Asher still had made little headway in finding his family. He was on the west coast right now, trying to track down a Crescent pack they had been a part of for a short time when they first met.

"Have you talked to Asher today?" Ruthy asked, walking into the library.

I looked up from the map on the table. "Not yet."

"What are you looking at?"

"I'm getting a few reports from some packs there have been increased Red Crows movement in these areas." I pointed to the red circle spots on the map.

"What do you think it means?"

"I'm not sure."

Ruthy pressed her palms to the table and studied the map, too. "Do we still think they're using their old compound?" She pointed to the red x on the map.

"I don't know. I would have to think not, but they also don't have anywhere else to go."

"Do you want me to see if Drake can portal some scouts there to look around?"

I tapped my fingers on the table. "It couldn't hurt, right?"

"I don't think so. I know your vision has your brother showing up on our doorstep in a few weeks, but if we can find them before that time... maybe we can prevent anything else from happening."

I hesitated. "Ok." Then looked back at the map. Part of me wanted to find out, but the other part was nervous that, like my other visions, this would shift them just enough to change the timeline and the vision. I looked up at Ruthy, but didn't speak. We needed to know if they were planning something and I couldn't let my fear of my visions prevent me from protecting my pack.

I called for the pack to meet me in the common room in ten minutes. This was my first official meeting as sole pack alpha and I'd be lying if I didn't say the nerves were getting to me.

"Hey," Ruthy stopped us at the door.

"What's up?"

"You got this!" She winked and then walked to the platform, falling backwards off of it with her hands spread out.

I laughed, peeking over the edge to watch her turn at the last second and land on her foot and knee. She really had the super hero landing nailed.

I stepped off and landed with a thud. I stood up straight and pulled down the hem of my shirt before I walked into the kitchen.

Most of the pack members were there, and the rest were straggling in. I nervously checked my watch a few times, gathering all my thoughts I wanted to say. My hands were getting clammy, so I tried to wipe them on my shirt without being obvious.

Breathe. Ruthy urged.

I cleared my throat and stepped forward. "Pack."

The talking stopped and everyone shifted in their seat or stance to look at me.

"There have been reports of increased Red Crows activity in several pockets around the country."

Someone in the back sighed, but I ignored it and kept talking.

"We don't know what this means as of now, but we... I want to send a few of you out to the Red Crows compound they were using last year to see if you can get any information. I don't want you to engage with the Crows if they are there. Again, this is solely a recon mission."

"Alpha." A man in the back stood up.

"Yes, Maxwell?" He was newer to the pack, only a couple of months in. He was older than most of the other members and had been one of the stronger fighters when the Red Crows came. Aside from that, however, I had little interaction with him... he seemed to keep to himself, mostly.

"Do you think they're still using the compound?"

"I don't know. That's what I'm hoping this group will tell us. I don't think they would continue to use the same compound, but I also don't know where else they could go. Thanks to a lot of the work that Asher has done with the treaties, we've made a lot of territories unavailable to them."

"Would it not be best to work with the Crescents and have some of their winged shifters do a fly over instead?"

"I don't want to get the Crescent's involved right now."

His brow furrowed. "Aren't they already involved since it's the Red Crows. I mean the Crows are wolves not shifters and they don't have a problem with most of us."

I looked around the pack and saw several people nodding their heads and could feel Ruthy getting anxious behind me. I could tell she was biting her tongue.

"They are working on other things involving the Red Crows, so I don't need them to run this quick recon mission."

"What if the Crows are there?"

"Again. I don't want anyone engaging with them. The team will be small, only a couple of wolves, ideally positioned on the hill overlooking the encampment. We're just looking for any kind of movement."

"I don't feel like this is a good idea. If they are using the compound and preparing for an attack, then there will be a lot of movement there and after what happened last time, they will be ready for it."

"The team will need to maintain a safe distance."

"Maintain a safe distance, but get close enough to get intel? Seems counterintuitive."

"Maxwell." I growled, getting irritated at the fact he continued to question me. "Since you seem to have so many thoughts and opinions about this simple request, you can go." He started to shake his head, so I continued. "You can pick two or three other wolves to travel with. You will leave within the hour, and Drake will portal you there."

I could tell he wasn't happy with me. "How will we get home?" He huffed.

"You can run back or mindlink myself or Ruthy and we will have Drake portal you back."

"Your witch doesn't mind being a paranormal Uber?" He snarked.

Ruthy stood up defensively, but I held my hand out. "Maxwell. We will talk when you get back. I'm the alpha and Ruthy is your beta. If you don't like that, then you can leave. But you will not sit here and disrespect us or talk back to us." I snapped.

"Merely having a conversation alpha. I thought the pack welcomed open dialogue." He sat back down.

I could feel my heart beating out of my chest and tried to calm down. I had initially wanted to give them an update on Asher, but I was so flustered and partially embarrassed from snapping that I wanted to end this meeting and retreat into a dark hole.

"Once you pick your team, meet Ruthy and I in the library where we will go over the plan. The rest of you are dismissed."

I turned and walked out of the room with Ruthy on my heels.

I leapt to the fourth floor and felt her right behind me, but I didn't want to talk right now. I wanted to be alone.

No.

I wanted to be with Asher. I missed him. My wolf missed him.

"I need a minute." I held up my hand and walked into my room, shutting the door. I didn't even turn around to face her, but I knew she was there. It wasn't her fault, but I couldn't deal right now.

I walked to the bed and started punching it while I screamed. Fortunately, the alpha's room had a cloaking spell of sorts on it, so anything I said or did in here was private and just for me.

Babe, babe, babe. What's going on? Asher chimed in.

Nothing.

Not nothing. Your blood is boiling right now.

Is it or did Ruthy tattle?

Ruthy? What happened Cami? His tone shifted from jovial to serious, and I realized Ruthy hadn't reached out to him.

Nothing happened... really.

Nice qualifier.

Ha. Nothing. I told you we've been getting messages from other packs about the Crows.

Yea. Are you going to send out a recon team to the compound?

Why would I do that? I asked, playing coy.

To get an idea of their numbers, see if they're going to act soon... I don't know... lots of reasons.

Yep. Ok. *Ruthy and I thought the same thing, but when we present-ed it to the pack, Maxwell spoke up.*

Oh.

Yea.

What did he say?

He kept questioning me and then when I called him out, he got snarky and tried to throw our conversational approach to the pack back in my face.

You're the alpha. He shouldn't be questioning you.

I know he shouldn't, but that doesn't mean he won't. A few of the others nodded in agreement.

Who?

It's not important. I will handle it.

Do I need to come home?

No. I have it under control, plus what would that say about our dynamic if you came running the first time someone spoke up at a meeting?

I know. I just hate being away from you, and I could have been using it as an excuse.

I laughed. I appreciate that. I miss you too. Have you had any luck?

No. I met with the pack in Seattle, but they didn't know my parents.

Did they ever talk about your grandparents... anyone?

No.

Do you think there's something at your house?

You mean our house?

Yes. I still hadn't gotten used to the fact we were practically married.

Potentially, but I have looked there several times for anything and have come up empty-handed.

Ok. So where are you now?

Traveling down to California. I figured I would stop at a few more packs along the way and then stop in to see Benji.

That's nice.

I don't really want to, but I don't feel like hearing how I didn't go see him for the next fifty years.

There was a knock on the door.

Ok, I need to go. We're about to meet with Maxwell and his team to run over the plans.

Be careful.

I'm staying put.

I know. Just... be careful.

I love you and you be careful too!

Love you pup!

There was another soft knock.

"I'm coming." I walked over to the door and swung it open.

"Sorry to interrupt, alpha. Maxwell and his team are in the library."

I nodded and walked down the hall with a renewed confidence. I felt good knowing Asher would have made the same call Ruthy, and I did.

When I walked into the room, I saw Maxwell first with two others standing behind him. The three of them joined around the same time, so perhaps they felt a certain connection with one another over the others.

"Thank you." I said, nodding at each of them.

Maxwell lifted his head but didn't speak.

I moved to the table and pointed at the map. "As you can see here in the red areas are reports of increased Red Crow activity. We feel they will make a move in the coming weeks to use the moonstone to get rid of the Crescents." I watched their reactions when I said the last part, but none of them flinched. I was looking for any sign they agreed with the Red Crows. I knew, rather, I felt strongly they weren't with the Crows, but that didn't mean they shared some of their ideologies. With them all being newer, part of me still didn't trust them completely. I continued, "This is the compound and as you can see, a lot of the movement is centered around here."

"So you do expect them to be there?" Maxwell asked.

"Yes. That is why we're going to portal you in here." I pointed about a hundred miles east of the compound. "You can make the trek, I would recommend in your human form, but you can decide what you think is best." I stood up, "Again. I know I have already said this several times, but I don't want you to engage. This is simply a recon mission. If they are there, and they're planning on using the moonstone soon, that could mean extra Crows and they will severely outnumber you."

I saw the two in the back shift from side to side uneasily.

"If any of you have a problem with this, then we will find someone else." I know I told Maxwell he was going, and imagined he wouldn't back down now, but I at least wanted to give the option.

"So you're all good?" Ruthy asked.

They nodded.

"I don't expect this will take very long. Perhaps sit at the compound for an hour or two and then head back to the portal point and mindlink us."

"I hope it's as easy as you expect, alpha." Maxwell said flatly.

"Me too." I sighed. "Asher supports the decision and would have made the same call if that makes you all feel better."

They all looked up but didn't speak.

"Any other questions?"

"No, alpha." I tried to ignore the slight bite in his words.

"Ok. I will give you some time to gather your thoughts. See you in the field within the hour."

CHALLENGED

RUTHY, DRAKE, AND I sat outside on the patio enjoying the weather.

Ruthy looked at Drake and swirled her hand in the air. "Cone, captain."

He shimmied his shoulders, "Captain."

"Oh my..." I sighed.

"This is no worse than you and Asher." Ruthy crossed her arms over her chest.

I rolled my eyes at her while Drake cast the privacy spell.

"How are you doing... from earlier?" She asked, leaning forward, resting her elbow on her knee.

"I'm fine. I expected it honestly. My introduction to the pack hasn't been the easiest... first I was Asher's mate, then a Crescent, then their alpha... all in a brief span of time. I don't blame them for questioning me."

"No. Don't do that. Don't sell yourself short."

I cocked my head to the side, smiling at her. "Thank you, but it's true. I mean, I'm not even at the one year mark yet for knowing about werewolves and shifters and here I am alpha to a pack on my own... well, you know what I mean." I rubbed my hands on my legs. "A bunch of these people have grown up with Asher. He's always been in the pack and a lot of them felt Dixon was wrong for what he did, so probably thought Asher should have been the alpha all along and I just got it because I happened to be mated to him."

Ruthy rolled her eyes. "Look. I hear a lot of your insecurities coming out, and that's understandable. I just want you to know you're an amazing alpha. You don't have to be like Dixon and bully the pack to follow you. A true leader will get the pack to follow them because they support the alpha and have trust in them."

"So you're saying that commanding Maxwell to go on this mission wasn't the act of a genuine leader?" I smiled.

"Everyone needs a different type of alpha. Maxwell seems to me like he needs a more authoritative leader."

I laughed. "You always have an answer for everything."

"Yes. She does." Drake groaned.

"Shut up." She smacked his arm. "You love that about me."

"It is one of the things I love."

I looked up to see Maxwell and the others leaping off the balcony.

Drake removed the privacy spell as Ruthy and I walked over to them.

"Are you ready?"

"Yes alpha." Maxwell said.

Drake began casting the portal spell as I fought the urge to tell them one more time not to engage, but I felt it would be overkill and I didn't want to come across as an overbearing mother type. "Good luck."

"Thanks." Maxwell said, stepping through the portal.

"Let us know when you want to come back." The little devil on my shoulder laughed and made some snide comment about them not coming back.

The portal closed, and we just stood in the middle of the field for a minute or two.

"Now what?" Ruthy asked.

"We wait, I guess."

"What are we waiting for?" Xander said, appearing from the ground.

"What?" Ruthy said, confused.

"Trying out Fangs the snake."

"Oh my Goddess." Ruthy signed. "Had I known you were down there, I would have stepped on you."

He threw his head back in laughter. "Ruthy. So funny. Always cracking a joke."

"I wasn't joking." She mumbled.

"What can I do for you, Xander?"

"I wanted to see if Levi could come out to play."

"I'm not his mother." I smiled.

"You two have been spending a lot more time together lately." Ruthy teased.

"I think he likes me."

"I'm glad at least one person does." Ruthy teased.

Xander closed the distance between them in a flash, wrapping his arms around her. She swiftly took him to the ground. "Dude, put some clothes on."

He laid on the ground for a minute, looking up at her and then at Drake. "Does she treat you like this?"

Drake shook his head. "You should be glad I trust you both. Any other dude coming at my girl stark ass naked would get laid out. Imagine all the spells I could cast on you to make your life miserable."

Xander popped back up and squeezed Drake's arms. "So strong."

Drake reared his free arm back.

"Ok, ok. You two."

With a pop, Xander changed back into a snake and slithered away. *Tell Levi to chat me up when he's ready.*

Ready for what? Ruthy asked.

None- ya bizzzz-nasssss!

She looked at me and huffed. "I'm going to kill him."

I laughed. "You like him."

She narrowed her eyes at me.

I held my hands up in defense. "I'm just saying."

"You better be glad you're my alpha or..."

"Or what?" I laughed. I knew Ruthy could easily kick my ass.

"You want to find out?" She playfully stepped forward.

"Your girl is feisty today." I looked at Drake.

"He likes me this way." She said, snaking her arm around him.

"I do." He kissed the top of her head.

"How do you think Maxwell and the team are?" I looked at my watch. "They should be at the compound by now."

"I'm sure everything's fine."

"I wish we would have sent Bryson with them so we could get updates."

Drake cast the privacy spell again. "Probably why Maxwell didn't ask Bryson."

"What do you mean?"

"Bryson volunteered to go, but Maxwell told him no."

"He told him no?"

"Yea. He was kind of rude about it, apparently. Bryson said Maxwell told the other two they were going with him."

"So they didn't want to go?"

"I don't know, but from what Bryson said, it didn't sound like it."

"Then why didn't they say something to me earlier?" I frowned.

"I'm sure they didn't want to appear weak or say they had reservations about going and perhaps they were a little scared of Maxwell."

"I need to have a talk with him when he gets back."

"What are you going to say?" Ruthy asked.

"I don't know, but he seems to have a chip on his shoulder... one that's gotten bigger the longer he's been here. I don't need him commanding others in the pack and getting the wrong idea."

"What do we know about him?" Drake asked.

"Not a lot. I wish we knew more, but he's been here for a couple of months. He's late twenties, came without anyone, doesn't have a mate, carries around a permanent grimace, but is a good fighter."

"Yea, I remember seeing him during the Trinity ceremony."

"There was a lot happening that day, but I remember bits and pieces of him fighting... there was a lot of rage and anger there, so I don't think he's Red Crows... but I don't know."

"I agree. I'm not thinking Red Crows either, but I don't know. I just have an odd feeling about him."

"Asher said to keep an eye out and be careful."

"How's he doing?" Drake wondered.

"Good. Well, I guess as good as can be expected. He struck out in the northwest and is now moving down the coast. I think he's going to stop by Benji's."

"Benji will love that." Ruthy said.

"That's what I said, but Asher was so blah about it."

"Hopefully, he can find something soon." Drake wrapped his arm around Ruthy.

"Should we cookout tonight?" I asked Ruthy and Drake, changing the topic.

"It is a pleasant night out."

I nodded. "Let's do it. I feel like after the meeting this morning, I just need to regroup with the pack and have a relaxing night."

"That sounds great." Ruthy smiled.

"I'll grab Bryson and Connor and head to the store to get some stuff after Maxwell and the team are back." Drake offered.

"Thanks!" I looked over his shoulder and saw Levi jumping off the balcony, making his way towards us.

Ruthy teased. "Your boyfriend was over just a little bit ago looking for you."

"What?" Levi recoiled.

"Xander." Ruthy rolled her eyes. "He was a snake in the grass. Literally."

Levi laughed. "Yea. He said he's been working on her for a while."

"Her?"

"Yea. He calls her a girl. I always assumed it would be a boy, but I don't know. Shifters are so different." He rolled his eyes.

"Interesting."

"Do you want–"

Alpha! Maxwell's voice was panicked and out of breath.

I looked at Ruthy.

"What?" Concern spread over her face.

What's wrong?

Open the portal now! Get support at the portal. We have company.

How many?

I don't know. Seven? Ten?

"Open the portal!" I barked at Drake. *Back up at the portal now!* I commanded the pack.

Within seconds, Drake was opening the portal, and pictured in front of us was a wooden landscape of trees and bushes as far as the eye could see, with bits of sun shining through the filtered canopy.

"What's wrong?" Ruthy asked, peering in with her feet wide in a defensive stance.

Maxwell is coming in hot. Up to ten Red Crows in pursuit. "Drake, as soon as our three are through, close the portal as fast as you can."

He looked at me confused, then looked through the portal and saw our three wolves running towards us with the Red Crows gaining on them fast. I wondered why our guys were running so slow then noticed one in the front was running with a limp and bleeding from their leg.

"Get ready!" I commanded, shifting into my wolf as the others followed.

It felt like the world started moving in slow motion as I watched and waited for our pack to make it through the portal. What happened? They were supposed to just look around the compound. How were they attacked?

Paw after paw pounded the earth, the thumping echoed through a hollow chamber, as the huffs of the wolves breathing bounced around through the woods. I was hyper focused on the wolves. Five... four... three... two... one!

Now!

Our pack formed a line in front of the portal as the Red Crows continued to barrel towards us. I watched as Drake worked to close the portal and saw it was getting smaller as they were getting closer, but they weren't slowing down. What would happen if they tried to jump through when it closed?

The portal snapped closed at the last second and they were gone.

I immediately turned and looked at Maxwell and his group and saw the first wolf, James, shift back. He was lying on the ground with a deep gash in his forearm and another wound on his abdomen. Maxwell shifted and was hovering over him, pressing his hand to the wound on his abdomen while Drake was looking at the forearm.

I darted off to the base level of the house and quickly shifted and changed into a set of clothes and then raced back out and saw most of the pack had shifted and were standing around them. Maxwell was looking at several people barking out orders and they darted off, causing a twinge on the back of my neck. Something about his actions made me feel uncomfortable.

I ran over to Drake. "What can I do?"

Drake looked at me with sad eyes while his hands continued to feverishly work the salve and hold it over the wounds.

I looked between Maxwell and James.

"Where did you go?" Maxwell demanded, then looked up at me. "You left to change while your pack member is in need?" He scoffed.

I stared at him incredulously. "What do you need, Drake?" I asked pointedly.

Maxwell interjected. "I've already sent several people off to get what he needs."

I took a calming breath and waited for Drake to speak.

"Nothing. Maxwell is working on it." His face dropped.

I nodded and looked around at the others. "Those of you still here can leave if you need or you're welcome to stay."

The one's standing around shifted and walked away, so it was just Drake, Ruthy, and Maxwell left. I started to say something to Maxwell, but the others started coming back out with the supplies Drake had apparently requested.

"He won't stop bleeding!" Drake yelled in exasperation.

Xander and Levi ran up. "What can we do?"

"Nice of you to join us." Maxwell mumbled.

"Maxwell. Enough! You are dismissed." I barked in my alpha voice.

"The hell I am!"

"Excuse me?" I recoiled.

"You're a weak alpha. We shouldn't have gone."

"You're out of line." I saw Ruthy step forward in my peripheral, but stop.

"You have no experience and it nearly got him killed- if it still doesn't!"

"You didn't follow orders! I said to go and surveil. How in the hell did this even happen?"

He glared at me.

"Speak." I commanded. I felt the hairs across my whole body stand on end.

"We walked around the property and coming to the field at the compound, we saw a man and a woman tied to a tree. I recognized the man as a wolf from one of the packs out west when I was moving across the country and the girl was here at our pack house recently."

"The girl?" I wracked my brain trying to figure out the girl he was referring to and the only one I landed on was Luna. "Did she have long, dark hair?"

He nodded.

I snapped my head towards Drake. "Is he talking about Luna?"

Drake looked at me and sighed, which told me all I needed to know. "Why is she at the Red Crows compound? What's going on? What aren't you telling us?"

He shook his head slowly.

"Drake." Ruthy demanded.

"I can't." He sighed, reluctantly.

"Damn it, Drake!" I yelled and then spun back to Maxwell. "Continue with your story."

"We went after the wolf-"

"Not Luna?"

"I don't care about her. She's a witch, not a wolf."

"A witch for the coven that looks over us."

"Not us. You. Crescents." He fired back quickly.

"Is that a problem? The Crescents."

He snarled, but didn't speak.

"So you saw them and decided to go after them? Without a plan? Without permission?"

"I decided in the moment. I didn't have time to get your permission. The guards protecting them had gone inside and when the girl, Lena or whatever her name is... called out for help... which was stupid, I might add." He rolled his eyes. "Anyhow, she called out for help and when we hesitated, she told us the wolf was in a bad way. So we jumped the fence. She insisted we get him first." He shrugged. "They had wolfsbane or something else on the ropes. It was enough to prevent him from using his strength to get out, and it burned me when I touched it." He showed me his hand. "But it didn't kill or paralyze him, so it had to be cut with something, but I don't know what."

I watched Drake walk over and look at his hand.

"Where is he now?"

Maxwell's head fell.

"Where is he?" I demanded again.

"I don't know. He was weak. It took two of us to help him over the fence and when we landed on the other side, the guard came back out and saw us, sounding the alarm. The wolf ran with us for a little while, but couldn't shift and he told us to go ahead of him because he knew he was slowing us down."

"So you left him?"

"He told us too." He defended, yelling. "He said he knew the area pretty well and knew of a hiding spot. Before we could talk about it any further, he ran in the opposite direction. We didn't have time to chase him down since the Crows were gaining on us. I hoped we were a distraction."

I stared at him, trying to process everything he was telling me. "Do you know who he was?"

"We didn't exchange names."

I ignored the snark. "And you left Luna there?"

"Yes."

"Was she injured?"

"Couldn't tell. I smelled her blood in the air and she had a few cuts on her face."

"Damn it." I yelled, spinning in a circle grabbing fistfuls of hair.

"We shouldn't have gone in. We weren't prepared. You almost got us killed with your inexperience."

"No." I pointed my finger in his face. "No. You don't get to stand here and try to point the finger at me. I sent you on a recon mission to see what was going on around the perimeter. You decided to go in without my permission. Had you followed protocol, you would have talked with your alpha prior to doing anything and I would have told you not to engage. You," I paused pointedly, "Almost got you and your team killed because you have a chip on your shoulder and can't follow a simple command."

"You wouldn't have been able to decide quick enough."

I stepped towards him aggressively, barely able to contain my rage. "You don't know what I would have done, because you didn't give me the chance, because you think you know better than your alpha. You are relieved from your duties and this pack. I banish you."

"You can't do that." He clapped back.

"I'm the alpha of this pack and can do whatever in the hell I please. I've had it with your snarky comments and disrespect!"

"I'm not leaving."

"You don't have a choice." I shifted into my wolf and could feel my gums pulled back over my teeth, and heard the low growl vibrating through my chest. I felt an electricity pulsing through my body, causing my hair to stand on end.

Maxwell shifted into his wolf and squared off in front of me, followed immediately by Ruthy and several others who had been watching from a distance.

Leave. You aren't welcome here anymore.

Maxwell's wolf took a step towards me and my wolf met him, nose to nose.

I don't know how long his wolf stared at me, but I didn't back down. I would fight him if that's what it took, but I stood by my decision.

A second later, he tore off across the field. I watched as his wolf ran further and further away until he was just a speck in the tree line.

CONNECTIONS

I FOCUSED ON MY breathing, allowing it to steady before I turned to Ruthy. *I need to run. Can you manage while I'm gone?*

She stared at me in shock, then nodded. "Yea, yea. I got this. Go. Go." She looked at Drake in surprise.

I stepped towards Drake.

Tell him we're going to talk when I get back.

Ruthy relayed the message and his head recoiled in concern before nodding.

I tore off in the opposite direction from Maxwell. I didn't need to accidentally run into him right now.

What's wrong? Asher mindlinked.

Nothing. I'm fine.

The hell you are. What's wrong? He demanded.

Maxwell.

What did he do? He barked in an overly concerned tone.

I'm fine. Ruthy and I talked and sent a recon team to track down the Red Crows.

Right. I remember. I thought it was a good idea.

While he was there, he found Luna and a man- a wolf from a neighboring pack- tied to a tree in the compound's yard.

Luna?

I don't know. Drake knows something, but insists he can't tell us.

He can't or won't?

I assume can't. Anyhow, the guards went inside and Luna called out saying the wolf was in terrible shape so Maxwell jumped the fence and tried to rescue him.

Without talking to you first?

Correct. When he did that, they were able to get the wolf over the fence, but the guard came back out soon after, sounding the alarm. They took off running, but Maxwell said the wolf was slowing them down because he was injured. He darted off in the opposite direction to hide and Maxwell and the team kept running. I guess along the way one was injured, and that's when he called for us to portal him home.

We will need to talk to him when I get back.

No need.

What happened?

It came to blows and I feel like he challenged me to alpha even though he never spoke the words. I shifted and so did he, and he didn't back down. My body felt charged.

What happened to Maxwell?

He left. I banished him from the pack.

I'm sorry I'm not there.

Don't be sorry. You needed to do this.

Not now. I should have waited. There's so much going on. We should be together looking for the Red Crows and preparing for what's coming. Instead, I ran off to track down my family.

No. No. It's because of the Red Crows you had to leave. What if the curse does something to the Crescents... beyond what they think? What if it kills us? Maye doesn't know, neither does Ellsmire. No. You need to find them now, in case anything horrible happens.

But...

No buts. You have to do this. We have a couple more weeks before my brother shows up on our doorstep. They aren't doing anything with the moonstone right now, so we have time.

Why were Luna and the werewolf there?

What?

Sorry. I jumped back to your story from before.

I don't know. After I'm done talking with you, I'm going back to the pack house to get information out of Drake.

You aren't there now?

No. I needed to get away... to clear my head.

So you're by yourself?

Yes.

I don't like that.

I'm fine.

Famous last words.

I chuckled. *Tell me about you.*

What do you mean?

Where are you? Did you see Benji?

No. On the way there I met another pack and after a several hour discussion and persuading them I wasn't a threat, we got to talking.

Talking?

Yes. They said there was a Hunter who looked similar to me in a pack in Montana, but they said that was years ago.

Do you think that Hunter could have been your dad? What if it's another Hunter?

It could be. They also said he was married to a woman with long brown hair who had a birthmark on her shoulder. My mother had a birthmark on her shoulder.

So you think it was them? I felt a nervous excitement tingle through my body.

I don't know. The confusing thing is they didn't call her Gwendolyn or any other variation.

What did they call her?

Mariel.

Do you recognize the name?

Not at all. I've never heard of it.

But they also said she had a twin.

A twin?

Yea. I don't know what it means... but maybe I'm getting closer.

That's really great Asher. It sounds like you have a solid lead on finding your parents' old pack. A man named Hunter that looks like you, who was married to a woman with a birthmark on her shoulder that has a sister. Did you reach out to Benji to see if he recognizes the name Mariel?

Not yet. I wanted to check on you first. I had just finished the conversation when I felt something was wrong with you.

I'm better now that I've talked to you. I miss you.

I miss you too. I'm hoping this pack knows something and I'm able to head home soon so I can wrap you in my arms and just inhale your sweet scent.

I felt a tightness stir in my stomach as I imagined his citrusy, sweet scent swirling around me.

Well, I'm headed home now. Hopefully, Ruthy has convinced Drake to talk.

Eesh. I will have Ruthy wish him luck.
Stop. I laughed.
I love you.
Love you too.

With the connection cut off between us, I turned towards the house with one thing on my mind. Figure out what Drake knew about Luna at the Red Crows compound.

I let the cooler night air dance around me as my feet pounded the earth, its hard floor not giving an inch under the weight of my paws. I could hear the crickets chirp growing louder and saw flecks of lightning bugs flittering through the air.

I hit the field behind the house in a matter of minutes and saw a flurry of bugs flying into the sky, lighting it up, a warning to anyone watching that I was coming- and there was someone watching. I felt their eyes rake over me, even though I couldn't see them.

I ignored the feeling and pressed on towards the pack house. Its outline glowed in the distance as lights from most of the rooms illuminated the night sky. I saw Ruthy and Drake in the distance sitting on the rocking chairs on the back porch and tried to guess their mood, but I was too far away.

I got the strangest feeling again and couldn't help wonder if Maxwell was waiting in the woods around the pack house. I looked over my shoulder again.

Nothing, but that's when I felt it.

My front legs seized together and burned instantaneously. I couldn't react quick enough and was hurtling face first towards the ground, my front legs unable to move. I felt my wolf's muzzle hit the ground, but seconds later I felt my body- my human body- rolling hard and fast on the hard dirt surface.

When I came to a stop, I was lying on my back, looking up at the sky. The same lightning bugs I was enjoying only moments before buzzed around in a panic... or was that me?

I closed my eyes to take in large calming breaths, trying to understand what was happening, and before I could open my eyes, I heard feet rushing to my side. I opened my eyes and saw Ruthy standing there with a blanket in hand.

"What in the hell happened?"

I grabbed the blanket and let it fall over me, still too confused, disoriented, and sore to sit up. "I don't know."

"You're bleeding." She ripped her shirt off and dabbed my cheek before pressing it to my upper arm, near my shoulder.

"I'll be fine. It should heal soon." I lazily batted her hand away.

She removed her shirt. "It's not healing."

"What?"

"You're not healing!" She said, more panicked.

I raised my head enough to look at it and saw the gash in my arm was still pumping blood out. "I don't understand."

"Where did you go? What happened?"

"Nowhere. I just went for a run in the woods, talked to Asher and was coming-" I felt a strike against my face that knocked the words out of my mouth. "Ow."

"What?" Ruthy was looking around, confused.

My wrist burned again, and I saw welts and blisters slowly appearing.

"What in the hell?" Ruthy looked behind her. "Drake!" She yelled, and he began running towards us.

"What's happening?" I felt a pain in my chest like a rib had just snapped and then looked up at Ruthy as realization set in.

"What? What is it? What's happening?"

"Kayden."

"Your broth-" She realized what I was saying. "They're torturing him? Or do you think he's doing it to himself?"

I screamed out in pain again just as Drake showed up. When the wave of pain passed, I was able to speak. "He's being tortured. No way..." I grabbed my chest from the pain. "He's doing this to... himself." I screamed out in pain again. It was everywhere. Every part of my body felt like it was on fire.

Drake grabbed my wrists and looked at them. "They're using wolfsbane and something else on him... it's stopping him from shifting and healing."

"Which is why you shifted back to human." Ruthy chimed in.

"They are..." I winced in pain as I sat up. "Torturing him. My ribs."

Drake placed his hand on my forehead and chest and began to mumble something. Within seconds, I could feel the pain easing.

"What-"

"He's breaking the link between us... or rather, blocking it."

I could feel the pain ease off my wrists and my chests.

"You're healing." Ruthy said, lifting the shirt to look at my arm.

"I feel stronger."

"He can't keep doing this all night, though."

"I know."

Drake paused, looking at us. "Let's get you to your room. I'm hoping the spells around your room can help act as a barrier to block out most of the connection." He continued mumbling his spell again.

"Ok." I moved to stand up, so Drake stopped casting his spell.

"How do you feel?"

"Fine, right now. I don't know if it's because they stopped or what."

"Could be." He looked around. "But let's get you to your room just in case. Are you ok to walk?"

"Yea." I had made it two steps before I felt Ruthy's arm tucked around me. I looked over at her, but she was looking straight ahead, face set with determination. "I'm fine, you know."

She cut her eyes at me, but didn't speak.

When we got to the balcony, she helped me jump up to the railing before she unwound her arm. It took me a second to realize she had done it for me, so the rest of the pack house didn't see her helping me as we walked through the living room.

As much as I didn't want to admit it right now, after what happened earlier with Maxwell, I didn't want to show I was a weak leader in any sense of the word.

Don't collapse or anything.

I'm fine.

You say that... but I... you can't... She huffed. *Asher would kill me.*

Once we walked through the living room and kitchen, she looped her arm around me, then helped me to the fourth floor. She guided me down the hall and kicked open the door and directed me to the bed. She gently shoved me down before walking over to the dresser to get some clothes for me, which she tossed carelessly onto the bed before heading into the bathroom to run some water.

While she was away, I slipped into the clothes, already feeling a thousand times better. I bundled up the sweatshirt and brought it to my nose, taking in a deep breath. Ruthy had thankfully given me one of Asher's oversized sweatshirts and his scent swirled around me, comforting me.

She walked back out with a washcloth in her hand. "Here. Your face is covered in dirt." Her tone was direct and not overly motherly, but that was Ruthy- guarded and never wanting to show she cared. It was almost like she was angry with herself for having those emotions.

I smiled at her and took the washcloth while she glared at me playfully.

Drake walked in a minute later. "How are you feeling? Mama bear Ruthy taking care of you."

"You joke." Ruthy warned. It was hard to tell if she was kidding or not.

Drake looked at me and pulled his lip.

"I'm fine and yes, she's taking great care of me, even though I've told her several times that she doesn't need to."

"If something happened to you while Asher was away..."

"Then he will get over it." I fired back.

"I won't. I won't get over it. I have to protect you. That's my job and I haven't been doing very good."

"Ruthy." I felt my brows raise. "Your job is not to watch over me, but over this pack. You are my beta and a damn good one at that."

"It is." She stepped forward. "Yes. My job is beta, but you... you are more important."

"I'm not and if Asher made you think that-"

"He didn't. I just..."

I reached out and grabbed her hand. "I'll be ok."

"You keep saying that, but you don't know. You don't know anything. If the Red Crows reverse the crescent curse, then what happens to you... to Asher? What happens if you're killed as a result? I'll lose you and him... I can't... I can't do that. I can't handle that."

Drake reached out for her, but she batted his arm away.

"No. I'm mad at you too."

"Too?" I said in shock. I was confused what I had done.

She glanced from me to Drake. "You know what's going on and you aren't saying anything. You're choosing them over us... over, over... over me."

He took a deep breath. "I'm not."

"You are!" Ruthy stomped her foot down. "Why is Luna there? Why can't you tell us anything?"

He rubbed his hands through his hair, grabbing fistfuls in frustration. "Fine."

"Fine?" Ruthy stopped moving.

"Fine. I will tell you what I know."

PLANS REVEALED

RUTHY SAT QUIETLY ON the bed beside me as we watched Drake pace back and forth for what felt like hours. Neither one of us spoke, for fear if we said anything, he would lose whatever courage he was trying to muster within himself to tell us.

He stopped walking and looked at us for a second, then resumed walking again.

Ruthy grabbed my hand and squeezed fairly hard, making me wince in pain, but it scared me to say anything, so I turned my head slowly toward her with wide eyes.

She pulled her lips in apology and then released my hand.

I rubbed it to soothe the pain away.

"Ok." He said.

A word! We got a word out of him.

He shook his head, then continued walking.

I couldn't take it anymore. "Drake."

Ruthy snapped her head in my direction, casting daggers at me.

I shook my head. "Look. I don't know what's going on."

"Because he won't tell us." Ruthy spat out before realizing what she said and clamped her hand over her mouth.

I looked back at Drake. "I don't know what's going on and I would like to. We both would." Ruthy still had her hand over her mouth. "But if you really can't tell us... then we don't want to put you in that spot."

He sighed and walked over to us. "I want to tell you. I really do."

I wanted to pry into why he couldn't, but I kept my mouth shut.

He stared at the ceiling, then looked back at us. "Luna and I, and several others, had a meeting with the council regarding the Trinity Curse, the Crescent mark, Red Crows and the moonstone." He took a deep breath, still shaking his head. "If they find out I told you anything... they will banish me. It will be my third strike in a very short amount of time."

"Banish?" Ruthy mumbled.

"Send me away... like far away. Like I never see you all again."

I could feel Ruthy's body soften in worry as the internal battle waged within her. Does she find out what he knows at the risk of losing him?

He shook his head. "Damn it."

"Is there anything you can tell us that wouldn't get you in hot water?"

"That's what I've been trying to figure out."

"Why is Luna at the compound?"

"Wait." Ruthy grabbed my arm. "Luna was at the compound trying to get the moonstone."

Drake didn't say anything, but also didn't correct Ruthy.

"Ok, well, that's obvious," I said.

"If it was obvious, then why did you ask?"

"Maybe because I needed to hear she isn't an evil, vindictive, little-"

Drake interrupted. "Despite everything she's done in the past, she really is trying to make amends... the way she knows how." He added after Ruthy choked on the air.

"Ok, she was trying to get the moonstone back, but obviously something didn't go the way it was supposed to. Do the others know? Ellsmire?"

"I would have to assume they do now since they haven't heard from her." Drake offered.

Ruthy continued to talk slowly, "Because they sent her on her own? Why would they send her on her own? That makes no sense."

"Unless..." I started waving my finger in the air. "Unless they wanted her to get caught?"

"Why?" Ruthy shifted on the bed, bending her leg under.

"Because of her background with Lucian and Dixon. When they banished her from Ellsmire all those years ago... they think she can use that somehow to get in with the Red Crows."

"So she was going in undercover?" Ruthy shook her head. "That doesn't make sense. Maye is there and would know that's not the case."

"Would she? Luna can be pretty despicable when she tries. She seems to have a genuine dislike for me, which helps sell any story."

Ruthy pulled her face.

"I mean, think about it. They turned their back on her for years and just recently she got in contact with her mom. But who's not to say Luna was playing us all along, trying to get back in with Ellsmire to get information for Lucian, and when Lucian died, she went straight to the source?"

"I mean, I guess it can be believable."

"I think it totally could."

We looked at Drake, who was listening to us, but not offering anything contrary to what we were saying.

"Ok. So we have that Luna showed up to weasel her way into the Crows to get information for Ellsmire, but I have to believe that part of her plan didn't involve getting beat and tied to a tree with a werewolf."

"No."

"So why then?"

I rubbed my hands together and then my wrists. "What if..." I looked down at my wrist. "What if... for the curse to be broken, they have to have the power of three again?"

"They already got the moonstone through the Trinity curse."

"Yes. I know. But what if it's a different three... what if they need..." I paused, thinking through everything I wanted to say as thoughts bombarded me. I nodded. "What if they need a witch, a werewolf, and a crescent?"

I watched Drake's head slowly look up and felt I was on to something, so I continued.

"They kidnapped a werewolf."

"They have a witch... Maye."

"Right, but I bet Maye isn't willing to sacrifice herself."

Ruthy nodded. "So then Luna showed up, all too timely."

"Yes, and then Kayden was always a willing participant."

"Until recently." Ruthy pointed at my stomach, my face, then all over.

"Until recently, because Maye had been keeping him in the dark, and when Maxwell showed up and helped the wolf escape, it messed up her plans, and perhaps Kayden found out they had to sacrifice him. He obviously wasn't ok with that so he fought them and that's why he's probably bound to a tree with Luna. He was probably trying to reach out to me." As things continued to click, I nodded. "I felt like someone was watching me on my way back here, before everything happened. I wonder if it was my connection to him. I wonder if he was trying to reach out to me."

Ruthy was also nodding excitedly, then stopped. "Wait, you think he was trying to warn you?"

"I don't know. I didn't understand what was happening so we never fully mindlinked, but he had made enough of a connection and when they bound him, that's why I shifted and felt everything else." I ran my fingers through my hair. "Ok. So, they don't have a werewolf right now, but they have Luna and Kayden."

"It won't be hard for them to get another werewolf."

I frowned. "No. It won't. We should send out a warning to all the other packs to let them know what's going on."

"We could, but the red zone packs would probably be all too happy to give up one of their own for this worthy sacrifice."

I rolled my eyes.

"I still don't understand how Luna got there so quickly."

"Maybe she thought the same thing we did and portaled there to see if the Crows were still using the compound."

"Maybe." I looked at Drake and his lips were pressed into a flat line, which told me there was something else I was missing, but he couldn't say.

"I also don't know how this plays into the vision I had with Kayden."

Ruthy shrugged.

"I mean, according to the vision, there are still a couple of weeks before he comes knocking, but based on what we know now... I just don't know. It would make sense that it would be sooner."

"Your visions aren't set in stone. They change. They changed when you were looking for your sister. Perhaps when we sent Maxwell and he removed their wolf, it changed the timeline. Without your vision, we may not have acted so quickly to find the Crows. Every time you have a vision, that gives us insight, which changes the way we act, which changes the future just a little."

I nodded, thinking back to all of my visions and how they had all changed slightly. "Right. So you think this one will too? Will he show up at all? Sooner? Later? He's bound to a tree and being tortured. Prior to us changing the future, was he bound?" I screamed out in frustration.

"I don't know." Ruthy squeezed my hand sympathetically. "I wish I had the answers." She gave a pointed look at Drake.

"Woah." He said holding his hands up.

I fell backwards onto the bed and stared at the ceiling, trying to process everything that was going on while Ruthy walked over to the window to look outside, and Drake found a chair in the corner on the opposite side of the room.

"What do we know about the sacrifice?"

"Drake?" Ruthy looked.

"We seem to know that a witch, a werewolf, and a crescent are needed as part of the trinity." He said, carefully replaying our words back to us.

"We do." I sat up, looking at him.

Drake continued speaking in generalities and fake conversations. "You're right Ruthy. Their blood has to be bound before they are sacrificed, most likely in some sort of circle."

"It's amazing how much we know, since we didn't seem to know anything days ago." Ruthy said, glaring at Drake. "How could *we* have learned so much in such a short amount of time? Unless *we* knew all along." She continued to use we in place of Drake and I could see him getting antsy.

Continuing the charade, Drake said, "We didn't know all along. We just found out recently when we had to go to Ellsmire. We also couldn't tell you."

"Then why is we telling us now?"

"We are tired of hiding the truth from you."

"Why could we not tell us before? Cami is a crescent, one of the three needed to make this curse apparently succeed, so maybe we should have told us so that we..." she paused for a second, confusing herself, "so we could protect her and Chloe?"

"Please, dear Goddess, can we stop using we in place of Drake? It's driving me crazy and is very confusing!"

"Fine." Ruthy pouted, then continued. "Why would Ellsmire not want to tell us about this information? If Cami, Chloe and Kayden are the only three people needed that can pull this off, then it would reason, we should all know so we can protect them." Her voice got louder the longer she talked.

"They weren't certain and didn't want to alarm. They found some documents that Maye had apparently compiled and they are trying to decipher them. They found a piece of paper that has werewolf, witch and crescent scribbled on it, but nothing else."

"I still don't get it. We need to know."

"You're right and I didn't agree with them not telling you. They have been keeping an extra eye on you, just in case."

"But not Kayden?"

He shrugged.

"Luna?"

"Her mission was two-fold. Try to get in with Maye to figure out what was going on, and also look after Kayden."

"But something happened."

"It seems so."

"What are they doing to help her?"

"I don't know. Luna knew it was a dangerous mission going in, but she was one of the few that could pull it off. She had a somewhat believable back story, came from Ellsmire and is strong enough- magically speaking."

"Ok. So they have a witch and a crescent, but they still need a wolf. I would have to imagine they will have one soon enough, which means they could perform the ceremony any day now." I fell back on the bed again. "I don't understand. My vision."

"Not to be rude... but I think we can't rely on those as fact." Drake said quietly.

I looked at him, and while the words he said made sense and I agreed with him, something inside of me wanted to argue and tell him he was being harsh. I don't know if it was because on some level I knew the visions couldn't be completely trusted... I mean they haven't been exactly right, ever... but the other part of me knew if I accepted I couldn't trust them, then everything I have been holding on to, everything I've based these last few weeks on is... not a lie... but... I don't know. I sent Asher away to find his family, when maybe instead I should have kept him here with me selfishly because the time we have left is less than we thought.

"Cami?" Ruthy whispered.

"I'm fine..." I looked at Drake. "I know we can't trust them... but... I don't know. Feeling like I knew part of what was going to happen in the future gave me hope everything would be ok because I would know. I would know what was going to happen and could fix it, prevent it... something. Now... I have nothing..."

"We will still find a way to fix all of this."

"I feel like we're running out of time. An hour ago I felt we had two more weeks at the very least. Now I'm not sure if we even have two hours."

"Are you going to tell Asher?"

"No."

"Really?"

"He's getting close to finding his family. He needs to focus on that right now, especially since we don't have a plan."

"You're his family too... don't forget that."

"I know... but... it's different. He needs to do this." I shifted on the bed, tucking my foot underneath me. "He told me he found a pack that had a man named Hunter married to a woman with a birthmark on her shoulder... like his mother. This woman also had a twin sister."

"A twin? You're a triplet and his mother was a twin? When you two have kids, watch out!" Ruthy joked, trying to lighten the heavy mood in the room.

"Oh my!" I hadn't even thought about that, although to be fair, I haven't had time.

"Let's get some rest tonight, and then we'll regroup in the morning. We need to adjust the timetables for the plans and assume they'll have a wolf within the next two days. We need to stop them."

BROTHER BROKEN

THE WARMTH OF THE sun shining on my face woke me up. I cracked an eye open to see the light filtering in through the windows with a bright blue sky in the distance.

We really needed to get curtains for those windows, I thought as I buried my head in the pillow, willing myself to climb out of bed.

Wakey, wakey, eggs and bakey.

Asher! Are you here?

I quickly rolled out of bed and grabbed my phone to see what time it was.

9:09 AM.

He chuckled. Not yet. I'm getting close, though.

You're coming home?!

I am.

Relief poured through me. *I can't wait to see you!*

That was the truth.

The last couple of days had been fairly uneventful, thankfully. Maxwell hadn't tried to come back, I didn't have any more phantom pains from Kayden, and I hadn't had any more visions... which I still wasn't sure if that was a good thing or a bad thing.

Me too! I have so much to tell you.

You could just tell me now.

Not going to happen.

Come on... just a hint. Did you find anyone at the pack house?

Cami. He playfully warned.

Asher.

I promise I'll tell you everything when I see you in a little bit.

You could tell me where you are and I could have Drake create a portal.

That's ok. I'd rather run.

And torture me by making me wait?

Of course. What kind of mate would I be if I didn't enjoy needlessly torturing you?

I laughed.

The doorbell rang, and I ran out of the room in excitement. *You sly devil.*

What?

I leapt off the platform and landed with a thud at the same time Ruthy was opening the front door. "I can't believe you tried to trick me!" I yelled out, then stopped when I saw who it was.

"Well, hello sister." Kayden said, leaning heavily on the door for support. "I didn't think you would be so happy... to see me." He winced in pain, grabbing his chest.

"She's not." Ruthy said flatly.

I looked at Ruthy. "I'm not." I said in a bit of a softer tone.

He rolled his eyes. "I need your help."

"Of course you do." Ruthy spat.

"Ruthy. I got this."

Her eyes nearly bulged out of her head. "No way in hell I'm leaving you with this jackhole."

I laughed. "I appreciate your concern, but-"

"Save it." She held up her hand. "I don't care what you're going to say. I'm not leaving. End of discussion. You will literally have to banish me from the pack to get me to leave, so unless you're willing to do that then..." she held her hands out towards Kayden, inviting me to ignore her and continue the conversation with him.

I sighed and while I tried not to show it on the outside, I was touched by her care for me. She truly was one of the greatest people I had ever met.

"You're going to let her talk to you like that... alpha." Kayden sniped.

"Shut it." I said.

He huffed and readjusted his weight on the door. "So... I'm in a bad way."

"I wonder why? Have something to do with the fact the Red Crows want to use you in the ceremony for the moonstone?"

"How did you know?"

"We didn't know for sure, but Ruthy and I started putting theories together after Maxwell came back a few days ago."

"How intuitive you two are..."

"How did you escape? I assume they had you tied to a tree with Luna?"

A smile spread across his face. "So you got my message?"

"You mean when you tried to mindlink with me so I could feel you being tortured?"

"Well, it wasn't so you could feel me being tortured, but I was reaching out for help. I just didn't have enough time." He stood up. "Thank your boy toy for me." He looked at Ruthy. "When he was helping Camilla out, it helped me out, too."

"That's a shame." Ruthy snapped.

"I know you don't mean that."

She scrunched her nose. "But I do."

I sighed. "What do you want?"

"I would like to see your healer. They injected me with something and whatever it is, I think it's preventing me from healing."

I felt the smallest amount of worry flicker across my face and hoped he hadn't noticed, but he had.

"Oh, you're concerned. That's refreshing."

"Because I'm a decent person and don't enjoy seeing people in pain. It's less to do with you."

"I'll pretend that's not the case and you actually care for me."

"I could have. I did, but that was before you had me kidnapped and locked in a room while you pretended to be someone else and then forced me to perform a ceremony to create a moonstone that is now trying to be used to rid us of our crescent powers."

"Yea... about that."

"What?" Ruthy stepped towards him, causing him to reflexively step back.

He winced in pain as he stepped forward again. "I'd really like to see that healer now."

"I'd really like it if you hadn't shown up on this doorstep, so I guess we both aren't getting what we want."

"Ruthy." I lightly scolded.

"What? It's true and I'm not sorry for saying it. The things he's done."

"I know." I turned back to Kayden and watched him for a second... I think part of me was trying to figure out if he was legitimately hurt or trying to deceive me. I looked back at Ruthy. "We'd be no better than him if we turned him away."

Ruthy sighed and rolled her eyes.

"Put him in the cellar."

"The cellar?"

I chuckled. "It was in my vision... and apparently it's the same room you locked Levi in when you pranked him."

"You had a vision of me coming here?" His interest was piqued.

"Yes. Although you're a little early."

"Early?"

"Yes." I didn't want to expand on it anymore. My visions felt personal and something I only wanted to share with people I was close to... and trusted.

A gust of wind hit me in the face.

Anastasia and Liam slid to a stop right behind Kayden, with Chloe following a second later, slumped over with her hands on her knees.

"They may be old, but man, are they fast." She said between gasps of air.

"Look at that. A family affair." Kayden remarked.

"What are you doing here?" I asked them all.

"They're here for me, sister."

I glared at Kayden. "Stop calling me sister." I turned to study my parent's faces.

"Kayden reached out to us." Liam said.

"You did?" I looked at him.

"I wasn't sure if you were going to throw me to the wolves." He chuckled, then stopped when it seemed to hurt. "See what I did there?"

"Are you ok?" Anastasia rushed forward to examine him, brushing the hair out of his face.

I watched her with him, hands delicate, but swift, and then I watched him. It was interesting... like a boy who wanted to be touched, wanted to feel compassion while at the same time hated himself for it.

I didn't know what kind of bond or relationship they had built when he was here before. Whatever it was, it didn't seem to be that strong since he left us the first chance he got.

"Is she serious?" Ruthy started, but I shot a quick glance at her, reminding her that while she may be our mother, she was still the alpha of the Crescent pack. "I'll be back. I'm going to go prepare the cellar." As she was walking away, I heard her mumble.

"What happened?" Anastasia asked again.

Kayden winced in pain, and his voice dropped an octave. "They tied me to a tree and beat me."

I rolled my eyes. "Must suck to be held against your will."

Anastasia shot a glance at me as Chloe came to stand beside me. "Are you ok?" she whispered.

"Her?" Kayden spat, then realized he was no longer playing the sad victim, so he corrected.

"The Red Crows? Maye? They betrayed you?"

"Shocker." I sighed. Where was Ruthy when I needed her? She could make all these snide comments while I cast disapproving glances at her. Now it was my mother looking at me and I wasn't liking it.

"Yes." He said, scrunching his nose at me, as if he'd scored a point in his imaginary game.

"Why? What happened?"

"They need to sacrifice him... well, one of us," I pointed between Kayden, Chloe and myself.

"Sacrifice?"

I nodded and then filled them in on everything that had happened with Maxwell, as well as our working theory on the sacrifice, being sure to leave Drake's name out of everything.

"So they want to kill one of you."

"I don't know anything, obviously. It's just a theory Ruthy and me were working on."

"Came up with it all on your own, did you?" Kayden remarked.

"We did." I looked at Liam and Anastasia. "Can we borrow your healer? Ours is out in the field right now and won't be back until tomorrow at the earliest. Kayden thinks he's been injected-"

"Knows. Kayden knows he's been injected with something that is preventing him. Me, from healing."

"Yes, of course." Liam nodded.

"What could they have used?" Anastasia asked.

"Something laced with wolfsbane, I think. It burned terribly when they were injecting it and it held a slightly bluish color."

"Why are you here?" Chloe asked.

"What do you mean?"

"We aren't your home, so why come?"

He looked down. "This is the closest thing I have to a home... to family."

"Oh brother." Ruthy said, walking back in. "Gag me with a spoon. You don't give a damn about any of these people. You're selfish with a 'damn the rest of them' mentality."

"Not true."

Ruthy cocked her head down.

"Ok, maybe a little true, but I'm trying to change my ways. I'm here to help you stop the Red Crows."

"To stop them. You realize there would be nothing to stop if you hadn't-" Ruthy caught her breath and turned in a circle. "I can't right now." She said, throwing her hands in the air.

"You can go. Thank you and we'll talk later." I said, dismissing her.

"Yes alpha." She blurted the words and darted off.

"Alpha... like father, like daughter." Kayden remarked snidely.

"The healer should be here soon." Liam added.

"Let's get you downstairs so you can rest." I suggested.

"I would like to get off my feet."

As we walked through the house, I felt the energy shift and knew the pack was on high alert. Kayden waved at people as we passed like one would an old friend, only none of these people were his friends. The last time he was here, he brought death and destruction.

We made it downstairs and found Ruthy standing in front of the shifting rooms. "You're home awaits." She said, directing him into a room near the back.

"You shouldn't have." He snidely remarked.

"I know." She said bluntly, before running out of the back door towards the field.

He walked in then turned to say something, with his hand reaching beyond the door frame, but a white light shot out and jammed his hand.

He looked at his hand, then back at me. "Very funny. You think I'm going to go somewhere?"

The spell must still be in place from when Ruthy put Levi in there? But how did she get him out? I would have to ask Drake or her when she got home, but I wanted to give her some space now. "I have no idea what you're going to do or not do because I don't know you. What little I know it's all been pretty horrible things, so am I going to take precautions to protect my pack house? One hundred percent."

"Such a good alpha." He walked across the room to the small bed in the corner and fell gently onto it.

"I'll let you know when the healer is here."

"Can't wait." He propped his head up. "Would you mind fetching me a glass of water while I'm waiting?"

"I'll get it." Chloe offered.

When she was running up the stairs, I stared at him for a second. "Are you really done with the Red Crows?" I wanted to believe him so badly, against all my better judgement, because I still hoped he could change.

"Well, they tried to kill me... so I think they wanted to break up."

"Why did you ever trust them to begin with? They hate Crescents."

"Because I didn't have anyone else." His words were simple and short and held a note of sadness in them.

"You have us now." Anastasia said, while Liam put his hand on her shoulder.

Part of me was disgusted and wanted to yell at my parents- our parents- for trusting him so openly, but they weren't there. They weren't locked in a room with him and forced to perform a curse against their will. No, to them, he was their child, their baby, that had to deal with unspeakable things and was broken. The child who has come home. I shook my head as I felt my blood beginning to boil.

I walked upstairs as Chloe was walking down with the glass of water, and I couldn't help but wonder how she felt. Did she feel the same as me? Probably not. She seemed to be more forgiving than me, more happy.

I got upstairs and saw several pack members gathered in the kitchen watching the stairs- waiting for me.

Bryson stepped forward, but I held up my hand to stop him and he fell back in line. I stopped in front of them and gathered my thoughts for a moment before speaking. "Kayden is here in one of the shifting rooms downstairs. There is a spell on the room, which is essentially locking him in so he cannot escape. This does not mean you are permitted to go in after him." A few people look disappointed. "I understand the ill feelings towards him, as I harbor them myself, even though he's my brother." I looked over my shoulder as hundreds of conflicting thoughts swam around in my head. "He says he's no longer part of the Red Crows. Part of me believes him, but the other part is cautious. We've learned in order for the Red Crows to reverse the Crescent curse, they'll need to have a witch, a wolf and a Crescent."

"So, you or your siblings." Bryson said.

"Yes."

There was a hushed whisper that spread across the group. "You're all under one roof. What's stopping them from coming here and attacking us again?"

I nodded. "I know. I need to talk with Asher, Liam and Anastasia to figure out what we can do to protect this house. I will probably pull Drake and Ellsmire in as well. While having all three of us in one location makes it more attractive for them to attack, it also makes it easier to protect us. We can centralize our forces instead of spreading them out."

"Well, I would happily kill some Red Crows after all they've done." A voice spoke up, and the crowd cheered in unison.

I smiled. "I understand, probably more than anyone. I hope it won't come to that again, but we need to be ready. I'm not prepared to send any more of our pack to their death."

The pack threw their fists into the air and began grunting like a wolf.

I gave them a minute, then patted the air to regain control. "Asher should be home soon and together we will come up with a plan. In the meantime, I'm going to talk to Drake and Ellsmire to put protections in place."

Chloe burst into the room.

"What is it? Is everything ok?" I asked, feeling my body tense.

She looked around. "Yea. Sorry."

Is this how it was going to be with him here? Every time someone walked into the room too quickly, I was going to think the worst. I don't know if my nerves could handle it.

"He wants to talk to you."

"Kayden?"

"Yes."

I rolled my eyes, and Chloe smirked at me.

Ruthy took off. I think she needed some space. Can you get a hold of Drake? Tell him what's going on and tell him I need to see him as soon as possible.

Sure thing... and try to be patient.

With Kayden?

Yea. He seems to have gone through a lot.

Are you kidding me right now?

Not completely. I haven't forgiven him by any means, but it's more for mom and dad.

Mom and dad?

They seem really concerned about him. I think they feel guilty for all the bad things he's done because they blame themselves.

I took a deep breath. *I will see what I can do.*

She smiled, then pranced off through the house to the balcony.

I walked downstairs and saw Anastasia and Liam steadfast at Kayden's door.

"I heard you needed to see me?" I tried to bite the irritation out of my voice.

"Sister." He smirked, obviously feeling more comfortable in his surroundings.

"You seem to be feeling better."

"What can I say... this place seems to have the magic touch." He laughed, trying to stick his hand through the threshold... and again, a white light shot out, "Literally." His face fell, unamused.

Liam stuck his nose in the air, then looked at me. "My healer's here. Do they have permission to come onto your property?"

"Yes." I mindlinked the pack to let them know what was going on and have them direct the healer downstairs, then looked back at Kayden. "We can talk when they're done." I turned away.

"Stay sister." There was a note in his voice I couldn't place. Part of me wondered if it was a genuine desire for my company cloaked in his lackadaisical sarcasm.

I looked from him to my parents and back to him and decided to stay. He clapped his hands together, then winced slightly. A moment later, Liam and Anastasia's healer was entering through the back door.

"Thank you for coming Bex."

I nearly choked at the man standing in front of me. He was tall. Six four? Six five? He had dark skin and long bright blonde dreads that hung past his shoulders and was very muscular. Nothing at all what I would expect a healer to look like, but very much like the type of man Chloe would fawn after. Greek God and all. I'm surprised there wasn't a horse waiting outside for him.

I saw Kayden scoot backwards in his bed, closer to the corner, staring at the healer.

"No problem Alphas."

"I'm feeling better." Kayden said, grabbing his knees, eyes wide open.

Bex looked at Anastasia and Liam, who both shook their heads.

"Kayden, let him help you. He's very good."

"At what? Grinding people into dust?"

I realized the joke was a cover. He seemed genuinely nervous of this man, and I couldn't understand why.

Bex's laugh boomed. "I get that a lot." He took a step forward but was still in the hall. "I would like to come in and take a look at you. With your permission, of course."

"Of course." Kayden mocked. "What if I say no?"

"Kayden." Anastasia reprimanded.

Bex held his hand out. "You could do that and I will leave. However," he paused. "If it's what I think, you'll likely be dead before the sun sets tonight."

Kayden scrunched his nose. "Well, that's not ideal."

Bex chuckled, "No. I would think not." He took another step. "May I examine you?"

"Are you going to kill me?"

"No. But if I was, would I actually tell you?"

Kayden stared at him for a second. "No, I guess not." Then nodded. "You may enter. Warning though, their little witch friend but a spell on the door, so you may be stuck in here with me."

"I think I'll manage." He entered the room and walked over to Kayden, laying him back on the bed. He placed his hand on his forehead and chest and began to speak slowly. A light began to emanate around Bex's hands, and then his arms tensed and he jerked upright.

I looked at Anastasia and Liam as they looked at me, concerned, but didn't speak. I turned back to Kayden and saw his eyes had glossed over and his back was arching off the bed. "Is everything ok?"

Bex didn't respond or even acknowledge he heard me. I looked back at Liam, who gently squeezed my shoulder to calm me down, and Anastasia who had her arms crossed in front of her chest, anxiously watching Kayden.

Bex inhaled a deep breath with his head turned towards the sky. Moments later, a black sort of dust began to seep out of Kayden's pores and floated up into a sphere above his chest. It looked beautiful with flecks of silver sparkles throughout, although I was fairly certain it was deadly.

There was a slight whistling noise, then everything got quiet. Bex's head leveled out, while Kayden remained laying on his back and the small sphere of black sparkly mist hovered in midair.

Bex looked at Liam. "Look in my satchel and grab out a jar."

Liam immediately dug through the brown leather bag and pulled out a glass jar with a cork plug.

"Yes. That. Bring it here, but stay back."

Kayden propped up on his elbows. "Careful. I'm toxic."

"Not anymore, you aren't." Bex said, scooping and guiding the dust into the jar before sealing it.

"Well, that was fun."

Bex walked over and placed the jar in his satchel, then looked at Kayden. "I'd recommended you to take it pretty easy for the next few days. Whoever injected you with that stuff knew what they were doing."

"How so?"

"Wolfsbane laced with monk's toe and frog poison."

"Frog poison? Sounds dangerous." He wiggled his fingers in the air, laughing.

Bex was obviously not catching the humor. "It is a serious thing. I overestimated your life expectancy because I didn't account for the frog poison." He sounded disappointed with himself.

"You overestimated?" Kayden asked, as the realization of his actual predicament set in.

"Yes. You had maybe an hour left."

Kayden swallowed hard.

"So, whoever injected you with that must have really wanted you dead."

"Good to know." Kayden's face fell.

So he was at least telling the truth about that. It seemed the Red Crows cut ties with him. I couldn't help but wonder if they were playing some sort of long game, and this was always their plan. It's the only thing that makes remote sense. Why else would a group that loathed Crescent's let a Crescent be their alpha?

Short loss for a future gain.

I shook my head. They picked the right one, the one who was broken and angry. They put up a little resistance to manipulate him, and it worked. He led them straight to the moonstone and the solution to their problem.

Crescents.

TAKING A PIECE OFF THE BOARD

BEX CHATTED WITH LIAM and Anastasia in the hall for a moment after he was done.

I watched them for a second, then turned back to Kayden. "You said you had to talk to me?"

He nodded, but didn't speak.

I raised my eyebrows, irritated I was still having to pry information out of him.

His face contorted.

"If this is some game to you, to see how long I'll wait around, I'm not going to play it." I turned and started walking down the hall and almost got to Anastasia and Liam when I heard him call out.

"Wait!"

I paused, but didn't move back towards his room.

When he realized I wasn't walking back, he added, "It's about Asher."

Asher? My heart stopped, and I stomped back to his room.

"What about Asher?"

He smiled mirthlessly. "I thought that would bring you back."

"Stop playing games or I'll kick you out on your ass. Remember, you supposedly have no other place to go."

"Seems like mommy and father dearest will take me in." He smirked, then added, "But I don't want to stay with them. I want to get to know you better."

"I will not play these cat and mouse games with you."

He sighed. "I'm trying. It's just so easy to revert to my old ways."

I rolled my eyes.

"Asher's in trouble. The Crows know he's out on his own and close to their compound. They sent a scout team out for him yesterday."

"A scout team? How close is he?"

"I don't know."

"What do they want with him?"

"Insurance, I think... for you. Maye wants you. Part of the reason I became... expendable."

Asher!

Silence.

Asher! Where are you? I yelled, panicked. What if it was already too late?

Silence.

Asher Evans!

Sile-

Hey pup, calm down. He said casually.

Kayden is here and he-

What is he doing there? Are you ok?

Yes. He says you're in danger.

I'm fine.

Asher. I warned. *I don't have a good feeling about this. He said the Crows know you're on your own and sent a scout team after you.*

I haven't seen or heard anything out of the ordinary.

Please be careful.

I am. He laughed. *I'm not going to let anything get in the way of me getting home to see you. Now tell me... what is Kayden doing there?*

There's a lot to tell you, most of which can wait until I see you, but basically he showed up because Maye and the Crows tried to kill him. I'm not sure how he got here though, because he could barely walk. They injected him with a poison to kill him, Bex, my parent's healer, just extracted it out of him.

Silence.

Asher?

Sorry. I thought I heard something.

We should stop talking so you can focus.

It was nothing. A deer or something.

They want to kill him? He chuckled. That partnership didn't turn out too well. Maye surprises me though, because I thought she cared for him.

I guess he thought so, too.

And you have no idea how he escaped? Do you think Maye did it?
I don't think so. Luna is there, so maybe she helped him.
Luna?
They think a witch, a werewolf and a crescent are needed for the ceremony.
So all three of you are at the pack house right now?
Yes.
Silence.
Asher?
Silence.
My eyes fell on Kayden, and I was getting an uneasy feeling. Was he some sort of distraction? Was this all a ploy in the Crow's evil scheme?
Asher.
I'm here.
Stop disappearing like that. You're making me nervous.
Sorry. There's just–
Asher?
Silence.
Asher? Talk to me.
Silence.
Dread crept in, starting at my feet and working its way up my legs.
"Everything ok sister?"
"Shut up!" I was shaking.
"What's going on?" Anastasia ran over and placed her hand on my back.
I glared at her. "Ask your son."
He held his hands up. "I did nothing. I've been here."
"Acting as what? A decoy?"
"No. Why would I tell you about him if I was a decoy?"
"You took your time telling me though, didn't you? Giving them more time."
"Giving who more time? What's going on?" Anastasia asked.
"Asher. Asher's in trouble. I can feel it." *Asher. Please respond.*
Re– His voice was tired.
Was he going to say the Red Crows found him?
I raced into the room, grabbing Kayden by the collar of his shirt, and threw him against the wall. "What's going on?"

"I don't know, I swear." He said, kicking his feet and trying to claw at my hands.

"I don't believe you." I said through set teeth.

"Cami."

I felt Anastasia's hand on my shoulder and turned to look at her. "No. No! He knows something about what happened to Asher. The Red Crows have him."

She removed her hand and looked at Kayden.

He stopped fighting me and frowned. "Well, I can see who the favorite child is."

"Knock it off!" I yelled, scooting him further up the wall.

He grabbed my hands. "Chill. I didn't do anything. Really."

I let go of him and watched him fall to the floor in a heap. "Talk."

I felt a gust of wind behind me and didn't need to look to know it was Ruthy.

"What have you done you sorry sack of-"

"Ruthy." Anastasia warned in her alpha voice, making the hairs on my neck stand.

Ruthy regained her composure and I continued.

"I didn't do anything. I swear. I came here to warn you."

"You came here to warn us? How did you get here?"

"I don't buy it." Ruthy snapped.

I cut my eyes at her, then looked back at Kayden.

"Luna. Luna sent me. She overheard the Crows talking out in the field and knew she had to get word out."

"Why not come herself?"

"She couldn't hold the portal open long enough for the both of us. Her magic is weak, and she wanted me out of there so they couldn't use me. Taking a piece off the board, she said. And I also think she was waiting to find out if they were going to get Asher."

Damn Luna. Had she really changed?

"Why didn't you say something sooner?"

His eyes grew wide with shock. "Because I was dying. I needed to take care of myself first."

I heard a puff of disbelief behind me.

"Ruthy. Can you please gather the pack and let them know what's going on?"

"What exactly is going on?"

I shook my head. "I don't know yet, but Asher has likely been kidnapped by the Crows."

"They won't kill him yet." Kayden clarified my unspoken worry.

"Yet?"

"Sacrifice sister. They needed a wolf. They got one."

Ruthy looked at me and I knew what she was thinking. Asher wasn't a wolf, but they didn't know.

"What?" Kayden asked, picking up on our silent exchange.

"Nothing." I snapped. "Ruthy, go."

She nodded. "Yes alpha."

"Anastasia."

"Already done. Xander and the others should be here soon."

"Wow. Mobilize the troops." Kayden remarked.

"Shut up. Was this part of your plan?"

He looked at me, but didn't speak.

"Tell me! Enough with the games!" I was fuming angry and wanted to physically hurt him to get the answers I needed, but I tried to maintain control. I was the alpha, after all.

"You told me to shut up and then you ask me questions. Very confusing."

I ran my fingers through my hair and pulled, taking in a deep calming breath, but it didn't help much.

"Kayden." Anastasia reprimanded.

"What?" He asked innocently.

"If you're here as you state, on the run from the Crows and you want to help us out, then stop playing games and help us out. We can't mend if you keep acting like the enemy." Her voice was soft, with a thread of steel laced throughout.

Kayden sighed. "Sorry. I was... I am, still angry."

"We'll work on that, but the first step is telling us everything you know and helping us get Asher back."

He sighed. "After you all took their wolf, they were very upset and blamed me. I think they were just using it as an excuse to come after me because Maye had decided I was no longer of use to her. She wants you." He mumbled something else under his breath, but I ignored him and he continued. "Anyway, she was angry about the wolf then she got word Asher was in the area. She was beyond excited, thanking the Goddess for this good fortune. She was talking a lot about the moon goddess looking favorably on her for some reason."

"Why?"

"I don't know. She seems to have gone a little crazy since her brother was killed."

"You mean since she killed him? She's the one who killed him to get his power." I was completely dumbfounded by the way he said 'her brother was killed', as if it was something that happened to her rather than a situation she created. Was he really that obtuse?

"Yes, but we were supposed to create the moonstone that day so she could use it to bring him back." He defended, which only further irritated me.

My eyes nearly bulged out of my head with the absurdity of this conversation, unable to form one solid sentence. "From the dead. Because she killed him. He even said he didn't want to be brought back. Us not completing the ceremony was the best thing for everyone."

"She doesn't see it that way."

"Because she's lost her damn mind!"

He bobbled his head from side to side, "Anyway, she became hyper focused on you. I assume because she blames you, though I'm not sure. But she started talking about getting Asher to get you to the compound and it would give her the three she needed. A witch, a wolf, and a crescent. So you obviously can't go or she'll be able to complete the curse."

"If I don't show up, she'll likely kill Asher."

"You'd risk the entire crescent species for Asher?"

Words got stuck in my throat. I knew I should say no. No, I wouldn't be selfish and risk them all for Asher, but he was my mate. He was my everything. I couldn't not go after him. I couldn't carry on with the conversation. I turned to Anastasia, whose face was torn, and walked past her.

I saw Liam finishing the conversation with Bex as I was walking towards them. Liam waved me down.

"Hey." I was short and felt bad, but the conversation with Kayden still had me annoyed.

His lips flattened into a line in sympathy. "Pack will be here in less than five minutes."

"Thanks."

I walked up the stairs and saw Ruthy had gathered the pack in the kitchen. "We'll be meeting on the back patio in five minutes." I continued walking through the kitchen to the foyer. I jumped to the fourth level and walked into our bedroom and slammed the door, pressing my back against it. I felt a wave of emotion pass through me and felt the muscles in my jaw tighten as tears began to flow.

Maye had taken Asher to get to me. I was just talking to him and he was so happy... excited. I could hear it in his voice that something big had happened. He had probably found his family, but wanted to surprise me. I shook my head.

The joy.

It was gone.

She took it away.

Those last seconds, he was scared, terrified.

I screamed out in anger. In pain. In fear. I wanted to tear every-thing apart, which reminded me of Asher when I was taken, and I chuckled briefly in the midst of my tears. We were one and the same. My true mate.

I walked to the bathroom and wet a towel to wipe my face. I couldn't show any weakness or tears when I went downstairs to address the two pack houses.

No. I needed to be strong.

I needed to be the alpha.

OPERATION G.A.B.

"THANK YOU ALL FOR coming." I decided to stand on the balcony overlooking the packs on the patio. "As you're all probably aware of by now, Asher has been kidnapped by Maye and the Red Crows." The lack of shock across the crowd told me they all knew, but a few passed side glances. "I believe this was in retaliation for us taking their werewolf and because Maye wants me." As murmurs rose, I patted the air to calm the crowds. "I don't think they know Asher is part Crescent, which is a good thing. They're more likely to keep him alive if they think they can use him."

The shifting around from the pack told me they were confused.

"We believe in order for Maye to reverse the Crescent curse, she needs the moonstone, a witch, a wolf, and a crescent- me, specifically." I took a deep breath and continued. "They have Luna and they have Asher."

"Why not Kayden?" A person yelled out.

"How did he get here? Do you trust him?" Another person asked.

"Is he going to stay here?" A third asked.

"What are we going to do about Asher? When are we going after him?" A fourth asked.

I stepped forward, holding up my hand to stop the questions. "I don't have all the answers, but I will tell you what I know. Luna found out they were going after Asher, so she took the opportunity to get Kayden here via a portal to deliver the message. Her magic is weak, which is why she couldn't come through and she wanted to stay in case they captured Asher. Kayden will stay here for now. He is locked in a room with magic, preventing his escape, but as I said earlier, he is off limits to you all. I wouldn't put it past him to have more information he's holding on to. He is a survivalist, after all." I took another deep breath. "As far as Asher is concerned, yes, I'm obviously going to figure out a way to get him back, but in a way that hopefully doesn't put the entire crescent species at risk."

I looked at Ruthy for a second. "I don't think the Crows are going to come after me here. She's going to make me come to her." And the thoughts of how she would make me do that made me sick and I could tell Ruthy felt the same.

"But we still need to be prepared." Ruthy stood up. "I will work on assigning you all shifts to watch the perimeter."

Liam spoke up, "Crescents, you will also listen to Ruthy and do as she commands regarding these shifts."

I nodded in his direction as he slipped his arm around Anastasia.

"Thank you. Liam, Anastasia, and Chloe, can you please meet me in the library?"

Chloe looked from me to Theo and Lily, but I shook my head. Not that I didn't trust them, but I needed them to get their assignments from Ruthy. They would better serve us on the field, protecting us, not in a room strategizing.

"Thank you all. If you see something, please call for backup before you approach. Do not go off on your own. Everyone should have a partner. Crescents, any of your aerials that can take to the air and surveil would be helpful." I clapped and walked back inside and headed towards the fourth floor.

Drake should be here within the hour.

Perfect. Send him up when he gets here.

Do you want me to join?

Yes. Once you have all the assignments posted and everyone knows what they need to do.

Yes, alpha.

One more thing. I need two people that you trust to be posted outside Kayden's door. I don't want Maye to try and grab him back. I don't think she will, but... he needs to be protected.

She grumbled.

Thank you Ruthy.

We will get him back.

I know. I hoped we weren't lying.

Asher?

Silence.

If you can hear me, we're coming for you.

I pulled out the rolled-up map from the cubby and spread it on the table. I felt like this map should be a permanent fixture on the table with as much as we've been using it lately. I stared at it, hoping it would tell me where Asher was and, more importantly, that he was ok.

I studied the large red circle near the center of the map where the Red Crows compound was.

The door opened and Chloe, Anastasia, and Liam walked in.

"How are you holding up?" Anastasia asked, walking around the table to give me a hug- a very motherly thing for her to do.

"I'm ok. I'll be better when I have him home, safe."

"What can we do?" Liam boomed.

I pointed at the map. "It's safe to say they have him at the compound. She won't try to hide him, because she wants me to come after him. Only thing is that he's not a wolf, but she doesn't know that yet."

"Do you think they'll kill him when they find out?" Chloe asked.

"If they find out he's a hybrid? Possibly, but not before they get me."

Liam nodded. "Makes sense." He tapped the paper. "So what do we do?"

"I'll take any advice you have."

He placed his palm on the table. "May I?"

I nodded, and he turned the map around to study it.

"We can send some aerials out to surveil and report back-"

There was a knock at the door.

"Come in."

Drake.

"I came back as soon as I heard."

I smiled warmly. "We're just going over plans right now. Ruthy-"

"Is here." She said, walking into the room. She wrapped her arm around Drake, but stayed focused on me.

"Is everyone squared away on responsibilities?"

"Yes. We split up into groups of three for rotations, taking eight-hour shifts. I have paired at least one Crescent with every group of two, as well as have the aerials flying overhead in the area."

"Perfect." I smiled appreciatively at her. "We'll need you," I pointed at Drake, "to portal us and some aerials to the compound so we can find out what's going on."

"Us?" Ruthy chimed. "All due respect, alpha, but you need to stay here."

"She's right," Anastasia concurred.

"No. I have to go. I have to get Asher back."

"You will be doing exactly what Maye wants."

"I don't care." I snapped.

"I do!" Ruthy snapped, unapologetically.

I backed down and stared at her for a second before speaking. "It's Asher."

"I know." She breathed. "I'll go and report back any and everything down to the way the air feels on my skin." She smiled. "But you can't go. You're the alpha of the pack and one of the only three that can reverse the Crescent curse, and apparently the only one she wants."

I knew she was right, but that didn't change the feelings I had inside. I needed to see him, needed to know he was ok. I needed to go after him.

"Cami. I promise-"

I held up my hand. "I know. I trust you."

She sighed, relieved.

"Drake. We need Ellsmire on standby to help us when needed. We need to put an end to Maye and the Crows for good."

"Understood." He said reluctantly.

"Has Asher shifted yet? Into his second?" Liam asked.

"No, not yet."

"Good, that will help him."

I know his words were meant to be comforting, and they were, in some ways. The fact he hadn't shifted and fully completed the transition into his second meant his Crescent scent was still muted. Asher needed all the help he could get. He needed to stay safe.

"Drake, we need to meet with the Council."

He rubbed his face, then nodded. I could tell he wasn't eager about setting up a meeting with them, but I couldn't figure out why. "I'll reach out to Mira."

"Ok, but we need to get the Council on board as well."

"I know," he whispered.

Ruthy looked at him, but didn't say anything. She must have noticed the same reluctance I did and was also confused.

I ignored his apprehension. "Great. You can go now and bring her back while we finalize plans to send a team to the Crow's compound."

He nodded and walked out of the room.

I briefly glanced at Ruthy, who subtly shrugged her shoulders.

What had happened at the meeting with him and Luna that had him so quiet and on edge? Why didn't he want us to meet with Mira or the Council?

I directed my attention back to the group as we worked through a plan for Ruthy to lead the charge to the Crow's compound.

Drake and Mira arrived at the pack house an hour later. I still couldn't shake the feeling something was going on with Drake that he didn't want to talk about, but I didn't have time to figure it out now.

"Cami darling. How are you doing?" Mira asked, holding out her arms as she walked over to me.

I went in for the hug by reflex. She felt like... I couldn't quite place the feeling, but she felt like family. "I'm doing ok. Better when you get Ellsmire on board."

She looked at Drake with an unreadable expression, then back to me.

"What is it?" I pressed.

"Nothing."

I didn't believe her. There was definitely something there.

Ruthy walked in a minute later and walked to Drake, but he didn't move towards her. I guess it was to be expected in front of - for all intents and purposes - your boss, your mentor, your teacher.

"We need your help, Mira. We have come up with a plan. Ruthy and nine others are going to the compound to get information on Asher, Luna, and the Crows."

"Ten? You're going to the compound?"

"Yes. Ten. Ruthy will lead our pack and Xander will lead the Crescents. We're only sending people we trust to obey orders and we'll have several aerial crescents to surveil from above. This is purely a recon mission."

"Like your other one?"

"That was a mistake sending someone I couldn't fully trust, and he's been dealt with."

"Banished?"

"Yes."

She nodded, but didn't speak. A silent disagreement with my choice that she would not get into right now.

"Will you help us with the portal?"

"Why come to me and not ask Drake? He seems to be all too eager to portal you where you all need to go." Her tone was obviously disapproving, causing him to shift uncomfortably beside her.

My eyes flicked from Ruthy to Drake, back to Mira. "Drake has done a phenomenal job of protecting us."

She lifted her head.

"But we would like to know that we can trust Ellsmire to support us. I fear taking Asher back will spark the beginning of the battle to end all battles. There will be a showdown with Maye and the Red Crows. We need to know we can count on your support."

She took in a deep breath. "Yes. Of course."

I felt like there was a lingering 'but', however, silence just filled the air.

"We would like to portal out of here around ten this evening."

"So late."

"Yes. With the time change at the Crow's compound, it should turn dark around then."

"Should you not go when it's darker, then?"

"We fear that's what they'll be expecting."

She nodded.

"I assume you know Luna is there."

Her lips pinched in a hard line. "I do."

"And you haven't sent anyone after her?"

"We haven't."

"Why not?"

She hesitated before speaking, glancing at Drake. "She is serving a purpose."

"What purpose is that?"

"I'm not at liberty to discuss that with you."

"Since when?" I spat back.

"Cami." Drake warned.

My brow furrowed and I looked at him. "What in the hell is going on?"

"Cami," he said again, nearly pleading for me to drop it.

"No! What is going on? You went away with Luna and since then have been off. No one has told me how or why Luna is there and now Mira is admitting she's fine, leaving her daughter beaten and bound to a tree because she's serving some purpose." I spun around, losing what little patience I had left. "What kind of mother-"

Mira's voice boomed. "Silence."

My mouth clamped shut.

"You will not disrespect me when you don't know what's going on."

I started to speak, then caught myself.

"Luna is not on her own, but she is staying put."

"Why?"

"We are not ready to discuss that with you yet."

I sighed. "So Luna helped Kayden get out..." I looked at Drake. "How did you know he'd come here?"

"What do you mean?" he asked.

"You bound the cellar with magic."

He nodded. "Based on your vision, I figured he'd come back."

"And how did you know which room?"

"I figured the one Levi called the cellar, but just in case, I put a spell on all the rooms. I didn't know how long I'd be gone or when he'd come, so I wanted to make sure you all were protected."

"But we've been in those rooms and we aren't bound."

He looked at Mira, and she nodded.

"We used his blood from the day the moonstone was created and tied it to his blood specifically."

"You can do that? Tie spells to blood?" I laughed. "Have you done that with me?"

They looked at one another.

"You haven't done that, have you?"

Mira shook her head. "No."

"That didn't sound very convincing."

Mira looked at me and I could tell she was done with this conversation. "Drake and I need to go back to Ellsmire. We will be back at ten till ten."

I nodded, and in a flash, she had created a portal and was gone.

I looked at Ruthy. "Something's going on."

"Yea, I don't like it. He's been more distant lately, and quiet."

I looked over the space in the room where the portal had just been.

"What if they've asked him to move?"

"What do you mean?"

"Remember, he said if there was another incident, they'd make him move and he didn't want that. What if that's what's going on?" The words rushed out of her mouth in a panic.

"But he's not done anything." I defended.

She paced in a circle. "I know I said I would not let myself get attached to him, but damn it... I did."

I laughed. "I know you did."

"I don't want him to go." She grabbed me by the shoulders, shaking gently.

"I know."

"My Goddess, I'm so sorry. I'm standing here rambling about not having Drake leave and your mate has been captured by an evil and vile witch with too much power for her own good!"

"It's ok."

"No, it's not. I'm horrible. I'm going to hell."

"Oh, need a ride?" I turned and saw Xander sauntering over with Chloe and Levi behind him.

"Not with you."

His brow furrowed. "That hurts."

"You'll get over it." She smiled.

I could tell she was coming around to him, especially since it appeared Levi had. The three of them had earned the name the three musketeers, because they always seemed to be together, which I was happy about. I'm glad Chloe was finding her people. For so long, she'd been alone and now she wasn't anymore.

"Are we good for this evening?"

Xander pumped his fist in the air. "We are."

"I wish I could go with." Chloe whined.

"No!" we all said in unison.

She scrunched her nose and her eyes grew wide. "Well, obvious-ly, I know I can't. I was just saying."

"I'm going to go to my room for a little before dinner."

"If you need anything, let me know." Ruthy said.

I nodded, then left. When I walked into my room, I shut the door and stood there with my back pressed against it, replaying everything we had talked about this afternoon. There were a lot of missing pieces with Kayden, Drake, Ellsmire and Asher and I needed to figure out how they all fit.

Only a couple more hours until they had eyes on Asher, hopefully. I needed to know he was ok. I couldn't feel him and that loss of our connection was driving me insane.

Just a few more hours, Asher.

HISTORY

THE BRIGHT BLUE LIGHT of the portal was illuminating the dark, star-filled sky. I cast a knowing glance over at Ruthy and her lips flattened into a hardline, while my stomach twisted and turned in knots. I was filled with so many thoughts and feelings- worry for Asher, scared for the pack, curious about Kayden's true intentions and motivations. There was so much going on and I didn't know how to process. I needed Asher here. I wanted him here.

"I'll find our boy." Ruthy's eyes grew wide with excitement and anticipation. She loved action and the unexpected... I did not. I've had enough action and unexpected events in the last year to last a lifetime. I wanted slow. I wanted predictable.

I let my gaze rest on Ruthy, soaking up her energy, and could almost feel it radiating off her. She was worried about Asher, but she was also thrilled at the chance to go do something.

I smiled and squeezed her shoulder.

Chloe hugged both Levi and Xander before they took their spot by Ruthy, hands gripped together with an unreadable expression between their eyes.

I felt like I should remind them one last time what kind of mission this was, likely a mixture of guilt from last time coupled with my anxiety. "This is recon only. If you see him, you can't get him." I shook my head to reinforce my statement. The last thing I needed right now was any of them being injured or killed. "I doubt it will be safe. Maye will know we'll come for him and there will probably be traps, especially after what happened last time."

"You got it alpha. Recon only." Ruthy repeated, looking at each person. She was pumped. She was thriving.

"Why did you look at me longer?" Xander asked, holding his hands up, dropping Levi's hand.

"If you're going to cause trouble, you can stay here. I can't babysit you." Ruthy snapped.

"Noted. No tom-foolery around serious Ruthy."

I tilted my head down looking at him and he raised his brows in a 'what did I do' sort of look.

"Thank you all for this. Asher would be so proud."

"It's time." Mira commanded.

Ruthy gave me one last look before she ducked through the portal followed by Xander, Levi and several other crescents and wolves. We had decided on nine with several aerials so they could scout over the area. Drake walked through last, his motions subdued, then the portal snapped shut.

Just like that, they were gone and transported to the Midwest in the blink of an eye. I looked at the gathered pack as we stood around in the dark field. A lone light in the distance on the back corner of the house shined on the patio, but the stars were the only light out this far.

"Well." Chloe clapped her hands. "What do we do now?"

"We wait." Mira said, solemnly.

I caught myself shaking my head as all the feelings starting bubbling out of control. "Mira."

"Yes, darling?"

I huffed, trying to calm the wave of emotions that was coursing through me right now. "We need to talk."

She cocked her head to the side and then, picking up on my tense demeanor, nodded her head. "Yes, I guess we do."

She nearly glided across the ground and when she got beside me, we continued walking, putting distance between us and the rest of the pack.

When we were far enough away, she waved her hand in the air to cast the privacy spell and then nodded her head towards me, waiting for me to speak.

"I..." I didn't know what to say. The entire walk over here, I was going through the list, the demands, but now the words escaped me. I knew why... it was because I was scared. Scared to hear the answer, because whatever it was, it would not be good. I could feel it deep down in my gut.

Mira continued to look at me. She had played this game before and would give nothing away.

"Mira."

"Yes?"

I shook my head, frustrated with myself for not being able to put two words together. Literally two words. I took a deep breath and stared at the stars for a moment. "I need to know the truth."

"What truth is that?"

"What is going on with Luna? What is going on with Drake? What is going on in general? I feel like I'm being kept in that dark and I'm tired of it. I thought we had moved past this point, but I feel like we haven't." The words finally flew out of my mouth like someone had unclogged a backed up drain.

An awkward silence filled the air as she looked at me. So much time had passed that I went to apologize, scared I had overstepped when she cleared her throat.

"Cami." She clasped her hands in front of her and I felt like I was about to get a lecture. I never had a mom growing up, but this was what I feel the moment would feel like when I was about to get scolded in that type of way that you didn't know you were being scolded, but at the end you were like oh, yea I will not do whatever it was I did, again.

"I'm sorry... I'm just worried and confused... and..."

Her tone softened and her clasped hands fell to her sides. "You don't need to apologize or explain. You've had a rough... well, life. You don't trust easily and your one rock, your mate, your love, has been kidnapped by someone who wants to do you, your family and your entire species harm."

I nodded.

"I can't tell you everything. You are a Crescent, you are part of the Trinity, and you created the moonstone. You are also alpha to a wolf pack and, on top of all that, you hold a very special place in my heart. I have looked after you since the day your mother and father came to me and said they were having triplets. When you were born, I was there. I actually held you in my arms after your mother delivered you. You were the first. Headstrong, but silent. Then came Kayden, followed my Chloe." She closed her eyes, like she was replaying the memory.

I hadn't asked my parents about that day. I don't know why it never came up, but I found myself curious now about the details.

She chuckled. "You. The healer pulled you out and you wouldn't cry. She quickly handed you to me so I could look you over, but you just stared at me, beautiful and bright eyed. You were observing the world around you, taking it all in. The other two... they came out flailing and crying, but not you. I held you in my arms until your mother and father were ready to hold you and you just stared at me."

I loved hearing all of this, but I didn't know if she was stalling or what the point of this story was. As if answering my unasked question, she continued. "All of this to say, that you are observant. You watch your surroundings, you learn and adjust. It's what has made you the survivor you are today. I can't tell you everything you have asked because part of it is not my story to tell."

She must have been talking about Drake, which all but confirmed there was something going on that he needed to tell us, or at the very least Ruthy and again, my gut was telling me it would not be good.

"After the Trinity curse was completed, and the moonstone created... we took a sample of your blood."

"Yes. I remember." Remembering back to Luna drawing it, still not sure about the reason, but too concerned with Asher to really care.

"We took the sample to see if we could use it to help you and the other crescents out. We know Maye is powerful. Since the gemini ceremony, she may be more powerful than many of our council members, though I'm not sure if she knows that yet."

That made my stomach turn. Someone with that much power... isn't a good thing. I had always thought she was doing all this because of some disgusting infatuation with Kayden, but now she's turned her back on him and I have to wonder what's driving it. What lengths will she go to get whatever it is she wants? A chill ran up my spine.

"We have our best, working on a solution- a protection."

"I don't understand what my blood can do."

"We don't either, but you have power within you. I've seen it twice now. The burst of light that you emit is a shifter power that few have ever had."

"What is it?

"Stories call it many things, but what we know is that when you first emitted your light, it sent out a beacon to Asher. It broke through the magic chains that were binding you, preventing you from talking with him and then the second time, when you thought Asher was in trouble, you did it again. It broke you out of the Trinity and knocked us all back."

"Yes, but what is it? I remember when Maye saw it, she panicked and ran."

"Some of the older council members called it Shiban Sori."

I shook my head, never hearing of that before.

"Shiban Sori is an ancient magic that basically pulls power from all kinds of shifters, wolf or crescent. It collects the energy and can be focused and emitted in powerful gusts."

"I'm not doing anything, though."

She laughed. "Just because you aren't trying to do it doesn't mean you aren't. You seem to pull from others in times of need."

"What does this mean? I'm still confused."

She nodded. "We drew your blood, along with your sisters, to see if we could extract any differences between the two. Isolate it, if you will."

"And?"

"The blood was very similar. Yours had something else, but we are still trying to figure it out."

"What would it mean? What does it mean?"

"We still don't know yet. But I'm hoping we can somehow use it as a weapon against Maye should the need arise."

"You want to weaponize my blood?"

"We want to learn more about it, so when the time comes, you can use your power on command."

"To do what?"

"Protect your species."

I laughed, causing Mira to look at me. I continued laughing and bent over, placing my hands on my knees to catch my breath. "You know. I was told I was a wolf and that werewolves existed in my little town. Did I bat an eye? No, not really. I was then told I was actually a Crescent, who is hunted by wolves and the alpha of the local pack hated my kind and wanted me dead, but for some reason couldn't sense I was a Crescent. Did that strike me as odd? No. I was then told I have an entire family that was essentially hidden from me and I was angry, but I accepted it. Then we have the mate bond and everything else. All of these things, I just took as the truth and moved on, but now you're telling me I have some sort of voodoo magic."

"Not voodoo. Definitely not voodoo." Her brow pinched together, like I had clearly mis-stepped.

"Ok. That I have some not voodoo, ancient magic that can emit light, siphoning from those around me and..." I threw my hands up in the air. "I can't believe it."

"I know. It's not in many texts. I have a close ally that is an elder, and I reached out to them about it. They're aware of your power and have been monitoring you from afar."

I looked at her in disbelief.

"They don't feel you're a threat." She added, as if that was where my problem lay, then continued, "Elder Heldalore."

My eyes perked up, recognizing her name.

"Yes. She told me she met with you and Asher." She smiled. "She said you had a fighter's aura. Anyway, she said there have been less than five in the history of the wolf who have had this power."

"I'm so lucky." I said deadpan.

"You are."

"Did she happen to tell you what I can do with this power? How to use it? Why me?"

She smoothed out the bottom of her dress. "The moon goddess has her reasonings for who she chooses to bestow this power of the light to, that we don't understand. It's not meant for us to understand, only to accept."

"So I have a power that I don't know how to use or why I have it, only that I do?"

She nodded. "We're still working on it, though."

I wasn't confident that her, or the council, were going to be able to tell me anything and I needed to move on from this for now. "Can you tell me what Luna is doing?"

She stared at me for a moment before speaking.

"Look. I felt like we were a team, Crescents and Ellsmire, you and me, but lately, I feel like we've reverted to the old way it used to be. The time you knew things about me or what was going on, but didn't tell me. I don't want to get back to that point again."

She nodded in understanding. "There are times I don't tell you something, because I don't have all the facts and I don't want to give you misinformation."

"Regardless, I want to know." I realized that sounded a little selfish and entitled, but I didn't care.

"Luna went to the Red Crows compound to get information. She was going in undercover, using... the history she has with you."

"Glad I could help." I mumbled.

"She's made a lot of progress towards you. She viewed you for a long time as an adversary, as the reason they banned her. We worked a lot on that over these last several months."

"I'm glad she can finally see I had nothing to do with any of that." I said sarcastically.

Mira cocked her head. "She was going to try to befriend Maye to get us information, but it appears they are using her instead. We had suspected they needed a witch, a werewolf and a crescent to break the curse based on some documents we found of Maye's at Ellsmire, but unsure what the purpose was or her plan was."

"What is she going to do?"

"At this point, she's just gathering information."

"So you knew she was tied to a tree and beaten?"

"I did not know the full extent of her situation, but she is strong and was prepared for this. She knew it wouldn't be easy and yet she still volunteered." She sighed. "I think part of her feels guilty for all the things Dixon had done when she was with him."

"She could have-" I held my hand up, stopping myself. "Never-mind, it's in the past. So what can we do? What needs to be done?"

"Probably need to talk with your brother and try to get more information from him."

I nodded, checking the time. It hadn't been long since our team went through the portal and I needed to do something to keep my mind active so I didn't worry. "I'll go talk to him now."

"I'll send for you if anything changes out here."

I was standing at Kayden's door a few minutes later and saw him lying on his bed with his hands propped under his head.

"How's it going out there, sister?" He asked, lifting his head slightly.

"Fine."

"You just missed mom and dad." He said solemnly, putting his head back down and staring at the ceiling.

I didn't know what kind of game he was playing at, but I would not let him get to me. "What can you tell me about Luna and the compound?"

He looked at me again before fully sitting up, a smile spreading across his face. "Can you get me some water? I'm a little parched."

I looked at the cup on the table beside him and his eyes followed mine. "Empty."

I reached my hand out for the cup and he held it out, still short of my grasp on purpose.

"If you want water, you need to bring me the cup."

"Sister. Why won't you come in here? Are you scared you'll get stuck with me?"

"I know I won't. I just can't stand being close to you. This is close enough and even this is making me nauseous."

"Sister, you kid."

"Do I?"

He sat the cup down. "How is everyone outside? I assume you've sent a crew after your beloved?"

"That's none of your concern. Can you tell me about Luna and the compound?"

His lips twisted.

"Look. I'm happy to kick you out. There are plenty of wolves in the area who would love to have a few words with you after the trouble you've caused."

"No need to threaten."

"It wasn't a threat."

He shimmied his shoulders. "Yes, alpha."

I took in a deep breath.

"Fine."

I shifted, standing upright in the doorframe.

"That Luna. She seems a bit crazy, but I like her. Do you?"

"You're stalling."

"Am I?"

"Bye." I turned and started walking down the hall.

"Wait!"

I didn't stop and heard a zap and a loud groan. I turned around and saw he had tried to leave the room and shocked himself in the process.

"I'm sorry."

I didn't move.

He sighed dramatically. "I'm sorry. I'm just used to being the bad guy. It comes so easily."

I still didn't move.

"I will tell you." He backed away from the door and mumbled, "It isn't that great of a story, anyway."

I slowly walked back to his room and found him sitting on the edge of the bed with his elbows propped on his knees and his face in his hands. He looked up at me and took in a deep breath.

"She showed up at the compound," he was trying to think back, "I don't know... like six, seven, eight days ago... I'm not sure." He slid his foot under his thigh. "She said she had information that could help us."

I started to speak, but caught myself.

He shook his head. "I don't know what information she had. Maye was skeptical and took her into a room to talk. When I tried to follow them, Maye shut me out and said she wanted to talk to her alone and had sealed the room with magic, so I couldn't listen. They were in there for several hours while I waited outside. When they came out, Maye directed one of the Crows to put Luna in a room and when I tried to talk to her, she shut me out."

"That's odd."

"Yea. It was the start of whatever happened between us."

"What could Luna have said?"

"Nothing. I don't know. Anyway, Maye then got the wolf and Luna did or said something, which angered Maye and that's how she ended up outside. When your team came and got the wolf, Maye started to lose it. I tried to talk to her about it and that's when I got put outside by the tree. She was furious."

"Sounds like she was- is- losing her mind."

He nodded. "I don't know what I saw in her."

"You saw a partner. You saw acceptance."

"Maybe. She was a friend. She had been one for so long." He shrugged. "We were going to change the world together." He sighed. "Well, that train has sailed." He laughed. "Ship. I guess trains don't really sail, do they?"

"No." I smiled.

"I tried to get information out of Luna when I was outside, but she wouldn't speak. The Crows came out and started questioning me about you and Asher and the pack and lots of other things. I told them what I knew, which was nothing. Well, nothing more than she did. She injected me with something and my Goddess did it burn. After a while, when I still wasn't giving Maye whatever answer she was looking for, even after the beatings, she left me outside with Luna."

"Did they hurt her?"

"A little, but she took it like a champ. She didn't even flinch... it was unbelievable. After a while, she started asking me questions about you and our connection. Again, I told her what I knew, but it wasn't what she was looking for specifically."

"What was she looking for?"

"I don't know, but she wouldn't say."

"Maye came out the next day. I guess she hoped a whole night tied to a tree would make me remember whatever it was she wanted to hear, but it didn't because, again, I have no information. She was talking as if my short time with mom and dad, before we completed the Trinity, had somehow turned me against her. She thought I was a spy."

I choked on a laugh.

"Pretty crazy, I know, and that's when we heard Asher was in the area. She thought he was coming for me or for Luna, but we tried to assure her that wasn't the case." He looked down at his hands.

"What? What's wrong?"

"Nothing."

"Not nothing. What is it? Do you know something you aren't telling me?"

"They said he was with someone."

"So."

"They said it was another woman, a Crescent. They thought it was you and immediately sent a team after him. But it wasn't you."

"No."

"Do you know who it was?"

I shook my head.

"You don't?"

"No. I don't." I could have made a guess to say he found his aunt, and that's why he seemed so excited, but I didn't want to share that information with Kayden, because I didn't know what game he was playing.

He groaned. "Well, when Luna heard that, something in her changed. She was worried about him and she said she knew they needed a wolf to complete the spell. She told me we were going to be sacrificed for the goddess as a reparation for the acts of the Crescent. She said she had to get me to you."

"Why?"

He hesitated for a second. "She didn't say, but it seemed important to her. When the guards weren't around, we started trying to get my hands untied. They were spellbound, and she didn't have her magic. Maye had somehow suppressed it. We used the tree and a few rocks and were able to break the ropes, which we learned broke the suppression. I got her out of her ropes and she opened a portal to send me here."

"And then she stayed for Asher?"

He nodded. "But I'm fairly certain she suffered for it."

"What do you mean?"

"As the portal was opening, the guards ran out and started yelling. She used her magic to stop them, but she was weak. I was barely able to make it through the portal before it snapped closed. I heard them attacking her behind me and wanted to go back to help her."

"You did?"

"I'm not a complete monster... I have rules."

I raised my brows in surprise and wondered what that list of rules looked like.

"Ok. Well, I'm trying to learn." He batted his hand. "Anyway, they yanked her backwards, and that was all I heard."

"So she didn't tell you why she was there?"

"No. But I assume she knew they needed to complete a sacrifice."

"So you think she volunteered for that?" I was completely confused. Who would knowingly volunteer themselves to be killed? It made little sense.

He shrugged. "I don't know. Seems kind of odd."

"Yea."

"So anyway, that's why I'm here."

"Do you know anything that can help us?"

He cocked his head to the side. "Are you going after him tonight?"

"No."

"You aren't?" He was shocked.

"No. I figured Maye would expect it and have more guards in place and we aren't ready for another fight just yet."

"If you got a moderate sized group together, you could take them."

I laughed.

"You could. Their arrogance makes them weak." He held up his hand. "I know… how weak I must be." He rolled his eyes.

"Maye is strong, though."

"She is, but she doesn't know, and I didn't tell her."

"Why not?"

"I liked Maye. I thought we had a good thing going, but when she started… acting differently, it wasn't safe for anyone if she knew how strong she was. Luna also seemed concerned."

Alpha.

Ruthy.

We're back.

"What is it?" Kayden asked.

"Ruthy. They're back."

THE OTHER WOMAN

I RACED OUTSIDE AND found Ruthy and her team standing in the middle of the field. Drake had his hand on her shoulder, and she angrily shrugged it off before she bent over and grabbed her knees.

"What's going on?" I asked, cautiously running up to them.

Drake looked at me, his face torn, and walked away to talk with Mira. Xander and Levi walked over to Chloe and the others dispersed, the trepidation clear on their faces. They were giving Ruthy space, which told me this was not good. A knot formed in my stomach as I continued closing the distance between us.

"Ruthy?" I asked cautiously when I got to her.

She glanced at me before looking back at the ground, still bent over, almost like she had run miles and was trying to catch her breath- which was something she never had to do.

I looked around at the others and they sort of watched from a distance and shook their heads. The longer people went without talking, the more fear crept in. Was Asher gone? Was that what they had to tell me, but they didn't know how? They left it up to Ruthy, who was not only struggling to process but also trying to figure out how to let me know?

I could feel my knees going weak.

"Ruthy. I need to know. Is he... alive?"

She looked up at me, tears filling her eyes.

I cocked my head to the side. "Ruthy?" I felt my throat constricting, slowly cutting off the air supply. He wasn't gone. I could still feel him. I would know. Right? He's not gone.

She stood up and looked at me. "He's alive." Her words were slow, the silent but hanging in the air. "Cami..." She stepped forward and wrapped her arms around me.

"What is it?" I pushed her off after a second, holding her by her shoulders. "What aren't you telling me?"

She shook her head. "He... Aerials surveilled the area from above. We stayed back. As soon as Xander took flight, he said there were dozens of Crows not even a mile from where we were, so we backed up some, not wanting to start anything. Xander took off towards the compound and found Asher and Luna."

I looked at Drake and assumed he was filling in Mira.

"Xander said he was bloodied and bruised, with torn clothes and dirt covering every inch of him, and said it looked like they dragged him behind them. I don't know if that's true or not."

It was obvious he'd be tortured. He was my mate, and they thought he probably had information that could help, which he probably did, but it wasn't information he was going to give them. Ever.

Stupid.

Why not tell them what he had so they didn't beat him?

"Xander was able to fly to the compound, but said there was a force field or something around it protecting them. He could feel it, almost like a dome. Xander relayed his exact location and Drake portaled there quickly, without being seen. Drake held his hands out in the air and apparently could feel it. He tried to counter the spell and could get it down momentarily while Xander flew in and sat in the tree above them."

"Why? This was just a recon."

"They weren't trying to break them out. Not yet anyway, just get information. Apparently, Asher saw Xander and had that look on his face." Ruthy shook her head. "Those were Xander's words, not mine. Drake had to continually move around to stay hidden while also monitoring Xander. Maye has nearly fortified the compound, up to a mile around it. It won't be easy getting them out."

"Maybe we don't."

Ruthy snapped her head in shock.

"No. I'm not saying we don't get them out. I'm saying we go in. I don't know. This needs to be handled once and for all. They won't stop coming."

She smiled. "Asher told Xander the same thing. Xander in his stupid infinite wisdom, shifted and sat against the base of the tree and looked like a prisoner."

"Wouldn't they know?"

Ruthy laughed. "Most of the guards are patrolling around the compound, not in the compound. No one, besides Xander, would be stupid enough–"

"Brave."

She smacked her lips. "Regardless, no one would dare walk into enemy territory and post up with the prisoners nonchalantly."

I shook my head, looking at him. He just pumped his eyebrows at me, then went back to his conversation with Levi and Chloe, his arms causally resting on both their shoulders.

"He talked to Asher, who said he was fine. Sore, but fine. He was asking about a woman. Xander thought he was talking about you. He was panicked."

"No. I think it's his aunt or someone in his family. I think he found them and they were coming back with him so he could introduce me. Last time we spoke, he wouldn't tell me why he was so excited, but I could hear it in his voice and feel it through our bond." Replaying that last conversation in my head, hearing his excitement and then hearing his current state was breaking my heart and filling me with a level of rage I'd never experienced.

"Did Asher tell him a name, a location, anything?"

She held up her hand. "Xander." She called out.

His head snapped up and his eyes grew wide.

"Come here."

He hesitantly walked over.

"Can you tell Cami everything about the woman Asher was talking about?"

His face fell. "I'm sorry. I thought he was talking about you. He seemed a little delirious and some of what he was saying wasn't making sense. I thought he was just confused."

"What was he saying?" I leaned forward, eager to feel and hear any piece of him, and my wolf did too. She missed his wolf and her ache was only adding to my feelings of worry.

Xander shook his head guiltily. "I'm sorry, I don't remember much."

"Tell me what you do remember." I stepped forward urgently.

He took a deep breath and looked at the sky as he gathered his thoughts. "Not much. He was talking about a woman and that we had to find her. He was scared they killed her and just kept repeating we had to find her while he rocked back and forth."

The image nearly tore me apart.

"I thought he was talking about you, so I was trying to convince him you were safe, but he kept on."

"Did he say where she was? Where he was taken from?"

"No, because, again..."

"Yes. Yes. You couldn't have known." I was frustrated and knew my words held a sting behind them, but it wasn't directed at him. "We need to find her though. She may be in trouble."

"Do you know who she is?"

"No. He didn't tell me. He was on his way back, I assumed with her... right before he was taken." I unclenched my hands, my nails biting into my skin. "I thought he had surprised me when I heard the doorbell ring, but it ended up being Kayden." I sighed. "He said he was close."

"Ok. We can work with that. Based on that information and where he was coming from and anything else you can remember, we can try to create a search area." Xander fired out in rapid succession. I could tell he felt guilty and wanted to make his perceived wrong, right.

I nodded with the slightest bit of hope seeping in. "Let's head to the library and we can map it out."

Xander and I started walking towards the house. I looked over my shoulder. "Ruthy?"

She batted her hand in the air. "I'll be there in a minute." She glanced at Drake and I had a feeling she was going to talk with him. She knew something was up and she wasn't the type to sit around and wait for things to happen to her, especially when it felt as big as this did.

I nodded and gave her a half smile in support and she returned it. I could almost feel her nerves running through me.

Chloe and Levi ended up following us up. While they took a spot around the table, I grabbed a marker and started marking up the map with anything I could remember. We had our location and the Crow's compound and I knew roughly where he was going and roughly how long he'd been traveling. Based on the assumption he wouldn't have detoured for any reason, I drew two lines on the map- the external perimeter of his path home.

"Ok. Ok." Xander said, walking around the table to stand beside me. "This is a good start."

"I can ask dad if he knows where the pack is in that area." Chloe offered, and I nodded.

Xander grabbed a marker and started scribing numbers on the board, with Levi looking over his shoulder.

Asher.

Silence.

Asher. If you can hear me, we're planning to come after you. We're going to find whoever you were traveling with. I love you.

I knew it was unlikely he could hear me. I had been where he was not so long ago, but reaching out to him like this and talking to him helped put my mind at ease and right now I would take anything I could get.

Ruthy and Drake walked in a minute later and she didn't look at me. I wanted to reach out to her to see if she was ok, but I knew.

She wasn't.

She was grieving, but why? I looked at Drake and he looked equally sad.

The only thing I could come up with is they had broken up, but that didn't make sense. They were both crazy about each other. Maybe it was something else. I realized I was lying to myself, because I didn't want any more sadness right now. I don't think my heart could handle it.

Ruthy came to stand beside me while Drake stayed on the other side of the table. I leaned into her without saying anything and she laid her head on my shoulder for a second, then popped up. "What do we have?" I could feel her walls going back up.

Xander walked over a second later and stared at the map before drawing a large circle and then a smaller one within it. "This is the search area I think we should hit first." He said, pointing to the smaller circle. "Based on my," he paused and looked at Levi, "our calculations, we think he was somewhere in this area."

"The larger circle being the buffer?"

He nodded.

Levi spoke. "Based on how fast he runs, assuming he isn't running at full speed and the fact he said he was close, I really think this is an excellent shot."

I looked out the window and saw the moonlight filtering through as a bout of exhaustion hit me. It was late, and it had been a long day.

"Ok." I tapped my fingers on the paper. "Let's get some rest tonight and then we'll head out first thing in the morning." I looked at Drake. "Do you think you can portal us there?"

He nodded, but before he could speak, Ruthy jumped in. "We can run. It will be good for us."

The entire room looked between the two of them, feeling the tension.

I nodded and then announced, "Great idea. It would be good to run. We've gotten so used to portaling. We don't need to spoil our animals."

Drake shrugged and walked out of the room.

I looked at Ruthy, who watched after him, her face taut.

"Ok. Well, I'm going to head to bed." Xander clapped and swung his legs towards the door.

Levi pointed at himself and then to Xander, letting me know he was going too, followed by Chloe.

When it was just Ruthy and me in the room, I looked at her, causing her to puff and cross her arms, but I didn't say anything.

"Don't." She threatened so weakly it came out as a plea.

"We don't have to talk. If you want to come lay in my room, I can be your big spoon." I smiled, and she cut her eyes at me so fast it caused me to laugh out loud.

She continued to glare as the hint of a smile played on her lips. She didn't move to leave, so neither did I. I could tell she wanted to talk about whatever had happened, but at the same time she didn't want to say the words because they would hurt too much. So I waited.

She pulled out a seat and sat down, so I followed, sitting three chairs down from her.

Ruthy stretched her arms out across the table and put her forehead on it, letting out a low growl.

She popped her head up and looked at me, then laid it on her arm, her eyes still on me.

I gave her a sympathetic smile.

"You know." She started, then stopped and shook her head. "I knew." She rolled her eyes and I could see the tears forming on the rim and see the hurt in her eyes. "I knew it wasn't a good idea and did I listen to myself? No. No, I did not, so I guess this only serves me right."

"That's not fair to you. You didn't know."

She sat up. "I one hundred percent knew I was going to get hurt, because he wasn't my mate. It was stupid to get involved with someone who isn't your mate, especially," she pointed her finger rapidly, "especially someone who isn't even your same species."

I went to speak, but she didn't give me the chance.

"I mean seriously. What was I thinking? It should have only been for fun, but no. No. I got attached and let myself..." She rubbed her face, screaming.

The unspoken words were that she let herself love him.

"It was a lie. I lied to myself."

"You let yourself live."

"Well, it sucks." She pointed. "And the shitty part." She sat up in her seat, "Is that it's not him."

"What do you mean?"

"It's me."

"What's you?" I was confused now. I had assumed he had broken up with her.

She laughed. "He's amazing in so many ways." She stood up and looked out of the window. "Ellsmire is promoting him."

"They are?"

She nodded. "Yep, and they are sending him away."

"Where?"

"He doesn't know yet, but probably somewhere on the west coast. There are a few covens out there who are struggling and the council needs someone they can trust to help right the ship."

"That's great for him."

"Yea. I know. He's the youngest. Yet, again."

"Why can't you-"

"Don't even ask why I can't go with him."

I stopped talking and looked away awkwardly.

"I can't go with him. What am I going to do? Follow him across the country?" She smacked her lips like that was the most ridiculous idea she'd ever heard of.

"Yes. There are packs out there who I'm sure would love to have you."

"I'm not leaving you and Asher." She raised her eyebrows in finality, leaving no room for question.

I shrugged my shoulders. "I don't want you to leave, but I also don't want you to stay and miss out on what could be with Drake."

She spun quickly and yelled, losing all formality. "You don't get it!" She shook her head. "I'm sorry. I shouldn't speak to you like that."

"I'm your friend first and foremost, not your alpha. Talk to me. Get it all out." I reached my hand across the table towards her, letting her reach out and take it if she wanted.

Her shoulders slumped over in defeat. "There is no Drake and me. I've been living in a dream. Our relationship was always going to end this way, it's just ending sooner, before anyone got their feelings hurt too badly."

I nodded, but didn't speak.

"Stop."

"What?" I asked, shocked.

"Whatever it is, you're thinking."

"I'm not thinking anything." Anything that I was willing to share with her, at least. "I'm going to say this and then we can be done talking about it, unless you want to talk more."

She shook her head.

"Ok. I think Drake is good for you and he makes you happy. I think you should at least consider the idea of going with him. You're young and have time to explore the world. Don't let fear of the future hold you back today."

"How prophetic."

I playfully snarled my lip at her, causing a hint of a smile. "And don't forget he can portal you here whenever you want."

"It's not like that. He will be busy there. I can't use him as my personal portal transporter every time I want to see you. I mean sure, every once in a while, but not all the time. Plus, I don't think Mira or the council would appreciate it. They already seem to have a problem with his portaling as it is."

"Fair point, but I think you two could make it work."

"I don't know. I think it's too late because I already broke up with him."

I nodded. "Yea, Drake seems like the type of guy to just walk away immediately."

Her brow furrowed, not catching my sarcasm.

"Obviously, I'm kidding."

"I don't think he's very happy with me."

"Well, duh. You broke up with him. You both looked miserable up here."

"I am." She puckered out her lips, frowning.

I shrugged and raised my eyebrows, showing I wasn't talking anymore on the matter, but she knew my thoughts and I would continue to say the same thing if needed.

She let out a low growl, then left. "Good night. I'll see you tomorrow."

"Offer still stands if you want to be little spoon. Although we can take turns if it makes you feel better."

She didn't speak as she walked out of the room, giving me the bird over her shoulder.

I laughed for a second before my sad reality sank back in.

I studied the map, trying to memorize as much as I could.

We will find whoever was with you Asher and we'll protect them and then we're coming for you.

I smacked the table in finality and walked out of the room.

INTRUSION

I WAS WALKING THROUGH the woods as my hand gently skimmed across the tops of some wild bushes. In front of me were an endless number of trees and broken branches scattered around, with a soft sunlight filtering through. In the background, off in the distance, the roar of a waterfall echoed through the trees, softly vibrating my bones.

I looked behind me and saw Xander and Levi joking around and was immediately transported back to the time we were in the woods on the way to find my sister.

A second later, I heard a voice call out.

Ruthy.

She wasn't there before and realization hit me this could be a vision.

I felt my pulse race at the thought, paying attention to every detail. The way the air felt, the sound of the waterfall and other creatures, the feel of the dirt beneath my feet. I needed to focus and find what didn't belong.

The whoosh of the waterfall grew louder and the echoes of the banter faded.

I must be walking away from them. I tried to turn around to see them, but they were fading away.

The smell of iron pulled my attention.

Blood.

I chased it, my pace picking up as each second ticked. I called over my shoulder to let them know, but the sounds of the waterfall continued to grow louder and louder.

I looked to my right down the hill, close to the water's edge and saw a flesh-colored heap laying in a ball. Had this person fallen down the cliff?

I slid down the hill sideways, leaning hard to keep my balance.

"Hello? Hello? Can you hear me?"

Silence.

It took a minute for me to get down the hill, losing my footing several times.

"Hello?" I called out again, falling to my knees as soon as I was close to her.

I looked over her naked body before touching her and saw several patches of dried blood lines. She didn't have any open wounds, but she must have before.

I felt her throat and felt a very slow pulse. She was alive, barely.

"Over here!" I called out to the others, but there was no response. I gently rolled her over onto her back. She had long dark hair and tan skin.

Where were Xander and the others? "Xander! Ruthy! Levi!" I looked up the hill and waited for their answer, but heard nothing.

I shook my head, frustrated. They were just behind me. Where had they gone?

I gently circled my knuckles on the woman's chest, trying to wake her up. I needed a healer and wished Drake had been here with us.

"Hello?"

Something shifted in the air. I felt a breeze cross over my skin and it was like I was being sucked backwards into a hole, only I wasn't moving. Sounds started to fade, and the picture was getting blurry.

"Hello?" I called out, "Can anyone hear me?"

"Shhh," was the response, creepily echoing through the dark chamber.

I looked around to see who had shushed me and realized I was now standing in a black void. "Hello?"

"Quiet down." The female's voice said.

Was it the one from the ground? Where was I?

I looked around, looking for any clue, but the room was pitch black. "Hello?"

"Cami. You never listen." The voice held a sinister note in it, and that's when I recognized it.

Maye.

"Maye?"

"Ding, ding, ding, ding, ding. Fredrick, tell her what she's won."

I looked around, trying to find her, but there was still nothing.

"You won't be able to see me."

"But you can see me?"

She laughed. "No silly. I just figured you were looking around."

"What do you want?" I snapped. "And what is this?"

"I would've thought you'd be a little nicer to me since I have your mate. And as far as what this is, I was hoping to talk to you uninterrupted."

"How?"

She laughed. "Magic dear girl."

"Where am I?"

"You're still sleeping in your bed at your pack house. You have that thing really locked down. Not enough to prevent me from getting in, but it would take some time and, frankly, I don't care that much."

"So you thought you would just, what, come attack me in my dreams?"

She laughed again. "I think you're being a little too dramatic."

"Dramatic?"

"You took my mate. For what?"

"Well, that's what I'm trying to talk to you about, but you won't stop running your mouth for two seconds."

I started to say something, then closed my lips and huffed.

"I know that was hard for you."

I felt my blood boiling and wished I was standing in front of her so I could snatch her by her throat and make her sorry for ever crossing my family.

"You seem to be a little angry right now."

Could she hear my thoughts? I panicked before I realized I didn't care. I hope she could. "What do you want?"

"Down to business. I love it. I want to make a trade."

"Let me guess. Asher for me."

"And smart too."

I rolled my eyes.

"What assurances do I have, you'll keep your word?"

"You don't. But I can tell you where the woman is."

Could she see my visions, too? My heart fluttered.

"Asher won't stop going on about her. Who is she?"

"I don't know." I sighed in relief.

She laughed. "I don't believe that."

"I don't know who she is." I snapped back. "I'm not lying. I didn't know he was with another woman. I don't know her name and I have never met her."All of those things were convenient truths.

She hesitated for a second, then continued. "She's somewhere around the Tallamaehee waterfall. That's where we picked up Asher and may have thrown her over a cliff."

The waterfall and cliff were at least matching my vision.

"I'll give you today to find her and expect to see you at the Red Crows compound by nightfall." She hissed, then added. "If not, I will send you Asher's body, piece by piece." Her words cut sharp. "Ta-ta lovebird."

It felt like I was being sucked backwards through darkness again with an invisible rope tied around my waist.

Moments later, I was waking up screaming. I looked out of the window and saw the sun was just starting to peek over the horizon. I threw the covers off and quickly got dressed and brushed my teeth, making my way to the library.

I sent a call out to the team and they were in the room less than two minutes later. Everyone but Ruthy looked like they were sleepwalking.

"Good morning." I said, pressing my hands to the table.

"Is it even morning yet?" Xander asked, rubbing his eyes, before getting an elbow in the chest from Levi. "Ouch." He mumbled, now rubbing his ribs.

"So I know where the woman is."

"How?" Ruthy asked, stepping forward, a look of concern clear on her face.

"That's not important."

"Bull!" Ruthy snapped, holding nothing back. "Was it a vision or something else?"

I studied her, knowing there was no way she could have known Maye spoke with me. But the fact, she asked if there was something else made the hairs on the back of my neck stand up.

"A vision." I drawled.

Ruthy continued to glare at me.

"Goddess! What?" I said, losing my patience.

Drake walked in a moment later and gave a quick glance between Ruthy and me.

"Where is she?" Xander interjected, mostly awake now.

I hesitated and pulled my glance from Ruthy, who somehow seemed to know more than she was willing to tell me right now.

"She's at the base of the Tallamaehee falls."

Ruthy made a noise but didn't say anything, while Xander and Levi walked over to the map to find the falls.

"Hot dog!" Xander shouted, pointing in the smaller circle. "I was-"

Levi cleared his throat.

Xander put his arm around Levi's shoulders, pulling him into a headlock, "Apologies, we were right! Here in this smaller circle."

"Perfect!" I looked at Drake, raising my eyebrows.

He cautiously looked at Ruthy, who rolled her eyes. "Yes. I will portal you there."

I clapped my hands. "Perfect." I know we had talked about running, but that was before we knew the exact location and before the clock was ticking.

"Let's go!" Ruthy said bitterly.

She obviously had woken up on the wrong side of the bed.

"We need to put a team together."

"To portal in and portal out?" Ruthy asked condescendingly.

I snapped. "What is your problem?"

"Nothing." She said, holding her hands out to the side.

"Bull!"

"We're going to go get some breakfast," Xander whispered, walking slowly towards the door, pulling Levi with him.

I saw Drake look between the two of us and then he slowly backed out of the room too, leaving just Ruthy and me.

"What is your problem?" I asked again, this time in a softer, more concerned tone.

She threw her hands up in the air and walked around the table to look out the window without speaking.

"Ruthy? I know something's up."

She looked at me, then back out of the window.

When Ruthy got protective, she often got curt and defensive. I just don't know what was setting her off right now.

"Ruthy?" I pushed, softer.

"You're lying to me."

"I'm lying?"

She turned to face me, arms crossed over her chest. "I know you are."

"Lying about what?"

"How did you find out where this woman was?"

"I told you I had a vision."

She rubbed her face in frustration and let out a sigh, looking back out of the window. "See!"

"I did."

"So your vision told you the name of the falls?"

How could she know Maye had found a way to talk to me? There was no way. "Is there something you want to tell me?" I pressed back.

"No." She said way too quickly.

The only way, and still I didn't even know how probable it was, was if Drake somehow found out and told her, which meant they had to have been together this morning. The look he gave her when he walked in... "There's nothing you want to tell me... about you and Drake."

She cut her eyes at me, shaking her head slowly.

"I saw the way you looked at him this morning when he walked in, the way he looked at you, and I'm sure if I tried in the slightest, I would be able to smell him on you."

"Fine!" She turned around, exasperated. "He slept in my room last night." She held up a finger. "But nothing happened!"

I raised my brows.

"Well, nothing much." She started rubbing her face in frustration. "Damn it Cami. I don't want him to go."

I wrapped my arms around her. "I know. What are you going to do?"

She let me hold her for longer than I thought she would, then pushed away. "I don't know. I really don't. I want to go with him, but I also don't want to leave you and Asher. You both need me."

I laughed. "We will always need and want you, but we also don't want you to put your life on hold for us. You deserve all the happiness."

She snarled. "Don't get too mushy."

I smiled and a heavy silence filled the room.

"Cami," she said, her voice soft. "Drake said he felt something last night and again this morning."

"I don't need to hear this."

"Shut up." She smacked me on the arm. "I'm serious. He felt his skin prickle."

"What does that mean?"

"Stop being obtuse."

I stared at her, my heart in my throat. I didn't want to tell her Maye had visited me, even though it seemed like she already knew, because that would lead to the next question which would ultimately lead to the answer of me trading my life for Asher's which wouldn't settle well with her.

She grabbed me, placing her hands on either side of my head, staring me dead in the eyes.

"Oh, goddess no! Ruthy! Don't do it! She's our alpha! Think of Asher!" Xander yelled, running into the room.

She dropped her hands and looked at him. "What in Goddess's name are you talking about?"

"I thought you were going to kill her!"

He pressed his hands on the back of the chair.

"She is feisty, but I don't think she has a death wish!" Drake smiled before he winked at Ruthy.

I watched Ruthy melt into a pile of goo when he looked at her, but then quickly regained her composure. "No. I don't." She looked at me, cutting her eyes, and I knew whatever she was about to say next I would not like. "Cami is keeping something from us, something I think we should all hear."

I cocked my head at Ruthy, willing my eyes to cut lasers through her.

Without backing down, she pressed. "Let's hear it Cami."

"Hear what?"

"The truth about how you learned the location of Asher's other woman."

I glared at her, and she realized what she said, then shrugged, knowing we all knew what she really meant.

"I already told you I had a vision. I was walking through the woods and there was a waterfall in the background... I kept searching and found a woman who was laying in the fetal position at the bottom of the cliff near the waterfall. She was naked and had areas of dried blood on her. I felt for a pulse and it was weak."

"Did the waterfall have a name?"

"What? No."

"So how do you know it's the Tallamaehee waterfall?"

I knew she could hear my pulse pounding out of my chest. Hell, she could probably feel my nerves rising, which is why she kept pressing. Somehow Drake knew, or at the very least suspected something was wrong this morning and my reaction is giving her enough to keep pushing.

"Fine."

I saw Ruthy exhale a breath before glancing at Drake, who stepped forward.

"I wasn't lying. I did have that vision, but what I left out..." I paused, looking around the room. "Was that somehow Maye managed to get inside my head." I ignored the mumbles and side glances and continued talking, "I don't know how to explain it, but it felt like I was being pulled through time and space- through darkness. I was in this... this kind of large open area and then Maye appeared, not visually, but more audibly. She must have tried to get in around the house because she noted it was locked down pretty tight."

I couldn't help but notice Drake's smile of satisfaction.

"Anyway, she said she wanted to trade my life for Asher's."

"Which you said hell no to. Right?" Ruthy lashed out.

"Which I agreed to." I flinched, waiting for the incoming assault.

Ruthy rolled her eyes. "Shocking," she said dismissively.

"I asked her for a guarantee that he'd be safe and she said no." I shrugged, "Which is fine. I'm not quite certain I would've believed her otherwise."

Ruthy looked around the room, not speaking. I could almost see the gears turning in her head.

"I have until tonight." I said quietly, again bracing for backlash.

"Tonight?" Ruthy barked, clearly not expecting that. "That's not enough time."

"I know."

She shook her head.

"So you're just going to go? Just like that? Screw everyone else? Screw us, Ellsmire, the freaking crescent packs!"

The floodgates had been opened.

"It's-"

She stepped forward, raising her voice. "I'm not done."

I instinctively flinched.

"Ruthy." Drake cautioned, placing his hand on her arm.

"No! No Drake!" She pulled her arm from his hand. "First, Asher was taken and then you're leaving and now Cami." She looked at me and shook her head. "I'm not losing you Cami! Damn it! You have been like a whirlwind since you first came into our lives. That first day of school, I walked by your desk and saw you doodling in the front of the room... I knew there was something about you, and then here you go, end up being Asher's mate. Asher, of all people!" She threw her hands in the air. "He asked me before he left to look after you and make sure you don't do anything crazy and you make it so freaking hard sometimes!"

I felt tears stingy my eyes, because I was seeing the real Ruthy. The one she kept hidden, the one who feared losing those close to her and the one who fought like hell to keep them protected. If she was a Crescent, she would definitely be some sort of bear for sure.

She stopped yelling for a minute and just looked at me. I saw her eyes glistening, but she had done better than me by holding back the tears. "I don't know what else to do." I squeaked out. "She said she was going to send me pieces of him if I didn't come. I can't allow that."

She walked forward, wrapping me in her arms and squeezed a little too tight, which I felt was on purpose because she was still irritated with me. "You come to me for help and we will figure something out."

I let her hold me for another second, hoping it would buy me a reprieve from her verbal assault.

"This is getting awkward." Xander chimed in. He looked at Levi, with his arms open wide, "Can I hold you?"

Levi pushed Xander's chest. "Man, no. Why do you have to always make things weird?"

Xander grabbed his chest, feigning pain. "Levi." He tsked.

Ruthy pushed me away, but still held on to my shoulders. "Ok. Let's think through this and make some plans."

"Ok."

"Yes! I love making plans!" Xander clapped.

Ruthy glanced at me, "Why do we keep letting him tag along?"

Xander answered before I could speak. "Because even though you won't admit it, deep down, like deep, deep, deep down in your littttttle bitty heart, you love me. I would hate to think what you would do if I were missing. Probably burn the whole place down."

"Because of the celebration I would have?"

Xander puckered his lips playfully at her and Ruthy just rolled her eyes, trying to hide the smile tugging at her lips.

Drake stepped beside Ruthy and leaned over the table. I noticed he got right beside her, so their hips and shoulders were touching, and saw the little play of his pinky as he reached out and stroked hers. I hoped when all this was done, Ruthy would decide to go with him wherever he went because while their relationship may have started out as just a simple prom request, it had blossomed into so much more. They were made for each other.

"We don't have a lot of time to put a plan together." Ruthy chimed. "Do we think Maye will be at the falls waiting for us, for Cami?"

"I don't know. If she thinks we're going after the woman, then possibly."

"Maye won't give you the chance to not turn yourself over." Drake added.

"What if we were to get a large group together and split up? Send most of the people to the compound, to make it look like we're going after Asher and Luna instead, to pull anyone away from the woman. A small group of us can pick her up and portal out. Do you think that would work?"

"It could, but I'm scared that would cause Maye to retaliate against Asher." Ruthy said.

"Could we do both then at the same time? Like actually pull it off?"

"I don't know how we would get into the compound."

"We have someone downstairs that does?" Xander added.

"Kayden?" Ruthy scoffed. "I wouldn't trust a word out of his mouth if my life depended on it."

Xander shrugged. "Just a thought. I mean, couldn't your boyfriend make a potion or something to force him tell the truth?"

Ruthy looked between Drake and Xander and when Drake wasn't correcting him, she asked, "Could you?"

He nodded. "I've only done it a few times in practice, but it can be done. I'd have to go to Ellsmire and get a few things."

"How long would it take?"

"Not too long."

She shook her head. "I feel like we're rushing this and playing right into Maye's hands."

"I don't know if we have another choice." I said, feeling the same as her, but also scared of what would happen if we didn't. The woman in my vision didn't seem like she had much longer. Enough time had passed where she should have healed herself, but she wasn't. She was Asher's family, and I needed to get her, but I also needed to get to Asher.

I slammed by hands on the table in frustration.

"What's going on in here?" Chloe asked, yawning and stretching as she walked into the room, then she looked up at me. "What happened? What did I miss?"

"I'm going to head to Ellsmire while you fill her in. Be back soon." Drake said, excusing himself. He moved to kiss Ruthy goodbye, then stopped, squeezing her shoulder instead and letting his hand run down her arm to her hand.

"Oh my Goddess. You guys. That was so romantic and sad at the same time." Xander clasped his hands under his chin. "Will they? Won't they?" He rubbed his face.

Ruthy cut her eyes so hard at him, he took a step back.

"Not cool dude." Levi mumbled.

I looked at my watch. "We have a couple of hours. Let's go prepare the groups."

BEST LAID PLANS

EXCITED MURMURS FILTERED AROUND the field as Liam and Anastasia's pack joined ours. I stood on the chair on the patio and looked around as the two packs came together, smiling and shaking hands. I didn't speak for a minute, relishing in the unity and camaraderie between the packs.

We had spent the last two hours questioning Kayden on the ins and outs of the compound with the potion Drake had created. Kayden pleaded with us, promising several times he would tell us without the potion, however we were on a time crunch and needed to know for certain he was telling the truth. I think the idea of his vulnerability made him nervous, because there were still things he wanted hidden, which I honestly couldn't fault him for. I'm sure I'd be the same way.

He finally agreed to the potion- not that he had a choice- if Liam and Anastasia stayed in the room to help ensure we were only asking pertinent questions. Anastasia took this as a sign he was starting to trust her, and while I wanted to tell her not to get her hopes up and that he was just using her, I kept my mouth shut.

Kayden said that several years after he'd been at the compound, they let him roam the halls freely. One day, he stumbled across a furnace room and heard a ticking noise. When he went to investigate, he found a rusty grate hanging by a screw behind a broken furnace. He climbed in and followed to see where it led- a straight shot to a door that was about a mile or two away from the compound. He turned around and swore he told no one, including Maye, in case his position at the compound changed and he needed a way out. We asked if he could lead a team to the exit, so we could get into the compound, but he wasn't sure he'd be able to find it again from the outside, since the woods all look the same and it was a door hidden in the side of a hill, camouflaged by leaves and debris.

So that left us with no way in...

"Hello all." I sighed a little. "I feel like this is a common speech lately and I'm terrible at speeches." I laughed, mostly at myself. "As many of you know, Asher was looking for his family and we think he found his aunt and was bringing her back here when he was kidnapped by the Red Crows. I had a vision last night that she was near the base of a waterfall and after Xander and Levi did some calculations, we feel like we have a good idea which one." I thought it important to leave out the piece about Maye.

I continued. "A small group of us are going to pop in to the location we think she's at to retrieve her. However, we think the Red Crows may guard the area she's in, knowing we would come after her." I shifted on the chair. "What we're hoping to do is have the rest of you head towards the compound."

"Are we getting Asher?" Conner asked.

I sighed. "I don't think that's a good idea yet. We'll obviously be met with a lot of resistance and I fear the Crows numbers have only grown since they were here."

"We should get other packs, too. This isn't just our fight. This is a fight for all Crescent's and their allies." Conner continued.

I nodded. "Yes. We're working on creating a plan to reach out to other packs across the country, but we have to be careful. We don't know a lot of those packs and we would hate to let the wrong pack into our group and have them turn on us."

Most of the group nodded in agreement.

"I promise, though. We're working on several plans to get him. Right now, our priority is to get Asher's traveling companion back here safely. To do that, we need a distraction at the compound. One that's not close enough to start a full out battle, because we aren't prepared for that, but close enough to make them think we are, to pull them from this woman. At the same time this is going on, I need several of you," I looked at the Crescents, "Aerials especially, to get an overview of the compound. Try to get a count on the size of their army and any other pertinent information. I fear we will have to act soon to save Asher and Luna."

"Luna." Someone scoffed.

"Yes, Luna too. While I'm not her biggest fan, she has saved my life at least twice and Ellsmire, for the most part, has seemed to have forgiven her." I looked at Drake, who nodded. "She also helped us on the day the moonstone was created."

There were murmurs filtering around the crowd, causing Ruthy to clap and hop onto a chair. "Aerials, over on this side." She pointed to the right and they all sort of stared at her without moving.

Liam stood up. "You have permission to follow any and all orders commanded by Camilla or Ruthy for this mission."

With his words, the crowds shifted and there were about ten people that stood off to the right.

"Levi, Xander, Drake, you three are with Cami and me."

I saw Chloe huff, and I glanced at Anastasia. She had seen it too and gave me a slight nod, letting me know she would take care of it.

She can't go. I can't risk her. I said to Anastasia.

I know. I'll talk to her.

She's not going to like it.

I know. You two seem to not like being told what to do or kept from any sort of action.

Not when it's my loved one's lives at stake. I hadn't told her about Maye's threat to dismember Asher if I didn't trade myself. Ruthy still thought we could figure a way out of it, but I was prepared to do what I needed, to protect him. I knew I was being selfish, but I had to hope trading myself for Asher's safety would buy our pack enough time to figure out how to get us out of the mess and perhaps force Ellsmire to help.

Or your own, if I recall correctly.

I didn't say anything.

What's going on? She prodded softly.

What do you mean?

Camilla. I can feel your nerves.

I don't want this mission to go wrong.

You think it will?

I hope not.

It seems fairly straightforward. Drake will portal you four in a distance from the waterfall, then open a portal for the rest of the team near the compound. He'll portal back to you and get you all home before heading back to the others and getting them home. She laughed. *Drake has the worst of it, ping ponging back-and-forth portaling you all.*

Yes. He's been great.

He is a great friend. He's been a little more absent lately, and more reserved when he's here. Is everything ok?

He's basically getting a promotion at Ellsmire and has to leave. It's hard because he's built a life here, but he also has several strikes against him... because of me. So I think part of this is punishment and a way to protect him at the same time. Ruthy is torn up because she doesn't want to leave.

That can be hard.

Mom.

Yes?

I just wanted to say, if something happens to me today...

Don't speak like that Cami.

No. I need to say this.

Ok.

Try to get Asher back and don't let him blame himself, and please do whatever you can to look after Ruthy.

What aren't you telling us... telling me?

Nothing.

She sighed.

I love you.

Oh Camilla. She had tears streaming down her face. *I love you so much too.*

I felt tears stinging my eyes, but refocused my attention back on the crowd. Ruthy had them all sorted into groups and was giving them instructions. She had a small group to the far left that could engage in battle if needed, but only if it was necessary. We needed to pressure test their pack, isolate the alpha and figure out how big they were. It seemed like she had separated another group of the younger and newer pack members to scour the areas around the woods to find the hidden door Kayden had described.

"Are we ready?" I asked after a few more minutes.

Ruthy nodded, then studied my face. *What's wrong? Your face.*

That's really nice.

Shut up. What's going on? I swear, if you're planning on giving yourself over to her, I will kick your ass.

I'm not planning on it. And I wasn't. I hoped everything would work out the way it was supposed to and we could pop in and pop out with Asher's travel companion and we could basically keep Maye and the Crows confused without actually have to fight anyone.

I laughed, because there was a lot of possibility for things to go wrong. Maye wasn't dumb, and I feared she would see our plan coming from a mile away, but one could hope.

I still don't like your face.

I love you too, Ruthy.

I'm serious. If you do anything stupid. I won't forgive you.

I smiled at her and nodded.

Ruthy ran through the plan one more time with everyone, then looked at Drake.

"Pack. Liam is your alpha on the field. Follow his orders as if they were mine."

My pack crossed their arms in front of their face taking a knee to Liam.

I nodded and looked at Drake. "Let's do this."

I glanced back at Chloe and mouthed 'I'm sorry'.

She glared at me. *Screw your apology. You're side lining me.*

I walked towards the portal Drake had created. Ruthy and Levi had walked through and Xander was going in now.

"I'll be there as soon as I can." Drake said. I nodded and started to step in.

"Wait!" Chloe called out, running over to me.

I took a step back and saw Anastasia running after her.

"I'm not going to sneak in. I'll obey my alpha." She rolled her eyes. "Even though I don't want to."

I smiled at her.

She slipped her necklace off. "Take this." She said, clasping it around my neck. "It's my lucky rabbit's foot. My parents gave it to me on my first day of school."

"Chloe." I sighed. "I can't take this."

"Shut up. You aren't taking it, I'm loaning it to you and this doesn't mean I forgive you for benching me, but I do love you and I want you to be safe." She gave me a quick hug, then pushed me through, peeking through the hole. "Boys, Ruthy. Keep her safe." She pointed, then nodded and walked back towards Anastasia, who had a look of relief spread across her face.

"She's scary sometimes." Xander said, watching the portal close behind me.

Ruthy nodded, then crossed her arms. "She means well, plus she knows Cami is going to do something stupid."

"I'm not."

Ruthy laughed a fake, loud laugh. "What's funny is we all know it but you."

I scrunched my nose, looking at both Levi and Xander who nodded.

"You know what? Screw you both, too."

"But we love you for it." Xander said, grabbing my shoulders.

I looked around, trying to get my bearings while also trying to figure out if any of this felt familiar, but it didn't.

I was getting the creeping feeling that Maye had lied. Which I don't know why I wouldn't have thought of that before. I think I was so eager to believe she was telling the truth.

LIFE FOR A LIFE

THERE WAS A FLOCK of birds that shifted in the trees, taking to the air about a few hundred yards to the north. It made the hairs on the back of my neck stand up.

"Let me see if I can see anything up ahead." Xander whispered. He walked behind a tree and stripped out of his clothes and took to the air a minute later.

"That's shocking. He usually just shreds his clothes. Oh wait. That's just mine." Levi joked.

Still so bitter about that, I see. He chimed. *So far, everything looks good from up here. Waterfall looks to be to the northwest of where you are right now, about three miles away.*

We're good to move that way?

Yes. I don't-

What is it? I tensed.

Getting a closer look.

Please be careful.

I'm invis- Shit!

What? Levi asked, concerned.

Silence.

Pookie, are you concerned about me?

Levi rolled his eyes. *Not in the least.*

I ran into a tree branch, because I wasn't paying attention.

Idiot. Ruthy chuckled, batting at the top of a bush.

Love you too, boo boo bear.

"I'm going to strangle him when he lands."

"Let's head that way." I jumped in, trying to redirect our focus.

Look at that fine group of people down there.

We all looked up and saw him gliding over our head- his dark speckled wings were a stark contrast against the light blue sky.

"Shouldn't you be paying attention or something?" Ruthy barked.

All looks good to the waterfall.

Did you see the woman?

No, but I didn't know where to look and also wanted to double back just in case I missed anyone the first time.

So there's no one here?

Not at all, which seems kind of strange.

Yea. I agree. Ruthy said, looking in my direction with a perplexed look on her face.

I felt it too. There was something that definitely felt off about this. Maye would know we'd be coming. If she thought I was going to back out of the exchange, she would have a trap waiting. Unless she was lying about the waterfall and I just believed her because it fit with the narrative I saw.

I wracked my brain, trying to think through everything as panic crept in and settled into a hard lump in my stomach. What if Maye had created the vision I saw? Could she do that? I didn't even think to ask Drake.

I shook my head. No. Xander and Levi had calculated speeds, probable locations and everything else and this waterfall fit right in the spot they thought we should search.

I stopped walking, grabbing the arms of Levi and Ruthy.

"What's wrong?" Ruthy panicked, looking around.

"Something's off."

"Yea. I agree. I have this prickly feeling on my skin like I'm being watched."

Sometimes I feel like... somebody's watchinggg meee.

"Shut up, Xander, this could be serious."

I'm telling you... from up here, the woods are ours and ours alone.

I stuck my nose in the air, smelling it for any trace of animal. "Do you smell that?"

They all followed suit, then shook their head.

"I don't smell anything." Ruthy said.

"Me either," said Levi. "We should be able to smell something. Right?"

"Yea. Some animal, any animal." I said, looking around for any sign of an animal, big or small.

"Do you think it's been magically suppressed?" Ruthy asked. "Where's Drake?"

Anastasia, is Drake almost done?

Silence.

Anastasia?

Silence.

Chloe?

"I don't like the look on your face." Ruthy stepped closer to me.

"I can't get hold of Anastasia or Chloe."

"Do you think something happened to them?"

"I don't know."

Xander landed and walked over towards us. "What's going on?"

"Cami can't get in touch with anyone."

Xander looked away for a minute, then looked back. "Me either. Liam isn't responding."

"Ok, well, that's probably good then." Ruthy said unconvincingly. "Chances are the problem is us, not them."

"Yea, super good." Xander said, grabbing his clothes from Levi, who was nice enough to grab them before we started walking.

"We can communicate with one another, but not outside of whatever bubble we're in."

I nodded. "Which means there's magic, which means Maye is or was here, which means..."

"Could mean the prickly feeling we're all feeling is Crows watching us, who have also somehow been suppressed." Levi said, looking around.

"Shit." Xander said.

"What?" I looked around quickly, trying to keep my wits about me.

"I lost a button on my pants."

Ruthy's eyes grew wide. "Why is everything such a freaking game to you?"

"It's not. I can't button my pants now, which basically renders them useless."

"Levi, can you take Xander and go that way?" I pointed up a small hill. "Ruthy and I are going to continue heading towards the falls down here. If we're in some sort of trap, then I don't want us all grouped together. If something happens, the other group needs to run back to the portal location. Hopefully, Drake will be there and can portal us out so we can get help. We need to be smart since there are only four of us. No one needs to play the hero."

"Cami." They all said in unison.

"Give me a break." I said, rolling my eyes.

Levi and Xander started walking up the hill, taking the higher path further from the water.

"Thank you." Ruthy said. "I do like him, but sometimes..." she shook her head.

"I know. He keeps things light through intense situations, but he can also take it too far."

She shook her head, but didn't speak.

We continued to walk along the water's edge in silence. I could hear the waterfall in the distance growing louder, but still recognized nothing, although it was the woods and everything looked the same.

"I hope," I started, then stopped.

She looked at me.

I sighed. "When all this is over, I want you to go with Drake." I chuckled, "Obviously if you want to. I don't want to force you to leave because I will miss you greatly, but I also don't want you to feel like you have to stay..." I smiled. "Plus, he can portal you to me anytime."

She chuckled. "I don't know."

"I-"

There was a rustle in the bushes ahead and we both stopped walking. I looked up the hill and didn't see Levi and Xander, causing my heart to thump. I looked at Ruthy quickly, then back towards the bush. She had closed her eyes and was concentrating and I was reminded of the time she and Asher were training me in the field by his parent's old house. They blindfolded me and taught me to use my ears to sense an attack. I thought about doing that now, but wasn't as confident as Ruthy.

A moment later, my decision was made for me. A squirrel darted out of the bush and up the tree beside us. I patted Ruthy's arm at the same time she opened her eyes and we chuckled.

We continued to walk and I felt like the closer we got to the falls, the heavier the air became, almost suffocating. It may have been my own nerves, but Ruthy seemed to feel it too.

"Does anything look familiar?" She asked, taking deep breaths.

"It's hard to say." I pointed up ahead. "That area up there seems a little familiar. There should be a flat area and to the left, a larger cliff facing."

"Seems like it. Could you see the waterfall in your vision?"

I shook my head. "I don't remember. It's all a little fuzzy. I know I heard it. It was loud, but then everything faded away."

She nodded and then ran up ahead. "Come on, let's go!"

I followed her, the pit forming in my stomach. We weren't running toward anything. No body lying on the ground, nothing. It was just more dirt and branches and bushes, and then suddenly Ruthy disappeared.

I skidded to a stop, panicked. "Ruthy!" I called out, looking around for any sign of Maye. Had she just zapped her away? "Ruthy!" I yelled out again, no regard for my safety. If Maye or any of the Red Crows were here, they would know our place.

"What?" she asked, appearing again right in front of me, completely unaware of why I was so worried. "I think-"

"You... you..." I grabbed her in my arms.

"What are you doing?"

"I thought I lost you."

"Are you feeling ok?"

I shook my head. "Watch me." I started walking from where she'd come from and felt a warmness pass over my body and then saw a woman laying in front of me.

We had found her!

I bent down beside her and felt for a pulse at the same time Ruthy walked up behind me.

"Ok I get it." She said, looking around. "Maye must have put up some sort of barrier around her."

"Yea, they had something similar at Ellsmire."

"So we know Maye has been here at some point." She looked around and shivered. "I feel like she's watching."

I looked up the hill from where I'd come down in my vision. "Me too. It was soon after this moment in my vision that she pulled me into whatever mind place, so I'm not sure what happens next."

"Let's hurry then." Ruthy bent down beside me and felt for a pulse. "It's weak, but it's there. Do we know her name?"

"No."

Ruthy shook her hard to wake her.

"Easy." I warned.

"I don't feel like we have a lot of time and she's a shifter- her wounds aren't bleeding anymore. I will not hurt her, but I need her to wake up."

"What if Maye did something to her?"

"Oh. Right. I wouldn't put it past her." Ruthy moved to grab the woman and throw her over her shoulder. "We'll just carry her and figure it out later."

"Good call." I looked around again, but still only saw trees. The hairs on the back of my neck were standing on end and my body was nearly yelling at me that there was danger nearby, but I couldn't see it. I didn't know how much of it was spells and illusions and how much was my nerves trying to get the better of me. "Let's get out of here."

Levi. Xander. We found the –

"Going somewhere?" The smooth, grating voiced echoed around us.

I turned, trying to find the source, but didn't see anyone. Shit! She was here. "Show yourself!" I demanded.

She laughed. "Where's the fun in that?" She said from a different spot.

Ruthy gently, but not so gently, let the woman fall to the ground.

I glanced at the woman, but she was still unmoving. "What did you do to her?"

"What do you mean?" She asked from a different location.

I turned to face the sound while Ruthy scooted over behind me, our backs pressed together.

"Are you nervous?" There was a gust of air that blew our hair.

"Oh that bitch." Ruthy seethed, through set teeth.

"That's not very nice." Maye mocked.

"Close your eyes." Ruthy whispered.

"What?"

"Do it."

I could tell Ruthy had closed hers, because I felt her body relax as she took in a deep breath. The training exercise.

"I'm not some monster that will go away if you close your eyes, dear Ruthy." Maye taunted, and that's when I heard it. It was faint, but there. The moving of the air around her as she traveled, the gentle whoosh- a whisper of a wind.

"I know." Ruthy muttered and after a second she lunged to her right with incredible speed and threw a punch into the air.

A wail echoed before Ruthy exploded backwards, pushed by some invisible force, landing several feet away. Maye mumbled some words and then the invisible barrier had dropped. She was standing where Ruthy had just been, rubbing her cheek in a white shirt and pair of khaki pants and boots. "Neat parlor trick." She spat in Ruthy's direction.

I'd forgotten how good she was at that.

"Not a parlor trick." Ruthy said, standing up wiping her pants off.

"I'd suggest you not try that again or I won't be so kind next time."

Ruthy scoffed, moving to stand beside me.

"I'm impressed you found her so quickly. I thought you were trying to pull me away when I got reports of your packs near the compound, so I added a few protections, then went to go check. When I didn't see you there, I figured it was a decoy. No way you'd be dumb enough to try and get Asher out, not when we had a deal."

"Deal's off." Ruthy spat.

Maye cocked her head confused, "Is it?"

"She's not going with you."

"Since when did the alpha of the house not speak for herself?"

"Since her beta will die to protect her." Ruthy stepped forward.

"Ruthy." I reprimanded. I would not let her give her life for me. That is ludicrous.

"Good to know." Maye held out her hand and Ruthy's back shot straight stiff and her head snapped back as she hovered off the ground. Ruthy's hands were grabbing onto an invisible rope around her neck, trying to pull it off with no luck.

"Maye! Stop!" I cried out.

Garbled noises came out of Ruthy as her face was turning a darker shade of red and her feet continued to kick wildly.

"She can't breathe Maye, put her down!"

"She said she would die protecting you. You should probably run or her death would be for nothing." Maye said calmly, watching Ruthy's face change colors with intense curiosity.

"I'm not leaving!"

"Ruthy!" Xander and Levi yelled in unison from the top of the hill.

Xander lunged off the cliff, landing right behind Maye, while Levi jumped towards Ruthy.

"No, you don't crescent." Maye used her other hand to throw a spell, doing the same thing to Xander. "Do you think a Crescent would die differently than a wolf? Let's find out."

"Xander!" Levi cried out, his eyes panicked. I could see he was torn between staying with Ruthy and running after Xander.

"STOP!" I shouted again. "You're going to kill them."

"Yes. I am." She said without a hint of remorse.

Ruthy had stopped kicking and her hands hung limply, while her head bobbled lifelessly from side to side.

"Please Maye. What happened to you? What made you like this? Please put them down." Tears were streaming out of my eyes. "Please stop." I fell to my knees. "You have me. Just let them live."

I saw Xander's eyes snap in my direction and could tell he wasn't happy and the fact there was no reaction from Ruthy told me she was dead or very close to it.

"One more time. I don't think I heard you."

"Put them down. They live and I will go with you."

"No Cami." Levi said.

"Shut up Levi." I spat back, standing up as I regained some of my strength. I glanced at Ruthy as panic tore through me. "Now, Maye! Put them down. They live and I come with you."

She began to lower her hands. Ruthy's toes hit the ground, but her legs continued to crumble under the weight like a limp noodle. Levi was there, guiding her down, cradling her in his arms. "You know I could just kill them and still make you come with me. I have the one thing you absolutely can't live without. Your dear Asher." She started raising her hands back up and Ruthy rotated more vertically.

"Maye!" I commanded, and felt a force pulse out around me.

Both Ruthy and Xander crumpled to the ground and Maye took a step back. I'd forgotten how scared she was of whatever this light force thing was that I had. Too bad I couldn't use it on command, because it would come in really handy right about now.

I heard Levi yelling at Ruthy behind me and fought the urge to look away. Xander was trying to suck in as much air as he could while on the ground.

I took a step forward and Maye took a step back, but she was watching, waiting, studying me. She was fairly certain I didn't have control over what this was, but she didn't want to risk her life on it.

I held out my hand in her direction and she took another step back. I didn't know what I was doing and was fairly certain nothing would shoot out of it, but I used Maye's fear to sneak a look at

Ruthy. Her face was still blue and Levi had started compressions. Xander had made it over to her and was helping.

"If she dies, you die." I threatened to Maye.

I could tell whatever fear she had of me was wearing off. Damn it!

"What?" I heard his voice, then looked behind me.

"Drake." I moaned regrettably, as a pit formed in my stomach. Maye could take me out right here. These were my closest friends, and all she had to do was flick her wrist. I took another step toward Maye, my hand still outstretched. "Take them all. Portal them out of here now." I commanded Drake.

"And you?"

"Get them out of here."

"Cami." Xander said, his tone a cross between anger and understanding.

"It was always going to be this way. We all knew it." I whispered. "Xander. Get the woman and get Levi and Ruthy out. Drake. Save Ruthy and don't come back for me."

Xander hesitated a moment, then sprinted to get the woman off the ground.

"She won't forgive you." Drake said.

"At least she'll be alive to be mad at me. Tell her I love her and that I'm sorry."

Drake opened a portal with one hand while looking at me. Xander ran the woman through and was looking back, waiting for Levi to bring Ruthy through.

"Go." I commanded softly. "I get to go see Asher." I smiled, a single tear rolling down my cheek.

He stepped through the portal, saying nothing. Before the portal completely closed, an image of the pack house stood in the background with a woman in a flowing dress on the balcony.

Anastasia.

She was looking out across the night sky, waiting for us to come home. Could she see me? Did she know I wasn't coming back? Would she understand my decision?

I wiped my cheek, then turned back to Maye, dropping my hand.

"That was so emotional." She mocked.

"Eat glass."

HISTORY OF THE MOON GODDESS

MAYE PORTALED US TO the front of the large gray compound. It was tucked away in the middle of the woods, with tall trees surrounding it and pine needles scattered on the ground. There were several single doors that lined the front of the long building, but only one set of double doors which had two men standing in front of them. There were several others walking around looking confused, not sure if they should prepare to leave for a fight or not. Maye didn't seem to care. She had what she wanted.

Me.

I tried reaching out to Ruthy or Xander several times to see if she was ok, but I was met with silence. I figured I would be, but I had to try. Images of the moment she passed through the portal replayed in my mind. She looked so blue, and I could see the worry in Drake's eyes. Maye had her in the air for a while and I knew there was no way a human could make it that long. My only hope was Drake could pull off a miracle... he had to.

A large clack startled me, bringing me back to the compound. I looked around, trying to find the source, but nothing stood out and Maye seemed unfazed.

She brushed past the two guards and pushed the doors open with a flick of her wrist. Once inside, I immediately started taking notes of hallways, doors, exits, anything to help me formulate a plan of escape.

"I wouldn't waste your time." Maye called over her shoulder.

"What do you mean?"

"What you're doing... trying to figure out how to get out of here. It's not going to happen. All the exits have magic on them."

"What kind of magic?"

She looked over her shoulder, a sly smile playing on her lips. "Wouldn't you like to know? I guess it doesn't matter since you aren't a witch and you may or may not be dead soon."

Her confidence and my lack of plan caused a shiver to shoot down my spine.

"The doors only open for me and a select few... blood magic."

I grimaced. Even the name blood magic sounded dark. "So not all the Crows could get out?"

She laughed and clapped her hands at a Crow standing by the wall and pointed. He obviously knew what she meant, even though she didn't speak. A moment later, he was opening a door I hadn't even noticed because it blended into the wall so well. This was going to be impossible!

"No. I made a few changes when I took over, doled out ranks and such, making it more official and creating more loyalty among those closest to me."

"So if something happens, then what? All the other Crows are stuck either inside or out?"

She looked over her shoulder again and smiled. I couldn't help but wonder if all the Crows knew that.

A moment later, I recognized the hall we were in from the last time I was here. The flickering lights still cast ominous shadows on the drabby, gray stone and the clacking of heels danced around with the faint hint of mildew. I saw the door up ahead, which led to the outside courtyard where Luna and Asher were waiting. I felt my heart flutter with excitement and then panic. I desperately wanted to see him, but the other part of me was nervous about what I would find. What would he look like? Had Maye and the Crows tortured him more? My excitement transformed into anger.

"I really wish this could have worked out differently, you know." Maye said, pulling me back to the present.

"There's still time."

She laughed. "Such the optimist."

"Realist." I mumbled under my breath, slowing at the door to the courtyard.

"Oh no. We're not going out there." She said as the Crow behind me shoved me forward.

Asher! I'm here. Can you hear me?

Silence.

The Crow pushed me forward again, but I glared at him and pushed back toward the door. I grabbed the handle, twisting, but it wouldn't open. Damn it! "Asher!" I yelled, pounding on the door. "Asher!"

The Crow grabbed my wrist and tried to pull it off, but I felt my wolf come just to the surface, letting out a ferocious growl. The Crow stutter stepped backwards.

"Get control of her!" Maye shouted.

"Don't touch me!" I seethed. "Asher!" I banged again and then grabbed at the handle, pulling it from the door.

"Cami?" I heard from the other side and excitement shot through me like a firework exploding into the sky.

"Asher!" I banged again. "I'm coming for you! I'm coming for you!"

Maye mocked in a high-pitched voice. "Asher, I'm coming for you."

My hardened gaze narrowed on her face.

She shivered in mock terror. "It's really sweet how much you two love one another... too bad it won't last."

"Shut up!" I barked.

The Crow seemed to have regained his courage because he grabbed both my arms, pinning them behind my back, causing my shoulders to scream out in pain. "Let's go!" He pushed forward, nearly lifting me off the ground, causing me to cry out in agony.

"Gentle James. We don't want to break her before the ceremony."

I heard a growl from the other side of the door.

"Someone go put that wolf in his place!" Maye shouted, but there was no one else in the hall. She spun around in annoyance. "It's so hard to find good help."

I shrugged, apathetic to her problem.

"Let's go."

I started moving forward on my own because I didn't want to have my shoulder dislocated, nor did I want to be the reason Asher got hurt.

"I love the compliance."

I rolled my eyes. "Where are we going?"

"Wouldn't you like to know?"

She sounded like a grade schooler, if only she'd added a na na na na boo boo behind it. "Yes, I would like to know, which is why I asked. Typically, how those things work."

She snarled her upper lip and then turned around, continuing to walk down the hall.

I glanced over my shoulder at the door to Asher.

"Keep moving!" He barked.

"I am!"

"We're here." Maye said, opening a door.

"Goody."

"I love your enthusiasm. You keep it up and I'll let you go see your beloved."

I sighed, but didn't speak. My mouth would get me in trouble.

I walked into an open room with only a large table in the middle and chairs scattered around the perimeter, like someone had shoved them out of the way in a hurry. There were a dozen open books on the table, some candles, a small golden bowl that looked like it was a thousand years old, and maps tacked to the walls. I realized this was her makeshift library.

"Leave us!" she commanded to the Crow.

He backed out of the room, shutting the door.

I stood near the door, watching her as she moved around the table, letting her fingers gently glide across the surface, flipping a page here or there in the books. I waited for her to speak as I glanced around the room, trying to figure out what I was looking at.

The map tacked to the wall had red circles around the country with numbers written in each circle. They ranged from the teens to several hundred. I felt bile rising in my throat as I realized that was probably the number of Red Crows in those specific areas. I did the quick math and determined there were close to one thousands she knew about. Had she reached out to all of them? Were they here or close to here or on their way? What did these numbers mean? If that was the case, we were severely outnumbered and there was no way I could get word to Ruthy... if she was even alive.

Damn it! I wish I could reach out to them! How was I going to break that news to Asher? Did I even try or just not say anything and hope for the best since I didn't know?

"There's a lot of people who hate you and your kind." She said, following my eyes to the map.

"Sucks, because I did nothing to them."

She shrugged. "A little."

I waited for some other snide remark, but it never came. I moved closer to the table. "What I don't get is why?" She looked up at me, but didn't speak, so I continued. "Why do all of this? I thought we were friends, or at the very least, not enemies."

"We aren't enemies."

I choked out a laugh.

"We aren't. At least you're not my enemy. You're more of a means to an end."

"A means to an end? Not your enemy? How can you say that when you want to kill me and everyone I love?"

She looked up at me like she wanted to say something, but held it back. "Sometimes sacrifices have to be made for the greater good."

"Your brother?"

She nodded and placed her hand on the center of a book. "There's so much you don't know... that we don't know about the power of the moonstone."

"Because everyone has died."

She nodded. "Everyone but you and the other shifters."

"The book from Ellsmire."

She nodded. "Yes. I placed that book in your room, hoping it would catch your attention. I wanted it to give you hope, to show you that your siblings and you could complete the ceremony and not die... not like the others. Witches can't go through the transformation like shifters can."

"Transformation?"

She bobbled her head from side to side. "In a way. You felt it inside of you? Yes? Kayden said he felt it, clawing at him from within."

"You make it sound like it's alive."

"It is, in a way. The Trinity ceremony awakens it within you. You all angered it when you didn't complete the ceremony the first time, which caused it to feed off you, making you all weak."

I scrunched my nose as a shiver shot down my spine. "Again, please stop talking about it like that. It's creeping me out."

She shrugged.

"What do you know about it?" I rolled my eyes, realizing I called it an it.

She smiled briefly at my mistake. "There are not a lot of books." Her hands trailed along the table. "This book though." She picked up a small notebook wrapped in leather and twine. "This one supposedly belonged to the family of the late Alexandria."

The name rang a bell. "The original shifter?" I questioned.

"Yes!" Maye clapped her hands together. "You paid attention." She carefully thumbed through the cream-colored pages. "This is an ancient book that I... acquired from a storage facility in Virginia."

"You stole it?"

She chuckled. "I plan to give it back. I was merely borrowing it. Anyway, it is full of information about that day."

"How? It happened how many years ago?"

"Many years ago, in 600 sometime. The stories were passed down from generation to generation to generation and eventually written in this book."

"What does it say?" I couldn't help but get caught up in the mystery of it all, I thought regrettably.

A satisfied smile spread across her lips. I had walked into the trap she skillfully laid out. "Take a look."

"Really?"

She nodded, holding the book out.

I walked over and gently grabbed it from her. I felt like the book was going to crumble in my hands if I moved too fast.

She laughed, and as if reading my mind, she said, "It isn't that old."

I opened the book and saw a barely legible hand writing slanted across the page in black thick ink. I tried reading the words on the page, but couldn't understand anything. Was this some sort of test? I flipped through a few more pages and they were all the same. In the middle of the book were a few charts and pictures which looked to be the moon or the sun and some other figures or shapes around it. There were lines connecting shapes and interconnected triangles and other symbols I couldn't quite make out. "What is all this?"

She looked across the table at the page I was on and answered, "I'm still trying to figure it out, but I think that's detailing information about what they understood the Trinity curse and ceremony to be."

"What do the pages say?"

"I haven't been able to decipher all of them yet. But from what I can gather, they performed the ceremony and created the moon-stone and went back into the woods, which corroborates what the old lady saw who everyone dismissed. They didn't know what had happened or what the moonstone was, but said they felt a calling to them for weeks leading up to the ceremony. It mentions that her and her brothers had been apart for several years, but something drew them to this place out of the woods. She mentioned a sort of humming that connected them all and the feeling of what I think she calls a Gichun or their spirit animal moving through them."

I nodded, "I wouldn't really call it a spirit animal... there was this energy, though, for sure."

"Kayden said the same thing when he was trying to help me figure these out."

I nodded and watched as she showed no hint of emotion when she said his name.

"Did you ever like him? Love him?" I caught myself asking before I could stop.

She looked up, startled by the question, probably no less shocked than me trying to figure out why I was asking it. Why did I care if she liked him or not?

"Your brother?" She shrugged. "I don't know. He gave me attention, and I liked it. I enjoyed knowing I was his person, the one he depended on." She looked at the ceiling for a minute, "But no, I don't think I ever liked him like he thought I did." She shrugged apathetically and looked back at the books on the table. "Do you want to keep talking about your brother or the books?" She glanced at her watch. "I'd say we don't have much time."

"Time until what?"

She smiled mirthlessly. "You'll see." She motioned towards the book in my hand.

I looked down at it, confused because I couldn't make out what any of it said and the pictures were confusing.

"Keep flipping." She encouraged.

There was more text followed by more pictures. These pages had more triangles and circles with dotted lines connecting them and symbols drawn. "What does all this mean?"

"Alexandria was very curious about the moonstone and the powers it held. Her brothers could not care less, it seems. She talked with many witches and their elders at the time about it, but no one had any information. After so many questions and her describing what she and her brothers went through and what she had felt, people began to doubt her and she was eventually shunned and had to leave her village."

"That sucks."

"But she didn't stop believing. She knew she had something special, but didn't know how to use it or why it had been granted to her- she felt chosen. She wrapped it in a wire basket to hang it around her neck, keeping it close to her. After years, she began noticing the people around her were aging, but not her."

I could see the excitement in her eyes. She thought it would give her immortality? I shook my head at the absurdity. "So she was immortal?"

She held her finger up. "I'm not sure. She didn't get enough time to figure it out." She walked down the edge of the table, resting her hand on another book. "When she would go into the nearby village to get supplies, others noticed the same thing, and they started calling her the Uhmbata."

"Uhmbata?"

"Magic Goddess." She smiled. "They thought she had special powers and could grant wishes, health, good crops, and so on. They would bring her food and other things as payment and as word spread of the Uhmbata, people far and wide traveled to see her. She used her wolf to scare off bandits and would boil the moonstone in water to heal them."

"Did it work?"

She shrugged. "The townspeople thought it did, but no one can say for certain. Witch councils from all around descended on the small village and tried to kill her."

"Why?" I stepped back in shock.

She chuckled. "They felt like she was using some sort of dark magic because she had been tainted with the Trinity curse. She was a shifter and shifters don't have magic. She tried to run, but they teamed up against her and when they cast a spell onto her, it hit the moonstone, sending her backwards. A pulse of light shot out from around her before retracting and shooting up into the sky. The book says the sky illuminated, and the stars created thousands of dancing animals and the moon shined its light down, absorbing her into the sky."

"They killed her?"

She shook her head. Irritation spread across her face at the fact I had missed the major point of the story. "The moon absorbed her into the sky, welcoming her there... she was a goddess." She sighed at my dumbfounded look. "She became the moon goddess."

"Alexandria became the Moon Goddess?"

Maye nodded. "Yes. The power of the moonstone had protected her from those who sought to do her harm."

I was trying to wrap my head around everything. "And that's what you want?"

She shrugged her shoulders and answered unconvincingly, "Not really the Moon Goddess, no."

"So, what do you want? Out of the stone?"

"I want power."

"You seem to already have that."

She laughed. "I don't have enough."

"What do you want to do with the power? Alexandria seemed to do good with it. Not quite certain you fall into the same category."

She shook her head. "It's easy for you to sit here and condemn me for my actions, but not look at your own."

My head snapped back in confusion. "What are you talking about?"

"You've killed people, but you're not a monster."

"Because you sent them after me!" I yelled back. "I wanted none of this!" I said, spinning around with my arms in the air. "I wanted to live my life in peace with Asher and my family, but no. I can't have that because of the Red Crows and you."

She shook her head. "You don't deserve to have a family, not when you're the reason mine was taken from me!"

"How am I the reason? You killed your own brother because of your greed. Because you wanted more power. I had nothing to do with that."

"Not my brother, my parents. Though I blame you for George's death, too. Yes, I did initially kill him, but I had a plan to bring him back and you impeded that when you didn't complete the ceremony the first time."

I shrugged apathetically. "I didn't even know your parents... so not sure how I'm responsible for their death."

"The night the Red Crows attacked when you were just over two years old. Ellsmire was in a panic. I remember everyone running around. Oh the Crescents, oh the Crescents, must protect the Donovan Crescents. My parents were part of the team sent to protect you all." She looked at the wall to her left, gathering her thoughts before looking back at me. "You know. They didn't tell my brother and me for weeks they were dead. Here we were taking care of you, loving on you, never knowing that it was because of you three that our parents died."

"You're blaming me- us, for your parent's death even though it was the Crows hatred of us. Things we couldn't help like being a baby, being a Crescent and being a triplet. Those are the things you focus on and blame? Not the hate filled group of the Red Crows who attacked us? Are you really that mental?"

"I blame you all!" She spat back and then caught herself regaining control.

I studied her for a minute because she was acting like she had spilled some secret instead of lashing out.

"I think I've had enough of you for one day." She moved toward me quickly and I flinched. She grabbed my arm and pushed me out of the door. "Take her outside with the others." She snapped at the Crow standing in the hall.

He jumped to attention, grabbing my other arm and pushed me down the hall. His grip was so firm on my arm that my hand was tingling by the time we reached the door. He grabbed a pair of shackles off a hook on the wall and pushed the door open. I quickly scanned the yard, looking for Asher. My heart nearly burst out of my chest when I saw him. I was so happy to see him and I felt a light stirring within, which was no doubt my wolf, happy to see him as well.

The Crow shoved me on the ground and reached down for my wrist to bind them and hook me to the tree. I looked at Asher, eager to touch him, kiss him, just be near him, but I waited until the Crow was gone.

The door shut, and I slid my butt over to be near him and he did the same. I leaned forward, eager for his kiss and the feel of his lips on mine. When they touched, I felt my body ignite and the world around us melt away. I savored his sweet kiss, not wanting to pull our lips apart, but also needed to breathe and to see him- just rest my eyes on him.

He looked mostly ok, a few scratch marks here and there across his dirt covered face. His hair was tousled and his clothes had a few rips, but mostly he looked good.

"Asher." I breathed out his name.

"Cami." His eyes twinkled.

"Are you ok?"

"Better now I can see you. I heard you banging and screaming earlier, and then there was nothing. I was so scared they had done something to you."

"No, not really."

He shook his head. "How are things? How's everyone? Why are you here?"

I panicked for a second. How was I going to tell him about Ruthy, or did I lie to him? I stared at him for a second too long.

"He's not going to disappear you know." Luna said, sliding around the tree.

I had forgotten she was here, but thankful for the interruption.

"You seem the same." I said, looking at her.

She smirked. "I'm fine, if that's what you're asking."

"I wasn't."

She sucked her teeth, sneering at me. After a beat she asked in a more sincere tone, "I'm taking it that your brother is still the duplicitous jackhole he was before?"

I shook my head at both her accusation and the fact I wanted to defend him. "I don't know what you're talking about."

She shook her head in disbelief.

I looked between the two of them. "What's going on?"

Asher grimaced. "He didn't tell you, did he?"

"Tell me what?" My heart sank.

BLOODLINES

"UNBELIEVABLE!" LUNA SHOUTED. "I should have known." She put her face in her hands and rubbed before looking up at the sky, as if it was going to have answers for her.

"What's going on?" I asked again.

"I shouldn't have trusted him. My gut told me not to trust him." She yelled out, clenching her fists.

"Luna." Asher tried to calm her.

She snapped her head at him with her finger in the air. "Don't Luna me. How are you not angrier than me? She's your mate and I can barely stand her!"

"Can someone please tell me what in the hell is going on?" I yelled.

Luna and Asher both looked at me, but didn't speak.

"Today would be nice."

Luna sighed. "I risked my life! My life! To get your low down, deceitful, prick of a brother to you because he promised to deliver a very important message."

"Which is?"

"You can't be here." Luna continued. "He was supposed to tell you under no circumstances were you to come here. I was hoping Maye would not get Asher, but even if she did, he was supposed to tell you not to come!" She gazed at Asher, who shrugged his shoulders. "When I saw Asher, I had hoped your brother would give you the message. I was ready to die for you, and I'm sure Asher would be more than willing."

He nodded as a pit formed in my stomach. I started shaking, putting any and all ideas of Asher dying out of my head. "He delivered the message." I said under my breath.

"He what?" Luna snapped her head in my direction.

"He told me. He landed on our front doorstep and he told me."

"Why are you here, then?" She questioned slowly, anger dripping off every word.

My gaze paused on Asher and she understood.

"Unbelievable." She spat, causing me to flinch. "You..." She sighed. "You're willing to give up your entire species, potentially your life, to protect him." She threw her hands out in Asher's direction.

Asher looked at me, his voice low and disappointed. "Cami."

I tried to defend myself, but knew the words I said wouldn't make it any better. "It was a trade. Me for you."

"And you believed her?" Luna yelled.

"She said she would send him back to me piece by piece if I didn't. What other choice did I have?"

Luna sighed and looked away. "I get it... but... you can't be here. You should have found another way. Sent Ruthy or someone else, put a plan together." She sounded defeated.

"Why?"

"Aside from the obvious reasons and you're the only person who can help her..."

"Only person?"

"Pretty much. It's why she poisoned Kayden."

"Chloe?"

"Not ideal."

"I don't understand."

Luna ran her fingers through her hair. "Where do I even start?"

"At the beginning Luna. That's where you start!"

Her eyes narrowed before she spoke. "Several hundred years ago-"

"Hilarious." I said sarcastically.

"This isn't a joke." She answered with a straight face. "As I was saying... several hundred years ago, there were a group of shifters who were triplets."

"Yes. I know. Alexandria and her two brothers." I had forgotten their names, but remembered the spot in the History of the Trinity book.

"So you know about her?" Luna seemed surprised.

"Yes. I read about them in the book that I just found out Maye had planted in my room at Ellsmire, and then we just spoke about it a minute ago."

"In her war room?"

I nodded.

"What else did you see in there?" Luna asked, getting off topic.

I shrugged. "There were books on the table and maps on the wall, which looked to be locations of Red Crows. Quick math said there are close to a thousand."

Luna flinched. "That's more than I counted."

I looked at her and she continued.

"Briefly. I tried to get information for the Council, but she figured out I was snooping and threw me out here." She paused for a second, looking around. "She doesn't trust anyone, but I was able to put together bits and pieces of her plan. Even if she is a psychopathic jackhole, she is very smart."

"Were you able to find out anything or get any information back to Ellsmire?"

She shook her head and then shifted the topic. "Did she tell you about the books?"

"I thought you were supposed to be telling me what's going on."

"Well, you obviously have some of the pieces and I don't want to waste time repeating them, plus I need to have the information you have to see if anything has changed."

"Like what?"

"Her plan for you." She stated matter-of-factly.

"For me?"

Luna nodded impatiently. "I'm getting there. Let's get back to what was in the room first."

I sighed heavily, but played along with whatever she had going on right now. "The books. I didn't really see them. She handed me a small one, and it was written in some old language I couldn't read, and there were maps and drawings of circles and triangles and dotted lines."

"Did she say anything about them?"

"No, not really. I mean, she told me the story about Alexandria."

"Yes, yes. That. What did she say?" Luna scooted closer to me, leaning in.

"She told me Alexandria studied the stone and tried to learn more about it, but was banished and then ended up becoming the Yumlata or something of another village."

"The Uhmbata."

"Yes, that."

Luna rolled her eyes.

"I can't remember everything. There was a lot going on. Plus, I didn't think it was that important."

Luna stifled a chuckle.

"Am I wrong?" I looked at Asher, who still wasn't talking much.

"Yes. So wrong."

"Care to explain?" I quickly added. "The only other thing she said was the witch council came and when they heard about the Uhmbata, they cast a spell, essentially killing her... kind of. Maye said that star animals danced in the sky and the moon pulled her up or something and that Alexandria is the moon goddess."

Luna nodded, smiling. "That's it."

"That's what?" I was getting really tired of asking what was going on.

"Ok, this is going to sound weird and I still have a hard time believing it, but it makes the most sense."

"Well, that sounds reassuring."

Luna looked around again, before scooting in even closer- uncomfortably close. "There is no Crescent curse... rather, no breaking of the Crescent curse."

Relief poured through me, but it was short-lived. "If there's no Crescent curse, then why are we here? Why lie?"

She nodded. "Ok, now I will start over, but you can't interrupt me. I don't have a lot of time."

I nodded, not knowing what she meant, since they chained us to a tree.

"After the Council learned about Maye, they had us dig into everything she had touched or been a part of. The council found out she was reading a lot of books about the Trinity curse and Alexandria Delavagne. So naturally, I too started researching her to put all the pieces together. I had a working theory, but I wasn't sure until after you all completed the ceremony. I gathered everything I needed and took it back to Ellsmire to test." She leaned in so her lips were lightly brushing my ear. "You're a descendant of Alexandria." She pulled away and watched me, waiting for a reaction.

I stared at her, completely dumbfounded. "The moon goddess?"

She bobbled her head from side to side. "Yes. It was hard to track, but Maye had managed to put the pieces together. The Donovan line comes from Delavagne, Alexandria Delvagne. I mean, so did a lot of others, but they aren't a triplet and, in your case, an alpha."

"Some alpha I am." I threw my hands out, showing I had got myself caught.

"It's fine. I'm sure Ruthy's having a blast bossing everyone around. She was always a bit much, but I imagine she's very good at beta."

I didn't speak, and she tilted her head for a second, clearly picking up on my awkwardness, but continued talking. "Maye has orchestrated this whole thing to get you here. Well, not just you, but she wants a big fight, including the Council."

"She wants to recreate what happened to the moon goddess."

Luna touched her nose, then pointed at me. "Yes."

"Does she really think that's going to work? I mean sure, Alexandria existed, we can prove that, but do we really think Alexandria transcended the celestial plane and became the moon goddess? And how exactly did you prove I'm a descendant of hers?"

"I might have used some of your blood that I drew after the battle to do some research of my own."

"You took my blood and tested it without me knowing?"

"You knew I was taking your blood."

"Yes, and to be fair, you took it at the height of confusion when I was distracted by Asher's state and the betrayal of my brother."

"I may have known you wouldn't fight me or know what was going on, so I seized the opportunity." She patted my knee. "If it makes you feel better, I had my mother's permission."

"Mira?"

She nodded. "She understood how important it was to get a sample of your blood."

I stared at her without speaking for a moment, not really sure what to say. I felt like I should be angrier, but I trusted Mira.

After a few minutes had passed, and I said nothing, she chuckled. "Wow, you took that better than I expected and way better than Asher did."

I leaned against him, eager for his touch. "I'm not happy about it, but oddly enough, I feel like your intentions were good even though I wish you would have told me or asked."

"So you could have said no and fought me on it or asked a thousand questions I didn't have answers to?"

"Yes." I chuckled.

She rolled her eyes. "And that's why I didn't."

I curled into Asher and could almost feel my wolf inside of me purring in delight.

"So cute," she mocked, before continuing, "So anyway, Maye believes you're the answer to all her problems. She pretended there was a spell to break the crescent curse so she could get the Red Crows to protect her." She started using her finger to draw in the dirt. "She also wanted to create enough tension with the Crows and the Crescents so the covens would get involved. She needs their magic, and I practically fell right into her lap when I portaled through the front door." She wiped away the picture she was doodling. "I feel like she's always ten steps ahead. She's been planning this for who knows how long, and she's willing to sacrifice anyone to get what she wants."

"She has lost her ever loving mind."

"Yes." Luna agreed, then continued. "So she had your brother and apparently she tested his blood." She pulled her lips. "I did too, obviously not together, but after the battle. It's how I was able to track him here so quickly."

"You tracked his blood?"

"A little blood spell? Sure. It's very handy." She smiled.

I didn't know how I felt about knowing she had my blood and could track me with magic. It felt very big brother, or sister in this case, I guess.

Luna tapped her chin, perplexed, then huffed. "These chains really do suck," she said, shaking them before letting her hands fall back to her lap. "So I think that's everything."

I stared between her and Asher, trying to think of any questions I had, but was coming up empty. "Wait." I realized. "What does she need me for again?"

"Your blood. You have Alexandria's blood."

"And why not use Kayden's?"

"She feels she needs a female's blood- a powerful female's blood and what's stronger than an alpha's blood."

"So, what is she going to do with it?" I feared the answer.

Luna shrugged. "I don't know how she plans on using it, only that whatever her plan is, she thinks it will set Alexandria free from her curse and she will be repaid with immense amount of power or possibly even ascend the throne of the moon goddess."

"She's using Alexandria as her personal genie in a bottle?"

"Something like that."

The door opened from the compound out into the yard and two Crows walked out.

"Right on time." Luna said, scooting away from me.

I looked at Asher and he shook his head like he knew Luna was planning something, but didn't agree with it.

She whistled to get their attention. The first Crow, a large woman with long brown hair and tattered jean shorts, walked over, gagging as she stepped past me.

"Real mature."

"Watch your mouth Crescent. You may be the alpha of your pack, but you're nothing here. You're worse than nothing." She spat, kicking dirt at me.

"If I was nothing, then why do you have me chained to a tree as a hostage?"

Luna clapped her hands lightly, drawing the attention back to her. "So I need to use the ladies room. I was told by the last set of you all, I'd be able to go."

"Here's your bathroom," the Crow waved her hand to the ground.

"Are you- that's gross. I'm not an animal like all of you."

I watched Luna play this pretentious, prissy character and found it amusing, especially since she had lived in the woods for years when she was partnered with Lucian.

"I could always call Maye out here."

The Crow's eyes shot open. "No. I'll take you." She looked at Asher and me, "But one at a time, and don't get any ideas."

Luna held up her fingers. "Scouts honor."

The Crow bent down and started working the cuffs around Luna's wrist. When she was unhooked from the tree, she rubbed her wrist and circled them in the air, stretching them and then her back, reaching up to the sky. I couldn't figure out what she was doing and the other Crow must have also got curious because he stepped closer.

"Let's go." The female Crow said, pushing her towards the door.

Luna stumbled a few times and then regained her footing. "You could have just asked." She huffed, looking over her shoulder at us.

What is she doing? I sighed, forgetting we couldn't mindlink. "What is she doing?"

He watched them walk into the compound. "I don't know. When we realized you were here, she started rambling about some sort of plan."

"About that." I looked up at him. "You were prepared to die for me?"

"Seems cliche, I know, but it's true. I showed up right after your brother left and Luna was mad. Like mad, mad. I guess she had devised some other plan to get herself out, and then I came along. She filled me in on everything, so I only hoped your brother had gotten back like he was supposed to. What happened when he got back?"

"Yes. Right when we were cut off." I snuggled in close to him, resting my head on his chest listening to the steady thump of his heartbeat. "I thought the knock on the door was you, surprising me, but it wasn't." My lips pinched into a hard line. "I was so worried about you."

"I know, I'm sorry."

"What happened?"

"I was talking to you and not paying attention. They ambushed us. They knocked Cecile out and threw her down an embankment. Is she... is she ok?"

I nodded. "Yes, I think so. She was breathing, but wasn't alert. Her body had stopped bleeding and had started to heal, but there were still scrapes on her and she wasn't awake. Drake and the team took her back to the pack house to get her cleaned up. Xander and Levi had done some math and calculated where you were likely abducted from and then..." I paused and he picked up on it and gently shook my arm. "I was having a vision and Maye had somehow pried herself into my vision. She told me she wanted to make a trade."

"I feel so guilty."

"Why?"

"She was running with me back to the pack house when they attacked us."

"You couldn't have known what was going to happen."

"No, I know that, but..." His words drifted away while he absent-mindedly rubbed my back as best he could.

"Tell me about her."

He shifted and looked down at me as tears slowly filled his eyes. "She looks like my mom Cami, at least what I can remember. When I first saw her, I stopped dead in my tracks. I knew my mother was dead, but seeing her twin... I nearly crumpled to the ground."

I grabbed his hand, interlacing our fingers.

"She saw me and her mouth dropped open. She knew me instantly and ran over to give me a hug. I told her what had happened when she asked about my parents. She seemed to have already known, but was looking for confirmation. She had mentioned she felt something through their twin bond all those years ago and was scared something had happened. She tried finding me, but couldn't." He added. "My parents had gone to great lengths to hide me and their relationship from everyone."

"They were scared of the Crescent curse?"

He nodded and then continued, "Cecile is the beta of her back. She's strong like my mother. I also met my uncle and a few cousins and," he shifted. "I met my grandparents."

"Asher, that's amazing!"

"I can't wait for you to meet them all. They all said my mother would have loved you."

I smiled, feeling a warmness move throughout my body, then yawned as the mental and physical exhaustion caught up to me. I scooted into Asher, letting him wrap his arms around me, and sat there by the tree, under the stars. If I tried hard enough, I could ignore the chains on our wrists and pretend we were in the field at our house, his parent's old house, camping out after a deliciously prepared picnic.

"I love you Cams."

"I love you, Ash." I smiled and turned to look up at him. As we basked in this moment, I gave him a soft kiss, letting our lips linger for a moment.

The door to the compound swung open with such force it startled both of us into an upright position.

"What has Luna done?" Asher mumbled under his breath.

"You two. Stand." The Crow commanded.

We shifted awkwardly, standing with a slight hunch since our chains were caught around a root on the tree.

He unclamped the chains. "You try to escape or fight us in any way and we'll end you."

"You won't." I said sharply.

The Crow snapped his head in my direction and raised his hand at me.

Asher stepped between us. "I wouldn't do that if I were you," he said in his low alpha voice.

Heat rose in my core with his show of dominance, though I felt it was partially my wolf responding because I could almost feel her prancing with glee inside.

The Crow lowered his hand and turned to walk inside while Asher cast a glance over his shoulder.

I shrugged and mouthed sorry, but I wasn't. I hated what the Crows stood for, I hated being here and I hated not knowing what was going on or what we were possibly walking into.

"Down the hall." A second Crow grunted from inside, pointing down the way.

The first opened a door and sitting at a table was Luna, with a tray of food in front of her.

"Welcome." She said, before placing a chicken leg in her mouth.

RACE AGAINST THE CLOCK

ASHER AND I WALKED in before they slammed the door behind us.

"Come in, come in." Luna motioned forward, before taking another bite of food. "I'm starving," she moaned. "Here. I got you both some as well." She pointed to two plates on the table.

"What did you do?" Asher asked skeptically, eyeing the food.

She took another bite and looked up at him while she chewed. Once she swallowed, she smiled. "I may have worked out a deal to get us reasonable-ish accommodations and some food."

"Maye isn't that kind, so what did you have to negotiate with?" His words were clipped, like he already knew the answer, but needed to hear her confirm it.

She scrunched her nose up. "I may have used Cami."

"You what?" Asher growled, stepping forward. Luna hurriedly stood from the table and backed away, causing her fork to clang loudly on the cement floor.

"Asher." I stepped forward and placed my hand on his arm.

He looked over at me and noticeably calmed down.

"Easy Romeo." Luna said, regaining control of herself.

I cocked a glance at her, telling her not to push it. "What exactly did you use me for?"

"Nothing you wouldn't have done. I just used it to get us a bed to sleep in and food. Although there are only two beds. Who wants to be my little spoon?"

"Pass." I sat at the table. The smell of chicken wafting up was becoming almost unbearable. I, too, was starving.

"Asher. Care to join us?" Luna motioned to the table.

"Do you plan to tell us what mess you got us into?"

She cackled. "I did not get you into any mess, simply trying to get us, mostly me, out of it alive. But yes, I will tell you."

He sat at the table and it was probably the most awkward dinner I had ever had. Asher was breathing deeply, Luna would take a bite and then look up at us, watching silently, and I stuffed my mouth like it was the first time I ever had food.

After a few minutes had passed, Asher casually reminded, "We're waiting."

"So impatient, isn't he?" she asked before looking at him.

I don't understand why she tried to push us sometimes. It was like she could almost be a decent, likable person if she stopped trying to be such a bitch all the time.

"Fine." She sat her fork down. "I was done anyway, since I don't think they're planning on bringing us dessert."

"Unlikely." I rolled my eyes.

"So on my way back outside, I ran across Maye. She seemed to be in a bit of a tuff so I merely inquired what her problem was. She told me she was having a hard time cracking the last bit of the book, so I said being a descendant of Alexandria perhaps you had latent genetic memories."

"Latent genetic memories? What does that even mean?"

She cut her eyes at the wall, "That perhaps... she would be able to retrieve or cause you to activate those memories-"

"Are you-" I stood up from the table, throwing my chair back. Had Asher not been eating, I probably would have flipped it over on her. "Are you crazy?"

She stared at me like a doe in headlights.

"That doesn't even make any sense. What is she going to do? Stick needles in my brain to access-" I stopped speaking as panic swept over me. Would she do that? She doesn't have the tools, the knowhow, or the knowledge if it could even be done. She would kill me trying. I was going to be sick. The bile was rising fast in my throat and I lurched forward, puking on the ground. Asher ran to stand beside me a second later. I heard a whisper of his voice reprimanding Luna, but I couldn't focus right now. I could only hear the thumping of my heart in my ears, pounding like loud drums. My skin felt clammy and I could feel my hands shaking as I stood up and looked at Luna.

She was standing there with her brows raised, like I was overreacting.

"How could you? She's going to stick needles into my brain and poke and prod for nothing."

"She thought so too."

I continued, without listening to her, still visualizing dozens of long skinny tubular rods sticking out of my head. "That's worse than torture."

"I know."

"How could you? Is there any proof that anything like that exists?"

"Not that I know of."

"It's a waste of time."

"She thought so too."

"I- wait. What?"

She sat down in her chair and grabbed a chicken leg off my plate and started eating it. "You sort of interrupted me, so all that was for nothing." She stretched her neck across the table. "Would you mind cleaning up your vomit? I don't feel like looking at it while I eat or smelling it tonight."

"Wait."

"What?" she whined.

"She's not doing that?" I pointed my finger at my head. "The genetic memories?"

"Goddess no."

"What in the hell Luna?" I stepped forward, wanting to wrap my hands around her throat and squeeze her until she passed out.

"You interrupted me." She said again, more slowly this time, like I hadn't heard her before.

"I heard you the first time. Why would you even say that?" I couldn't finish the sentence because I was so mad at her.

Asher guided me back to the table and picked up my chair off the ground.

Luna took a deep breath and continued eating.

I said as calmly as I could. "Please finish your story and I will try not to interrupt you this time." I was digging my nails into the palm of my hand to help me keep an even tone. Asher must have seen because he gently grabbed my hand and pried it open and slipped his fingers through.

She smiled. "As I was saying, I offered the retrieval of genetic memories, but she didn't think that was a good option. So I may have told her you are the sentimental type and after hearing you're a descendant of the moon goddess, you would probably have a natural curiosity about your family history, since yours has been a bit... turbulent."

I bit my tongue to prevent myself from speaking or lashing out.

She nodded in approval of my silence and kept talking. "You merely need to be your inquisitive, passionate self and go learn about your ancestor and try to help her figure out what happened exactly at the end so she can recreate it."

"And if I don't?"

Luna pulled her face and stuck her fingers in her head like long needles. She laughed, "Too soon? No, but in all seriousness, I imagine if we can't figure out what happened, she will take a best guess, and that will most certainly mean your death. The way I look at it is this way you have an infinitesimal chance of not being bled like a pig and killed." When I didn't speak, she looked at my plate. "Are you going to eat that?"

I pushed it towards her. "I'm not hungry."

"Goody." She pumped her eyebrows up and down.

"No." Asher said, sliding it back to me. "She's going to eat it." He looked at me. "You're going to eat it. You need to keep your strength up."

I cut my eyes at him, watching him as he picked up the fork and stabbed a few green beans and held them to my mouth.

"Is this some sort of kink thing? If you start calling him daddy, I'll turn myself over to Maye happily."

"Thank you, daddy." I said, biting the green beans off the fork and cutting my eyes at Luna.

She burst out in laughter. "Classic Cami. I love it."

"Should I ring for your shuttle for Maye to come get you now?"

"Oh stop it."

I took the fork from Asher and finished eating while Luna climbed into one of the beds and laid on her back with her arms folded under her head.

"How did you get us in here, though?" I asked curiously, cleaning the puke off the floor with the extra napkins we had.

"I just told her you may be more willing to help if you weren't as pissed and that a bed and food would be a good start."

Asher climbed into the little metal framed twin bed and held his arms open, inviting me to join him. It was going to be a tight fit, but I didn't care. I would sleep on the floor as long as I could be in his arms again.

"No funny business over there, you two. I know how mates act when they're in bed."

"Shut up Luna." Asher mumbled and then pulled me in close to him, so my body molded into his.

"I've missed this so much," he said, breathing into my hair, causing a shiver to go down my spine.

"I missed you too. I was so worried about you." I rolled over so I was facing him. "Please never do anything scary like that again."

"I will try not to, but sometimes being an alpha is going to put us in tight situations."

I rested my hand on his face and stared into his beautiful, bright blue eyes. "Goddess, I love you. With every part of me, I love you."

"Samesies." He said, pressing his lips against mine.

I wrapped my arms around his neck, pulling him towards me and pressing my body against his. My body responded like it usually did around him, but I had to remember where we were and who was in the room with us.

"We should probably go to sleep." He said, panting.

"Probably." I gave him one more quick kiss and then rolled over, pressing my body into his and grabbing his hands that were wrapped around me.

I breathed a few deep breaths to slow my heartbeat down and get my mind relaxed so I could go to sleep. I needed to get as much rest as I could because I felt like tomorrow and the days after were going to be endless days and I just hoped I survived them.

"Wakey, wakey, eggs and bakey."

I heard Maye's voice echo through the room and didn't want to open my eyes because I still felt exhausted, but didn't trust her enough to keep them shut.

"There they are. I hope you had a restful night, because we have a lot ahead of us today."

She thumbed over her shoulder at Luna. "You didn't kill her, did you?"

"Not this time."

"I'm awake," she moaned, sitting up in her bed looking like the bride of Frankenstein.

"She's not a morning person," Maye said, scrunching her nose.

"What time is it?" She moaned again.

"Time to get up. I have your breakfast here. So eat up quickly and give three taps on the door when you're ready. I will need you all in my special room to help me. Just think... you get to help me find a way to get what I want without having to kill you to do it." She pointed her fingers like they were guns before walking out of the room.

"Are we really going to help her?"

"Yea." Luna said, matter-of-factly. "We need to buy as much time as possible to give Ruthy a chance to get a team together."

I took a bite of toast.

"Right Cami?" Luna pressed both her hands on the table and looked at me. I guess it was too much to hope she would let it go a second time.

"What is it?" Asher asked.

I sat my fork down and looked at him, my heart speeding up.

"Cami."

"I didn't know how to tell you."

"Tell me what?" His body tensed and he shifted in his chair so he was looking straight at me.

"When we found Cecile, it was a trap Maye had set. Long story short, Maye cast some spell on Ruthy, essentially strangling her." I tried to erase the images from my mind, but they replayed over and over again.

"Is she dead?" He choked out.

I took a deep breath and my face fell. "I don't know."

"You don't know?" Asher said loudly, causing me to jump back in my seat.

I pinched my eyes shut, trying to hold back the tears. "I don't. Her lips were blue, and she was unresponsive by the time Drake found us and portaled them all home."

"All?"

"Xander, Levi, Ruthy and Cecile."

He was pacing in a circle. "Damn it!" He shouted, causing me to flinch again.

After a few minutes of watching him walk in a circle, he looked up at me. His expression softened, and he walked over and pulled me into his arms. "I'm sorry I yelled. It wasn't directed at you."

"I know." I wrapped my arms around him and let him pull me in tight. "I didn't want to tell you... I didn't know how to tell you because I didn't want to worry you unnecessarily." I hope that's what this was. There was a pit deep in my stomach, wondering how she was doing and if she was alive.

Goddess, I hoped so. My life wouldn't be the same without her in it.

I inhaled Asher's scent to calm my worry. I had to trust in Ruthy, Drake, my parents, and everyone else. Drake would bring in the best healers from Ellsmire.

The door opened, and we all shifted our gaze to Maye, who walked in smiling, then stopped. "Who died?"

I felt Asher's muscles flex under my fingers and squeezed him a little tighter before I pulled away from him. "We're concerned about Ruthy."

She drew her finger to her chin. "Ah yes, your little beta. Unfortunate, really."

Asher took a step forward, and I grabbed his arm, but he pulled it away easily, so I grabbed it again, this time using my strength to hold on. He looked over his shoulder at me, his eyes blazing.

"She's not worth it." I said through clenched teeth.

"Usually I would take offense to that, but this time I agree."

"What do you want?" I asked, stepping in front of Asher, feeling I needed to be some sort of obstacle for him in case he decided to lunge.

"I want you, of course." She cackled. "Well, all of you could be of some use." She looked over our shoulders, "Were you all not going to eat? I don't want to waste food."

I glanced back and realized the conversation around Ruthy had distracted us from eating. "We'll eat that."

Her eyes narrowed into slivers. "I don't want to wait much longer. Next time I won't be as lenient. You have five minutes to eat as much as you can. We have a lot to do today and I don't need you stalling. You stall... well, let's just say you don't want to find out what happens."

"Noted." I nodded, and she left a second later. "Come on." I pulled Asher's hand towards the table. "Someone told me it's best to eat to keep up strength." I winked.

He rolled his eyes as the hint of a smile played on his lips. I could tell he was still worried about Ruthy and I was too, but we had to hope she was fine and not let it distract us from getting back to her and everyone else in one piece.

I grabbed the toast and eggs and piled them on top of one another, taking bite after bite, barely giving myself enough time to breathe. Maye seemed to be a rather fickle individual, so while she was generous and providing food right now, I wanted to take full advantage of it because the next meal was not guaranteed.

In the blink of an eye later, the door was opening again. "Let's go," she barked.

I scooped up the last bit of eggs and toast and shoved it in my mouth, following Asher and Luna out.

We started walking down the hall as Maye passed by me to the front, where Luna was. "I would advise you to not try anything or you will end up like your dear friend, Ruthy."

I placed my hand on my Asher's back. I couldn't feel his emotions, but could tell he was nearly climbing out of his skin.

"In here." Maye directed us into the war room.

I looked at the map on the wall and noticed the numbers hadn't changed, but locations did. Was she actively moving them around the country? I couldn't help but look in the area our pack house was and saw several circles, totaling close to five hundred just off the perimeter, surrounding it on all sides.

I caught Asher's eye and nodded my head towards the map, and he saw the same thing.

Goddess, I wish we could mindlink. It had been so long since I'd heard his voice in my head and I missed that connection. I sighed, then looked at Maye. "What are we doing in here?"

"Luna and Asher are going to help me filter through all of these books and find any and all references of Alexandria, and you're going to look at this book." She held up the small little book she had shown me last night. "I need you to help me decipher the words and find the spell the council had used."

"What if I can't decipher it or the spell isn't in here?"

"I'd rather not think in can'ts and start thinking in cans... for your sake." She shrugged before walking over to the table.

Asher grabbed my hand and I know it was meant to be encouraging or supportive, but I was irritated. I wanted to get out of here. I needed to get out of here.

I picked up the book and started mindlessly flipping through pages.

"There we go! That's the spirit. Isn't this better than sitting outside in the blistering sun chained to a tree all day?"

"So much better." I sniped.

"She means to say thank you." Luna added and I looked at her confused. Since when did she become a kiss ass? She shrugged. "I don't want to go back out there. I hate bugs... and dirt. I'm not a shifter like you two."

I shook my head and continued flipping through the book. "Do you have notes on what you have deciphered so far, or any page references?" I asked in a noncommittal monotone.

"Yes!" She slid over a notebook. "All of my notes are in here."

I opened a page and found the corresponding notes sections and just stared at it. I needed to formulate a plan and figure out how to get to the furnace room Kayden told us about. Even though he was under Drake's truth serum, parts of me wondered if it had worked or if he was just tricking us. We had little time to test anything out, and it was Drake's first time on a shifter.

In some ways, in those last few conversations I had with Kayden, he seemed... different. Something had definitely changed, but I couldn't put my finger on it. I know he'd been spending a lot of time with mom and dad and perhaps they were rubbing off on him, giving him what he'd been missing his entire life.

I needed to find the furnace room, but how was I going to do that with Maye watching me... us?

"You've been on that page for a while."

I looked up, startled. "Yea. I know. I'm trying to figure out what you've done... to get a better understanding, so it will help me on the other pages." I know I completely butchered that excuse, but I was never good on my feet.

She nodded but didn't speak, just watching for a long minute before turning back to Asher and Luna. I flipped a few more pages to show I had progressed if she looked over, but I knew I couldn't keep this up the entire time, so I found the second set of drawings with the symbols and studied it. I grabbed a pencil and paper and recreated the drawing and flipped back and forth through the pages, noting other uses of the symbols in her text, and jotted those down. I had no idea what I was doing, but as long as she thought I did or could help her, then she would leave me alone, which would buy us a little more time. And that's what we needed.

I looked at the clock and saw it had already been several hours. "Maye." I called after her.

"Did you find something?"

"Not yet, but I need the ladies' room."

"Right."

"Me too." Luna chimed. "I've been holding it for a while now."

"I'm not letting you both go at the same time." She looked at Asher. "Although, I guess it doesn't matter. I have your mate, so you wouldn't do anything stupid."

"Wouldn't dream of it." I said deadpan.

She raised her brows. "Down the hall, third door on your right."

We opened the door and the Crow standing outside looked at us, but didn't move or speak, so we plodded past him down the hall.

"Are you finding anything?" Luna whispered.

"No, you?"

"Nothing."

"We need to get out of here."

"No shit. Do you have a plan?"

"Working on it." I still wasn't sure I could trust her. Even though I didn't feel like she was working with Maye, she would also be the type to try and escape without warning and leave us to pick up the pieces.

I grabbed the handle on the door to my left, but it was locked.

"She said on the right dummy."

"Oh. My mistake." I walked across the hall to the bathroom and closed the door in one of the three stalls.

"What's going on?"

"What do you mean?" My voice echoed in the small room.

"That. What was that you just did?"

"I went to the wrong door. Careless mistake."

"Unlikely. The Cami I know is calculated."

I shrugged. "That's the truth. I thought she said third door on the left."

We were washing our hands and with the water still running, she leaned over and whispered, "I have my magic."

I snapped my head in her direction so fast, our lips nearly met. "You what? Can you portal us out of here? Does Maye know?"

She continued washing her hands. "It's weak and I assume Maye has to know. The chains binding us outside stopped it. They had ropes holding me before your brother, but when I got them off, I was able to create a portal, but only for a second. It snapped back so quickly that I think it cut off a piece of his shirt as he was going through. If I were to do that now, I know we all couldn't make it."

"So then, why don't you just go?"

"And leave my ex-lover and BFF? Not a chance."

Again, she could almost be likable...

She cut the water off. "Did I say too much?"

"Not at all. Asher had told me about you two. It was before me, he was in a dark place, and he said it meant nothing." I said coolly before walking out of the door.

"We're back to the left. I know how you get your directions confused."

"Thanks." I said, holding out my thumb and index finger in front of me to make an L.

Luna grabbed my arm and looked at me, her eyes intense and penetrating. "Don't leave me here. When you make a run for it, don't leave me. I know you're working on a plan because I don't think you'd be stupid enough to come here without something."

I nodded. What she didn't know wouldn't hurt...

We got back to the room and Maye looked at us curiously. "Everything come out ok? You were gone for some time."

"Gross." Luna walked over to the notebooks with Asher and continued flipping through the pages.

After several more minutes, Maye clapped her hands. "Who's ready for lunch?"

I was. I needed a break from these pages, from this room. "I could eat something."

Maye looked at the others. "You as well? You didn't say anything so you can stay in here and continue working."

Her voice and her words grated on me. She knew she was in control and was toying with us, throwing it in our face.

Luna and Asher nodded, and we were all walking down the hall a moment later. I saw another door on the left and purposely tripped myself, grabbing the handle to see if it twisted.

Locked. I had hoped the boiler room Kayden talked about would stay unlocked, because who would want to go into that room? I also should have asked more questions about where it was located.

"Did you forget how to walk?" Maye chimed without looking over her shoulder.

"Sorry. I wasn't paying attention and tripped over Luna's feet."

Luna looked over her shoulder at me. "Please watch where you're going. These are my only shoes and I don't need your clumsy self messing them up."

"I said I was sorry."

We walked into another room on the right that was several doors past the bathrooms. There were long tables in the middle of the room with a small kitchen on the back wall, with bins of food lined up, reminding me of the school cafeteria.

"You can grab a plate and fix yourself some food." She pointed.

We all stood around looking at her for a second before making our way over. I had to believe it wasn't poisoned, because that would mean all the food was, although I wouldn't put it past her to poison the entire compound to get to us.

She must have seen our hesitation and stomped over, snatching a plate and grabbed a sandwich and bag of chips and started eating it. "It's all fine." She shook her head.

I went first, mostly because my stomach was growling and because I had high hopes she still needed me for whatever convoluted plan she had. I took two sandwiches and a bag of Doritos and a bag of BBQ Lays and sat at a table different from hers. Asher and Luna came to sit beside me, leaving Maye on her own.

"Well, this is like Ellsmire all over again." She mumbled.

She quickly finished her sandwich, then stood up to leave. She walked to the door, propping her hand on it. "You have about seven minutes before the bell rings and the Crows come in here to eat. I wouldn't get too comfortable if I were you..." She smiled. "I will see you back in my room when you're done."

I took a huge bite of my sandwich and quickly chewed it, swallowing a piece slightly bigger than I should have. I felt the pressure on my throat and through my chest as it made its way down.

I leaned in. "We need to get out of here."

"No shit Sherlock."

I took in a deep breath and continued. "We need to find the boiler room."

"Why?"

I took another bite of food and started chewing it. "We just do."

I looked at the clock. One minute.

I stood up from the table and grabbed the two bags of chips and shoved them in my pockets. I opened a small hole in the top to let the air out and then pinched the bag, causing all the chips to break apart. Bite size. Great. I grabbed what was left of my second sandwich and walked out of the door when I heard the bell ring.

I heard doors opening along the hall from all different directions. While it sucked being in a hall with who knows how many Crows, it was allowing me to peek in each of the rooms and that's when I saw it- a door leading to a staircase.

I made eye contact with Asher and Luna, and they nodded, picking up on the same thing. Hopefully, those stairs led to the boiler room.

We walked back into Maye's room and saw her flipping through pages at the table. She sat the book down. "Oh good. I'm glad you could get out before they came in."

No one spoke, but went back to doing our job- looking through the text to find whatever was needed to get Maye off our backs.

We got back to our room late. Dinner had already been served and while I felt guilty eating two sandwiches at lunch, I wasn't regretting it now.

Maye walked in with a tray of food. "In case you're hungry." She stated simply, with no hint of maliciousness. This was the same Maye I had met at Ellsmire the first time- the one I liked.

"Thanks."

"Are there showers we can use?"

She studied me for a second, then responded. "We have some downstairs. I will have someone guide you all down there in a little."

That worked out better than I had imagined. I tried to contain my excitement. We were getting to go downstairs, giving us a chance to find the boiler room. We could leave tonight or very soon.

"Also, not to be the bearer of bad news, but you have about three days left before the moon is full. After that, regardless of what the books say, I'm moving forward with the spell and that way doesn't bode so well for all of you."

I nodded.

"Eat up and I will send someone by soon." She smiled, then tapped the door frame before leaving.

I was beginning to think she was a legitimate psychopath- her manipulation, intelligence, instant mood swings, her detachment from things. That made her so much more dangerous.

BINDERS PROTECTION

THE NEXT TWO DAYS passed much like the first. Asher, Luna and I were sitting at the table eating our breakfast as we had been doing, looking at each other in silence. Luna had got a piece of lead that fell out of a pencil on the first day, which she pocketed, and that's what we've been using to communicate anything we didn't want anyone else hearing. I had told Asher and Luna what Kayden had shared with me about the furnace room, but we still hadn't found it yet. There were so many doors in this blasted place, and being attached to an invisible tether made it almost impossible to locate it.

But we had to, and soon.

Today was the day.

We find the solution to our problem, escape, or die.

Maye hadn't tried hiding the last option. I guess she thought it would give us extra motivation to find the solution she wanted, but it was hard to find something that didn't exist.

The last two days hadn't been a complete bust, though. I had learned about Alexandria, mostly from Asher, who would tell me what he read about her at night- almost like a bedtime story of a woman's history who had long been forgotten until now. It didn't feel real, to know she was related to me- just the woman, not the supposed moon goddess, which I still wasn't buying. She was a strong woman, not easily swayed off opinions that weren't her own. She had fought in many battles before she was eighteen and had a child- a son named Caldon, who had no named father, but many suspected was the alpha of the pack. He was taken away when they banished her from the pack, which left her heartbroken and eager to return to him. There were rumors after she was supposedly cursed and passed through the celestial plane you could hear her wails of sorrow on a cool night's wind.

It wasn't until Caldon was much older he learned the truth about who he was and where he came from. His grandparents, Alexandria's parents, said little about her, only that she had left when he was very young. He asked around, trying to find out who his father was, but was eventually banished from the pack as well. Not wanting his mother to be forgotten, he began telling stories of the woman who visited the moon and made the stars dance. They were passed down from generation to generation until they compiled them in the book that was written.

"It's almost time." Luna said, looking at the door.

"We're running out of time. Who knows when she's going to say enough is enough?"

"When the moon is at its peak."

"Which is?"

"How am I supposed to know? You two are the shifters."

"You seem to have all the answers."

"Next time, before I'm held hostage, I will study the moon cycles just in case I need to know when the full moon is at its peak."

"Thank you. That's all I can ask for." I said sarcastically, with a smile.

She smiled back, then stopped. "Oh, Goddess no. No. No. No. No."

"What?" I asked, concerned by her sudden panic.

"We're not friends. We're not becoming friends and I don't like you."

"Samesies." I said, smirking.

She sighed, then stood up from the table.

I chuckled before walking over to Asher to wrap my arms around him. I wanted to feel him and hold him as much as I could today. We would find a way out of this, I was certain... just not sure how.

I felt isolated and alone without the ability to mindlink. I wanted to know if Ruthy was okay and when they were planning to come get us. I had paid extra attention to any of the conversations the Crows were having when we were walking in the halls, hoping to hear something about attacks or movement... anything. But it was silent, which only further worried me. If there wasn't movement at the pack house, is that because they were in mourning and without both their alphas and the beta, they didn't know what to do?

I squeezed Asher tighter as fear settled deep in my stomach.

"Good morning." Maye said, entering like a broadway star. "Who is excited about today?"

Luna answered deadpan. "I can hardly contain my excitement."

Maye batted the air. "Today is a big day. Lots of nerves. Lots of plans."

"Do those plans still involve killing us?" I asked, unable to hold the bite from my tongue.

"I hope so." She checked the clock. "Full moon is at its peak tonight at nine after one in the morning, so I guess technically you have until tomorrow, but..." she shrugged.

We started walking towards the door and Maye chuckled. "I love it! Ready to start the day."

"Can we please stop pretending we are here of our own volition? We're here because you won't let us leave and are forcing us to decipher practically ancient text to find a curse... you know what... never mind. Disregard everything I said. I'm pumped for today! Big things are going to happen. I can feel it!" I said, walking faster, passing her in the hall. "Let's go!"

"Excellent!"

I walked into the room and grabbed the book I had been staring at for the last several days. I had gathered part of the drawings were of the trinity ceremony and the triangles represented Alexandria and her brothers and the moonstone was the circle with jagged lines drawn through it. There was another picture that I was trying to decipher, but I still didn't know what it meant. It had a triangle with a curvy line to a circle with another smaller circle inside of it.

I glanced over my shoulder and saw Asher and Luna with their heads huddled together. Luna peeked over Asher's shoulder and looked at me, and I saw something change in her eyes. She took her hand and placed it on Asher's back, scooting closer to him like she couldn't hear what he was saying.

Was she serious right now?

I stood there in shock as I watched her continue to rub his back without him stopping it.

"Are you kidding me?" I slammed the book on the table.

Maye looked up, startled.

"What?" Luna asked, turning around, but not moving away from Asher.

"Your hands Luna, that's what!"

She looked at her hand and then back at me. "We thought we found something, so we were talking about it."

I was fuming. I could feel the rage pouring out of me right now. "Did you need to grope him to do it?"

"What-" She stepped away. "Old habits."

"Old habits, my ass! You've been trying to come between us since the moment you found out he had moved on. Remember the first day you came back to the pack house, trying to weasel your way between us?"

"Cami." Asher patted the air. "Calm down. It's not like that."

"Calm down? Calm down. Did you just..." I spun in a circle. Who was he right now? Telling me to calm down? Letting Luna rub his back? How close had they gotten before I showed up? Oh Goddess! My mind started reeling. This wasn't happening. This was a dream, rather a nightmare. It had to be. I smacked myself in the face, so hard that both my hand and face were equally stinging and hard enough, it should have woken me up.

"What was that for?" Maye asked, curious.

"This has to be a nightmare."

Luna laughed her evil laugh. "Not a nightmare, sweetheart." She put her hand on Asher's arm and I waited for him to move it, but he didn't.

I glared at him, raising my eyebrows and he eventually took his hand, laid it on hers for a brief moment and then picked it up, removing it from his arm.

"Cami," he breathed, the pain in his eyes.

I shook my head. "I can't even. I need some air."

Maye was startled, but obviously enjoying the show.

"No." Luna interjected. "I'll go. You and Asher need to talk about some things."

Maye batted her hand. "Go. But don't stay gone for too long. Cami's life depends on it." She laughed. "Although I guess that doesn't matter to you." She laughed again.

Luna looked at me and then at Asher before leaving.

"I will leave you two as well, although I would love to see what happens."Maye said, walking towards the door.

"Wait!" Asher said. "I have a question. We were talking about something we had found." He watched Luna disappear around the corner and then grabbed the book. Something in the book was more important than talking about our relationship?

I stood watching in utter bewilderment as Maye's face contorted into confusion. Whatever he was showing her she couldn't care less about- it wasn't the big revelation they had thought it was and that's when it hit me. Oh my goddess. That bastard! He and Luna had planned this, so I would lose my mind. How could I have been so stupid? I took in a deep breath and watched him talk to Maye. I hadn't heard most of their conversation because my brain was still reeling.

"I'm going to let you two chat. You don't have long, but you need to find a way to continue to work. I would really hate to kill her. I do genuinely like her."

"I'm right here." I mumbled dryly.

Maye walked out of the room, shutting the door.

Asher rushed over towards me with his hands out, palms up, face torn.

"Stop!" I yelled. "I don't want to hear it!" Then whispered, "Why couldn't you just tell me?"

His face was breaking. Serves him right, I thought briefly, but then felt bad. I pulled him in and pressed my lips against his, taking him into a full kiss. I pulled away. "Of all places to find out! Of all ways to find out!" I pulled him in again, curling my fingers through his hair. I loved him so much and so hard right now.

"I'm sorry. I didn't know how to tell you." He shook his head and mouthed, I'm sorry.

"I don't want to hear it." I ran my fingers up his rippled chest and clasped them behind his neck, pulling his forehead to mine, and whispered, "I love you."

"I should have stopped her. You're my mate and I'm sorry. Please forgive me." He whispered, "It was her idea. She needed a distraction so she could go explore."

I whispered back. "She can't stay gone for too long."

"I know. I don't think she fully thought through the plan, but we're desperate."

I looked at the door, not sure if Maye was still listening or wandering around. "I don't know. It's hard for me to trust and you know I can't stand her. She's been looking for a way between us from day one. Day one. She never gives up."

"I love you Cami."

He reached his arms around me one more time and brought me in and I buried my face in his neck, taking in his scent and whispered. "I love you big."

The door was opening, and I pressed away from Asher like he was forcing me into a hug. "Well, you should have thought of that before." I turned, heartbroken, back to my desk and picked up the book. I felt bad now, slamming it down in anger. It was practically an artifact, hundreds of years old, and should have been treated better than me throwing it down. I patted the book in a silent apology.

"So things are better?" Maye asked.

"I will not blow my top, if that's what you're asking. He said it meant nothing, but I don't know." I looked at Maye. "Maybe I'm just too in my head reading about all of this. I think it's all just getting to me."

"Understandable."

I turned back to the book and didn't speak.

I don't know how much time had passed before Luna walked back in. I know she was gone for a while, but hoped it wasn't too long that Maye would get suspicious.

"Everything gravy in here?" She asked with her hands out to her side.

"Quite the little pot stirrer. You always were." Maye said in disgust.

Luna shrugged and looked at me, waiting for me to say something, but I didn't. I didn't know what to say, and I didn't want to over or under sell it, so I took the road of the silent treatment, which always seemed to speak volumes.

Before I knew it, it was lunchtime, and Maye released us to the cafeteria room. Asher, Luna, and I all walked separately, none of us talking. We grabbed our plates and helped ourselves to the food before sitting at different tables.

"You all try not to kill each other. That would definitely ruin the night."

I flicked my fingers from my head towards her, a sort of silent agreement.

When Maye was out of the room, I heard Luna mumble some-thing and before I could look up, she blurted. "Well, that was fun. The acting Cami. I didn't know you had it in you."

My eyes widened in shock.

"Oh, don't worry. I put up my little cone of silence, but," she held up her finger. "I don't have a lot of time. Whatever magic she has in this place makes me very weak."

"Did you find it?" Asher asked, getting right to the point.

I wanted to yell at her and tell her what she did wasn't cool and they should have told me, but I get why she didn't. She needed the genuine reaction for Maye to believe it. I kept my mouth shut and turned to her, waiting for the answer.

"I did."

"You did?" I asked, surprised, along with a half dozen other emotions.

"Yes. It's downstairs. It was in that corner that had all the boxes in it. The door was behind that. I peeked in, then put all the boxes back, so I don't know if everything else is there like Kayden said it was, but it's a start."

"I guess when we go, we'll have nothing to lose." I looked at the door and saw a Crow walking by. "Save your strength, we may need it later."

She nodded and mumbled something.

I finished eating my food as Maye barreled back in, looking at all of us suspiciously. Damn. The Crow must have seen us talking and when he heard nothing, he reported us.

"What's going on in here?" Maye asked.

"Eating." I said, holding up the last bite of my sandwich.

"You aren't trying to play me, are you?" She pointed to the three of us.

"How?"

"That whole scene earlier."

I put my food down and sighed. "I appreciate you think I'm that good of an actress. No. Everything you saw from me was one hundred percent real and Luna has been a thorn in my side since the day I met her and I don't know what mine and Asher's future holds after today." I pushed back from the table. "If you're done, we can go back to the room."

She studied me for a second. "I believe you."

"Good, because it's the truth." I said apathetically, walking past her and down the hall.

It technically was all the truth. I wasn't acting early, Luna has been a thorn in my side and I really didn't know what our relationship looked like after today since I didn't know what Maye's plan were.

I started backing into how much time we had left. If knowing the peak of the moon was just after one in the morning, she would want us out there definitely an hour before to make sure we were in our places. I couldn't think of why she would have us out earlier than that, but let's say eleven, just to be safe. I looked at the clock when we got back in the room.

Ten hours.

I had ten hours to figure out how to get us all down to the furnace.

We sat in the room, each at our little corners. Luna seemed to have put extra distance between her and Asher to prove to me it was all staged. I knew now it was and I should have known then, but I let my fears and insecurities get to me. But she knew that- Luna knew how I would react and that's what she needed- a blow up.

I stared at the book, planning out our evening. Finish up in here at five, go back to the room, dinner at six, showers at seven, escape soon after. Easy peasy lemon squeezy.

"Something funny?" Maye asked.

I shook my head, not realizing I was smiling.

"Not at all. Just laughing at myself because I've been staring at this book for days and can't seem to figure anything out."

Maye walked over and stood behind me. "Oh, I figured that picture out at lunch."

"Just like that?"

"Just like that. It really makes a lot of sense once you know what it means."

The tone in her voice caused a shiver to go down my spine. I felt like a trap had been set and I was heading straight for it, even though I couldn't see it. Asher must have felt the same thing because I saw him slowly turn in his chair, eyeing us cautiously.

The tension in the room grew heavy as I waited for her to explain what the picture meant. The only thing I could gather was that it was one of the three, likely Alexandria, and the moonstone. There was some connection between them, which was the squiggly lines. I saw that, but not sure what a psychopath would see and how she would twist it to tell the story she wanted.

"I need your blood." She said simply.

"The book says you need my blood?" I know Luna had mentioned it days ago, but I was getting hopeful she was wrong since Maye had said nothing about it.

She chuckled. "Not in so many words." She reached into her pocket and pulled out a little black stone and I felt the air leave my lungs.

The moonstone.

"Is that the?"

She beamed pridefully. "It is."

"May I hold it?"

She turned her head to the side just barely, reaching her hand out to mine. I opened my palm, eager to feel it in my hand, but before she dropped it, she pulled it back. "No. I don't think so." She said before stuffing it back in her pocket.

"All of this for that stupid rock." I said, turning back to the table.

"It's not stupid. This rock holds so much power." I could tell she squeezed the rock through her pants before pulling her hand out.

"That rock causes death and destruction. How many people have been killed over it?"

"You don't understand."

"You're right. I don't."

Maye sighed. "This rock can bring back life. The rock gives the power of the moon to the one who holds it."

"What is the purpose of the rock? Have any of these books talked about it? Given a hint?"

Maye looked around the room, but didn't speak.

"That's what I thought." I spat. "You know what? I'm done." And I was done, both mentally and physically. I had enough of her threats. I had enough of the constant worrying. If it was up to me, I would take that rock and smash it into one thousand pieces.

"You aren't done. You are the opposite of done. We are only just beginning."

"No." I stood up and started walking out of the room and felt a rope wrap itself around my neck. I reached up to pull it away, but there was nothing there. I heard myself gasping for air and I continued scratching at my throat, hoping for a brief reprieve.

"You do not walk out on me." Maye said through clenched teeth.

I felt myself being lifted off the ground, my feet dangling, and the only thing running through my head was a flash of Ruthy in the woods.

I heard a high-pitched whine ringing in my ears and realized it was me trying to suck in air.

"Put her down!" Asher commanded, standing from his seat.

"Stay put Romeo." Maye held her hand out towards him, but waited for him to move.

"She can't breathe!" He cried out.

"I know. It's called punishment."

Luna chimed in, "If she's dead, she can't help you."

"I only need her blood."

"Willingly given. If she doesn't willingly give you her blood, then the spell doesn't work."

"What?" Maye asked, startled. "No." She said uncertainly.

"Yes. It's in the book."

"No. Where? Show me. Show me!" She demanded, looking at the book that Luna was shoving in front of her.

She dropped her arm, and I crashed to the floor in a heap of clothes, gasping for breath, unable to get it in fast enough. Asher was by my side, rubbing my back.

"It's ok. Just breathe, slow breaths." He repeated over and over again.

"She'll be fine." Maye said nonchalantly, like she hadn't almost just killed me.

I used Asher to push off the floor and stood wobbly on my two legs. "You can kill me now because I'll never willingly give you my blood."

She faced me quickly, excited about the challenge I had just laid out in front of her. "Dearest Cami... why do you say things like that? I know you don't mean it and if you thought about it for more than two seconds, you would also know. You will give me your blood willingly. I'm certain of that. Do you know how I know?" She asked with a cocky expression on her face.

I crossed my arms and stared at her.

She chuckled. "You will, because I have what you care about most in this world. What you care about more than your own life."

Asher.

I would do anything to protect him, and she knew it. She didn't even have to say his name, and I felt my heart racing with panic at the thought of what she would do to him just to get me to comply.

"There it is," she grinned maliciously. "The look of realization."

"Cami. No." Asher said, stepping forward. "I'm willing to die to prevent her from getting what she needs to complete the curse."

I looked at him, my heart breaking. "You may be willing to, but I'm not." I said sadly. "I can't be the reason you die. I couldn't handle it."

I heard a gagging sound and looked at Maye, who was pointing in her mouth. "Seriously, you two. Vomit."

I wanted to yell at her. I wanted to lash out. Just because she was a psychopath and pushed everyone close to her away didn't make our love gross. It was beautiful.

"Shall we?"

"What?"

She cocked her head to the side, confused about what I was seeking clarification for.

"Your blood."

My stomach twisted into knots. "Now?"

"No time like the present."

"But the moon."

"We aren't doing the ceremony yet." She laughed, as if I had told the funniest joke. "That will be later tonight."

"Then why do you need my blood now?"

"I'm getting really impatient." She seethed. "I don't need to explain to you why I need it now or if I need it two hours from now. I want it now and you will give it to me now. End of discussion."

I bit my bottom lip, my mind racing, trying to figure out how to get us out of this mess.

Maye raised her eyebrows.

Literally, every fiber of my being wanted to shake my head no and run away, but I couldn't. I couldn't force myself to move, to speak, to act. I just stood there, frozen.

"Cami." Asher quietly urged. "You can't."

I looked at him and felt tears pooling in my eyes.

"I can't not do it." I whispered.

"I'm one person. Think of all the people she will hurt if she gets this power. She will be unstoppable. She will be stronger than anything or anyone."

"We don't know that." I mumbled.

"Cami." He scolded and repeated. "I am one person."

"I heard you the first time, but it doesn't change things. One person or not, you are *my* person."

I felt like I had a truck sitting on my chest. The pressure was almost too much to handle.

"You got this." He reassured me, holding my hand.

"I don't." I started shaking my head quickly. He was giving up. He was giving his life up. "No, Asher. Don't make me do this. Don't." I started sobbing. "I can't do this life without you."

"You can."

"No. I won't." I stopped shaking my head and stood up straight. "I won't live this life without you."I turned to face Maye. "You can kill us both."

"NO!" Asher yelled out.

"Oh my Goddess!" Maye shouted, throwing her hands in the air. "The theatrics."

I jerked to look at Asher. "What?" I asked incredulously. "You can try to save my life, but I can't try to save yours."

His eyes thinned into narrow slits.

"I'm not sorry. Either she gets my blood or she kills us both. I'm not living my life without you."

"How do you even know she will not get your blood and then kill one or both of us?" He rubbed his face.

I had been so concerned with Asher I hadn't thought about that. How naïve was I? My head started reeling, thinking through all the potential outcomes, and nothing was a definite.

"Binders protection magic." Luna jumped in.

I looked at her hopeful. I had no idea what binders magic was, but she seemed upbeat about it and Maye's head dropped, so it seemed like it was something.

Luna repeated, as if she was reciting a textbook definition. "Binders protection magic. A magical contract created by two or more parties and bound through magic. Think of it as a quid pro quo, bound by magic- you do something for her and she does something for you. You could state in the contract, she can willingly have your blood in exchange for protection for the three of us. She won't be able to kill us, at least not immediately, because the spell wears off overtime."

"Wear off? How long?"

Luna shrugged. "It really depends on how big or wide spread your request is. For example, if you ask for protection for yourself, then it would last a lot longer than if you requested to protect the entire world. Magical output or protection, in this case, is the same. It just depends on how many times you split it up."

I nodded slowly, taking it all in. I looked at Maye and she seemed angry, which sent a jolt of hope and joy through me. There was no way she would be this pissed about something that was good for her. "You always were good with the legalities of witchcraft." She boiled, glaring at Luna.

"It was my favorite class." Luna sniped back.

Maye snarled, then conceded. "Yes. Luna is correct. You can create a binder's protection spell."

"So I just say what I want?"

Maye looked at the ceiling. "Yes."

I nodded, "Ok."

"Cami." Asher whispered.

"Stop." I said sternly. "I will not let you die and I can do this binder protection thing to keep us safe, which means she can't kill us, so if the curse she comes up with involves one of us dying, she can't do it." I looked at Maye, waiting for her to correct me.

"She's right."

I nodded again. "Ok. Ok." I felt like a kept repeating myself, because I had so many competing thoughts filtering through my mind and was hopeful for the first time in a long time that Asher or me would not die.

"So... are you going to say it?"

"What do I say?"

"You have to say-"

Luna interrupted. "I will tell her."

I turned all of my attention to Luna. I felt like the next words out of her mouth were going to be the most important ones I had ever heard.

"You will say, I, Camilla Donovan Porter Evans," she rolled her eyes, "creating a binding protection spell with-" she turned to Maye.

"Mabel Marie Manus."

I felt my neck jerk back in shock at her name.

"Mabel Marie Manus, offer to willingly give a small sample of my blood to Mabel and in exchange, she cannot kill myself, Asher

Evans, or Luna Ashwater." She paused, thinking about it for a second. "You need to be specific in your phrasing."

"Ok, thank you."

"Perfect. Can we please get on with it now? I'm growing impatient."

"Yes." I looked between Asher and Maye. Both seemed less than excited, but for very different reasons. "I, Camilla Donovan Porter Evans, creating a binding protection spell with Mabel Marie Manus, offer to willingly give a small, very small sample, of my blood to Mabel and in exchange she cannot kill," I paused looking around the room. "Anyone important to me."

Maye waved her hand in the air. "Fine. Accepted."

I felt a warmth swirl around me and then heard a snap in the air like an electric charge going off.

"Well, that sucked." Luna sulked.

"Kind of a crappy move you just made, especially after she told you about the binders spell." She bobbled her head from side to side. "Although, I guess she hit on your boyfriend in front of your face."

"You all are assuming she's not important to me. I will have you know I think Luna is very important. She has saved my life more times than I want to admit and even though I don't like her most of the time, well... never mind. I just don't like her. She is a thorn in my side."

"Cold." Maye said.

I walked over to Maye. "You may have a small sample."

"A very small sample." She recited my words back to me, however, there was a look in her eye that made me feel uncomfortable, as if she had somehow one upped me, like this was all part of her plan. She grabbed my wrist, twisting it over, and felt for the vein on the inside of my elbow. "Yes, this will do." She grabbed a needle and jabbed it into my arm without care.

I felt a warmth spread across me like my body was emitting some sort of heat and Maye took a step back, staring at me ominously. Could she see it? I looked at Asher and Luna, and their eyes widened.

Maye stepped back in and quickly popped the vial off and pulled the needle from my arm, grabbing a tissue and tossing it at me, hurriedly backing away.

I grabbed the tissue and pressed it on the small bead of blood pooling on the inside of my elbow and the warmth disappeared. I looked at Asher and he gave me a half-hearted smile and I knew he was grateful to still be alive, but not happy with what I had to give up. But really, what was that? A little blood? I don't think she could do much with what I gave her. I started walking out of the room, ready to put all of this behind me once and for all, but she stopped me.

Her voice was silky smooth with a thread of cold, hard steel centered through it. "Cami."

I nervously turned around, afraid of what I would find. I looked at her and saw it, the joyful gleam of celebration on her face. What I had just done?

She stood up straight. The nervousness from a few minutes ago had passed. "You realize when you make those binding spells, you have to be very specific, don't you?"

I nodded slowly.

"Ok." She responded without speaking. I had a shiver go down my back. I looked at Luna, but she didn't know what was going on.

"You're all dismissed for now. I'll see you later tonight, before the ceremony."

I stared at her for one more minute before heading down the hall. "That was weird, right?"

"Yes." Asher said. "She was acting like she won. But how?"

Luna was reciting my binder's agreement silently to herself, occasionally saying a word out loud and pausing on it.

I looked at Asher. "Why were you all looking at me funny in there?"

He looked at me, shocked. "Your eyes were glowing."

"Glowing?"

I wondered if it was the Shiban Sori Mira had told me about. I didn't feel any different aside from the warmth that was dancing over my skin.

We walked into the room and Luna grabbed both of our arms and yelled crap at the same time.

All hope I had quickly vanished.

"What? What happened? Why was she so giddy?"

"You said Maye can't kill the people you love. You left it open for the Crows or anyone else at her request on top of the fact you cast the net so damn wide, who knows how long it will actually last."

"No." I whispered out. My skin got clammy, and I started shaking.

"I told you." She looked up at the ceiling. "I warned you, but you didn't listen. Keep it small Cami... not too wide, and what did you do?" She clasped her hands together and rested her chin on them, batting her lashes, and spoke in a high pitched girly voice. "I want to protect everyone I care about and the entire world and the little animals and the blades of grass." She grabbed her hair. "Waste of time!"

THROUGH THE TUNNEL

DINNER HAD JUST COME and Luna and Asher were sitting at the table, eating. I walked over to join them, but the bundles of nerves in my stomach made me feel like I would vomit if I took a bite of food.

"You have to eat." Luna motioned.

"I know I have to... I just don't want to." I paced in a circle around them. "We have to get out of here."

"I know." Luna said, setting her fork down. "When they come to take us to the showers, we'll leave then. There's usually only one guard down there at that time."

I nodded.

They finished eating, while I picked at a few fries on the plate, waiting patiently for the turn of the door handle. Hours passed, but no one came.

"Do you think they're coming tonight?"

Luna looked between the both of us. "I thought they would." She pulled her face. "The one thing I can't figure out, though, is how she expects the ceremony to go. If she needs the battle and the coven's magic... she is counting on them to show up and rescue us, but what if they don't?"

I tilted my head to the side. "That's true. She's cut us off to coordinate any sort of plan and I have heard no chatter from the Crows about a hint of activity from our packs."

"There's something we're missing. She's smart and I feel like she's planned every detail down to the nth degree."

"Do you think she knows?"

"There's no way."

"Well, obviously, something's changed."

Luna walked over to the door and twisted the handle and it squeaked open. She turned back to look at us, hesitant.

I walked over to stand beside her and looked down the hall. I heard echoes of people in other rooms, but didn't see anyone.

"Do we go?"

She looked from me to Asher, then nodded.

My heart started beating faster. We were doing this. We were going to get out of here.

Luna pressed her finger to her lips, then patted the air down with both her hands. We both nodded and peeked down the hall.

She waved her hand over her shoulder and inched out of the room, back pressed to the wall. We moved quickly, but silently, a few times pausing when we heard Crows getting louder. We reached the door that led downstairs in under a minute. Luna gently twisted the handle, and it also opened. She waved us through and closed the door behind us.

I paused at the top of the steps, listening, but it was quiet. At the bottom of the stairs was a large unfinished room with cement poles reaching floor to ceiling scattered throughout, with a few doors off the perimeter. One was an oversized group shower room with individual stalls, and the second being the furnace room. There were a couple of other doors, but we hadn't gotten the chance to explore those. We were usually followed in and out by guards, which made it difficult, but there was no one here now. Were they getting ready for tonight or was it something else?

We dashed across the empty floor and reached the furnace room. Luna pushed the door open, and we were met with the low hum of the tanks working. We hurried in and shut the door.

The last stop.

I looked around at Asher and Luna, and we all held the same confused look on our face.

This felt too easy.

Without wanting to waste time, Luna shrugged her shoulders, placing her hands palm up, not knowing where to go next. I went back and tried to remember everything Kayden had said and prayed to the goddess he was under Drake's serum and telling the truth. I just had a strange feeling about all this, but didn't want to wait to find out.

There were several furnaces, and he said it was the one in the back which wasn't working. We made our way through the tight space and found one that looked to be very old. I pointed at the furnace and then gave a thumbs up. We could probably talk now because the hum of the furnaces would drown out any noise, but I guess it was better to be safe than sorry since we had made it this far.

I crouched down and saw a rusty grate on the wall, so I squeezed behind the furnace and gripped my finger tips to the rusted metal slats and gave it a gentle shake. I felt it give a little under my fingers, then saw two rusty screws at the top, barely holding it in place. I quickly reached up and twisted. I gripped the grate and gently pulled it off and sat it on the floor. I stuck my head into the opening and felt a cool breeze brush across my face, but couldn't see anything. I pulled back out and looked at both Luna and Asher and shrugged. I realized when Kayden came through, he probably had his powers so he could see in the dark and we were climbing in blind.

It didn't matter, though.

We needed to get out of this place before it was too late.

I started to climb in, but Luna grabbed my ankle. I looked over my shoulder and she pointed at herself, then held up her finger. She wanted to go first, but why? A second later, she wrapped her hands around an invisible ball and a light appeared.

I nodded and backed out so she could lead the way. Asher climbed in and dragged the grate over the hole in the wall. It was still resting on the ground so it didn't cover it all the way, but it was better than nothing.

Luna kept the ball of light floating in front of her while we moved along. I still couldn't get over how easy this was, which left me fearing this was some sort of trap. What would we face on the other side?

Luna stopped abruptly, and I was so caught up in my thoughts I nearly crawled right into her. She looked at me over her shoulder and then pointed ahead.

I peered over her shoulder and saw the tunnel split into a Y. I quickly thought back to my conversation with Kayden and realized he didn't mention a Y and my nerves started getting the better of me. If he was under the serum, he should have told us. We had gone through everything, making it difficult for him to omit key pieces of information. My lips pinched into a flat line as I shrugged. I looked behind me to see if Asher had any thoughts, but he also shook his head.

I looked back at Luna, nodded my head at her, letting her know she could choose a path. I just hoped it was the right one. I had no idea what time it was or how long we had been gone, but I knew the seconds were counting down. I didn't know how long it would take for Maye to realize we were gone, but once she did, it wouldn't take long for the hundreds of Crows to search us out.

I nodded my head at her again, telling her to hurry and decide.

I heard her huff and saw her hold her hand out in the air like she was feeling for something. For what, I had no clue, but she seemed to find what she was looking for because she was veering us to the right a moment later and was crawling a little faster. I had to imagine she also realized time was running out and if this was the wrong way, we needed to know sooner rather than later.

This can't all be for nothing.

It felt like we were crawling for a long time, which made me more and more nervous. If this was the wrong way, the time we had wasted was immeasurable.

We came to a T in the piping, but straight in front of us was a ladder climbing up.

I took a deep breath, staring at it. Was this it? Kayden hadn't mentioned a T either, another fact that could have been useful. I made a decision and pointed up. She pointed at me and then up with two walking fingers.

She wanted me to go first.

Probably in case we had made some wrong turn or were still at the compound, they would get me first. I scrunched my nose and shimmied past her and climbed the stairs.

Goddess, please let this open to the middle of the woods with no Crows in sight. I carefully climbed the worn metal rungs and saw a square door on the side of the wall near the top. I looked back down and saw Asher and Luna looking up at me, and then something caught my eye that caused my stomach to twist with excited anticipation.

Asher's eyes were glowing.

Babe?

He looked around excitedly.

Cami? Cami!

We're so close! We must be away from the compound, away from Maye's spell.

My hands started trembling as I reached for the door to push it open. I gave it a gentle push, but nothing happened. The door swung open after I gave it another firm push. I recoiled, waiting for Crows to descend, but nothing happened.

I poked my head through the hole and saw the woods.

We did it!

I motioned excitedly for Asher and Luna to come up.

I climbed out and stood at the opening, looking around, trying to get my bearings. The sun was setting in the distance, casting an orange glow across everything. I took in a deep breath and realized I could smell everything around me. The wet dirt, the owl in the distance, the sap seeping out of the nearby tree. I hadn't realized how much I had missed my shifter smell when I didn't have it, but to take a deep breath now and...

We did it, I thought again, still in shock.

I listened for any sound, any twigs breaking or hushed whispers, still expecting this to be a trap, but there was nothing.

Asher and Luna climbed out a second later and looked around.

"Where are we?" Luna asked.

"I have no idea, but I don't want to find out. Can you get us home?"

She nodded and started moving her hands around in a circle. "My magic is still a little weak, so when I get the portal open, run through. I don't want it snapping closed around you."

I nodded.

We were going home. I grabbed Asher's hand and squeezed before he pulled me into a deep kiss.

"Goddess, how I've missed you."

"Please wait a few more minutes so you can get a room." Luna said, as the portal was growing. I could see the fields by the pack house coming into view. "Get ready."

I glanced from her to Asher, back to her, just waiting on the signal.

"Ok... now!"

I ran through, followed by Asher.

We turned, waiting for Luna, but she stood there.

"Come on!" I yelled.

She winked before the portal snapped shut.

"What did she do? What happened?" I asked, confused.

"I don't know."

"Where's she going? What is she doing?" I yelled louder. I realized I was worried about her. "This wasn't the plan. She could've made it through."

Asher grabbed my hand, but a ferocious growl distracted us in the distance, quickly approaching. Glowing eyes filled the darkness and were closing in fast. A few at first, and then the number quickly multiplied.

I gripped Asher's hand.

At ease pack! Asher commanded, and the eyes stopped, forming a perimeter around us, but the air was still tense.... Waiting.

A moment later, something shot out of the sky and landed in front of us.

Xander.

"At ease." He mumbled before closing the distance between us. "Alphas!" He moved in and wrapped his arm around my neck before I could say anything. He released me, then hugged Asher.

"Dear Goddess, put some clothes on."

"It is you."

I cocked my head to the side. "Who else would it be?"

He started to speak, then stopped. "It doesn't matter." He hugged me again. "I thought I would never see you again. How did you escape?"

"I didn't think we would either, and as far as escaping... we found the tunnel behind the furnace Kayden had mentioned and escaped that way."

"Did you have any problems?"

"That's the thing. We didn't have a single problem."

He scrunched his nose.

"Right? I felt like we were in some sort of trap."

He looked around. "Let's get you inside."

I nodded, remembering the map on the wall in Maye's war room. There were a bunch of Red Crows around the border of our property. If any of them saw us, they have definitely reported back to her by now.

We need to be ready pack. There are almost a thousand Red Crows surrounding the area, ready to strike at the command.

Everyone looked around for any sign of them, but it was quiet—only the crickets and cicadas playing their nightly serenade.

We all started running back to the pack house, elation souring through me. I leapt into the air and shifted into my wolf, letting her run free. I felt a tingle shoot down my spine as she stretched her legs and took off towards the house. Asher followed suit and was beside me within seconds. My wolf howled into the night air before I could stop her as she, too, was beyond excited to be back home.

How's Ruthy? I mindlinked Xander.

Silence.

Ruthy? I mindlinked her, panicked.

Silence.

I glanced at Asher beside me. His wolf's mouth looked as if he was smiling as the wind raced through his hair. How would I tell him about Ruthy? I had hoped she was ok, that Drake had found a way to save her... but what if he hadn't?

I had noticed something at the field, but paid little attention to it at the time with all the excitement around being back home, but the wolves were acting differently around Xander. There was... a respect. It was brief, but I felt it. They were not stopping for us, but were waiting for him. It wasn't until he gave his power over to us they did as well. For him to do that... oh Goddess. That meant there was no beta, and he assumed the role of beta... of alpha.

My heart lurched, and I felt a weakness spread through me. I stumbled as my legs buckled under the weight.

What is it? Asher asked, worried, skidding to a stop.

I shook my head. How was I going to tell him that his closest friend was gone?

The rest of the pack stopped and stood around us. Asher must have sensed I didn't want them around, so he shifted and turned to face them. "Xander. Get a team of aerials and start patrolling the woods around our pack house. I have to imagine Maye knows we're gone and won't wait long to come after us. She plans on doing the ceremony tonight in a little over four hours. Bryson and Conner, take some wolves, stay in pairs and create a perimeter, use the Crescents too." He looked around. "Where's Ruthy and Drake? I can have her reach out to the other packs and get them here. We're going to need all the help we can get."

Bryson looked uncomfortable, his eyes shifting between Conner and me.

"*You all have your orders. Go.*" I commanded.

They all darted off without hesitation. I would like to think it was because I was their alpha and there was an impending war coming to their doorstep, but it was probably something much worse.

Avoidance.

They didn't want to have to answer the tough questions.

"What is it?" He asked, looking at me, a prickly feeling moving across my body as his nerves and mine combined.

I shifted and stood in front of him. "I don't think..." tears filled my eyes. "I don't think she made it. When we arrived, I felt Xander as alpha. It was brief, but it was there."

He shook his head.

"The only way... that could happen."

His head turned to the side, but his eyes stayed on me. "Don't say it."

"Asher." I used the back of my hand to wipe the tears from my face. "I tried to mindlink her when we got here and..."

"No." He continued to shake his head. "I want to see her."

We started walking towards the house as the world filtered every other noise out except for the pounding in my head as my pulse thumped, thumped, thumped. I chanced a glance at Asher, but his features were tight, his face showing no emotion. I could feel them, though. The pain, the hurt, the doubt, playing over and over again, like they were on a loop.

"What took you so long?" I heard the voice before I saw her. We froze, just by the fire pit. I looked up on the second-floor balcony and leaning against it with Drake by her side, was Ruthy.

I stared at her for a second and then ran full speed, leaping through the air, wrapping my arms around her.

"Put some clothes on, you perv." She said weakly, giving me a hug.

I pulled back, grabbing her by the shoulders as her arms hooked around mine for support. She was weak. Very weak. "What? How?" I looked at Drake and he looked as lost as we were.

Asher landed by me and gave her a slight nudge in the arm.

"I missed you too." She said, smiling. "Let's get inside so I can sit down. I heard all your hubbub out here... and had to come and show you... I'm still kicking."

I nearly carried her and sat her on the couch. There was a bed in the corner of the living room and sheets strewn across the back of the couch. If I had to guess, this is where Ruthy and Drake had been sleeping. "Tell me what happened."

She yawned. "I'm going to let Drake tell you, while I take this healing concoction he made for me." She said, lifting a cup of what looked like green goop.

I turned to Drake and raised my eyebrows, waiting for him to speak.

"I don't know, honestly."

"What do you mean, you don't know?"

Asher grabbed a blanket and wrapped it around me before he sat behind me. With all the commotion, I hadn't even noticed I was still naked.

"I mean, I was fairly certain she was dead. I could barely feel a pulse and then a couple of hours ago, she just sort of opened her eyes."

"Opened her eyes?" My brow furrowed.

"Yes. I brought her back here after you went with Maye. She was blue. I worked on her for hours, trying every trick in the book. I was able to get a pulse, but it was weak, but I didn't care. I called in several healers who looked at her and they all said the same thing... she was dying, but they couldn't figure out why so slow."

"Because I'm a fighter." She mumbled out before gagging on the drink in her hand. "This taste like shit." She pinched her nose and took another sip.

"Something." He winked, squeezing her leg. "Anyway, this morning I checked her pulse and couldn't feel it. I had the pack listen and they said they could barely hear it. And then something happened this afternoon. Like I said, she took a deep breath, gasped and sat up straight. The color started to return to her cheeks." He squeezed her leg again. "I have no idea what happened. A miracle."

Asher sat forward. "What time did you say it happened?"

"I don't know, around three or so, not exactly sure. I wasn't watching the clock or anything."

He looked at me, his eyes excited.

"What?"

"The binder protection spell you made with Maye."

I was confused.

"The spell. You said she can't kill anyone you care about it. Because she had hurt Ruthy... when you made the spell–"

"It brought her back to life!" I exclaimed. "Oh my Goddess. I hadn't even thought of that."

"You performed a binder protection spell? How do you even know about that?"

"Luna. She helped us out."

"Where is she now?" He looked around, like he was expecting her to walk around the corner.

"I don't know. We escaped, and she opened the portal and after we climbed through, she winked at me and the portal snapped shut."

"You don't think she went back, do you?" Asher asked.

I pinched my brows together. "No way. She wanted out of there as much as we did. It would be a death sentence if she went back because she wouldn't have her magic."

Ruthy grabbed my hand, her eyes still weak and tired, but I could see her there, under the surface, fighting. "You need to call on Benji. He's prepared to come out and fight with us. Tell him we're ready."

"How do you know?"

She smiled wickedly. "I've been preparing for this day for months. I knew it was going to come to this, just didn't know when. There are several packs around the country that are committed to fighting with us. I've been..." She took in a deep breath. "I've been watching and following the Red Crow movement for some time now. I didn't tell you because I didn't want you telling me to stop." She looked at the ceiling, then back at me. "There are a lot of them."

I frowned. "I know. We were in her war room." She looked confused, so I clarified, "It's like our library. Anyway, on the wall she had a map. It took me a minute to realize, but I'm pretty sure it was all the Crows around the country. There were a lot hovering around our area. I noticed several times the groups moved around like she's playing chess."

"Kayden says she's been moving them closer for a while now."

"How did we miss that?"

Drake chimed in. "You wouldn't know. They've been keeping a low profile, especially after the moonstone ceremony. Kayden said some of the Crows wanted to leave because they didn't like the direction things were going, but Maye made an example out of them." His lips flattened.

"I don't want to think about what she did."

"No, you don't."

"So, are you and Kayden like BFF now?"

"You know it." He replied sarcastically.

"But seriously... why all the Kayden chat?"

"I gave like two examples of conversations." He sighed, "Fine. When you were gone and Ruthy was hurt, I went to talk to him. I wanted to find out how I could get my family back."

I puckered out my bottom lip.

"Stop."

"You called us your family."

"Well, you're the closest thing. I haven't seen my parents in years. I talk to them on the phone occasionally, but they're always working."

"It's crazy to me I never noticed your parents were never home. I didn't question it one time." I chuckled, thinking back to the simpler days before I knew about wolves, crescents, and witches.

He shrugged.

"Oh my Goddess!" I heard, yelled across the room.

I looked over and saw Chloe walking in from downstairs.

She ran across the room and wrapped her arms around me. "I thought I heard you. Are you ok? She didn't hurt you, did she?"

"No. I'm fine." I rubbed the necklace Chloe gave me. "I think this helped."

She cocked her head to the side, smirking. "What's that?" She pointed to my arm. "You have a bruise."

"She took my blood."

"She did?" Drake asked, mildly concerned.

"I didn't really have a choice."

"You did." Asher mumbled.

I snapped my head in his direction, glaring at him. "I. Didn't."

He shrugged, giving up the fight.

"How did you get out?"

"Luna was able to find the furnace room Kayden told us about. It was really easy actually, almost too easy."

"How so?"

"There were no guards. The door to our room was unlocked, so we were able to walk down the hall to the door that led downstairs and not once did we pass a Crow, which is almost impossible, given how many were there."

"You think it was a trap?"

"It has to be, right?"

"Well, it's not like she didn't know you were going to come back here."

"I know, which is what I don't get. She was adamant about doing the ceremony tonight at the peak of the full moon. I don't understand why she would just let us walk."

"She got the blood from you."

"Still. She needs more. She needs a battle to end all battles." I shrugged. "I don't know. I need to talk to Kayden."

"He's waiting for you downstairs."

"He is?"

"He figured you'd want to talk when you got back."

I looked at Ruthy. "Are you ok?"

She gave me a thumbs up and closed her eyes. "Right as rain."

I glanced at Drake and he was rubbing her head.

I turned to Asher. "I'll be right back. I'm going to talk to Kayden and see if he can't shed some light on Maye."

"Do you want me to come with you?"

"No. You need to finish the work Ruthy has started and get packs here. Maye's coming tonight." I gazed at the moon. "And soon, by the looks of it."

"If he tries anything, call me. I'm going to check on Cecile."

BONDING

"Sister. I see you made it out in one piece." Kayden said, shifting to sit up in his bed, leaning his back against the wall.

"I did." I stood at his doorway.

"Thanks to me... I think you left that part out."

"I can see you haven't changed."

He shrugged. "How was Maye? Missing me I'm sure." While his tone was sarcastic, I got the impression he was using it as a defense mechanism and really wanted to know how she was doing.

"Thank you for telling me about the furnace."

He smiled. "There it is!" He tipped his invisible hat. "Anything for my sister."

"Cut the crap."

"Which crap would you like for me to cut?" He asked, looking around his room.

I bit my tongue.

We stared at each other in silence for a moment and it looked like a switch flipped in his eyes. The sarcastic Kayden was gone and replaced with a more tolerable version. "She'll be here soon."

"I know."

"What are we going to do?"

"We?"

He laughed. "You can't leave me in here. She'll march right in and kill me."

"I don't trust you."

He sighed, shifting to put his feet on the floor. "I know. I've... not been the best brother." He fiddled with his hands. "I try, but sometimes the other version of me comes out, the one who has a hard time forgiving and forgetting."

I stared at him without speaking.

"I tried to help... with the furnace."

"Yea, about that. You left out a couple of things."

"I did?" He asked coyly.

"You did."

He shrugged. "Maybe it was my way of showing you that Drake's little potion didn't work and I wanted you to see I was legitimately trying to help you..."

I nodded. It's what I had figured. "You also didn't tell me Luna risked her life to send you back so you could tell me not to go."

"I kind of told you." He cocked his head to the side. "Look. If I straight up told you not to go, you and I both know you would have left immediately. At least this way you had a way to get out."

I stared at him for a second, trying to process what he just said. I wanted to be mad at him, but at the same time I understood why he did what he did. He was right. If he had told me, I would have gone and not thought twice about it.

"I've been feeding as much information as I could to Xander, Chloe and our parents to help them prepare."

"Why?"

"I know you don't believe me and I wouldn't either, but I do want to help. Maye and the Crows made it very clear where I stand. Despite everything I've done, you still took me in, granted you keep me locked up." He waved his arms in the air to point out his current situation. "But hey. I get it. I don't like it, but I get it." He rubbed his face. "I want to make amends. I want to forgive. Mom and Dad have spent hours and hours here, trying to help me and I'm not there yet, but I'm slowly starting to understand why they did what they did."

"Yea, mom has a way with that." I laughed, playing back the countless times she tried to make amends with me.

"I can see where you get your determination from."

An awkward silence filled the air as we looked at one another. I heard people moving around upstairs, but didn't feel it was anything important. I found myself not wanting to leave right now. I wanted to spend more time with him, I wanted to get to know him- this version of him. I sat on the floor at the door's threshold. "What kind of information did you give everyone?"

He walked over and sat in front of me. "I gave them locations of their camps, although they moved around every couple days, probably more now that we are closer."

"That makes sense. I saw a map in her office and noticed the circles had moved around while we were there."

He nodded. "Yea, she's amassed quite a few number of people."

"Yea. I counted close to a thousand in this area earlier today. A few days ago, it was just around five hundred."

"Yea, there's a lot." He paused like he wanted to say something, but didn't know how.

I stood up because I needed to get back to Asher and wanted to check on Ruthy.

"Wait." He called out. "Before you go. I've already said this to Chloe, but I need to say it to you."

"What?"

"I'm... sorry." He swallowed like he had an unpleasant taste in his mouth. "I'm sorry." He repeated, more easily this time.

"Thanks." What do you say? I had no idea. He had hurt and betrayed me, while at the same time I wanted to forge a relationship with him. That is what I wanted for so long and then when he ended up betraying Chloe and me, locking us in that room and then forcing us to complete the ceremony... it's hard to come back from that.

I got a little further down the hall and he called out to me again. "Yea?"

"When Maye comes... I *will* help you. Don't leave me in here to die a coward's death." His voice held a note... an emotion... sadness? Fear? Something.

His eyes penetrated into the depths of my soul and it was like the blinders had been removed from my eyes. I was seeing the real him, the one I had wanted to see so many times. I now understood. He had abandonment issues and was terrified of being alone. He would lash out to get people to react, because that usually meant someone had to be down here with him, to watch him, to babysit him. He was never alone.

I walked back down to his door, and he stared at me. "What are you doing?"

"Please don't make me regret this."

"Regret what?" His tone had a slight uptick in it.

I grabbed a wooden cup off the side of the wall and poured the salt within, along the threshold of the door and then swiped my foot through the middle. When I spoke to Drake about the room, he gave me the instructions on how to get Kayden out if I needed to. Seemed silly, but the salt supposedly bound then broke the spell on the room.

"You're telling me, the entire time someone just had to pour out salt and then swipe it away?"

I shrugged. "Drake told me soon after you arrived."

"I really am sorry."

"We will see." I looked at the clock. "I don't imagine we have to wait much longer."

"No. She'll need some time before the ceremony begins, but she has to make sure everyone is here."

"Who is everyone?"

"She's going to bring in all the Crows. She has to make a big enough show so Ellsmire views it as a credible threat. They've been staying on the sidelines for most of this. She's going to make them choose."

"I can see that." I said, walking up the stairs.

Asher paused from talking to Drake and looked at me at the same time Kayden stepped behind me.

"What is he doing out?" Asher questioned, looking rather unhappy.

I took a step forward. "I let him out. He was the reason we escaped, and with Maye on her way, we need all the help we can get."

"You think you can trust him? He's also the reason you showed up at the compound!"

I bobbled my head back and forth. "I was going to end up there one way or another and you know that. He's why we were able to escape. He knew if he told me the message Luna sent coupled with the fact you had been taken, I would have left immediately. At least this way we had a plan to get out."

He huffed, but didn't say anything.

I looked up and saw Anastasia and Liam walk in. Their eyes scanned the room and then landed on Kayden standing behind me and mother smiled. She walked over and gave me a hug, cupping the back of my head in her hand, and then moved to Kayden.

She looked back at me. "I'm so glad you're home."

I smiled and looked at what she was wearing. She had abandoned her usual flowing dress for a pair of khaki cargos and a white shirt, with dark brown boots. She looked like she was going on a safari and the only thing she was missing was the hat and binoculars.

She was ready.

"Has there been an update on Maye?" Liam asked.

"Not yet."

"She won't show herself until the last second. If the full moon will peak here around three, then I'd say you won't see anything until at least one, one thirty." Kayden added. "She'll send in Crows around then to stir the pot."

"You think she'd cut it that close?" Asher asked.

"She's cocky. She has an enormous army, coupled with the fact she isn't thinking rationally."

I nodded, able to attest to that.

Liam stepped forward. "We have a massive army, too. We have been working with several Crescent packs for a while now. They are on their way here. Some by land and air, and others through portals."

While I hadn't admitted it out loud or even to myself, I was actually starting to feel hopeful we could win this. After I saw those numbers on the board in the war room, it made me sick to think about what I was asking our packs to do.

Asher glanced at me, his brow questioning. Could he sense the relief I felt?

There was a knock on the door.

Everyone looked around the room, anxiety increasing exponentially.

The door creaked open as several of us changed our stance, prepared to fight, and then we saw a hand slip through, waving up and down and then a head.

Luna.

"Hey party people." She said, smiling, before pushing the door open.

"Luna. Where did you go?" I asked, stomping over to her.

Her head snapped back. "You weren't worried about me, were you?"

"Not at all."

She pumped her eyebrows, then finished opening the door all the way open. "I needed to pick up a couple of people."

I looked out on the front lawn and saw at least a hundred, if not more, people dressed in dark clothing, some in cloaks.

Ellsmire had shown up. They finally decided to get into the fight. "Do you... all want to come in?"

Luna laughed. "No. If it's ok, we'll split up and stay out here on the front lawn and send some to the back."

"Yes, of course. What do you need from us?"

"Just let your packs know we're here. Don't want to startle or surprise them."

"Done."

"Ok... well..." She looked around and her eyes landed on Ruthy. "Oh! How is she doing?" Her concern seemed genuine.

"She's good. Apparently, when I made the deal with Maye, it saved her life. She's still getting her strength back, but overall, things are looking good."

She nodded. "Good to hear." She tapped the door awkwardly. "Ok, well, I'm going to head outside."

I looked over her shoulder. "Is the council here?"

"They will be here later. They are still searching for a way to end this before it gets to the point we all know it's going to get to."

"Thanks again."

"Saving your life seems to be a full-time job of mine now." She chuckled.

"How does that make you feel?"

She shivered, and I was still chuckling when I shut the door. I turned to see Ruthy and Drake, and the others staring at me with their mouths on the floor.

"What?" I asked meekly.

"When did you two become BFF?"

"We aren't. And she isn't that bad anymore..."

"My word." Ruthy said, clutching her chest. "I think I'm hallucinating. Drake, what did you put in this beastly concoction?"

"Stop. She brought at least a hundred people from Ellsmire and surrounding. They're going to stay outside for now." I quickly mindlinked the packs and let them know of Luna and her team.

The others in the room just nodded.

"Right, super hearing. I'm just nervous... I want this to be over."

"It will be." Asher said rubbing my back. "And then we'll go on a nice long vacation to celebrate our union. I was thinking Hawaii."

I beamed.

"What did I miss?" Chloe asked, bouncing back into the room. She saw Kayden and took a step back. "Wow."

"Hey sis."

She looked at me and then at our parents. "Ok then." She paused a moment. "I just talked to Xander and Levi. They're on the south side of the territory and said they found a small group of Crows, but that's it."

"What do you mean, that's it?"

"They haven't found any more."

"That makes no sense. In Maye's war room, there were hundreds."

"She has them shielded with magic." Kayden offered.

"Why didn't I think of that?"

"Wait." Ruthy sat up. "If it's the same spell she had used on Cecile, then they can move onto our property and we wouldn't even know."

My eyes grew wide. "I'll grab Luna and see what they can do. They could already be moving in and we'd have no idea." I felt my throat tightening up as fear shot through me.

CALL TO BATTLE

IT WAS TIME. I glanced at my watch before walking to the middle of the field. The moon hung bright in the sky, illuminating the grounds below and the air held a muggy warmth to it. It was so quiet outside, even the nightly insects were too scared to play their symphony. Did they know what was coming? Could they feel it?

I looked back at the house and saw all the lights were out except for the lone kitchen light on the second floor and painted in its silhouette was Ruthy. She was standing at the back railing, watching all of us below. While we were close to seven hundred people strong, it didn't feel crowded. We had created pockets in the woods surrounding the pack house, creating several layers Maye's Crows would have to go through to get to us. We figured she wouldn't portal them in because that would take too long and they would be an easier target.

I looked at Asher. "I'm tired of waiting."

"I know. It shouldn't-"

A howl echoed throughout the woods, carried closer and closer by each pack member. A call to battle. They were here.

My heart started pounding faster. I quickly shifted into my wolf and felt my hair stand on end like an electric shot pulsed through me.

I glanced from Asher, then up to the balcony. Ruthy was still standing there and I could sense her frustration, her anguish. She wanted to be on the battlefield, but she was still too weak. She knew she'd be a liability and we couldn't risk it.

I thought about reaching out to the pack members for an update, but didn't want to distract, so I continued to stare at the trees, waiting for a sign- any sign they were coming.

Silence.

I glanced at Asher, our wolves were tense and ready to spring, but we waited. He looked to the sky and let out a long, low howl.

Silence.

What's going on? Do you think they're ok?

I don't know. Their howl signaled incoming danger, but...

I looked across the field and saw animal after animal lined up, circling Asher and me, but spaced out enough that Luna and her team could be mixed in between.

Silence.

It was driving me crazy- the absolute silence. Not even a chirp from a cricket or a gentle blow of the wind.

Nothing.

And then I heard it. A twig breaking.

The heads of every animal snapped in the noise's direction, like a scene that had been rehearsed a million times. I looked at Luna and tossed my nose in the air.

"Ellsmire, get ready. Last time they used holograms as a distraction. This time, they could use invisibility. Move forward and knock down those walls if they exist." She nodded at me, then stepped forward one step at a time, pausing after each move. Her hands were moving in the air as she would conjure up something, then release it into the world.

What was taking so long for the Crows? I watched the tree line again, waiting.

Another howl echoed through the air.

Was that closer? I asked Asher.

Sounds like it.

What do you think they're doing?

They're trying to lure us into the woods. They know we have larger animals on our side, so they're trying to make us weaker. We just need to hold our ground.

She can't wait us out forever. She needs the battle. She needs me.

And she will not get you.

The field plunged into darkness as a floating cloud moved in front of the moon, its light glowing behind it. That's when we heard it.

The crashing through the woods.

They were here, and they were coming fast.

I felt the hair on the back of my neck stand on end as we all hunched lower, teeth bared.

The Crows erupted from the woods into the field in a fury. I don't know where our other wolves were, but they couldn't have done much to stop this wall of Crows.

The quiet night had erupted into sounds of growls, screams, whines and gurgling. Maye wanted her fight, she got it and it was then I realized this was the plan all along. She let us escape so we could run back here. She had been moving the Crows closer to our pack house because this is where she wanted the fight.

Damn it!

I saw a wolf lunging at me and tore off after it. My feet pounded the ground. The wolf leapt through the air, mouth open, drool hanging from its lips. I slid low to the ground, under it and then turning almost immediately, lunging after its neck. I clamped down and twisted.

He was dead.

My wolf looked to the sky and howled out just as the clouds parted. I took a moment to look around the field, there were so many people fighting. Fighting over a stupid rock, over a hatred for a group of people.

I started running, but I didn't know where I was going. I passed wolf after wolf, body after body. I darted around fights, occasionally biting at a leg or a tail to help our team out, but I kept moving. I needed to find Maye and put an end to this, but she was a coward. She was likely hiding somewhere watching the scene unfurl in front of her. *Has anyone seen Maye?*

Silence. I didn't expect an answer, but I had hoped.

I heard a growl from behind me and whipped my head around to find a large wolf stalking towards me out of the trees. He lunged at me, knocking me to the ground while he stood over top of me. My front paws were stiff as a board, pushing him away, while my back legs tried to move under him for extra leverage. His head snapped down at me, but I was able to move it just in time, feeling only his muzzle brush against the hairs on my neck.

You're an abomination. You shouldn't even exist. The wolf seethed.

You're an idiot and a coward. You fight me from a place of fear, not understanding, and for a witch that's only using you to complete a spell.

To get rid of you all!

Wrong. So she can ascend the moon goddess's throne. It's all for power. She's only using you.

You lie. He bit down again, getting my leg.

My wolf howled out in pain. I snapped at his nose, causing him to let go, but he was still over me. I was stuck with no way out. He was much too large and strong for me to fight him. I was scared to go into my mind temple to get my bear, because we hadn't practiced much with everything going on and I couldn't be stuck in the temple with a wolf actively trying to kill me. It was my only option though, because I couldn't fight the wolf on my own.

I closed my eyes and prepared, praying to the moon goddess the entire time that the bear would not fight me. A second later, I heard the huff of a wolf and looked up to see it barreling into the side of the Crow standing over me.

Miss me, sister?

Kayden?

The one and only.

I quickly rose to my feet as we squared off against the gigantic wolf, circling it. It lunged after me again, even though Kayden was right in front of it. It was after me.

I heard a loud roar and looked behind the wolf to see a large brown bear standing there.

Chloe?

A family affair. Kayden said.

Chloe's bear moved forward and swiped at the wolf, sending him flying into a tree.

So much more effective. She said, throwing her paws into the air like a boxer in a ring.

But slower. The Crow had come back, barreling at her, latching its mouth around her leg. The bear let out a roar of pain. Another wolf jumped on her, and then another.

Chloe! I screamed out, watching her thrash and shake. I stood, immobilized by fear.

Snap out of it! Kayden yelled, racing by me, latching on to one of the wolves and ripping.

I cleared my head and went into my mind temple and saw her there waiting, eager. I shifted into my bear in seconds and towered above the wolves. I used my paw to smack away a wolf gripped on Chloe's arm, then went after the enormous wolf on her leg. I bent over and clamped down on him with my mouth. A second later, he had released and was howling in pain. I bit down, silencing him, and tossed him back into the woods.

Well, that's unfair. Two bears?

Chloe and I looked at him. *What's your second animal?*

He didn't say anything.

I looked down at my bear's paws. I had only shifted into her one time, so I wasn't as familiar with the way she moved as Chloe was. I didn't use her earlier because I thought she'd be too slow, but she definitely had some advantages.

I need to find Maye.

She's here. Waiting. Kayden said, standing beside me and looking out.

But where? I looked around at the scene in front of me. *Waiting for what?*

The right time.

Is the council here yet? Chloe asked.

No.

I heard another low growl from behind and turned around to find five wolves stalking towards us. They all five leapt at me again, ignoring Chloe and Kayden. I used my large paw and knocked one out of the air, while Chloe did the same, but the three others latched on to me, sinking their teeth in. It felt like a hot razor cutting through my skin.

I tried kicking them off my leg, but I wasn't strong enough and she moved slow. Kayden grabbed one by the back legs, causing its mouth to release, so when I kicked they both moved through the air. *Sorry Kayden!*

I heard a large growl that caused a shiver to go down my spine. Asher.

I found him running full sprint towards us and I froze, watching him glide through the air like a fish in the water. He leapt and bit one wolf around the neck, ripping him away from me with no mercy. The last wolf scampered back off into the woods.

Are you ok? He asked, looking at the three of us.

Fine. You?

Fine. Several Red Crows have left. They seem to be retreating.
That's good.
That's not good. Kayden chimed.
Why not?
They're regrouping.
How do you know?
He looked up. *We're moving to the next phase.*
Should we pull back and regroup?

Before anyone could answer, a clack of lightning shot out in the center of the field and screams and howls echoed through the trees.

Chloe and I shifted back into our wolves and we ran as fast as our feet could carry us, dodging around bodies and fighting.

Another clack. Followed by another.

A blue glow reflected on the bottoms of the clouds in the distance. Was Ellsmire council showing up? Was someone leaving? I hated not knowing!

We broke through the trees lining the field and saw Maye standing on a heap of bodies. My stomach turned, nearly making me stumble. She was using the fallen as her pedestal. I quickly scanned the faces and didn't see anyone I knew immediately. They mostly looked like Red Crows, but we had so many other packs here I couldn't be certain.

Standing in front of Maye were several Ellsmire witches with Luna at the helm.

"Stop this now!" Luna warned.

"Why? We're just getting started."

"This won't end the way you want it to. You can't ascend the throne of the moon goddess."

Maye shook her head. "You know nothing."

"I know that after the battle, Alexandria fell."

"No."

"They buried her in her hometown under her mother's family name."

Maye shook her head.

"They didn't want her grave being dug up by lunatics eager for her presumed power."

"You lie!" Maye cast a spell that hit at the ground right below Luna's feet, causing her to jump back.

"Well, that wasn't very nice." Luna said, dusting off her arms. "It's all at Ellsmire."

I looked at Luna and had no idea if she was telling the truth or not. I had never heard any of this and she didn't have enough time to find it on her own, but I also wouldn't put it past her to withhold information, only doling it out when necessary.

"It's not! I pulled every piece of information on Alexandria and the moonstone."

Luna took a step forward, her head falling to the side. "Maye," she started in a slightly condescending tone. "You didn't have access to all the information. The council had other writings, journal entries, accounts of what happened they had locked away."

Maye was shaking her head.

"Yes Maye. Unfortunately, your rank at Ellsmire wasn't high enough to grant you access to key pieces of information you needed."

"You're lying!"

"Am I?" Luna pulled a rolled-up piece of parchment from under her robe. "I'm going to send this over to you." I watched as the paper floated through the air.

When it was within reach, Maye snatched it and unrolled it, causing a hush to blanket the field.

"This is lies. This is something you created!"

"When would I have time, Maye? You've had me held captive at your compound."

"Before! Or someone at Ellsmire did it!"

"Why? Why, Maye, would we create this lie?"

"Because!" Maye spattered, clearly flustered. "If you knew this, then why... why didn't you say something before?"

"I didn't need to. You're unpredictable. I mean, hell, you killed your own brother. You're unstable."

I glanced at Asher. *What is she doing? Luna is baiting her.*

I don't know. He sounded concerned. *I'm sure she has a reason, but if she keeps pushing, Maye could explode and send the entire field up in flames. Luna's already pointed out how unstable she is, if she feels like she has nothing left...*

I glanced around the field. *Have you seen the council members yet?*

No.

Mira?

No.

There's no way she would miss this.

Maybe Luna is stalling for them?

Maye threw her arm up in the air, causing Luna to retreat a bit. "You know. I have never liked you."

Luna rolled her eyes. "Feeling's mutual."

"You used to walk around Ellsmire like you were the Queen when, in reality, you were nothing."

"I was still more than you. You sought title, recognition, and power because you had none of it. You walked around like a wounded animal after your parents died."

"Died? They were killed!"

"By the Red Crows!" Luna pulled at her hair. "They are the ones who killed them! Your parents knew what they were getting into."

"It took days before anyone told us about them because they were too concerned about them!" She shot her gaze at my siblings and I. "It was always those three! How important they were." She laughed. "It was impossible to walk around the castle playing with them, babysitting them after I found out what they had done."

I started to speak, to defend myself. We were only two when her parents died! She was delusional if she thought we were the cause.

She looked at us, pointing her finger in the air. "You know." She paused. "I almost killed Chloe when she was there with us. It would have been so easy, too." She gripped her hand into a fist. "Goddess, I wanted to, but no, poor George walked in and caught me." She laughed. "I made up some story, and he believed me." She pumped her eyebrows once. "Oh well, I got the next best thing- I got rid of you."

Luna stepped forward and then caught herself.

"It was shocking how easy it was, especially with you being dear ol' Mira's daughter. Just a few planted pieces of evidence and sending you on specific missions and viola you were gone."

"Well, I guess joke's on you since I'm back with the coven now."

Maye looped her finger in the air. "I found the coven a little lacking in vision."

I saw Luna glance just behind Maye, who must have caught it also because she laughed.

A flash shot out of nowhere directed at Maye, but she must have had a spell around her because it shot back in the direction it came from and hit someone. Their invisibility spell vanished, and the woman was falling backwards onto the ground. The cloak she was wearing hid part of her face, so I couldn't see who it was, only that it wasn't Mira.

Maye looked over her shoulder. "Will you ever learn? I'm stronger than all of you!"

Luna shot out a spell, and when it ricocheted back, she dodged out of the way.

"Ballsy and stupid."

The rest of the coven changed their stances and held their arms out.

Maye laughed loudly. "Your magic won't be able to touch me. You don't have enough power." She reached into her pocket and pulled out the moonstone. "This. This right here is what this is all about, and this," she said, holding up a little vial of blood in her other hand. "Now. If you're done trying to distract me, we can carry on with this evening's, rather this morning's, plans."

"I can't let you do that." Luna said.

"You don't have a choice." Maye retorted, extending her arms towards me.

Before I knew what was happening, I was shifting and being pulled across the field by an invisible rope around my throat. I stiffened my legs to prevent myself from moving, but the spell was stronger than my tired legs were.

"Cami!" Asher yelled out.

I fought to look over my shoulder at him and saw him move towards me, but then I heard Maye warn him away and saw Kayden snatch his arm to hold him back. Asher's eyes cut so hard at Kayden I thought his head was going to explode, then Chloe stepped in and grabbed Asher's other arm and said something to him.

"So glad you decided to join me." Maye said when I got to her.

"You didn't give me a choice."

"Always so dramatic."

I looked around the field and saw everyone had gathered in a circle to watch what was going to happen next. I tried to pick out faces I knew to ensure they were all ok, but couldn't find Xander, Levi or Drake, and Ruthy wasn't standing on the balcony anymore.

Maye looked up at the moon and shivered with excitement. "It's almost time."

"What do you need me for? You have my blood."

Maye looked down at me. "You didn't think that was all I needed, was it?"

"Reverse the curse! Reverse the curse!" The Crows started chanting, getting louder and louder.

"She lied to you all. She's not reversing the curse." I said.

The chants continued.

"She can't do that. No, her plans are to use the moonstone to get an infinite amount of power." The chants got softer, so I continued. "She wants to ascend to the moon goddess's throne. She used you all, and you fell for it. Your blind hatred has made you all look like a bunch of idiots." I laughed. "What's sad is so many of you have died here tonight for nothing. She hates the Crows because they killed her parents, so she used you all."

The Crows were looking around and some began to understand the truth.

"That's a lie." Maye said, trying to ease the growing tension.

"Is it?" I asked.

"Absolutely."

"If the spell to reverse the curse also involves a witch and a werewolf, then why aren't they up here? Why don't you have their blood?" I saw the faces of several Crows and it was like I could almost see the lights going off in their head.

"Shut up!" Maye shouted, snatching my arm in her vice-like grip. She glanced up at the moon and then the stone in her hand, and I could tell she was getting antsy. She pulled a knife out of her pocket and those in the crowd closest to us took a step back.

I felt my heart race, but then reminded myself she couldn't kill me because of the deal we had made. "You can't touch me with that."

"I most certainly can."

"The binder's protection spell."

She lips twisted into an evil grin. "You said I can't kill anyone important to you."

I nodded, missing what she was getting at.

"One, I'm not going to kill you. I just need more blood and two, you said anyone important to you. Who or what do you think determines who is important to you?"

"I don't understand."

"I figured you wouldn't. The problem is that you don't see yourself as important. That much has been made clear by the number of times you have sacrificed yourself for others. You value so many more lives above your own... well, I think you get it now."

My heart sank to my stomach while my mind reeled. Had I really been so short-sighted? Do I really not value my life? That's absurd! Of course I do.

"And what's better is your request was so broad, I'm sure it's worn off by now." She scoffed. "Protect everyone I care about? Seriously, who says that? Do you not realize how many people that is? You should have just given me your blood without the binders protection spell, because that's about how long it lasted." She tapped the knife on her chin. "It was gone before you snuck out of the compound." She pointed the knife at me, "Which I will say was impressive. I still can't figure out how you did it. I had left all the doors to the front open for you and I waited- hidden, of course, but you never came out that way."

She walked around me, using the moonstone to draw a circle in the dirt. "It's almost time." She placed the moonstone at my feet on the ground and before I could act, she grabbed my arm and used the knife to slice down the length of it from the inside of my elbow to my wrist. "I'm going to need that blood now."

I screamed out in pain, looking down at the blood flowing out of my arm onto the moonstone. My eyes caught Asher fighting with Kayden and Chloe to get to me, but I shook my head. I met Chloe's eyes, and it nearly broke me. There was so much pain and sadness. I looked back at my arm, waiting for it to heal, but it wasn't. It just continued to bleed.

"Tricky little knife." She smiled, holding it up in the air. "Does it look familiar?"

I stared at it for a second, then recognized the curved blade and tip. "Dixon's knife? The Blade of Haldives."

"Yes. I'm borrowing it." She laughed. "Well, he's dead, so I guess it's mine now." She tapped the knife on the end of my nose. "You know. He had so much potential, but he was so angry. He made careless decisions, although I imagine it has something to do with that one." She nodded to Luna. "You know, the night they attacked you at your aunt and uncle's house..." She paused, looking around for my parents. "I had carefully planted little seeds along the way, tipping them off, but what I didn't plan on was Luna." She snarled. "I was there that night and had removed most of the spells Mira had put up, but then Luna comes along pretending. The lies! She starts putting them back up. All my hard work!" She laughed.

"You?" Luna asked, confused.

"Me." Maye smiled. "I was hiding in the woods watching everything happen and I couldn't figure out what was taking them so long. They should have been able to walk right in, but no. You. You got in the way again."

I watched the knife bounce loosely between her fingers while she spoke.

"But it's ok, because that was when your mother realized there was no saving you."

"You set it all up?"

"I did."

"How miserable of a person do you have to be?"

Maye gripped the knife in her hand tightly and my shot of taking it was gone. I moved my foot towards the stone and slowly shifted it outside of the circle, but it stopped at the edge and a white light shot up around me to the sky.

Maye snapped her head at me and then at the stone. "Tsk tsk, Cami." She picked up the bloodied moonstone and put it back in the middle. "Don't touch it or I will be forced to hurt someone you love. It really is a shame that Ruthy couldn't have joined us this evening."

"No!" I yelled out, lurching forward, but was stopped by the circle in the dirt again. "What did you do to her?" I looked back at the house and still couldn't see her.

"Me." She gasped, clutching her chest. "I haven't done anything... yet. She really is so weak."

I looked at Asher and saw him looking out into the field. A moment later, a handful of wolves tore off towards the house.

"They won't find her."

"Where is she?" I spat.

"I will tell you when I'm done with you."

"If you hurt her." I threatened.

"If I hurt her, you'll what? You can't do anything to me." She cackled.

I glared at her and then turned my attention to the house and saw the three men jump onto the balcony and move through the house, flicking lights on as they went.

Maye let out a dramatic sigh. "We really are wasting time." She looked at the moon again. "So close." She grabbed my hands and began speaking in an unfamiliar language. I quickly glanced from Luna to the witch on the ground to Asher, who was fighting to break free from Chloe and Kayden.

Don't let him go! I mindlinked Chloe.

She gave me the look like she was trying, but was having a difficult time. I was thankful that Kayden was there with her and that neither of them looked at him as an alpha. If so, he could easily command them to release him.

I felt myself growing weaker as the warm trail of red continued to pour down my arm onto the ground, moving straight for the moonstone, covering it like iron filings to a magnet. The moonstone glowed as the dark outer shell began to crack open, revealing a white, radiant stone within. My eyes grew wide at the transformation happening and I couldn't help but notice Maye was just as surprised.

She bent down and picked up the now creamy white stone. I watched the blood from my arm follow it up through the air, almost like the stone was taking from me. Was this why she needed my blood? I felt a warmth creep over me, starting at feet and working up my entire body, to my head and then finishing at my fingertips. It was the same warmth I had gotten the few times I had the Shiban Sori emit from me. Is that what this was, or at least the reason I had it? Did Maye know?

I watched as a shimmer seeped out of my body, much like one would expect to see a soul leave a body. It floated like a glittery dust through the air and poured into the moonstone and then a light shot straight up into the air, from Maye's palm. It was beautiful- mesmerizing.

"Can you feel it?" Maye shouted, her hair whipping around her face, as her eyes grew wide with excitement.

I was too shocked to speak. I felt an energy pulse through me, growing stronger and stronger, as I continued to watch the shimmery dust leave my body and go from the moonstone to the sky.

The wind picked up as Maye continued to chant whatever spell she was casting, causing my hair to swirl around my face. Lightning began to erupt, filling the night sky as it shot from cloud to cloud, almost like it was feeding the moonstone. It started to raise out of Maye's hand and was now floating between us. She placed her hands on either side of it, palms up with her eyes closed. If I could just grab the stone, I felt like I could put an end to this, but I was too scared to see what would happen.

Suddenly, the world began to slow down, and I became hyper focused on the stone as a voice began to speak to me.

You can end this. You must end this.

I looked up and saw a woman with long, dark brown hair floating in the sky, almost transparent.

Alexandria?

She smiled.

I don't know how to stop her. She's too strong.

Camilla. You are stronger than her, you just have to believe. You were created for this moment- for this day. The only person who can stop her is you. You have the ancestral power of the Shiban Sori, for this very reason. Our forefathers and foremothers spoke of a day when a trinity would be created who could withstand the power of the moonstone and this trinity would put an end to the curse.

What curse? The Crescents?

She chuckled. *No, the Trinity curse has been a curse on the magic community. The moonstone was forged many years ago to help create balance and heal the shifter community from a disease that was ravaging it. It's why, after my death, the shifter population plummeted. Without the moonstone to heal, there was no hope. When the coven feared the power of the moonstone and killed me, they angered the moon goddess, who created the curse. Every generation, a trinity, would be born who would be called upon on their nineteenth birthdays, the age I was when I was killed, and each time they'd be unable to complete the ceremony.*

The trinity had to be shifters.

Yes, and over the years, the magic community treated the shifter community as equals and that's when you were all born to be the trinity that ended it. Only now, Maye is on the brink of cursing the magic community again for who knows how many years.

I can't let her do that.

No. You must stop her.

But I don't know how.

You have the power within you. Your Shiban Sori. You can use the power to break the spell and end this. You can do this. She repeated, fading away into the night sky.

I stood there for a moment, stunned by what had just happened. I looked around and no one else seemed phased. Did they not see her? Not hear her? Slowly, the sounds crept back in and soon I was in the middle of a deafening whirlwind, as lightning continued to clap above. I looked at the stone and then at Maye and knew what I had to do.

The Shiban Sori had been pulsing through me for a while now, asking to be used, and now I knew why. I tried to move my arms, but it felt like they had lead weights attached to them. I could feel the energy pulsing through me, pushing them apart like it was fighting me. I tried again and screamed with all my might and felt them slowly start to move.

"No! What are you doing? No! Stop!" Maye shouted.

"I... can't... let you... do this!" I screamed one last time as my hands clapped together, arms straight out in front of me. A powerful gust of wind and a bright light shot out, knocking Maye and me backwards onto the ground.

Immediately the wind stopped, as did the lightning, and the moonstone fell to the ground, landing with a thump.

"No!" Maye shouted again. "I was so close." Her eyes bore into me like daggers. "You ruined it!"

"You weren't close." I rolled onto my side, resting on my elbow, trying to gather as much energy as I could. "The moonstone isn't full of power for you. It was created to protect shifters from the witches." I exhaled out, too weak to barely speak.

"What? No. That's not right." She cast a spell in my direction and it landed at my feet, blowing up dirt and small rocks.

I quickly scooted backwards. "Alexandria came... to me. She told me."

I noticed several witches had instinctively stepped forward to hear better, but still kept a safe distance.

"Alexandria and her siblings were the first to produce the moonstone. It created balance and was supposed to heal the shifter community. There was a disease ravaging them, which is why, after their Trinity, it was so hard to find a record of shifters. Everyone thought it was because the moonstone wiped shifters away, but that wasn't it." I paused, taking a breath. "When the witch community feared the power and went after Alexandria and killed her, this angered the moon goddess, who then created the Trinity Curse. Every generation for fourteen hundred years, the witch

Trinity, would be called upon to perform the ceremony, but they wouldn't be able to live through it, a reminder of what they had done." Feeling a little stronger, I sat up. "With the shifter and witch communities working together, this pleased the moon goddess, so she created my trinity to break the curse. You will not get the power you seek from this stone, because it's a healing stone. The only thing you will do is anger the moon goddess and doom your species to who knows how many more years of death."

"You lie!" She stood, hunched over, heaving loudly.

"I'm not. Alexandria came to me and told me I needed to end this."

"No!" Her face was contorted into so much rage, I wasn't sure how it wasn't hurting her. "You did this!"

She cast a spell in my direction, hitting me in the shoulder, knocking it back, and then cast another, hitting my other shoulder. I screamed out as pain exploded from the bloody patches. It felt like molten lava had flown through the air and struck me, burning my skin and making me dizzy with pain.

"You will pay with your life!" Her arm shot out, and I froze as the world moved in slow motion around me. I saw the red and silver ball of light leave the tips of her fingers coming straight for me. I watched as it spun clockwise in the air, like a fireball twisting, and knew I should move out of the way, because it would likely kill me when it hit me, but it was beautiful- mesmerizing. I could smell sulfur in the air, the closer it got to me, like it was burning specks of dust as it drew closer and then drops of rain began to fall. I watched the teardrop shapes fall slowly to earth, pulled by gravity.

As it was getting closer, I thought about Asher and wanted to turn and see him, but wouldn't be able to handle the pain on his face. I didn't want that to be the last image I saw, but I wasn't given the chance. I heard something from behind me and I instinctively turned around, only seeing a blur before I felt something hit me in the chest, sending me sliding backwards on the ground. I looked up at the sky as the raindrops continued to hit me in the face.

MOONSTONE

IN A WHOOSH, ALL the noises and sounds came back. My chest ached as water pelted down on my face. What happened? I was sure I was going to die.

I sat up and saw a naked body lying on the ground in front of me- a man's body, lying face down in the dirt with dark hair. I leaned over, throwing up as the bile rose from my stomach.

Asher.

Tears streamed down my face as I crawled over to him. I knew he was stronger than Kayden and Chloe, but I had only hoped.

"Asher, why did you do this?" I cried out, crawling over to him. I grabbed his shoulders and rolled him over, wanting to cradle him in my arms.

I felt the air leave my lungs.

Kayden.

I looked back to where he'd been standing and saw Asher running to a stop just behind me, with Chloe by his side. "Asher?" I looked from him back to Kayden. "Why? How?"

Asher shook his head. "I was trying to get to you and I was almost free, and then he knocked me on the back of my head. I nearly fell to the ground, disoriented, and by the time I could stand, I saw him racing towards you."

"Kayden..." I brushed the hair out of his face.

Maye sat up, confusion contorting her face, but not remorse. Never remorse. She was a psychopath, void of any feelings or rational thought.

316 CRESCENT MOON : TRINITY CURSE

I saw the knife laying beside me and before I knew what I was doing, I grabbed it and lunged toward her, stabbing her in the chest, pushing her to the ground. She grabbed the hilt of the knife and looked up at me, eyes wide with shock. She was struggling to breathe as blood trickled out of the corner of her mouth, but I could tell she wanted to say something.

"It... should... have been... you." She said as her last breath left her body with her eyes partially opened staring lifelessly at the ground.

I sat there, kneeling over her body with my hand on the hilt until I felt a delicate hand on my shoulder. Luna was standing there with a somber expression. "I've got her. Go be with your family."

I stood up, feeling numb, and trudged back over to Kayden. Asher met me halfway, sliding his arm under mine to help carry me. Anastasia was on her knees holding Kayden's head in her lap as tears were streaming down her face. Liam stood behind her with one hand on her shoulder and the other wrapped around Chloe, whose face was buried in his chest.

I fell to my knees on the other side of Kayden, gripping his hand in mine. Anastasia looked up at me, but didn't speak as she continually rubbed Kayden's hand. "I..." I started, but didn't know what to say.

His eyes fluttered opened, but they were weak. He searched through the faces, landing on mine. "Please... forgive me... sister."

I felt a bubble move up through my chest, lodging itself in my throat as my eyes began to burn. "Kayden, why did you do this? Why?" I started crying.

"It's... a brother's... job to... protect... his siiii." His words were getting slower and quieter. "Sister."

"Kayden! Don't you do this! Don't you leave me!"

He smiled, his lips barely turning up at the corners. His eyes were closed, and the color was draining out of his face.

"Forg..."

"I forgive you, Kayden." I looked up. "HELP!!!" I screamed out! "HELP!!!" I looked at Kayden's face and saw his eyes staring up at me- a blank void. "No. No, no, no, no." Tears were streaming down my face. "Kayden. Please come back. We're not done yet. We're not done. Don't you do this to me." I hit his chest between sobs. I had to save him. There was still so much we had to talk about, to learn about from one another.

I looked around frantically, searching for anything or anyone to save him. We had to heal him.

Heal.

That was it! I looked at the creamy white stone laying on the ground. A stone everyone had been so concerned with that now lay on its own, being ignored. I hurriedly crawled over to it and grabbed it in my hand, the exterior smooth but warm to the touch. How does this work?

"What are you doing?" Asher asked.

"Maye was going to use this to bring her brother back. I can do the same!" I looked between Asher and my mom, her eyes growing with apprehensive excitement. "But I don't know what to do?" My mind was racing, pinging between thought after thought. "I don't know what to do!" I cried out.

Bex was standing beside Liam a second later. I looked up at him, "Here! Here! Use this." I said, holding up the rock. "Save him. We have to."

He looked down at me, his face falling. "I don't know how to."

"Maye was going to do it. She was going to bring her brother back." I glanced down at Kayden's face. "We're running out of time! We have to try something!" I looked around again and saw a group of Ellsmire witches huddled around Maye.

I stood up, running over to them. Maye. She had to help. She would know what to do.

I pushed my way through the rows of witches and found Maye laying on the ground in Mira's arms.

Mira looked up at me, but didn't speak.

"I need Maye to tell me how to bring my brother back!"

"She's dead Cami." Mira said, her tone indecipherable.

I shook my head. "No. No. Not yet. She can't be." I knew I had stabbed her and wanted her dead, but part of me didn't think she was going to die. Not evil like her. Not someone with her kind of power. "I need her." The little voice in my head was yelling at me for killing her. I should have been able to control my emotions, but at the moment, I didn't know what I was doing.

I looked at the stone in my hand and took a deep breath. I needed to calm my mind. I needed to formulate a plan, any plan.

I ran back over to Kayden and sat the stone on him, letting my mind filter through all the stories and all the pages I read in the books at the compound.

Think. Think! I commanded myself. I closed my eyes and focused on the stone. Slowly, the sounds began to drop out one at a time until I was left with only the sound of my heart thumping slowly. I opened my eyes, and it was like everything was frozen, or moving so gradually it was barely detectable. Even the rain drops hovered in the air, barely falling.

I looked down at my hands, praying for them to do something, and watched the small rivers of red drop onto the earth. My arms had healed and the only thing that remained was the little bit of blood.

Blood.

It was like the Goddess had snapped her fingers and the world starting moving again. The rain drops fell, and the noises hit me all at once. "The knife."

"What?" the group asked.

"The knife. The knife!" I yelled. "Get me the knife!" I shook my arm in the air.

Without hesitation, Chloe ran towards Maye and pushed everyone out of the way. She grabbed the knife off the ground and ran back over to me, holding it in her hand. "What do I do?"

"Cut him. Here!" I pointed at his chest. Anastasia stood up and backed into Liam's waiting arms.

I heard a few people question the idea, but not Chloe. She dropped to her knees and cut. "Now what?"

I shook my head, not quite knowing what I was doing, but praying to the moon goddess the entire time it was going to work. I dropped the stone onto his chest where a pool of red was forming.

"Come on." I whispered under my breath over and over again. "Work. Work damn it!" The blood wasn't reacting. It continued to puddle and started spilling over his sides, leaving blurry red trails as it mixed with the rain.

I could feel everyone's eyes on me, wondering what I was doing.

"It's not working." I shook my head. "Why isn't it working? It should be working!" I looked up at the sky. "Why? Why isn't it working?" I don't know who I was talking to, but suddenly another thought popped into my head. "Knife." I commanded, holding my hand out.

"Cami?" Asher questioned, concerned.

"Knife." I demanded.

Chloe slowly handed the knife over.

I snatched it from her and cut across my palm and squeezed out the blood over the stone. Chloe looked at me and something clicked in her eyes. She grabbed the knife and did the same thing, both of our fists dripping blood onto the stone.

Nothing.

I grabbed Kayden's hand and her eyes grew wide with under-standing. She grabbed Kayden's other hand and then we clasped ours together.

The Trinity.

It was there.

The buzzing.

The wind started to pick up around us, causing everyone to stop and stare. This had to work. It was our last shot. Our only shot.

I squeezed Chloe and Kayden's hand, pleading with the goddess to help us–to help Kayden.

I closed my eyes to hold back the tears and to give me hope. Maybe if I believed hard enough that something would happen, then it would.

I heard a crack of lightning overhead, while the winds continued to whip my hair around.

"Cami..." Asher said apprehensively.

I ignored him. Scared if I opened my eyes, everything would be the same and it couldn't be. It couldn't be the same. Because if it was, that meant this didn't work and Kayden was still dead.

Another crack of lightning.

I waited for the energy to build in us like it did last time, but it wasn't. Why wasn't it?

I squeezed harder- so hard that my knuckles were burning. I felt the buzz between us, but it was different.

Moon Goddess. Alexandria. If you can hear me... please help me... help us. Please save my brother.

Another crack of lightning and then everything stopped- the wind, the rain, the buzzing.

It was all gone.

Dread filled me.

It hadn't worked. I felt tears building behind my eyelids. I took one last breath, as I accepted defeat and opened my eyes.

I felt my vision flicker for a second. The moonstone was floating in midair, hovering several inches off Kayden's chest with a ring of our combined blood around it- like rings around Saturn. I noticed everything hadn't stopped. We were in our own little bubble. Lightning was flashing wildly in the sky, like a strobe light, while the winds whipped around unforgivingly.

I gave Chloe's hand two gentle squeezes to get her attention. She opened her eyes and looked at me, then at the stone, then up towards the sky. Her eyes widened with astonishment. No one was looking at us, because the lightning was flashing so much. Anastasia's head was nestled in Liam's chest, while his arms shielded her from the lights, and Asher and Bex were covering their face.

The moonstone slowly turned one way while the ring of blood spun in the opposite direction, matching the stone's speed. Suddenly, a light struck down from the sky straight onto the stone, and then a bluish white thread danced between the stone and Kayden's chest.

Seconds later, the stone dropped, the bubble popped, and the skies cleared.

It was over.

Everyone dropped the shields from their face and I dropped Kayden and Chloe's hand while we all sat there and watched.

Seconds ticked by slowly.

My eyes met Anastasia's, who looked broken, but hopeful.

We heard a large gasp of air and all looked at Kayden, whose chest was rising up, arching off the ground before it fell back.

"Kayden?" I asked.

Nothing.

"Kayden? Can you hear us?"

His eyes slowly opened.

"Kayden! It worked. You're back."

Anastasia fell to her knees, lifting his head into her lap. "My precious boy. You're back." Tears were streaming down her face.

He was weak, but he was alive.

Bex dropped to the ground and ran his hands over Kayden's head and chest and then glanced at Liam and Anastasia and nodded.

I stood and wrapped my arms around Asher. He was going to live. I closed my eyes as all the emotions poured out of me. I looked down at Kayden and just watched him.

I don't know how much time had passed, but I noticed Ruthy, Drake, Levi or Xander still hadn't shown up and panic set in. They would be here with us if they could. Which meant something else if they weren't. Maye had threatened Ruthy and the wolves still hadn't come back from the house.

"Where's Ruthy?"

Asher shrugged.

"Drake? Xander? Levi?"

We looked around the field for any sign of them, but there were so many heads moving around, it was hard to locate them.

"Go." Anastasia said softly. "I'll stay here with him."

"Are you sure?"

She nodded.

I looked at Chloe and she nodded. *I'll stay here with her, but you need to find Xander and Levi. They aren't responding.*

I nodded. There was so much death and pain around us I didn't know where to start. Once everything started, I didn't know where Levi and Xander had gone.

Levi? Xander? I mindlinked the field.

Silence.

Has anyone seen them?

No's filtered in from so many people. I looked at Asher and shrugged my shoulders.

Let's go into the woods?

Crows?

They're gone.

They are?

The ones who were still around when Maye started left when they realized she'd lied to them.

Asher and I darted in and around the trees, passing several people sitting against the base of them, waiting to heal. I stuck my nose in the air, trying to see if I could scent Levi or Xander, but there were so many unfamiliar smells it was hard to pinpoint them.

Where could they have gone? It wasn't a question I expected to be answered, so I shifted into my falcon. *I'll take the air.*

Asher looked up at me, but didn't speak.

After taking a nosedive, I hit a pocket of air and rode it back up. I studied the ground, looking for any sign of Xander or Levi, but there was nothing. There were so many people laying on the ground either injured and dead and I felt so guilty. This was all because of me.

Here! Asher yelled.

I turned in the air and saw him in the distance through the canopy of trees and dove through the branches, twisting left, then right and ducking under the last branch, before shifting into my wolf, landing with a soft thud.

There was a body laying on the ground.

No!

I shifted into my human form and ran towards them. When I got closer, I saw Levi on his knees over Xander's body, holding his hand. He looked up at me and I saw his tear-stained cheeks. My head fell to the side in disbelief. "Is he?" I couldn't say the words.

"I don't know." Levi shrugged. "No. No, he's not," he corrected. "I hear his heart beating, albeit slowly. His leg was gashed opened and so was his abdomen and that's still healing. He needs a healer. Where is everyone? Where's Drake? We need to get him here. I don't know if we can move Xander." His thoughts were rapid and short, fraught with panic.

"We don't know where Drake is, or Ruthy."

He looked up at me, his face falling.

"Maye did something with Ruthy."

"Then ask her!"

"I... killed her."

"You what? Why?"

"She..." I felt the muscles in my jaw tightened as I could feel a wave of emotion pass over me. "She tried to kill Kayden. Well, she did, but we brought him back."

"Kayden?" His brow furrowed.

"He saved my life. Maye was going to kill me and he saved my life, taking the hit from her spell."

"Oh."

I grabbed Xander's hand. "Xander. It's time to open your eyes now."

"He won't." Levi rocked back and forth. "Come on, Xander." Levi shook him.

"How long has he been like this?"

"I don't know. We got separated. I found him a few minutes before you found us."

Xander's head fell to the side, and I panicked. I felt his neck for a pulse.

Nothing.

I moved my fingers around frantically. "Xander. Don't you do this to me!" I pleaded.

Levi felt around on his neck. "Xander... you come back to me." He smacked his chest. "You aren't going to leave me. You're a pain in the ass. Who's going to call me out... who's going to help me..."

I looked at Levi, trying to figure out what he was talking about. Whatever it was, he was still very guarded about it.

"Xander... don't make me..." Levi brought Xander's hand up to his forehead and closed his eyes. "Xander, I need you... I... I think I love you..."

I looked up at Asher and back down at Levi, but didn't speak. What in the world had I missed? I looked at Asher again and he was smiling and nodding in approval.

"Xander!" Levi said, dropping his hand and hitting him hard in the chest. "You can't leave me! I said it. You should be so happy! I finally said it. I finally admitted my feelings to you and nothing... you say nothing. Coward. Isn't that what you called me? A coward. Now who's being the coward? What did you want to hear? You were right? Well fine. You were right. I didn't know how to act, think, or feel, until you. Goddess, you! You freaking sauntered into my life and blew it up." He sighed dramatically. "You're so annoying! All the time! You're annoying when you talk and you're annoying when you don't." Levi hit him again in the chest as tears flowed down his face. "Just say something, you ass." Levi slumped over, resting his head on his stomach, Xander's hand clutched in his.

The wind blew softly as leaves floated down from the trees above.

I looked around at everything, trying to take it all in, and then saw Xander's foot twitch.

I looked from his foot to his face, hoping... waiting.

A smile started to spread across his lips, even though his eyes were still closed.

"Levi." I whispered. "Levi," I said a little louder when he didn't respond.

He sat up and I nodded at Xander and he looked at him and saw the smile on his face.

"You said... you... love me. It's about time."

"You're an asshole."

Xander opened his eyes and turned to look at Levi. "But I'm your asshole." Xander scrunched his face. "That... sounded better... in my head..." He closed his eyes again for a second. "Where's Ruthy?"

"We don't know. We can't find her."

"Maye..."

"She's dead." I said.

Xander shook his head weakly. "No. I think... Maye took her..."

"Where? We don't know where."

His eyes opened, and he looked at me. "I was in the air... and saw a blue light in the house."

"A portal."

"Then saw another, a moment later, several miles away."

"Where? Which direction?"

Xander pointed. "That way. I was headed there, but heard someone yell out and came to help... I'm sorry. I thought it was only going to take a second, but there were too many."

"It's not your fault. Thank you."

I looked at Levi and Asher. "Take him back to the house. I'm going after Ruthy."

"I don't think you should go by yourself."

"It's fine." I shifted without waiting and took to the air.

I looked back down briefly and saw the frustration on Asher's face, but I didn't have time to wait. I needed to get to her. I couldn't lose her.

When I got in the air above the trees, I looked in the direction Xander had pointed and realized where the portal had opened and my heart sank. I kept them out of this, praying they would stay safe. I pumped my wings harder.

She took them to Leo's.

I'll find a healer and have them portal us there.

He thought the same thing I did. Maye had gone after my family. It wasn't enough to go after the crescents, but she had to go after everyone. I was so filled with rage I wasn't paying attention and almost flew past the house. I swooped down at the last second and shifted in the front yard and ran up the stairs, throwing the door open.

All the lights were on and I heard voices coming from the kitchen. I grabbed the blanket off the back of the couch and wrapped it around me as I ran down the hall.

Will, Ems, Leo, Ruthy and Drake were sitting at the table. They were staring at me before I fell to the ground, overwhelmed by emotion.

"Will, get her some clothes. Ems, get her some water." Ruthy was by my side a moment later, holding my hand. "Are you ok? Where are you hurt?"

She threw the blanket off and was looking me over.

"Goddess, where is this blood coming from?" She lifted my side.

Ems dropped down and held the water out for Ruthy at the same time Will leapt down the stairs with clothes in his hand.

"Not mine. Xanders."

"Not that little shit stain."

I chuckled, trying to get my bearings, sitting up. "No. He's fine... rather, he will be."

"Thank Goddess. Where's Asher? I was so worried."

A pop sounded, and Drake peeked down the hall. "Did you nearly tear the door off?"

"Will, go get Asher some clothes." Ruthy commanded.

I stared at her, watching her command out orders.

"What happened? Is she ok?" Asher asked, tearing through the house.

"Yes. I'm fine."

"What happened?"

I held my hands out. "Everyone needs to pause."

No one moved as eyes darted around.

I slipped on the clothes and grabbed the water Ems was still holding out. "You're ok?" I asked Ruthy.

"Yes. I'm fine, but a little pissed. Well, a lot pissed." She glared at Drake.

His jaw muscles clenched, and he shook his head. "Be pissed all you want. You didn't need to be on that field."

A male healer walked down the hall and waved his hand awkwardly. "Hey all. Does anyone need me here?"

I looked around and everyone seemed fine.

"Drake might in a minute." Ruthy seethed.

Drake turned to the healer. "No, we're good. You're dismissed."

"Thank you, sir."

Everyone looked at Drake in shock while the front door slammed shut and a pop echoed through the house.

"There is so much to unpack." I said, looking at everyone, still completely confused.

"Let's take a seat at the table." Leo suggested.

"Only six seats," Ruthy said. "Drake can stand."

I glanced at Drake and he chuckled, rolling his eyes.

We all sat at the table quietly, looking at one another, no one speaking for a moment.

Will shifted in his chair. "Is it over?"

I looked from him to Ems, not sure how much she knew, although I was getting the impression she knew some, if not all, given the events that had just happened in the last five minutes alone.

"It's over." I breathed. Leo put his hand on mine and squeezed. "Maye..." I hesitated, looking at Ems.

Ruthy picked up on my hesitation. "She knows everything."

"Everything?"

Ruthy nodded. "When Drake plopped us right in the middle of their house in the middle of the night... we kind of had some explaining to do."

Drake inhaled deeply. Apparently, waiting for the verbal lashing that he expected to come, probably because he had already received it several times already.

"So Drake portaled you here?" I asked.

"Yes."

"I was trying to protect her." He sighed.

"That's bull!" She roared.

"I asked him to. He was following my orders." I interjected.

"That's also bull! You didn't know where I was, so don't pretend you gave him the order."

"You were weak." Drake defended.

"We don't need to go through this again." Leo commented.

I got the impression this had been an ongoing conversation.

Ruthy huffed then looked in the opposite direction from Drake.

"Maye had said she hurt you and hid you away."

Drake shook his head. "No. I think that was her plan. I was checking on Ruthy before I came outside to help and Ruthy." He glanced at her, "Was on her way outside."

She huffed.

"I knew the second I left her, she was headed to the field, even though she wasn't in any condition." He glared at her and she rolled her eyes. "We were arguing when Maye entered the house, calling out Ruthy's name. I portaled her here to hide her."

"You trapped us all inside."

"I kept Maye out. I had to protect you all!" He retorted.

Ruthy snarled, grabbing an apple out of the basket on the table and taking a huge bite. I hadn't noticed the three apple cores piled on the table in front of her already.

"Is everyone ok?" Ems asked.

I looked at Ruthy and then at Drake.

"Who?" Ruthy asked.

"Many people, all sides... and Kayden, almost. We were able to bring him back though... with the moonstone."

She looked at me, confused.

"Maye was going to kill me and he jumped in front of her spell. He died, but we were able to use the stone to bring him back. I can't explain how or why..."

"Oh, Cami." Leo said, rubbing the top of my hand with his thumb.

"Maye?" Ruthy asked.

My lips flattened into a hard line. "She's gone." *I killed her, stabbed her in the chest after I thought she killed Kayden.* I didn't want to say the words out loud because I didn't want Leo, Will, or Ems to look at me differently.

"Good." Ruthy nodded. "Xander, Levi and your... other family?"

"All good. Thought Xander was gone, but he's still kicking."

"I don't think he can be killed. He's too annoying."

I laughed. "You're probably right."

I looked at Ems, whose eyes were wide with shock. "How are you doing?"

She chuckled. "Well, this explains a lot."

"I'm so glad you know now."

"You just can't-" Asher started.

"I know. I can't say anything. Ruthy has already talked to me about it several times." She laughed. "Quite the mother bear."

"You have no idea." Drake chuckled.

Ruthy cut her eyes at him.

"But I love her. Goddess, help me." He added.

"Don't try to be all sweet and romantic. I'm still mad at you."

He walked over and started rubbing her shoulders. "You can be mad at me forever if you like, because you're alive to be mad at me." He bent over and kissed her forehead.

Leo yawned. "Assuming all is ok... this old man is going to head to bed. Do you all want to stay?"

"We have to get back to the pack house to sort things out."

"Am I allowed out?" Ruthy asked.

"Stop." Drake gently shook her shoulders.

"Ems and I are going to head to bed."

"Let's have a family dinner a few nights from now, once things on your end settle down. You're all invited."

"Even Drake?"

"Especially Drake." Will interjected.

"I liked you until now." She said, casting a side glance at him.

Will threw his head back and laughed. "Such spunk! I love it!" He pushed his chair from the table and placed his hand on Em's shoulder, signaling it was time.

The rest of us stood up and on the walk to the front door, Leo grabbed for my arm from behind. I turned around to face him and saw he was standing there with opened arms, so I walked into them, gripping him tightly. "I'm always here if you need to talk, kiddo."

"I could probably use one of your porch swing talks in a couple of days."

"I'll be waiting."

I squeezed him tightly, then grabbed Asher's hand, who was waiting on the front porch.

We caught up to Drake, who had his arms wrapped around Ruthy, his chest to her back, while they were waiting for us. Her head was rested on his shoulder, while she looked at the stars.

"Ready?" I asked, walking up. I wasn't, really. There was a lot of work to be done and I didn't want to go back now. I didn't want to deal with the sadness. I just wanted to stay here and pretend like none of this had happened, but I knew I couldn't do that.

Drake nodded and created the portal a moment later. Before I climbed in, I turned behind me and saw Leo, Will and Ems on the front porch watching us, while Em's mouth hung wide open. I waved, then stepped through.

Drake had portaled us to the front yard, which I was grateful for. We walked in and there were people moving all around the foyer and in the kitchen and living room. The smell of coffee and pizza permeated the entire space. It was late, or rather early, but people had different vices in times of stress. I saw Bryson and Conner walking around the kitchen with aprons on and trays of pizza in their hands, passing it out to any who wanted it.

Alphas. Please meet Cami and I in the fourth floor library. Asher mindlinked out.

Several people looked up and then went back to doing whatever it was they were doing.

"I'll go see where I'm needed." Ruthy said, then looked at Drake. "I feel fine."

He nodded. "I will also go see where I'm needed."

Asher looked at him. "Stay close. I want to start portaling people back to their home, to clear out space for those who need it."

"Understood."

Drake and Ruthy moved through the space, pausing and helping whoever they could while Asher and I leapt to the fourth floor landing.

The halls were empty, and it was quiet up here, almost like it existed separate from the rest of the house. We walked into the library and sat there for a moment, alone.

Asher grabbed my hand and rubbed it. "I love you."

I smiled at him. "I love you, too."

Benji was the first to walk in, followed by three other alphas I had never met and then by Liam and Anastasia. Her eyes were red and swollen and her cheeks were still wet from her tears. One of the three alphas, a female with dark brown skin, walked over to her and crossed her arms in front of her face and bowed.

Anastasia smiled meekly and nodded in appreciation.

Asher waited a moment before he spoke, letting others filter into the room. "Alphas. First, thank you so much for your support and your sacrifice. While we lost many people, we have successfully ended the Trinity curse and hopefully pushed the Red Crows underground permanently, if not disbanded them. For all of those able to transport, you may head home if you want to. If any of your pack need to stay or be seen by a healer, please let us know and we will have a room prepared for them. I'm not kicking you out," he smiled, "But wanted to give you the option of leaving if needed. You have helped us more than I can ever thank you or repay you for."

Another man and woman walked into the library and stood near the door. I didn't recognize them, but Asher did.

"Thank you all," I said, stepping forward. "Your help here today will never be forgotten and if you ever need us for anything, you only need to call and we will be there."

"Thank you alphas." They each said.

Liam stepped forward. "Our pack, along with Benji and Angelique's pack, has worked on clearing the field and surrounding woods, allowing for easy transport back to their respective packs for burial proceedings."

"Thank you so much." I was scared to ask how many we had lost because I didn't want to know the answer. How many people had died because of me?

Asher turned to look at me, sensing my sadness and guilt, and put his hand on my back, rubbing it.

"Thank you alphas." Each of the alphas said one at a time before walking out.

The last two who had walked in stepped further into the room.

"Cami, I want you to meet the alpha of Cecile's pack, Tabitha and Augustus."

I crossed my arms in front of my face and bowed.

They returned the gesture. "So nice to meet you Cami, although I wish it was under better circumstances."

"I, as well."

"Your brother was very brave."

I smiled. "Yes, he was."

"Cecile is doing better?" Augustus asked.

Asher nodded. "My healer said she will make a full recovery."

"That is excellent." Tabitha said.

"I'm sorry for putting her in danger."

"Nonsense." Augustus said. "Would she be able to stay here for a few more days while she continues to heal?"

"Absolutely. I would love nothing more than to introduce her to my pack and to Cami."

"Perfect. I think she'd like that." A silence filled the air again. "Ok, well, we may go see where we can help before we move our pack back home. I'm sure you want to get things back to order as quick as possible."

"We will follow you down." Asher said.

CELEBRATION OF LIFE

TWO DAYS HAD PASSED and everything still felt surreal. The pack house returned mostly to normal, although a somber weight hung in the air. Asher, Liam, Anastasia and I decided to hold a combined burning ceremony between our two houses. Kayden was still very weak, but it was interesting to see how the pack had changed around him. There still wasn't an acceptance, because it was hard to erase the memory of the things he had done, but there was a respect. Risking his life for their alpha had gone a long way with them and I could tell Anastasia appreciated it.

After the ceremony, we held a celebration of life at our pack house and brought both packs together. We grilled out hot dogs and hamburgers with s'mores and turned on some loud music. While those closest to Xander and Levi knew their secret, Levi was still nervous about letting the rest of the pack know. Ruthy was trying to push him to tell everyone because she was so excited he was finally out. She'd had a suspicion for months, but said nothing to anyone, knowing it was something he had to handle on his own when he understood his feelings better or trusted others with his secret.

I picked up a wooden stick and slipped a marshmallow on the end.

"Can you please try not to burn it this time?" Asher bellowed from his chair.

I stuck my tongue out at him. "I like them burned."

He laughed. "No, you don't! You're just too lazy to take the time needed to cook it to a perfect golden brown and you try to convince yourself you like them burned."

I puckered my lips at him.

"Do you want me to make you a s'more?"

I smiled coyly.

"Exactly." He teased, standing up.

"You know me so well." I gave him a quick peck on the cheek when he grabbed my stick.

"Yea, yea." He patted my butt before I went to sit in our chair.

Ruthy was sitting beside me, talking to Drake and Chloe while Levi was in the chair next to her, batting Xander's hand away. "Will you stop!" Levi shout whispered.

"Why? It's so much fun to screw with you." Xander poked him one last time in the cheek before walking to the fire pit to join Asher.

Ruthy looked at Levi and pumped her eyebrows.

"You too?" He playfully glowered.

"Has Ruthy told you yet?" Drake asked, squeezing her shoulder.

"No." She looked up at him.

"Tell us what?" Asher asked, walking back over with my s'more perfectly cooked.

"You can tell them, babe." She smiled.

He sighed, gathering his thoughts. "Well-"

Ruthy interrupted, "You're taking too long," she shifted in her chair to look at us. "Drake gets to stay here for another year and they'll reassess his location then."

My eyes grew wide with excitement. "That's amazing."

"Yea." She nodded. "He got promoted in rank." She squeezed his hand. "Which is why that guy at your house was all weird with him."

"It's really nothing." Drake said quietly, not wanting to draw attention to himself.

Ruthy cocked her head at us. "It is. He's just humble."

"Well, man, that's amazing! I'm so glad you can stay, at least for a little while longer."

"Thanks. I'm pretty happy too." He quickly kissed the top of Ruthy's head.

I watched the way he looked at her for probably longer than was normal, but fortunately, no one saw.

"So, you guys?" Drake pointed to Levi and Xander.

Xander put his finger over his lips. "We aren't supposed to really talk about it."

Levi elbowed him in the stomach. "Will you stop? You're making me regret telling you."

"You didn't have to tell me. I already knew."

"I'm glad someone did." Chloe said, smiling. "I had no idea."

"How is that even possible? You three were allllways together." Ruthy laughed.

"Yea. I thought they just really liked me. I didn't know I was Levi's buffer."

Our small crowd burst into laughter.

"You don't get it." Levi said, bringing a serious undertone back into the conversation. "One. I love you Chloe." He smiled. "And two. I don't even know what's going on. I used to like girls. Well, I thought I did. But I don't know. It's all still very new to me and I'm just scared that others are going to give me a hard time and not accept me."

"Who cares about them, anyway?" I said.

"What she said," Xander seconded, putting his elbow on Levi's shoulder. "But seriously, I get it. These looks, this charm... You aren't the first boy I turned gay."

Ruthy nearly fell out of her chair in a dramatic fashion. "Oh, brother."

"I don't even know if that's what I am." He flailed his hands in the air. "And thank goodness Drake cloaked our conversation."

"I've learned with this crowd to expect the unexpected." He laughed.

Xander leaned in close. "But seriously. If anyone gives you a hard time..." he looked at each of us. "You have an entire werewolf and shifter pack behind your back and a witch or two."

Levi smiled. "I know."

"We're your family." Ruthy said, squeezing his hand as her eyes held his for a moment.

"I'm going to check on Kayden." Chloe nodded in his direction.

After the ceremony, Liam and Anastasia took Kayden back to their pack house where he's been staying. When he came over to our house, he stayed close to them, I think in part because he felt awkward being around our pack, but also because he was still pretty weak. We hadn't gotten a chance to really talk at length since everything happened, but I had checked in on him a few times. He seemed different- less snarky. I think he was having a hard time processing everything that had happened and didn't know how to feel about being brought back from the dead.

"Sounds good. I'll come over in a minute." I smiled.

Xander and Levi walked out into the field while Ruthy and Drake went inside.

"It's just us, pup." Asher squeezed my thigh. "Well, over here anyway."

"It is." I leaned back on his chest, looking up at the stars. Was this all really over? It still didn't feel real. Dixon was gone, Lucian and Maye were gone. Luna and I were... I'm not sure what you would call it. Friends seemed too serious, acquaintances seemed too simple for what we had endured... I didn't have a word other than frenemy.

She had offered to help me study my Shiban Sori. I couldn't help but wonder what she was getting out of it, because why else would she offer to help, but I didn't press it. I was happy to learn more about it, although part of me wondered if I still had it, because ever since I saw Alexandria on the field and used it to break Maye's spell apart, I hadn't felt it. We had briefly looked at the moonstone, but she said she couldn't feel any power in it and when I held it, it no longer had its warmth, even though I'm not sure it ever did. That night I felt it, but there was so much going on I could have been mistaken.

"Whatcha thinking about?" Asher stroked my hair.

"Just everything and nothing. So much has happened this past year... it's just so hard to wrap my head around."

"Yes. That's true."

I watched Chloe talk with Theo, Lily, Kayden and our parents and was immediately drawn back to Asher. "Cecile seems nice."

"Right? She reminds me a lot of my mother."

"I hate I only got to see her a few times. It's just been so crazy with the stone, Kayden, and everything else."

"She understands and said she wants to come back and visit soon, after things calm down. She was feeling better and wanted to get home before her pack's burning ceremony for their fallen."

"It makes sense."

"Perhaps we can go out and visit her next time. I'd love for you to meet the rest of my family."

"That's a great idea!" I turned my head and kissed him softly on the temple. He looked up at me, our lips finding one another.

"I love you Cami Evans."

I smiled against his lips. "I love you Asher Evans."

EPILOGUE

4 MONTHS LATER

"I can't believe you talked me into doing this." I said, looking at Asher who seemed to have no issues, standing upright on his paddle board. The sun baked down on us as the gentle Hawaiian air swept across the crystal blue water.

"What? The brochure made it look fun." He chuckled.

"For you! Who's apparently a natural athlete at everything!"

"What can I say?" He said, throwing his hands up, which caused him to wobble on the board. His body stiffened, slumped over as he caught his balance, waiting for the water to calm down.

I sat with my butt planted firmly on the board and both of my legs overhanging either side.

"You have to try it." He encouraged.

"I did, several times and several times I ended up in the water."

"We can go back in." He sighed.

"Absolutely not. We're not going in because of me. I'm more than happy to sit out here and relax on this board and watch you." I pumped my eyebrows at him, beholding his beautifully sculpted torso with his tattoos. He had added a new one last month around his family crest that simply read Cami.

We had finally taken our two-week vacation and honeymoon. On the way out to Hawaii, we stopped by Cecile's pack and spent a few days with them. It was there that Asher shifted into his second animal, a brown owl. His grandparents were there to guide him through the transition, which I think made it a very special moment for Asher. He was so excited to be surrounded by his family, not only for the transition, but in general. I spent most of the days just watching him get to know each of them and at night we would stay up and listen to stories of his mom growing up. I would have liked her- feisty but loyal, strong willed and compassionate.

After that, we headed to Hawaii where Asher had reserved us a room with a butler and a private pool. We didn't leave the room for the first few days, just soaking up the sun in our private pool and using the butler for everything else. It was nice not having to worry about anyone trying to kill us or having to run the pack house. Although, at times, I wondered if leaving it in the hands of Ruthy and Xander was the best idea. We had Liam and Anastasia on standby if needed.

Anastasia was working through her guilt around Kayden, while also trying to help him process. Kayden was opening up more and more about his childhood and the things that scarred him, both physically and emotionally. While it was hard for Anastasia to hear, she needed to know and he needed to speak it so they could both heal. Liam had suggested they have individual therapy sessions, as well as, us all having family sessions. We had all been through a lot and the only way to get through it and have a cohesive future was to work on it together. I never thought Kayden would go for it, but when it was brought up he didn't hesitate to participate. I really think he wanted to change and for things to be different. I think he wanted it before the ceremony, but something about dying and coming back to life seemed to put everything in perspective for him. I think he realized how much we wanted him to be part of the family and the part of him he was keeping guarded finally tore down those walls.

Anastasia and Liam had grown close to Theo and Lily through this whole process which was great for Chloe. She had grown up without much family or a pack and now she had a multitude of both. Theo and Lily's son had stopped by after he heard about the ceremony to check on everyone and decided to stay the rest of the summer at their pack house when he realized they had a hundred foot long pool. Chloe took off near the end of the summer because she wanted to explore her crescent heritage, but I knew the real motivation- she was looking for her mate- which she didn't find. She visited several packs and came up empty, but she didn't let that dampen her spirits. She was still very optimistic.

Xander and Levi are doing great. Levi is still shy about his status and trying to understand his feelings. He had come out to the pack, and they all accepted him with open arms, although Levi was convinced Ruthy threatened them. He's finishing up his last year of school and then he and Xander plan to go on a trip over the summer. He wants to go back to his parent's old house because he says he's been having dreams of them lately and feels there is something he needs to know.

Ruthy and Drake are doing great. She was opening up more to the idea of traveling around the world with him. She was still finding it hard to commit to leaving us, but she knew we'd be in excellent hands. Drake had come to us privately to inform us he would have to leave at the beginning of next summer to take his post on the West Coast. In prep for that, we've been quietly trying to reassure Ruthy any chance we get because we know they can't live without each other. She hasn't fully given up on finding her mate, but she also hasn't been trying or worried about it. I think deep down, she's still scared, and she doesn't want to admit that.

Luna has come around the house a few times under the guise of research, but I think it's because she genuinely likes us and is having a hard time adjusting back to life at Ellsmire. She'd been gone from there for so long, I imagine in some ways this pack had become her new family, although she'd never admit it. Along the way, I've also developed a special fondness for her. I still don't enjoy being around her much, but find myself worried about what trouble she's potentially gotten herself into when we don't see her for a while. I agreed to come to Ellsmire for a few weeks after we get back from our honeymoon so she can do some light, non-evasive testing so we can better understand the Shiban Sori and also study the moonstone more, although I'm convinced it's nothing more than a rock now.

Mira got promoted to a seat on the council after Maye had killed one of the council members in battle that day. She seems to be adjusting to it well, but as a result, hasn't been around a lot. She's been holed away, learning rules, customs, law... Luna said that it's a lot more than they ever realized.

Will and Ems are doing great. Will is on the football team with Connor and Bryson, though he doesn't start as much as he would like, but he's also a freshman. Ems made the cheerleading team, so they can be together at all the games, which is nice. They're planning on moving into an apartment together off campus for their sophomore year, which is a pretty enormous commitment for Will, but I couldn't be happier. They are busy all the time, which means they can't go home as much as they want or I want, which causes me to worry about Leo, but he's doing well. Evelyn and he are living their best life, going to all of Will's games, going on fishing dates in the mornings and just enjoying their time together. I've gone over a few times to have our front porch swing chats and he's been tremendous with helping me move past the events of the ceremony, and I think is even helping Ruthy accept the idea of moving.

I watched Asher some more as I let the waves lull me into relaxation.

"Hey!" He shouted, grabbing my attention.

"What's up?"

"Race you back?"

I glared at him playfully. "It's on!" I grabbed the oar off my lap and starting pushing it through the water. We were neck and neck and both laughing.

I would remember this moment forever. He is my everything and I can't wait to start the next chapter of our life together.

THANK YOU! THANK YOU! THANK YOU!

Thank you so much for reading this trilogy. I hope you enjoyed it as much as I loved writing it. I would be so appreciative if you left a review on Amazon and shared this story with your friends. It helps me so much!!

I don't think this will be the last time you will see these characters. I have several ideas for spinoffs, but currently don't have any release dates yet. My goal is to work on getting these into audio formats, while I work on a few other projects. But I can tell you that I want to explore what happened to Levi's parents more and perhaps Kayden's history and Drake and Ruthy's story also intrigues me. So many options!

Thank you again!